Disenchanted

SUSAN CARROLL

One

Once upon a time... That is how a good story should begin or, so I have been told. These tales always involve a poor but sweet young maiden who attends a royal ball, falls in love with a charming prince and lives happily ever.

This is not my story. While I am certainly poor enough, no one would ever describe me as sweet, and our kingdom's prince is far from charming. When I did get the chance to go to a ball, my mind was more set on burglary than falling in love and... But I am getting ahead of myself.

My story starts on what promised to be another ordinary day until someone came hammering at my front door with enough force to snap the ancient brass knocker in half. At that moment, I was kneeling in front of the library hearth, ramming a long-handled broom up the chimney while soot sifted down over my face and hands, speckling the apron I wore over my old grey woolen gown. Only the kerchief knotted about my head prevented my hair from becoming a shade of ash blonde. I was in no fit state to receive callers.

When the insistent rapping continued, I shouted out, "Can someone please answer the front door?"

I knew both of my stepsisters were near at hand, entertaining one of their vapid beaux in the parlor. But when Amy and Netta were anywhere in the vicinity of an eligible young man, they tended to become so addle-pated that it affected their hearing. There was no response to my plea other than the sound of muffled giggling.

I sighed, hoping whoever was at the front door would have the wit to go away and come back later. I gave the broom another shove, but only succeeded in dislodging a little more soot. There was something up there blocking the flue, some poor swallow perhaps or even an owl. I flexed my shoulder muscles and rammed harder. There was a loud crack as the ancient broom snapped in half.

I rocked back on my haunches, staring in dismay at the splintered spear of wood in my hand. The top half of the broom was stuck somewhere up the shaft, further blocking the flue.

"Oh, frap!" I swore since there was no one around to frown or be shocked at my vulgarity.

Meanwhile the rapping continued; the idiot at the door as persistent as a hedge fly trying to get at the sugar bowl.

"Amy! Netta! Get the door," I bellowed.

At least this time, I managed to get a response.

"We are busy, Ella, dear," Amy sang out. There was more giggling.

As if I am not, I started to shout back only to give up, muttering, "Never mind."

I struggled to my feet, trying to wipe my hands clean on my apron, but it was only making matters worse. I stomped from the library, aware that I was leaving a trail of soot all along the main hall I would be obliged to clean up later. Just add that to the many other tasks facing me this afternoon. The thought did nothing to improve my mood.

I flung open the door, stopping the caller in mid-rap. "What?" I demanded.

The round florid-faced little man on the doorstep drew back in dismay at the sight of me. He was clad in all the accoutrements of a royal herald, a blue toque with a jaunty feather perched on top of his auburn curls. His costume was ridiculously antiquated, a sapphire blue doublet, the sleeves slashed with silver, the colors of the royal house of Helavalerian. The short baggy breeches and tight hose he wore were enough to make any man look absurd, never mind one as stout as him.

I was no more pleased to see him than he was me. If I had known the caller was a messenger from the palace, he could have rapped until the knocker disintegrated. I would never have opened the door.

Recovering from his initial dismay, the herald puffed out his cheeks and raised his trumpet to his lips.

"Don't do that!" I grabbed the trumpet and wrenched it away from him, stopping him mid-toot. He gasped in outrage, bouncing on his toes as he tried to retrieve the trumpet, but I held it easily out of his reach.

"Miss! I must sound the trumpet. It is protocol."

"You were supposed to have blown the horn before you knocked."

He sank back on his heels, looking disgruntled. "I was warned that people are unlikely to answer their doors if I sound the trumpet first. Especially at this house, Miss Upton."

Despite my layers of soot, the man knew who I was. Obviously, he had been warned.

"What happened to George, the herald who used to work this street?" I asked.

"He retired."

"Surely he is a little young for that."

"The poor man's nerves were a wreck. He's gone off to join the Loyal Order of Hermits in the Red Grove Forest. He simply couldn't endure any more of the abuse heaped upon him, all the insults and threats, being set upon by dogs or angry cats." The herald directed a pointed glare at me. "Or having pails of dirty water flung on his head."

"I was washing the second story windows and the bucket slipped from my hand," I protested. "It was an accident."

Well, almost. It was George's own fault for provoking me. When I refused to come down from the ladder to take his message, he had shouted the tidings up at me, that the palace had declared a new (and exorbitant) tax on windows. Dumping the wash water on his head had been a purely involuntary response. Still, if I had contributed in any way to poor George becoming a hermit, I felt a twinge of remorse.

"What is your name?" I asked.

The new herald bowed with a great flourish, his soft round stomach doubling over his belt. "Rhufawn Smythe, at your service, miss."

"Rhufawn?" I chuckled.

He straightened, scowling at me. "I am sure it is no more amusing than being called Prunella."

Although I utterly loathed my first name, I said, "Prunella is an old family name among the Uptons."

"So is Rhufawn among the Smythes." He sniffed. "You know, I think it very unfair that we royal heralds should constantly be subjected to such mockery and abuse. It is not our fault that the news coming from the palace is not always pleasant. We are simply doing our duty and—"

"All right!" I cut him off with an upraised gesture to call a truce. "So do your duty.

But no trumpet," I warned as I returned the instrument to him.

He pouted, but he attached the horn back to the loop on his belt. Rhufawn delved into the large leather pouch which I could see was crammed with rolled parchments. He produced one and prepared to unfurl it.

"Just give it here." I grabbed the parchment, but the new herald was prepared this time. His pudgy fingers clamped down, refusing to release it.

"I am supposed to read it to you."

"I have been reading since I was three." I tugged harder. He pulled just as stubbornly in the opposite direction.

"It is protocol, miss. I must make sure you have heard and understood the proclamation. And you will want to hear because I assure you it is good tidings."

Good tidings from the palace? That was as unlikely as the fabled cow being able to jump over the moon. Our tug of war continued until the royal parchment was likely to be torn in half. That would not have bothered me, but the prospect alarmed Rhufawn enough that he released his grip.

"Very well, Miss Upton. But you must promise me you will read it. You won't just chuck it into the fire or anything. Because it is really good news."

"Yes, yes." I waved him off, preparing to retreat into the house. But his hand shot out to stop the door being closed.

He cleared his throat, "Er... I understand it was the custom of old to offer the royal messenger a small token of appreciation. Just a penny or two. It wouldn't even have to be silver. Bronze would be quite acceptable."

Was he serious? "You expect me to tip you for bringing me bad tidings?"

"I told you it is good news, great news, exciting news. News so wonderful it has inspired many of your neighbors along the street to be quite generous to me. It would be such a nice gesture, welcoming me to my new route. A new beginning as it were, after what happened with poor George. Not that you were entirely to blame for his coming undone."

Rhufawn fluttered his pale lashes at me, his humble demeanor not quite able to disguise the sly calculation in his eyes.

I smiled sweetly at him. "Here's a tip for you." When he leaned eagerly forward, I used my forefinger to smudge his pug-like nose with soot. "Find yourself a better kind of employment."

Stepping back, I slammed the door in his face. I heard a muffled sound that could have been a curse or a pitiful "ow" because he had been standing too close.

My attention had already shifted away from the royal herald to the battered parchment I clutched in my hand. I stared at it, as though it might explode at any second. Despite all the herald's assurances, I could not believe the parchment held anything that could be construed as good news.

No doubt the proclamation would be worded with a cordial elegance. It would even contain a charming note of regret as the royal government went on to explain there was to be another new excise levied much as King August deplored the necessity of it. The new tax, whatever it was, would be made to sound very reasonable.

I regarded the parchment glumly, wondering what sort of tax our greedy king had dreamed up this time. We were already taxed on our food, our clothing, our wine, our candles, our livestock, our horses, our carriages, our dogs— providing that they were working dogs such as hunting hounds or herding collies. Household pets were exempt.

Whatever the latest exaction might prove to be, I did not feel up to dealing with it. I tossed the parchment atop the hall table next to a dapper-looking top hat and kid gloves. At that moment, the parlor door opened and my two stepsisters, Amy and Netta, fluttered out like two gauzy white moths released from the confinement of the winter cupboard.

Their proper names are Amethyst and Garnet, their late father, Albert Wendover, having been a wealthy and distinguished jeweler. At least he was until he had been caught trying to pass off colored glass as a costly dwarf sapphire in a medallion he'd designed for the king. His trial and subsequent execution had been swift and brutal.

Determined to distance herself from her husband's infamy, my stepmother, Imelda, had insisted her daughters adopt the Upton name when she married my father. She seldom referred to her girls as Amethyst and Garnet— not unless she was excessively vexed with them.

My stepsisters had inherited their mother's luxuriant ebony hair, but otherwise there was little resemblance between them even though Imelda still found it precious to insist the girls dress alike. This morning, they were clad in similar gowns cut according to the current fashion for high waists and puffed sleeves although in a small display of defiance, Netta had opted to wear a blue sash instead of pink.

At the age of eighteen, she was two years older than Amy. She was as tall and angular as Amy was short, dimpled, and plump. But their familial resemblance was marked as they drew up short, regarding me with twin expressions of horror.

"Oh, Ella, just look at you," Netta cried. "You are all covered in soot."

"Please tell me you didn't answer the door that way," Amy added.

"Gads, Miss Ella!" This last exclamation came from the young man who had followed Amy and Netta from the parlor. The girls made a frantic effort to shift position, blocking their beau's view into the hall. It was futile. Fortescue Bafton easily squeezed past Netta to gawk at me.

Fortescue was the only son of a prosperous and fashionable tailor, although you would never guess that from his attire. He was poured into a pair of yellow breeches so tight; they clearly outlined his less than impressive masculine accoutrements. He wore a pea-green frock coat tightly nipped in at the waist. The collar on his frilled shirt was so high, Fortescue's head poked out like a turtle emerging from its shell.

"Gads," he repeated again. "Whatever have you been doing, Miss Ella?"

I thought of several clever retorts I could make, but I discovered a long time ago that sarcasm was wasted upon Mr. Bafton.

"What does it look like I have been doing?" Recalling that he never understood rhetorical questions either, I added, "The library chimney has not been drawing properly. I am endeavoring to clear the flue."

"Why don't you just engage a chimney sweep?"

I heard Netta's and Amy's sharply indrawn breaths. They fixed pleading eyes on me, fearful of what I might say. They hated it whenever I let anything slip regarding our straitened circumstances, especially to one of their beaux.

So, I told Fortescue, "I have become so bored with my needlework, I am thinking of adopting chimney sweeping as my new favorite pastime."

"Truly? Then we may have to think of a new name for you. What about Miss Sooty-Ella?"

He guffawed and was echoed by Amy, who tended to laugh heartily at any lame joke a young man chanced to make. I had tried to hint to her that this makes her seem too eager, even a little desperate, but to no avail.

Netta joined in, but hers was more of an uncertain titter. She cast an uncomfortable look at me, anxious that my feelings might be hurt by this jest at my expense. It would take a man far wittier than the likes of Fortescue Bafton to wound me.

Encouraged by Amy's giggles, he continued, "No, wait! I have it— cinders! We should call you Cinder-Ella."

"Cinder-Ella!" Amy chortled.

I rolled my eyes as the pair of them went off into peals of laughter. "Vastly amusing, Mr. Bafton," I said. "If your wit were any sharper, it would be as keen as a butter knife."

Chuckling, Fortescue started to bob his head in agreement, only to stop, his brow creasing. I could tell that somewhere in the recesses of his brain, he was trying to work out whether he had just been complimented or insulted. Before he could arrive at any conclusion, I offered him my best smile.

"If you would be pleased to accompany me to the library, I could show you something truly remarkable. Do you know if you look up the chimney shaft in the daytime, you can see the stars?"

"Oh, no, no, no!" Fortescue wagged his finger at me. "I am familiar with that jest, Miss Cinder-Ella. You get me to look up the shaft and I end up with a face full of soot. You won't be catching me with that trick again. No, ma'am!"

I already had caught him with it— twice. I had wagered my best friend, Malcolm Hawkridge, that I could get Fortescue to fall for it a third time. I believe I could have coaxed him into doing so, but my attention veered toward Netta. My oldest stepsister was an irrepressibly curious girl. Having noticed the royal parchment on the hall table, she had pounced upon it.

"Don't bother with that," I began but she had already cracked the seal and unrolled the parchment. Netta was excessively self-conscious about her height. She tended to hunch forward which inspired me with the urge to gently push her shoulders back, but I refrained. The poor girl endured enough criticism from my stepmother about this habit. Her hunch was more pronounced as she bent over the message. Suddenly, she straightened upright with a gasp, and she motioned frantically for Amy to join her.

Their dark heads drawn close together, the girls appeared stunned as they perused the document, eyes wide and round, mouths hanging open. My stomach flopped over in apprehension.

"What kind of new horror has the king devised?" I asked. "How bad of a tax is it?"

Instead of answering me, they raised their gazes from the parchment and stared at each other. They broke into simultaneous grins. Whooping with joy, they hugged each other. Gripping each other's arms, they proceeded to bounce up and down, emitting delighted squeals shrill enough to crack my eardrums.

If my stepmother had been present, she would have rebuked the girls for behaving with a lack of ladylike dignity. Like Mr. Bafton, all I could do was stare at them in bewilderment. When I was finally able to make myself heard, I ventured, "So the royal herald was not trying to cozen me? It really is good news from the palace?"

"Oh! The best news in all in the world!" Netta trilled.

"The king has decided to refund some of our tax money?"

"No! Even better," Amy cried.

"Nothing could be better than that," I groused.

"You think so? Well, just look at this." Amy snatched the parchment from Netta and pranced over to dangle it before my eyes.

She was fluttering the paper about so much, I only caught glimpses of the words.

His Supreme Highness King August, the first of that name... by royal decree doth declare that the eve of high summer be set aside... a grand ball to be held in honor of our most beloved son and heir...

"Oh." I gave a disappointed shrug. "This is nothing but the announcement of the same ball the palace holds every summer."

"But this year is going to be very different," Amy cried. "This year we all are invited."

"What!"

"It says so right here." Amy flapped the parchment at me. "Look."

"Perhaps I could if you would hold still." I plucked the missive from her grasp and steadied it to read. Netta, Amy and Fortescue started to crowd closer but wary of my layers of soot, thought better of it.

Netta urged, "Oh please, read it aloud, Ella."

Clearing my throat, I obliged, "His Supreme Highness King August, the first of that name, descendent of the noble line of the house of Helavalerian, ruler of the great kingdom of Arcady—"

"No, skip all those boring bits," Amy interrupted. "The really good part is down here." Jabbing the paper with her finger, she directed my attention to a paragraph lower down the page.

I began to read again. "Our most beloved son and heir, Prince Florian, having recently returned from his tour of the neighboring kingdoms, was disappointed in his quest to find a bride. Despite the loveliness of these foreign princesses, none of them were able to win the favor of our noble prince."

I snorted. "More likely none of them would have the conceited fool."

"Ella!" Netta scolded.

"Keep reading," Amy insisted.

I glanced down and found my place again. "Therefore, our doughty prince— doughty? That makes him sound like a pan of bread left to rise too long."

"Ella!" Both my stepsisters shrieked.

"Oh, very well... our doughty prince has resolved to choose his bride from among the fair ladies of our own kingdom. Every eligible maiden, be she of high or low degree, is hereby invited to attend the royal summer ball. Come join us for an enchanted evening of supping and dancing wherein one fair maid will be fortunate enough to capture the heart of our valiant Prince Florian."

"Win the heart of the prince," Amy cooed, flinging her hand across her brow as if she would swoon at the thought. "It could be me."

"Or me," Netta said.

"Or neither of you," Fortescue said, looking rather peevish.

"What does that signify?" Amy said with a haughty toss of her curls. "The prince has four younger brothers, and the ball is bound to be teeming with other desirable young men as well. Dukes and earls and barons."

"Knights and lords," Netta added dreamily. "Rich, handsome and clever."

"Forget about clever." Amy giggled. "I just want one that is all rippled with muscles."

Fortescue flexed his arm in a feeble effort to display his own strength, but it would not have mattered if he could have produced biceps the size of a ham hock. The unfortunate young man was forgotten in my stepsisters' ecstasies over the ball.

When he announced in aggrieved tones that he might as well take his leave, the girls barely stopped their excited chatter to bid him goodbye. I was the one obliged to see him out. He snatched up his hat and gloves as I opened the door. Even though I thought Fortescue was a bit of an ass, he looked so crestfallen I felt sorry for him and rather ashamed of my stepsisters' behavior.

As he tugged on his gloves, I tried to cheer him up. "Never mind, Mr. Bafton. You have a sister so I daresay you will discover your family has received an invitation as well."

"What care I for that?" he asked in a wounded accent.

"If there are so many eligible noblemen at this ball, there will certainly be an even greater number of ladies, most of them in need of consoling because only one can win the prince."

"Why, that's perfectly true." He paused on the doorstep, looking much struck by my words. "It is possible that I might win the favor of some great lady, perhaps even the daughter of a duke or a countess. Gads, do you think that I could, Miss Ella?"

I smiled at him cheerfully. "Why not? Stranger things have happened."

He thanked me and said farewell. Perching his hat at a jaunty angle, he sauntered off down the walk, whistling off-key. I closed the door behind him, staring down in bemusement at the parchment in my hand. Every eligible woman in the kingdom invited to a ball that had until now been for only the wealthiest and noblest of families? The prince vowing to choose a bride from among all the maidens in attendance? I did not know what to make of this mad announcement from the palace, but I was by nature a suspicious person. When something sounded too good to be true, it generally was.

I scanned the parchment again and this time my gaze homed in on the fine print at the very bottom of the announcement, beneath the king's seal.

Present this invitation to the royal exchequer to procure the vouchers necessary for admittance to the ball. Each household may purchase an unlimited number of tickets at the cost of—

I nearly choked as I read the staggering sum per ticket. I stiffened as I realized what this was all about, just another way for the king to rake in money. This so-called grand ball was nothing more than a lottery with exorbitantly priced tickets and marriage to the royal heir dangled as the grand prize.

It was outrageous. It was diabolical. It was… frapping brilliant!

I was torn between disgust and a grudging admiration for our wily old king. Levying another tax would have increased the rumblings of discontent among his subjects. Among the more radical quarters in Arcady, there were even rumors of a possible rebellion arising.

But how many of the king's subjects, dazzled by the prospect of a royal ball, would even notice that once again His Majesty was successfully picking their pockets? At least for once it kept the royal treasury agents from delving into the Upton purse. As for those foolish enough to waste their money taking part in this princely lottery, good luck to them.

Shaking my head and chuckling a little over the king's audacity, I rolled up the parchment. But as my gaze traveled down the hall toward the open parlor door, I could see my stepsisters dancing around the room, practicing the waltz. My smirk faded.

Amy and Netta were glowing with girlish hopes and dreams. They looked as though they were floating off the ground, encased in a bubble of sheer happiness. As usual, I was going to have to be the one who administered the sharp prick of reality. I headed toward the parlor, girding myself for the unpleasant scene to come.

Two

Mercifully, by the time I entered the parlor, the girls had calmed down a little. They had collapsed on the settee and delved into the latest issue of Fantine's Designs for Fashionable Young Ladies.

"We are not dressing alike for the ball, no matter what Mama says," Amy said. "We must be firm with her this time. Agreed?"

Netta nodded vigorously.

I cleared my throat to get their attention. "Girls…"

"I am picturing myself in a pink silk while you should have mint green," Amy continued. "And for Ella, I am thinking a soft shade of sky blue."

"Indeed, Ella always looks well in blue. It brings out the color of her eyes."

"Girls!"

They dragged their attention from the fashion book long enough to look up at me. Amy frowned. "Ella, you must go bathe and get rid of that soot. We have so much planning to do. The ball is only a month away."

"We should get down to the Silk Emporium as soon as possible," Netta said.

"Oh, yes. Every woman in Midtown will be swarming the place."

"Girls!" I fortified myself with a deep breath. "We can't go."

"To the emporium? But, Ella, we must," Amy said. "There will not be a decent scrap of fabric left."

"I mean we can't go to the ball."

They stared at me blankly, as though I had started speaking in some incomprehensible language known only in the darkest regions of elf lands.

Amy was the first to recover. "Whatever do you mean, Ella? Of course, we can go. We have been invited."

"No, what we have been invited to do is bankrupt ourselves by purchasing tickets."

I read the passage they had overlooked in their excitement, laying particular emphasis on the sum required— twenty silver galoons.

"Twenty? Per ticket?" Netta faltered. She had a somewhat better grasp of money matters than Amy who said, "Surely that is not so very much."

"Not so very much? It is as much as a good plowman can make in a year."

"How very fortunate we are not plowmen."

"We are not as well off as plowmen because we don't earn money. We only spend it." I tossed the so-called invitation toward the empty fireplace grate. I missed and it rolled across the tapestry hearth rug my stepmother had embroidered. Netta gasped and pounced as though fearful I would destroy the precious parchment. She tucked it behind a cushion and leaned against it while Amy insisted, "We do earn money. We get an allowance every quarter from that trust thing your papa left."

"Two quarters' worth of the allowance would not cover the cost of attending this ball."

"Cannot we withdraw a little money from the trust reserves again?" Netta suggested timidly.

"No!" I said more forcefully than I intended, but the very thought of such a thing flooded me with panic. I had tried many times to explain to the girls and my stepmother that the modest inheritance my father had bequeathed was not inexhaustible. Once again, I might as well have been speaking in fairy tongue whenever I broached the subject of diminishing capital, declining interest rates and higher taxes.

"We have dipped into the reserve too many times," I said. "Do you want us to end up having to sell our house and move to one of those dismal cottages in Misty Bottoms?"

"N-no," Netta faltered, but Amy dismissed my concerns with an airy wave of her hand.

"Pooh. You always exaggerate how poor we are, Ella." Amy closed the fashion book and rose to her feet. "If we can't get the money from the trust, we must find another way."

She sidled over to me and grasped hold of my hand, gazing up at me with a coaxing smile. "I know you will contrive something, Ella. You always do. You are so very clever."

Netta leapt up and caught hold of my other hand. "Oh, yes, please find a way, Ella. We simply must go to that ball. It is the event of a lifetime."

"It could make all our fortunes," Amy said. "If one of us won the love of the prince or even a wealthy duke, we would never have to worry about money, ever again. Oh, please think of something."

"Please, please, Ella," Netta chimed in.

As they clung to me, pleading, I was stirred by a poignant memory of when Amy and Netta were little girls, and we all went to the fair. Me holding them tight by the hand for fear they would get lost, them skipping along and wheedling me into buying peppermint sticks with the pennies I had so carefully saved.

I sighed. If only it was still so easy to make my stepsisters that happy and content. At the ripe age of four and twenty, I was already too cynical to believe in the romance of a grand ball and the possibility of finding love during the lilt of a dance. The harsh truth was that a royal prince or grand duke would never become smitten enough to marry a poor maiden from Midtown. That sort of thing only happened in romance tales, but I would never be able to convince my naïve stepsisters of that.

They still believed in happily ever after and dreams coming true. Despite pretending to be anxious and pleading, I could tell that the girls were convinced I would somehow be able to conjure the money we needed out of thin air. Their absolute faith in me was both touching and a heavy burden, but it was my own fault that my stepsisters thought I could perform miracles.

In the past I had managed to grant their wishes, from the chocolate-colored miniature ponies housed in our tumbledown stable to the costly harp gracing one corner of the parlor. I had dug deep into the trust, unearthing the funds for music masters, dancing lessons, and refurbishing the parlor with the velvet settee and side chairs, the gleaming mahogany tea table, the elegant bird of paradise wallpaper so my stepmother and the girls need not feel ashamed to receive guests.

We had not been able to afford any of those things, but at least they were all tangible items, capable of giving enduring pleasure. This ridiculous ball was nothing but a one-night fantasy and likely to prove a great disappointment and waste of our dwindling resources.

No, this time I had to stand firm.

Easing my hands away from the girls, I said, "I am sorry, my dears. There simply is no way we can afford it. It is not only the outrageous price of the tickets that puts this ball beyond our reach. There would be other expenses as well, new gowns, the hire of a carriage. We would need some way to get to the palace and we could hardly walk or hitch the ponies up to the old cart."

"Oh no, Pookie and Pippa would hate that," Amy exclaimed. "They are too small to pull the weight of all four of us. It would be far too hard on my poor old darlings and think how ridiculous we should look arriving at the ball in such a fashion."

"I was only teasing, Amy."

"This is not a matter for jest." Amy frowned a little and then brightened. "I am sure one of our neighbors or friends would be kind enough to allow us to ride with them."

"Mr. Bafton, perhaps," Netta suggested.

"Highly unlikely after the rude way you girls dismissed him."

Netta had the grace to look ashamed, but Amy said, "I can always turn Fortescue sweet. As for our dresses, you are brilliant with a needle, Ella. When the fashion for hoop skirts ended, look how you contrived to redesign our frocks."

"That is because I had reams of material to work with. What would you have me do for fabric, Amy? Cut up the bedsheets?"

Amy pursed her lips stubbornly. "I am sure there must be some silk we can afford. As for the cost of tickets, we can economize on other things. I would be willing to do without a few luxuries."

"Like what?" I asked bluntly. "Fuel for this winter? Food?"

"We could certainly buy less food. Netta eats like a sparrow and when you are absorbed in one of your books, you forget to eat at all. Mama has a delicate appetite, and I am sure I need to skip a good many meals. I have grown fat as a little piglet, and I must shed a ton of pounds before the ball."

It saddened me to hear Amy speak thus of her weight. There was nothing wrong with her figure other than it did not conform to the sylphlike silhouette which was the current standard of feminine beauty. The notion that she was fat had been put into her head by my stepmother. From the time Amy was quite young, Imelda had subjected her youngest daughter to periodic starvation diets that had only increased Amy's craving for sweets. When she had been a little girl, she had taken to hiding treats up in her room like a desperate squirrel preparing for a long arctic winter. For all I knew, she still did.

But she asserted heroically, "I could live on bread and water if I had to."

"Me too," Netta added.

"And what about the fuel we will need when the snow flies?"

"We could close off some of the chambers. The chimney already isn't working in the library. Who cares about that pokey old room anyway?"

"No one of any importance," I said tartly. "Only me."

"But you could read in the parlor, Ella," Netta pleaded. "Amy and I would be ever so quiet and not disturb you."

"Maybe for about five minutes," I began but Amy interrupted me eagerly.

"I have an idea. We could sell something."

"Such as?"

The girls looked around the parlor as though in search of some overlooked treasures. There were only blank spaces on the walls where the sylvan paintings done by the famous fey artist Peccano had once been. They were the last things we had owned of any real value and had been sold off last year, so we did not fall into arrears with taxes.

Netta wandered over to the harp, running her fingers lovingly over the curve of the golden wood frame. Awkward and ungainly in so many other pursuits, when Netta sat down at the harp to play, she became grace personified, her nimble fingers coaxing the strings to sing the most plaintive and lovely melodies.

The notes she plucked out now sounded as mournful as her voice as she said, "We could sell the harp."

"No, dearest," I protested. "It would break your heart and to no purpose. No one would give us enough for a secondhand instrument to purchase even one ticket."

I heard Amy swallow hard before saying, "What if we sold the ponies as well?"

"You would be willing to part with your old friends?"

Amy's lip quivered but she bit down to still it. "They are like me. They are fat and they eat too much."

"Oh, Amy," I groaned. "My dears, can't you see? Even if we

sold the harp and the ponies, it still would not be enough. This ball is simply not worth sacrificing your treasures."

Amy cast me a look, half-defiant, half-guilty. "What if we sold these?" She swept back her dusky curls, exposing the emeralds glittering in her earlobes.

I gave a gasp of outrage. "Amy, those are my earrings. You have been in my room again and borrowing things without my permission."

"I am sure I am always willing to share my things. I do not know why you must be so selfish with yours."

"I am not being selfish. I wouldn't mind if you ever bothered to ask me or were not so careless, forever losing things or soiling them. I still haven't been able to get the stain out of my muslin shawl."

"It's an ugly shawl and doesn't become you at all," Amy muttered as she plucked the emeralds from her ears. "And it is not as if you ever wear these earrings anyway. They just sit there in your little treasure chest, gathering dust. But if we were to sell them, I bet—"

"No! Never," I said, snatching the earrings from her grasp. "These emeralds belonged to my mother and are all I have to remember her by."

"That isn't true. You have that flowered handkerchief with her initials. And if it meant you could go to the ball, I am sure your mother would want you to sell the earrings."

"I can hardly ask her, can I? Because she is dead and has been for the past eighteen years!"

In my agitation at Amy's callous suggestion, I realized I was close to shouting. When I saw Netta flinch, I took a deep breath. Shoving the emeralds into my apron pocket, I tried to stem my anger. But when Amy opened her mouth to continue the argument, I snapped, "Enough. I have already made it clear we cannot afford to go to the ball and that is the end of the matter. I don't want to hear any more about it."

Amy flushed, her blue eyes taking on a stormy hue, but worse than that, Netta began to cry.

"Oh, Netta, please don't," I begged, my frustration with this whole situation dissolving at the sight of the large silent tears trickling down her cheeks. My normal instinct would have been to comfort her with a hug, but if I soiled her dress that would only make everything that much worse.

"Listen, my dears. What about this idea?" I said. "The night of the ball we can have a party in the garden like you have always wanted to do. We'll string up paper lanterns and move the tea table out there, drape it with our finest cloth. I will get my friend Mal to obtain some inexpensive champagne from the smugglers' market and I am sure he will bring his fiddle and play for us. We can dance in the moonlight, and we will still be able to see the fireworks from the palace and you can invite all your friends."

My hopeful suggestion only produced a dolorous sniff from Netta and a stony glare from Amy.

"All of our friends will be up at the palace attending the ball," she said.

"If they want to waste money they don't have on such nonsense, the more fool they."

"You are the only one who thinks it is nonsense. For Netta and me, that ball is our only chance at happiness."

I managed not to roll my eyes. "Don't be so melodramatic, Amy."

She flushed, her eyes glinting with angry tears. "I would not expect you to understand. You are so mean, Ella. You used to be so kind and sympathetic and sweet. Well, you were never exactly sweet, but you were a great deal more fun. But you have turned bitter and nasty and— and old! You don't have any dreams about romance or finding your one true love and living happily ever after. All you want to do is shut yourself up in your musty library with your stupid books and you don't care what becomes of Netta or me. I am sure if I do not get to attend that ball, I shall simply die! I know I shall."

"I do hope not. We cannot afford to give you a decent burial."

I immediately regretted the retort when Amy burst into a flood of tears.

"I am sorry, Amy. I—"

She shoved past me, storming toward the parlor door. I turned to my other stepsister, holding out my hand.

"Netta, please, I—"

She shied away from me, averting her tearstained face. She hurried after her sister.

Amy paused on the threshold long enough to hurl a parting shot, but she was sobbing so hard, I could barely make out the words. "N-not the end of the matter. When Mama gets home, just see what she has to say."

The girls fled the parlor, but not before Amy slammed the door hard enough to make me wince.

I heaved a deep sigh, realizing my stepmother would have plenty to say about the ball and I dreaded the thought of another tempestuous encounter. No matter how she would scold or plead, I could not yield. Not this time.

My father had set up his will so that all control of the trust money rested with me. I hardly knew whether to applaud the wisdom of my father's foresight or curse him for it. I had just turned eighteen when Papa died and his decision to leave me in charge of the family coffers had placed a crushing burden on my youthful shoulders. My stepmother had no more notion of economy than my stepsisters did. The knowledge that it was entirely up to me to ensure we did not end up facing utter ruin was terrifying and kept me awake many a night, worrying.

I knew this next month until the cursed ball was over was going to be a nightmare. A veritable siege of tears and tantrums, frozen silences and verbal assaults designed to weaken my resolve. For all our sakes, I could not, would not let that happen, but the mere thought of it left me feeling drained and exhausted. I retreated to the library, resisting the urge to nail the door shut behind me.

I tried to return to what I had been doing before I had been interrupted, but I knew it was hopeless. I lacked both the proper tools and the ability to unstop the chimney. I sank down on the stool by the hearth, trying not to think of my stepsisters upstairs weeping into their pillows. Didn't they understand that I would happily have sent them to a hundred balls if I could afford to do it?

I dug my hand into my apron pocket and drew forth my mother's emeralds. I wondered if I was being selfish to cling to these relics of the past. It was true that I never wore them and would never have any occasion to do so. But the thought of parting with my mother's earrings made my heart ache.

I had been fascinated by those emeralds as a child, calling them Mama's "twinkles." Whenever she dressed to go out to some dinner or party with Papa, I liked to brush back her soft blonde hair just to look at them.

"The twinkles make your eyes sparkle, Mama. Like stars," I would say.

She would laugh and lean down to rub her nose against mine. "These earrings were a special gift from your papa when you were born, my Ella. And that is what puts the sparkle in my eyes, not the twinkles."

My eyes welled at the memory, and I hastily shoved the earrings back in my pocket. Leaning back against the brick frame of the hearth, I gazed around the room at the sheets I had draped over the furniture to protect it from the soot. White cotton shrouded the bookcases, the desk where Mama had taught me my numbers and letters, the large wingback chair that had been my father's domain. I felt surrounded by ghosts of happier times.

I was a very restless child, and the library was of little importance to me in those days. I much preferred tearing out of the house to play with my best friend, Mal, who lived next door to me.

This was long before the Hawkridge family had moved to Misty Bottoms. Mal and I had had glorious adventures, climbing trees to rescue imaginary royals from towers, dueling with stick swords upon boards we cobbled together to make pirate ships or grubbing in the dirt in a quest to find fairy gold.

No matter how inclement the weather, I chafed to be outside with Mal. During a particularly harsh winter, I had contracted a bad case of influenza that had obliged me to spend weeks indoors. I would have been utterly miserable but for my mother's ingenuity in devising entertainments, wonderful picnics on the library floor, treasure hunts for colored rocks and treats she hid among the bookshelves. She even draped a blanket over the desk turning it into a cave where the dread ogre Dirty Burt lived, appearing whenever I poked at him to chase me around the room, squealing with delight.

The part of the ogre was always played by my petite fair-haired mama because my father was not the sort of man to crawl about on the floor and play. But as the evening shadows lengthened, he would light the candles and draw me onto his lap to read from what would become my favorite book, The Life and Exploits of Queen Anthea, the Magnificently Wise.

My mother would sit nearby quietly stitching and smiling over some passage she particularly liked, often asking Papa to read it again. No matter how hard the wind howled or how high the snow drifted outside the library windows, I remembered feeling safe, warm, and loved. How could any of us guess that enchanted winter would end in tragedy? The same influenza that had made me so ill would eventually claim my mother's life.

My father was a quiet man, never as demonstrative with his affection as my mother. I tended to think of him as being like the moon, reflecting my mother's light and warmth. When she died, it was as though the moon fell into a state of permanent eclipse, stealing the stars from my sky as well.

Lost in his grief, my father spent much of his time shut away in the library. This situation did not improve when he married my stepmother a year later. If anything, he became even more withdrawn. The library became his fortress and the rest of us were forbidden to enter there.

It probably speaks volumes about the sort of little girl I was. Tell me something was forbidden, and it was the very thing I wanted. I had shown little interest in reading books heretofore, but my father's edict made me stubbornly determined to breach the library walls.

I would wait until late at night when my stepsisters and stepmother were fast asleep and creep downstairs. Tiptoeing to the library door, I would inch it open and peek inside. My father always sat up until all hours reading. Ensconced in his wingback chair, he would be absorbed by some heavy tome.

By dropping to my stomach and snaking across the carpet, I could creep across the room undetected. I would hold my breath as I inched past my father's chair, keeping a wary eye on him. But when my father was lost in a book, he was oblivious to the world. My stepmother often complained that the entire roof could cave in on all of us and he would never notice.

Stretching my arm out, I was able to snag the volume of Queen Anthea from the bottom shelf. I would scoot back carefully until I was hiding behind my father's chair, smug and triumphant, the book clutched in my arms.

I settled against the back of the chair, positioning myself so a flicker of light from the candle fell across the pages, just enough for me to read. It was difficult at first, but I was familiar enough with the story, I could figure out the harder words. But the more passages that I mastered, a strange thing began to happen. What had begun as an act of defiance became a labor of love as I learned the true magic of words and claimed them for my own.

Night after night I would return to the library and sneak another book to read behind the chair. I had soon devoured all the volumes that I could reach without drawing my father's notice. I would have been obliged to start reading the same books over again but for my father's habit of constantly rearranging his shelves. Just as I would finish the last story on the lowest shelf, a new collection would appear within my grasp.

I enjoyed my career as a nocturnal book brigand for a long time. But eventually the day came when I grew older and more rebellious. Then I would simply march into the library and pluck a volume from the shelf. My father would glance up from his book, but I would just glare at him in defiance, challenging him to say something.

He never did. He would just give me an odd, sad kind of look and return to his reading.

I have often suspected since then my father had been perfectly aware of my stealthy nighttime raids on his library and did not mind. But if that was true, why had he never acknowledged my presence or invited me to come out from behind the chair? I wished I had asked him, but it was far too late for that now. It was also too late to tell him I was sorry that the last words I ever spoke to him were angry ones.

When I was seventeen, I had begun stealing away for trysts with a young man my stepmother had considered highly unsuitable. She had complained to my father who had roused himself from his books enough to summon me to the library. Imelda had been concerned for my reputation. My father, forbidding me to see the boy again, warned me about ending up with a broken heart.

What would you know about my heart? I shouted at him. All that matters to you is your library and your books!

That was so like the accusation that Amy had hurled at me, it gave me a twinge and I was quick to thrust the painful memory aside. I could not afford to spend the rest of the afternoon indulging in maudlin recollections. Marketing needed to be done, if our supper tonight was to consist of anything besides turnip stew.

I levered myself off the stool and headed up to my bedchamber. All was mercifully quiet on the second floor. I surmised that my stepsisters were either napping or had retreated to the garden to await their mother's return. Imelda was off visiting her good friend Madam Dearling, the wife of a prosperous silk merchant. I did not particularly like the Dearling woman. I thought she was a simpering creature who enjoyed nothing more than crowing about her neighbors' misfortunes, but I was glad that Imelda had finally found a friend of sorts.

After her husband's fall from grace, all of Imelda's former acquaintances from the Heights deserted her. Imelda's patronizing airs had not found favor among the simpler ladies of Midtown. Even as a child, I had been able to perceive that Imelda's pride concealed a deep unhappiness and loneliness. I certainly did not begrudge her friendship with the unpleasant Madam Dearling. In fact, I hoped Imelda had a good long visit. It would give me more time to muster my defenses before she returned to harangue me about the ball.

I quickly stripped out of my sooty clothes and bathed in the cool water at the washstand. Rummaging in my wardrobe, I selected a clean chemise, petticoat and simple gown and shrugged into them.

My bedchamber had changed little from the days of my childhood. The same silk hangings embroidered with unicorns draped in tentlike fashion over my four-poster bed. Once a vivid sky blue, the silk had faded to a shade of mist, but even when these draperies became tattered shreds, I did not know if I could bear to take them down because my mother had fashioned them for me.

My old dollhouse still stood in the corner by the window. It was once an impressive two-story structure, four feet high. But the paint was chipped, and shingles knocked off the roof from the time Mal besieged it with his toy cannon during the Battle of Upton Castle. Whatever miniature furniture and dolls had survived the siege, I gave to Netta and Amy long ago. For many years, I had used the dollhouse as a bookshelf, my much-worn biography of Queen Anthea having pride of place in the upper bedchamber.

The hinged roof opened to reveal the attic and that was where I stored my treasure box. I kept the key to it hidden beneath a segment of loose carpet in the miniature parlor. Not the best hiding place, considering how easily Amy was able to find it. Even if I had kept the key on a chain around my neck, it would not have mattered because my stepsister was adept at picking locks with a hairpin, a circumstance that was entirely my own fault. Mal taught me this skill when we were children, and I passed this knowledge along to both Netta and Amy. I was not always the best influence on my little stepsisters.

Fetching the key, I unlocked the treasure box to restore my mother's emeralds to their velvet pouch. I had always called this small chest my treasure box although the earrings were the only thing of monetary value. Everything else was nothing but baubles and keepsakes such as the fake gold bracelet Mal won for me at a traveling fair.

Nor was it a repository of secrets... except for one. Delving into the bottom of the box, I unearthed my mother's handkerchief. As I unwrapped the folds of linen, I was relieved to discover what I had left tucked inside undisturbed, although even if Amy had come across this object, she would never have understood the significance of it. It was a pick that minstrels used to strum their lutes. Made of ivory, the pick was shaped like a teardrop, which, considering the pain its owner had inflicted upon me, was rather appropriate.

As I cradled the ivory pick in the palm of my hand, I was flooded with bittersweet memories of a youth with golden hair and a golden voice, with eyes of a deep cerulean blue capable of both tenderness and treachery. He called himself Harper and that was the only name I ever knew him by— this young man my step-mother and father had warned me about and were right to do so.

I folded the ivory pick carefully back inside the handkerchief and returned it to the bottom of the box. I no longer kept the pick for any sentimental reasons or as a memento, only as a grim reminder of a lesson harshly learned. Never give your heart to a strolling minstrel for inevitably he will wander off and leave it discarded along the wayside.

Three

It was deep in the afternoon when I finally left the house, my marketing basket hooked over my arm. The rhododendron bushes had started to overtake the path and brushed up against my skirts, dislodging a snow of soft pink petals in my wake.

Our house was very like most homes in Midtown; two stories with a bay front window, a pitched shingle roof and gables adorned with icing latticework (although ours needed a fresh coat of paint). While most of the other houses in the neighborhood were fronted by tidy gardens, ours had become more of a wilderness since I seldom had time to attend the weeding.

Besides the rhododendrons' encroachment upon the walkway, the day lilies had also run riot, the ivy had commenced a tender assault upon the picket fence and the roses had gone completely insane, threatening to crowd out the meek little violets. This abundance of roses was a source of great vexation to our nearest neighbor, Mrs. Biddlesworth. She prided herself on being the best gardener in Midtown, but no matter how carefully she nursed her rosebushes, she had difficulty getting them to thrive.

I told her it was because she fussed with them too much. Roses do not like to be touched. That is why they have thorns. I felt a peculiar kinship with these flowers so perhaps that was the reason my roses grew in such abundance. Mrs. Biddlesworth suspected that I had bewitched them. I was surprised she had never tried to lodge a complaint with the authorities, accusing me of practicing magic without a license.

As I made my way to the gate, Mrs. Biddlesworth was out in her garden as usual, sprinkling water on her tidy borders of alyssum. I called out cheerfully, "Good afternoon, Mrs. B."

She stopped watering to glare at me, her moon face framed beneath a straw bonnet. Instead of returning my greeting, she pointed at something beyond me and demanded, "And just what is that supposed to be?"

I followed the direction of her accusing finger and realized she was gesturing at a particularly tall weed growing in the corner of the yard near the fence. This weed had a heavy stalk, the thickness of a small sapling with broad, flat leaves. I had tried to uproot it many times, but it always grew back. I finally gave up and glued a pot around its base so that it would appear as though it was something I had meant to grow. I even gave it a name.

"Oh, that's just Frank," I told Mrs. Biddlesworth. "Its proper name is... um... Frankincense herbarium. It's a very rare plant."

Mrs. Biddlesworth came closer to the fence that divided our properties. She leaned forward to squint suspiciously at Frank with her small birdlike eyes.

"Wherever did you acquire such a thing?" she asked.

"I traded our pig to a peddler down in Misty Bottoms. He gave me the seeds."

"Magic ones?" she demanded with a fierce scowl.

"No, they looked quite ordinary to me. The peddler promised me that in time Frank will grow the most luscious melons, capable of feeding a small family for a month."

This was all such a blatant lie I was sure Mrs. B would never believe it. We had never owned a pig. If we had, we would have eaten it long ago. When I realized she was swallowing this tale, my evil genius prompted me to add, "I plan to enter Frank in next year's garden competition. I feel sure to win the prize for most exotic plant."

Mrs. B reared back, her cheeks reddening with the force of her indignation. She regarded every prize in the annual competition as her due and anyone who sought to challenge her right as little better than a thief. It was probably not wise to tease a woman who already suspected me of illegal sorcery. I started to assure her I was only joking, but with her chest puffed up like an angry pigeon, she growled, "There is to be a ball at the palace."

Expecting another accusation of witchcraft, her remark caught me off guard.

"What?" I asked, thinking I had not heard her correctly.

"There is to be a ball at the palace," she repeated tersely. "The prince is going to choose a maiden for his bride."

"Yes, so I have heard."

"I hope it is you," she spat out and stalked away before I could reply. I did not mistake her parting words as any sort of good wishes for my future happiness. Mrs. Biddlesworth had wanted to be rid of me ever since I was a child. Mal and I would sneak into her garden and raid her strawberry patch. No doubt she wished that I might marry the prince and move far away, and she would acquire a respectable neighbor who would garden in a normal, tidy fashion.

I thought of telling her that I had no intention of attending the ball, so there was not the least likelihood I would marry the prince or anyone else, but why disillusion the poor woman? Everyone was entitled to their little hopes and dreams, even Mrs. Biddlesworth.

Strolling down the front walkway, I let myself out the gate, which creaked loudly. I should oil the hinges, but I liked the idea of an early warning should trouble head my way. Closing the gate behind me, I emerged onto the cobblestone street, a broad avenue lined with oak trees and streetlamps whose whimsical shape reminded me of acorns.

To the north, this street stretched upward until it split into two forks. The left branch led out to the countryside, grazing meadows, fertile farmlands, and the Red Grove Forest. The right sloped up to the grand estates of the part of Arcady known as the Heights and eventually ended at the massive, gilded gates of the palace.

Going southward, our street curved down to Midtown proper where the markets and governing buildings were. I took that way, bracing my flat shoes against the gentle downward slope of the hill. This road was usually quiet at this time of day, but I was passed by an unusual number of grand carriages with coachmen in livery and footmen riding up behind. Many of these coaches were designed in the latest fashion for pumpkin-shaped carriages. The whimsical design was created by the Duchess of Tarkington. Unfortunately, it had been adopted by many of her acquaintances who carried the conceit to ridiculous lengths, bright orange coaches adorned with stems, curling vines and curtains shaped like seeds.

The duchess's rival, the Countess of Pangbourne, tried to set a trend of her own for a cucumber-shaped vehicle. It never caught on because the odd shape of her coach provoked ribald comments and catcalls from the more unruly elements of the town. Humiliated, the countess returned to her stables and the cucumber carriage was never seen again.

I would be glad to see the last of the pumpkin coaches as well. Besides looking ridiculous, they were far too wide and took up too much room on the road. More than once, as I made my way to town, I was obliged to shrink to the side to allow one of these monstrosities to lumber past.

The amount of traffic heading toward town dismayed me. There was a good reason I chose to do my shopping late in the day. The markets were never crowded and that was when you could get the best bargains from the butcher, the poultry shop and the greengrocer— when they were on the verge of closing.

I imagined the increased amount of coach traffic must be due to one reason. That wretched ball! I discerned that most of the occupants of the carriages were of the fairer sex, an army of ladies preparing to descend upon the milliners, the lace shops, the dress-makers, and the Silk Emporium. I did not plan to visit any of those places, but I would have to pass through that district to reach the food markets.

The street narrowed as I drew nearer to town. I glared resent-fully when I was obliged to leap into a ditch to avoid yet another pumpkin coach. I prepared to step back onto the roadway when I had to give way again, this time to a troop of the king's Royal Scutcheons. They marched past me, looking crisp in their blue jackets and dun-colored pantaloons, their high boots striking the pavement in a synchronized rhythm.

Their sergeant, a stout fellow with a bristling mustache, bellowed out the cadence, "Left, right, hup! Left, right, hup!"

On the "hup," the guards swung their right arms up and struck their fists across their chests in unison. I often wondered if they all ended up with bruised shoulders at the end of a day's march.

There are many branches of the Scutcheons. Their floppy black berets and sashes identified this group as part of the platoon whose task it was to maintain order in town, arrest malefactors and bring them to justice.

In their midst was a prisoner being prodded along. He attempted to keep step, his hands manacled before him, his grey hair straggling over a face lined with an expression of abject misery. I speculated on what the poor man might have done. It could not be anything too serious or he would have been incarcerated in the King's Royal Prison. The grim fortress had been nicknamed "The Dismal Dungeons," an accurate reflection of the miserable condi-tions of the place.

Most likely this poor fellow had committed some minor trans-gression which would result in his being whipped in the town square or confined for a day in the Yoke of Shame. I should have just kept my head averted as the troop marched past, but I could not help gazing with sympathy at the prisoner.

A shadow fell over me as the leader of this troop came up behind me. He was the only one mounted on horseback, a fierce-looking man, with a full dark beard. I recognized him at once but that was no great surprise. Everyone knew Commander Horatio Crushington, the head of the Midtown garrison. Nor was it any surprise that the commander was aware of who I was. Crushington made a point of knowing every resident of Midtown. He had a prodigious memory, never forgetting a name or a face.

He guided his roan gelding alongside me, a horse as massive as its master. Nodding down at me, Crushington said, "Good afternoon, Miss Upton."

I nodded back in acknowledgment. "Commander."

I slowed to a halt, expecting he would ride on by. I was dismayed when he reined his mount to a stop. The entire troop would have halted as well, but the commander motioned to the sergeant to keep them moving. I could not restrain a soft outcry when their prisoner stumbled and was hauled to his feet. I knew it would be far better to say nothing, but I could not restrain my curiosity.

Shielding my eyes against the sun, I craned my neck to gaze up at Crushington. "What did that man do?" I asked.

"Nothing to alarm you, Miss Upton. Farmer Grey merely sought to evade the tax on working animals. He tried to pass off his sheep-herding dog as a pet by keeping it shut up in the house. The poor beast was frantic, barking day and night until it finally managed to leap through an open window to return to its flock."

I lowered my gaze to conceal my disgust that this poor farmer should be dragged off in chains over such a small offense. "I was not aware that your authority extended into the countryside, Commander. How did you even know such a transgression had taken place?"

"One of Farmer Grey's neighbors rode into town to complain. When such a report is filed, I am obliged to take action."

"No doubt this neighbor was well paid for informing on Grey."

"That is our system."

I compressed my lips together to avoid telling him the system stank. Whoever had informed upon Grey had better hope none of his neighbors found out or he might endure reprisals in the form of a midnight beating. Our king's petty laws, high taxes and habit of rewarding informants was engendering a very ugly spirit in our kingdom, setting neighbor against neighbor.

"I congratulate you on apprehending a very desperate criminal," I said. My tone of voice was so mild another man might have missed the sarcasm, but Crushington was no fool.

I tensed when he dismounted from his horse and wished I had kept my mouth shut. The commander was just as formidable out of the saddle as when mounted. Although he frowned at me, he did not seem angry as he said, "I deplore the necessity for having to arrest men like Grey for such small offenses, but the law is the law, Miss Upton and I am sworn to enforce it. I would much rather spend my energies pursuing more dangerous criminals. That is why I need to speak to you."

"Oh, dear! Never say you have found me out already," I quipped.

He subjected me to such a piercing stare, I recollected how imprudent it was to jest with this man. I hastened to add, "No doubt someone has informed you I have been insulting royal heralds again."

Some of the tension in the commander's face relaxed. His lips twitched upward. This might have been some sort of tic or what passed for Crushington's smile. I was uncertain, but his voice sounded wry as he said, "Royal heralds are accustomed to being insulted. I believe it is part of their training. I am more concerned with some of the bad company you keep."

"Bad company?" I forced a smile to my lips, but it was a nervous one. I feared where Crushington might be going with this. "I assure you, sir, I number no hardened criminals among my acquaintance."

"No? Not even Malcolm Hawkridge?"

I tried not to flinch.

"Mr. Hawkridge is a respectable apothecary," I insisted.

Crushington's heavy brows rose upward. "I think we are both aware that is not strictly true, Miss Upton."

"Indeed, it is. Mr. Hawkridge has been my friend for years and I swear to you that I know nothing of him being involved in anything illegal."

This was true as far as it went. If I knew nothing of Mal's dodgier activities, it was because I chose not to know. I was aware that he occasionally dealt with smugglers, buying things on the black market. Although he was not licensed to act as a mage, he often brewed up magical potions or enchanted objects, but since Mal's spells invariably did not work, where was the harm in that?

Of late, I had suspected that Mal might be involved in something of a more serious and dangerous nature, but I preferred to remain in ignorance. Knowing what Mal was up to would only give me one more thing to worry about that I was helpless to remedy.

"I hope you are telling me the truth, Miss Upton," the commander said. "I have had your friend Hawkridge under observation for some time and I know he is not the simple herbalist he pretends to be. Whatever crime he is involved in, I will catch him out eventually so you would be very wise to keep your distance."

"Are you threatening me, sir?" I demanded.

"No, merely cautioning you. I should be grieved if I was ever obliged to arrest you, because— because I like you."

"How nice," I mumbled.

"No, I—" He startled me by seizing my hand in his massive grip. He continued gruffly, "I mean that I *really* like you."

Gazing up at him, I was horrified to see something akin to tenderness in those hard grey eyes. My jaw dropped open. When I was finally able to close it, I hardly knew what to reply to this astonishing declaration. I should make it plain that I was not interested in being really liked by him. But offending a man as powerful as the commander was not a prudent thing to do.

I finally managed to stammer, "Um, well, thank you. You are also extremely... ah... tolerable."

An awkward silence descended in which the seconds seemed to stretch into hours. I tried to slip my hand free, but it would have been easier to wriggle out of a carpenter's vise.

The commander cleared his throat. "I suppose like all the other Midtown ladies you are excited about the invitation from the palace and eager to attend the ball."

"Oh, frap, no!" I blurted out, without thinking.

I thought he would be appalled by my swearing, but he merely regarded me gravely. "Your refusal to attend the ball could be misconstrued as a sign of disloyalty to the king."

"Or a sign of my poverty," I retorted. "I cannot afford the cost of the ticket and even if I could..." For once I managed to check my wayward tongue before I added that I thought Prince Florian was a complete moron and I would not want to marry him, even if he came gold-plated and bearing the gift of a million books. Well, perhaps that many books might induce me to— no! Not even then.

Keeping my opinion of the prince to myself, I said, "I daresay I am a very strange woman because I have no interest in becoming a princess."

Something in the commander's eyes brightened. "I am very glad of that."

"Of what? That I am strange?"

"No, that you do not desire a prince, that perhaps in time, you might even consider—"

Terrified of what he might be about to say, I interrupted. "My goodness, how late it is getting! I fear I have detained you from your duties far too long. I am sure you must be a very busy man, reports to file, troops to drill, prisoners to whip. And I need to get on with my marketing."

"Of course," he agreed, but continued to grip my hand and regard me wistfully.

"And to do that, I really need you to release me. I have always been a two-handed shopper."

"Oh yes, certainly." He let go of me, his cheeks reddening with embarrassment. He looked as though he wanted to say more, but mercifully could not find the words. He settled for a stiff bow, clicking his boots together. He turned back to his mount. Any other horse might have used its master being distracted to wander off or crop at grass, but I could have sworn that gelding stood to attention the entire time.

Crushington swung up into the saddle. Looking down at me, his lips pulled upward in that peculiar twitch. "Farewell, Miss Upton. I hope we meet again soon."

I managed a stiff smile and shook my hand. He probably thought I was waving, but I was only trying to work the circulation back into my numbed fingers. That man did not know his own strength.

He gigged his horse into motion. I remained where I was until he trotted off down the road and disappeared around the bend. When he was gone, I had to resist the urge to flee back home and bolt myself inside my room, never to emerge again.

Heretofore Commander Crushington and I had been nothing more than passing acquaintances, the more distant, the better as far as I was concerned. Never in my wildest dreams did I imagine that he looked upon me with anything approaching a friendly eye. I could only wonder in dismay what I could have done to attract such a solemn, humorless man. If I ever figured it out, I vowed never, ever to do it again.

It was not that I considered the commander evil. He was

nothing like many of the other Scutcheon officers, corrupt, power-mad bullies. But he was something just as frightening, a man rigid in his sense of duty, incapable of seeing shades of grey or indulging in the quality of mercy. I was quite certain he would arrest his own grandmother if she were guilty of something he considered an infraction of the law.

Now this ruthless upholder of law and order had his stern gaze trained in my friend's direction. I wanted to race down to Misty Bottoms to warn Mal at once. But I was restrained by the fear that Crushington might still be lurking somewhere ahead. I was going to have to head for the market first. Even if the formidable Scutcheon commander had developed an alarming infatuation with me and threatened to clap my dearest friend in irons, the Upton family still needed to eat.

When I rounded the bend, I quailed at the scene that met my eyes. Midtown's shopping district had descended into utter madness. The dratted pumpkin coaches were everywhere, blocking the street as grooms tried to keep their restive horses calm. One of the carriages had locked wheels with an ale wagon. The carter and the bewigged coachman appeared ready to come to blows, swearing and shouting insults.

Such a dispute would have drawn a crowd on an ordinary day, but no one was paying much attention amid the rest of the chaos. Women and girls thronged the street, fighting to make their way to the shops. Grand ladies from the Heights were trailed by maids and footmen as they tried to sweep majestically forward. Midtown women, usually deferential, elbowed duchesses and countesses aside to get first pick of the merchandise.

The lacemaker's, the milliner's and the glove and ribbon shops looked crowded with clamoring females to the point of bursting out their bow front windows. The worse congestion was of course at the Silk Emporium. Dearling, the shop's proprietor, had conceived the brilliant notion he could relieve the crush inside his store by setting up a display outside.

The hapless clerk assigned to this task got as far as setting up a table. The young man, in his innocence, clearly expected the ladies to wait patiently while he unpacked the silks and arranged the fabrics in a pleasing display. As soon as he opened the first box, he was swarmed by the eager, squealing throng. The poor boy's arms flailed desperately as he struggled to remain upright before he disappeared completely, engulfed in a sea of petticoats.

Scutcheons were everywhere, frantically trying to keep order. One private made the mistake of trying to get between two stout dames fighting over a length of lace and ended up being scratched and bitten. I saw no sign of Commander Crushington, but I doubted that even his fierce demeanor could have gained control over these ravening hordes of women.

There was nothing like the prospect of wedding a handsome prince to rouse something feral in the bosom of the demurest maidens and their ambitious mamas. If I could have hung back and watched from a safe distance, I might have found the whole thing amusing, especially if I'd had Mal with me to enjoy this melee over fabric and furbelows.

Alas! If I wanted to reach the food markets, I was obliged to fling myself into the very heart of this insanity. Fortifying myself with a deep breath, I took the plunge, struggling for every inch of pavement that I gained. I was a slender person, but I still had to balance my basket on top of my head to squeeze through the thicket of savage shoppers. My toes were trampled, and I was stabbed in the rib cage with something— I believe it was some dowager's parasol. My basket tumbled from my grasp, but there was no hope of retrieving it. If I had tried to bend down to find it, I would have ended up flattened like one of those hot cakes that bakers smack thin with their spatulas.

By the time I reached the other end of the street, I was panting like a swimmer who had finally fought free of a powerful undertow. The area where the foodstuffs were sold appeared like a veritable haven. I staggered toward it, grateful to find these shops as empty as I would have expected at this time of day.

Unfortunately, I was about to encounter yet another unpleasant consequence of this royal ball madness— greed. My intention had been to splurge on a plump pullet, as though a fine chicken dinner might somehow console my stepsisters for their disappointment over the ball. A ridiculous ploy I knew, but it was the best that I could devise.

I discovered that even providing this small treat was impossible when I entered the poultry shop and Mr. Barclay quoted me the price of a small hen.

"What!" I cried. "That is almost quadruple of what you were charging last week!"

Mr. Barclay shrugged his bony shoulders. He was a scrawny man whose neck skin sagged like a rooster's wattle. "Prices can't stay the same forever, miss."

"Why? Have your hens started laying golden eggs?"

He crowed out a laugh, displaying the gap between his front teeth. "No, miss. If that was the case, I'd keep all the hens for myself."

"That must be what you are planning to do if you charge these prices. Is there a poultry shortage that I don't know about?"

"No, but I expect there will be. With this year's royal ball being a much larger and grander affair, I fancy the palace will be ready to buy up all the chicken I can supply and at any price I name." He hooked his thumbs beneath his apron straps and looked so smug, I wanted to smack him.

"This ball is a one-night affair. Do you think that makes it worth offending your regular customers?"

"You are hardly a regular customer. If I make enough money from this ball, maybe I can retire. Do you know how much I hate chickens? All that squawking and the smell! Plucking them clean is disgusting work. That is why I have decided to start charging more for that as well. If you want your hen killed, dressed, and stuffed with cornbread, that'll cost you extra."

I wanted to tell Barclay what he could do with his stuffing, but I just glared at him and stalked out of the shop. I soon discovered that he was not the only merchant determined to exploit this opportunity. The butcher, the greengrocer, the baker and even the spice seller had all hiked their prices as well. And the stupid ball was still an entire month away.

As I trudged from the cheese shop, empty-handed, I muttered, "We are all going to starve." I immediately chided myself for being as melodramatic as Amy.

Of course, we would not starve. We could always fall back on the one constant supply of cheap food in the kingdom, the great body of water that bordered Misty Bottoms— Conger River —so called because it teemed with a variety of eels.

I'd had recourse to the snigglers far more often than I or my family liked, even though I had grown quite ingenious in the many ways to prepare eels. Eel pie, eel ragout, creamed lampreys, eel fricassee. I could probably contrive another new recipe but the thought of eel again for supper left me completely dispirited.

My hair was coming undone, straggling about my cheeks. I had lost my basket; the hem of my dress was torn, and my rib felt bruised where that horrid old lady had poked me. I do not often give way to lachrymose emotions, but I felt so tired and overwhelmed by everything, I could have sunk down in the middle of the street and cried.

I forced myself to trudge onward. I managed to avoid the worst of the crowds by squeezing down a narrow alleyway between the Silk Emporium and the ribbon vendors. I emerged into the area of town behind Quad Hall, the old grey stone building that housed all the municipal governing departments. Covered in ivy, it resembled a small castle with four round towers. Somewhere behind those forbidding walls, Commander Crushington would have his office. It was likely situated near the Scutcheon barracks and the steel doors that led to the jail where the unfortunate Farmer Grey would be held, awaiting his punishment.

I was, thankfully, not familiar with that part of Quad Hall. I was regrettably too well acquainted with the Exchequer Tower, where you went to pay your taxes unless you wanted the king's revenue collectors to come hammering at your front door. Even when it was not Collection Day, townsfolk tended to creep past the Exchequer Tower as though fearful of waking a sleeping giant.

I was surprised to see a cheerful-looking crowd queued up outside the tower door until I remembered this was where the tickets to the ball were being sold. Unlike the unruly mobs outside the shops, the crowd here milled about docilely as a flock of sheep lined up to be fleeced. As vendors moved among the waiting crowd, selling ices and sugar nuts, everyone was laughing and chattering as though it was some sort of holiday.

I spotted Fortescue Bafton and his sister near the front of the line. Florence Bafton looked disheveled but smugly triumphant as she displayed the blue silk she had bought to several other girls I recognized as some of my stepsisters' friends. Amy and Netta should have been among them, instead of at home weeping into their pillows.

The thought did nothing to improve my mood. Ducking my head down, I slunk past the queue, in no humor to be hailed by Mr. Bafton or anyone else I happened to know. I made it, reaching the next point of the building, which contained the Ministry of Registrars. This was where one went to register births, marriages, deaths and apply for licenses to set up shopkeeping or practice magic.

It was also the tower that contained the infamous Aura Chamber, invented by the king's chief sorcerer, Mercato. This device measured and recorded each citizen's aura and stored it in the city's archives. It first came into use about seventeen years ago, when every subject had to register their aura or pay a hefty fine.

It was for the good of the realm, King August had insisted.

This registry would not only help protect his loyal subjects from criminal elements but would also aid in tracing children who strayed and became lost.

I was six years old at the time and was excited by the prospect of seeing this amazing Aura Chamber everyone was talking about. To my dismay and astonishment, my father balked at complying with this law. When I realized I was not to have my turn in the magic chamber, I burst into tears, wailing.

"B-but everyone has got to have their aura collected. Mal's grandmother even took him. It is for our safety. Don't you care if I get lost, Papa?"

My father scooped me up onto his lap, awkwardly brushing my tears away. He gave me one of his odd, sad smiles. "You will never get lost, Ella. You are far too clever for that. The only way you will ever disappear is because you wish to do so."

His words confused me, but I was so pleased to discover my father thought I was clever that I stopped crying and beamed at him. As a child, I could not imagine any reason I would want to disappear.

That of course has changed. There have been many moments when I have been so overwhelmed, I have wished I could simply vanish and today was turning out to be one of them.

Leaving Quad Hall behind me, I reached the fountain burbling in the middle of the town square. I bent down to splash the cool water over my face until I felt somewhat revived. This great fountain with its soothing sprays of water used to be one of my favorite places in the kingdom when I was a child. Back in those days, there had been an enormous statue erected in the center depicting my heroine, Queen Anthea, the Magnificently Wise.

The ancient sculpture had been commissioned to commemorate Queen Anthea's role in ending the Nodellian War before it ever began. She had formed a secret alliance with the enemy queen, and they had amassed an army of women from both kingdoms.

When the day for battle dawned, Queen Anthea led her considerable force of mothers, wives, daughters, sisters, aunts and grandmothers right down the middle of the field between the two opposing armies, thus preventing them from getting off a single cannon shot.

The women dispersed among their men folk, coaxing, cajoling and in many cases seizing them by the ear until the foot soldiers all threw down the arms and headed back home. Soon there was no one left but two pipsqueak kings and some fat, old generals. When they realized if they wanted a war, they were going to have to do the fighting themselves, they slunk homeward as well.

Hereinafter, Queen Anthea browbeat her son, the king and his council into enacting a law that no man would ever be able to go to war without written permission from his mother. The kingdom enjoyed a long period of peace until a plague swept through Arcady, killing the young king, his wife and infant son.

The aging Queen Anthea was obliged to surrender her crown to a distant cousin when he marched into the kingdom at the head of his army and thus the reign of the Helavalerians began. Some said that Arcady had never prospered since that ill-fated day Cuthbert theFirst claimed the throne. He immediately did away with all of Queen Anthea's wise laws and embarked on a series of disastrous wars that nearly left the treasury bankrupt. Thankfully, our present king, August, was not as bellicose as his ancestor. Except for a brief skirmish along the northern border, Arcady once again knew peace, mostly because wars are expensive, and August was too much of a miser to fund an army.

When the statue of the magnificent Anthea was damaged in a storm, King August used it as an excuse to tear the sculpture down and erect another in its place. What now loomed over me represented the cause of much of my present misery, Prince Florian. It was a decent likeness of the heir to the throne, depicting his strapping, muscular frame, and flowing locks of hair. His sword clutched in one hand, his shield in the other, he looked almost noble instead of the dolt that he truly was.

I had never actually met the prince, but I had heard many tales of Florian's idiocy, most of the stories acquired from my wandering minstrel. Harper had often been called to entertain at the palace. Afterward, he would reduce me to tears of laughter by imitating the way Florian liked to toss his thick mane and the prince's braying laugh.

Of course, that was all before Harper simply reduced me to tears. Peering down at my unhappy reflection in the fountain waters, I trailed my fingers through it as though I could erase all memories of my faithless bard.

Harper had proved to be so false; I might have been inclined to think that his stories about the prince were all lies. But I had caught a glimpse of Florian those rare times he had ridden through town, and he gave the impression of a man fond of gazing into his mirror. The way he liked to whip back his golden mane led Mal to dub our prince the "hair apparent." But he never said this too loudly because one could be heavily fined for mocking a member of the royal family.

There might be a touch of envy on Mal's part because all the Hawkridge men suffer from the curse of prematurely receding hairlines. Even though Mal was only a few months older than me, he had little hair left other than a fringe.

The mere thought of my friend was enough to bring the smile back to my lips. I know that if there was one person in the kingdom who I could count upon to remain sane and aloof from all this royal ball madness, it would be Malcolm Hawkridge. My longing to be with my friend was so acute, I turned away from Midtown and raced down the hill to Misty Bottoms.

Four

The area known as Misty Bottoms rested at the southern-most tip of Arcady near the border. It was situated on the Conger River and was usually bathed in a mist rising off the turgid waters. Some days, the mist could be so thick, one could not see two footsteps ahead. The Bottoms was such a twisted warren of lanes and narrow alleys, it would be quite easy to get lost in the fog, even for those familiar with the area.

This afternoon, nothing but the usual grey pall hung over the Bottoms. I made my way down Eel Splitch Lane, past a row of defeated-looking cottages, their windows boarded over to avoid paying the extra tax; many of them with their thatched roofs appearing in danger of collapse. I wrinkled my nose at the foul odor that permeated the air here, something that smelled like a combination of rotting fish and boiled cabbage. The stench was even worse in the winter when the cottage dwellers burned peat made from the compressed dung of mountain elks, otherwise known in the vulgar parlance as "frap."

Mal assured me that the Bottoms dwellers grew accustomed to the smell after a while. It saddened me that anyone should have to become used to living in such dismal conditions. I was terrified to think that someday my family and I might well end up here— or somewhere even worse.

As miserable as the Bottoms were, at least these folk still had a roof over their heads. The king's council had passed an edict making it illegal to be homeless. As King August had decreed, "It only makes the good citizens of our kingdom uncomfortable to look at beggars, and truly if these miscreants had been more industrious and thriftier, they would not have ended up in such a sorry state."

Consequently, vagrants were rounded up by the Border Scutcheons and exiled out into the swampland and unchartered forest beyond the river. What ultimately became of these wretched individuals no one knew.

As I followed the twists of the lane, the smell of fish grew stronger, the closer I got to the river. I stifled a shriek when something large and black skittered past my skirt. I tried to imagine it was nothing more than a scrawny cat.

The lane was largely empty at this hour of day. Folks in the Bottoms tended to retire to their homes well before dark and bolt their doors. What individuals I passed looked as worn and ragged as their homes. A few gave me sidelong hostile glares but for the most part, kept their heads down.

I did the same until I chanced upon someone I knew. My stomach knotted at the sight of the hunch-backed man with pointy features and a dandelion shock of white hair. He ran a small curio shop and was known as a purchaser of goods, especially from those desperate to acquire funds. I had had occasion to visit his establishment far too often, not a happy memory, but I forced a stiff smile to my lips.

"Good afternoon, Mr. Fugitate."

He responded with a grunt. "Shop is closed for today, miss. So, if you are bringing me something to sell—"

"I am not."

He grunted again and brushed past me. I never took Withypole

Fugitate's surliness amiss because I knew the reason for it. Mal believed that Withypole was one of the fairy folks. Most of them had been driven out of the kingdom a long time ago by the king's harsh regulations regarding the practice of magic and his ruinous tax on wings. Those few who stubbornly chose to remain were at pains to disguise these prominent appendages. Fugitate did so by crushing his into a sack and making it appear as if he had a hump beneath his shirt. I knew nothing about what it would be like to have wings, but I suspected that being obliged to compress them must be rather painful. Hence Fugitate's constant state of ill humor.

I quickened my steps, turning down another lane, up an alley and cutting across a narrow field where the burned out remains of several cottages stood. It was a longer and more roundabout route Mal had shown me to avoid going past the Winking Goblin, a dark, smoky tavern that tended to be frequented by some rather rough characters.

The next thoroughfare was wide enough that it almost merited the name of street. It was in fact called Rock Gunnel Street and Mal's place was in the middle of it, tucked between a chandlery and an old house whose upper stories were built in such crooked fashion, it resembled a layer cake constructed by a drunken pastry chef.

Mal's shop was constructed of weather-worn clapboards and had a dingy bow window and green door. A sign creaking on rusty chains hung from the upper story. The placard depicted a predatory bird with spread wings and hook talons. Painted beneath was the shop's name, THE HAWK'S NEST.

I told Mal that the name sounded more suited to a den of thieves, and he ought to think of a more respectable moniker for an herbalist's shop. Mal only laughed and replied that respectability had never been of great concern to Hawkridges.

Extreme poverty was not the only thing that drove people to live in Misty Bottoms. Some chose to settle here for murkier reasons. The heavy mists, the maze of lanes and the proximity to the border made it an ideal location for those engaged in activities that would not bear scrutiny by the law. My friend Mal fell into this category.

A CLOSED sign hung in the shop's window, but I ignored it, hammering loudly on the door. As I did so, I had the uncomfortable feeling of being watched. I knocked again while looking nervously around me.

"Rrreow."

A low growl caused me to glance down into the yellow eyes of Mal's sleek black cat. This creature had taken a marked dislike to me. It glared at me, arched its back and hissed. I hissed right back at it and started to knock again when the shop's door swung open.

"Can't you read? The sign says—" Mal snapped, then broke into a broad grin. "Ella, what an agreeable surprise."

I was likewise surprised, but I cannot say I found it agreeable. My friend Mal was a lean man of medium height and possessed of a rangy, almost catlike grace. His face was one of sharp, hard angles, softened by a pair of melting chocolate eyes. He had a wicked smile that I suspected had been more than one maiden's undoing, despite his receding hairline. As usual, he wore a stained apron over his breeches and an open-necked shirt.

He was also wearing a thick black wig styled into a pompadour.

I just stood there gaping at him, until Mal reached up and smoothed back a dark wave from his brow. He gave a self-conscious chuckle and asked, "Well, what do you think? Do you like it?"

"No," I said bluntly. "It looks like you scalped that wretched cat of yours and stuck it on your head."

Mal's hand dropped back to his side, and he scowled at me. "I have told you a hundred times. Ebony is not my cat. She belongs to the witch next door."

Mal was not being insulting when he referred to his neighbor thus. Delphine really was a witch, although most likely an unlicensed one.

"If that cat doesn't belong to you, perhaps you ought to tell her that."

The cat had insinuated itself between us, rubbing up against Mal's legs and purring. Before he could prevent her, the cat bolted past him into the shop. Mal swore and tore off after her, leaving me to follow and close the door behind me.

The cat had streaked up the stairs to the upper floor with Mal hard after her. I could hear him stomping about, alternately calling, "Here, kitty, kitty. Nice Ebony," and muttering, "frapping cat." Perhaps I should have gone to help him, but I knew from experience that if anyone ended up being scratched by that demon cat, it would be me. I believed it wiser to wait below.

The main floor of the herbal shop was warm and dim, dominated by a long counter upon which were laid out the tools of Mal's trade, mortar and pestle, a silver scale, empty vials, ladles, funnels, and wooden spoons. Behind the counter were shelves, every inch covered with bottles and jars containing liquids in a rainbow array of colors, anything from clear to blood red to the vilest hue of black. The bottles on the upper shelves required a ladder to reach and were the cloudiest looking, coated with a thick layering of dust.

Nothing was labeled and I often wondered how Mal kept from confusing potions for curing warts with the poisons for killing off weeds. But Mal had a phenomenal memory, and he knew right where to lay hands on the potion he needed, as long as no one else touched anything.

The beams on the ceiling had hooks that hung bundles of drying herbs. Usually, the shop was redolent with a fragrant blend of marjoram, fennel, basil, mint, and other spices. But Mal had some golden liquid bubbling in a small caldron suspended over a fire on the hearth. Whatever the potion was, it emanated a cloyingly sweet aroma that overpowered every other scent.

Before I had a chance to inspect this brew more closely, Mal tramped back down the stairs with the cat clutched in his arms. Ebony set up a loud purr, rubbing her head beneath Mal's chin, but he ignored her. Opening the door, he chucked her out, saying, "Shoo. Go home to your mistress and don't come back."

I heard Ebony's reproachful meow before Mal slammed the door shut.

"Oh, Mal, how can you be so unkind?" I teased. "Your kitty clearly adores you."

"Frapping cat! She's forever sneaking over here bringing me gifts of minnows she fishes out of the witch's pond. If any tax collector ever sees her, I will probably be accused of owning a working cat and have to pay a huge fine. One of these days, I really will scalp her."

"In case you need a spare hairpiece?"

Mal glowered at me. "Did you come here today just to insult me or is there some other reason for this unexpected visit? If there isn't, you'll have to excuse me. I am quite busy."

It was not like Mal to be so abrupt, either with the cat or me. I feared I had hurt his feelings with my usual tactlessness. Sidling closer, I said, "I am sorry if I was unkind."

I brushed a kiss against his cheek and smiled impishly at him. "But if your closest friend doesn't tell you when you look ridiculous, who will?"

"Humph," he said, but the taut set of his lips softened a little. "Does it really look that bad?"

"Yes, I am afraid it does. Why suddenly did you decide you need a wig?"

"It is not a wig, Ella." He bent closer, adding eagerly, "I managed to grow real hair. Go on. Touch it."

I reached up and gave his hair a gentle tug. Unfortunately, a clump of it came loose in my hand.

Mal reared back, protesting, "Not so hard." He combed his fingers through his hair to repair the damage and only succeeded in dislodging another handful. He emitted a deep sigh. "Apparently I need to refine the potion a bit more."

"Why would you even bother with such nonsense? You are an attractive enough man just as you are."

"Oh, you think so, my dear?" Mal leered, leaning closer with a mock growl. "I had no notion you found me so irresistible."

"Idiot," I said, giving him a playful shove.

Mal straightened with a grin. "While you might be smitten with my semi-bald head, alas, my customers are not. I have had several women tell me they find it difficult to believe in the skills of a sorcerer who cannot even manage to devise a potion to grow back his own hair."

"You are not supposed to be any kind of a sorcerer, Mal. With or without hair. You have no license to practice magic." I had lost track of the number of times I had reminded Mal of this and the equal number of times he had ignored me, just as he did now.

The caldron on the hearth gave a loud hiss, threatening to bubble over.

"Oh, frap!" Mal exclaimed. Rushing over, he snatched up a long rod with a hook on one end and used it to swing the caldron off the fire. He seized a wooden spoon and bent over the iron pot, stirring the golden liquid. I pulled a face at the sickly sweet aroma.

"Is that your hair potion?" I asked. "Besides looking like you skinned a cat, you are going to smell like a rose garden."

Mal paused in his stirring long enough to give me a disgruntled look. "No, this is not a hair tonic. It is something far more powerful."

When Mal showed no inclination to explain further, I drew closer. He scooped up a spoonful of the liquid and blew on it to cool it. He sniffed and took a cautious taste with the tip of his tongue.

"Ah!" He nodded, looking satisfied.

"Mal, what is that stuff?"

His mouth tipped in a mysterious smile. "Something I am planning to call the Elixir of Love."

"You are trying to brew up a love potion?"

"Yes, there should be a great demand for it, don't you think? With this royal ball in the offing and so many ladies hoping to win the heart of the prince, our golden hair apparent."

I groaned. "Oh, Mal, not you too!"

When he regarded me with surprise, I flung up my hands in exasperation. "All day long I have been surrounded by people going berserk over this ridiculous ball. First, my stepsisters wailing they will die if they do not get to go and then I was nearly run over by those stupid pumpkin coaches with the ladies from the Heights racing to be the first at the Silk Emporium. I was almost crushed in a riot over ribbons and beads and even the poultry man is out of control. The one person I counted upon to be untouched by all this royal ball insanity was you. And now I find you as caught up in the madness as everyone else."

"Calm down, Ella. I totally agree with you. This ball is ridiculous, but I would be insane not to try for a little profit from it. I imagine many women will pay quite handsomely for a potion that will give them an edge over their competition."

"Shame on you for seeking to trick them. You know as well as I do there is no such thing a true love potion."

"No, there isn't. And that is not what I am offering them."

"Then what is it?"

"A belief in possibilities."

When I rolled my eyes, Mal said, "Let me ask you a question, Ella. Have you ever observed that it is not always the fairest woman in the room who attracts the notice of every man present? That often a woman who is less beautiful is the one who receives the most attention. Now why do you think that is?"

"She has a large fortune?"

Mal laughed. "No, my dear cynical friend. What she has is a complete belief in herself, in her looks, her power of allurement, her worthiness to be loved. That belief communicates itself in the way she walks, the way she smiles, the way she carries herself. You probably have no idea how much courage it takes a man to woo a woman, his innate fear of making a fool of himself. The lady who can meet his gaze boldly and knows how to encourage him with her eyes will win out over the timid beauty almost every time."

While he spoke, Mal fetched a ladle and scooped up some of the liquid, pouring it into the bottle. Holding the golden liquid up to the light, he concluded, "The women who buy this potion will think that it has the magic to make them totally desirable and if they truly believe it, they will be. What I have brewed up in this bottle is confidence."

"No, what you have conjured up there is trouble. I don't care if your Elixir of Love works or not. If you are caught peddling that stuff, you are going to end up arrested for practicing magic without a license. Do you realize that Commander Crushington has you in his sights? He is just waiting for any excuse to lay charges against you. He told me so himself."

"When were you discussing me with the Crusher?"

"Just this afternoon. He warned me to stay away from you."

"Oh, don't worry about him. Do you think I cannot handle the Crusher?"

"What I think is you have been sniffing the fumes of your own potion and suffer from an overconfidence that is going to get you arrested or even killed one of these days."

Mal just grinned. "Recklessness has always been a characteristic of Hawkridge men. It is part of our charm."

I scowled at him and added hesitantly, "There is something else Crushington told me. I know this is going to sound unbelievable, but it appears that the commander has developed some sort of fondness for me."

To my indignation, Mal burst out laughing.

"I don't see what is so amusing about that."

"What is amusing, my dear, is how completely obtuse you are.

I cannot believe you never noticed how smitten the Crusher is with you. One time, he craned his neck so far for a glimpse of you; I thought he was going to fall off his horse."

"I never noticed that, and I am glad I didn't. I am sure I never did anything to offer him the least encouragement so I cannot imagine why he should have become so enamored."

"Can you not? You should try looking in a mirror sometime, on one of those days when you have found the time to wash your face and brush your hair. But you are also completely oblivious to how beautiful you are."

"If I am that attractive, it is no merit of mine. I did not create my face and I am sure I am no prettier than scores of other women."

"I could debate that with you, but I know it would be of little use," Mal said. "In any event, I do not know why you are so distressed about the Crusher. It could prove of great advantage having a Scutcheon commander infatuated with you."

"No, it couldn't. The commander is not the sort of man to allow his feelings for anyone to sway him from his duty. Even if he were, I am not the sort of woman to take advantage of his infatuation."

Mal smiled and cupped my chin. "I know you aren't. That is why I am rather madly in love with you myself."

"Oh, be serious, Mal," I said, pushing his hand away. "I did not come here to talk nonsense." I fetched a wearied sigh. "What I could really use is a cup of tea."

Mal swept me an exaggerated bow. "Your every wish is my command, milady. Allow me to escort you to the parlor."

Mal led the way through the curtain at the back of the shop. I followed him into his kitchen and tried not to cringe. When Mal's grandmother was alive, the place was so clean you could eat off the floor. Mal, on his own, was a total disaster. Dirty dishes were stacked everywhere, in the sink, on the counter and on the small oak table. When I walked across the hardwood floor, I could hear the grit crunch beneath my shoes. I had to skirt around a tumbled pile of wood that Mal had never gotten around to stacking in the log basket.

Mal chucked a few pieces of wood into the stove furnace to stoke up the fire. While he filled up the iron kettle, I tried to clear away some of the dishes, empty bottles, and books from the table.

"Just sit down," he commanded. "I'll take care of that."

Mal swept the table clean by dumping everything into the empty log basket. I sighed but said nothing. But when he squinted at the bottom of a stained teacup and began polishing it clean with the hem of his apron, it was more than I could endure.

"No, you sit down, and I'll prepare the tea," I said.

Mal voiced his usual token protests, but in the end was pleased to surrender. Mal enjoyed being taken care of and he truly missed his grandmother. I have often suggested he engage a charwoman. Mal insisted he could never trust anyone to clean as well as his grandmother had. What he really meant was, he did not want any stranger in the shop, stumbling upon some of his more dubious activities.

While I gave the teacups and saucers a proper scrubbing, Mal removed his dirty apron and lounged back in one of the kitchen chairs. It amused me to notice him tugging at his neckline and scratching. Obviously more of his hair had fallen out and slipped down inside his shirt. It was a loose-fitting garment with full sleeves that closed with laces that Mal never pulled too tight.

I have never known Mal to wear anything resembling a cravat. Mal said it was because something that constricted the neck was an uncomfortable reminder of strangling which was the current method of execution in our realm. Our king had such a horror of shedding his subjects' blood, that all condemned prisoners met their fates at an appointment with the Lord High Garroter and his thick, knotted rope, deep in the Dismal Dungeons.

This individual seldom ever came into town, but I do recall seeing him once when I was about nine years old. He was a giant of a man with thick beefy arms and hands the size of dinner plates. He had come lumbering into the sweetmeats shop where Imelda was treating me and my stepsisters to marzipan. Imelda had turned pale and hustled us all out without buying anything. Amy began to cry but was sharply hushed by her mother who declared we had to get away from "that evil man."

I didn't think that huge man looked evil, only rather sad and lonely. It was sometime later before I realized who the mournful giant was, the Lord High Garroter who had executed Imelda's first husband.

When the kettle came to a boil, I scooped some loose tea in the pot and added the hot water. The tea leaves must have been reasonably fresh because a fragrant aroma issued from the teapot. It was a pretty piece of crockery that had belonged to Mal's grandmother. The teapot was painted with vines and roses but had to be treated carefully because there was a crack in the handle where it had been glued back together.

This was not owing to any carelessness on Mal's part but to the time Grandmother Hawkridge had chucked the teapot at her husband's head. The teapot likely would have shattered but Granny had good aim. She hit Grandfather Hawkridge square between the eyes, and he managed to catch the teapot before it fell to the floor so only the handle was damaged.

I can only imagine what sort of skullduggery Mal's grandfather must have been planning to inspire his patient wife to such violence. I have often felt the urge to bounce something off Mal's head if I thought it would do any good.

As I took my place at the table and served the tea, I was tempted again to try to dissuade Mal from bottling and selling his "Elixir of Love." But he would never listen, and I was already weary of anything to do with the royal ball. I had come here to escape from any further discussion of it.

I took a soothing sip of my tea and relaxed back in my chair, feeling some of my tension melt. I nudged the sugar bowl closer to

Mal, smiling as I watched him ladle spoonsful into his cup. His grandmother used to scold him for that, declaring Mal might as well just take the sugar bowl and wet it down with a bit of tea.

I have such good memories of many cozy afternoons spent in this kitchen with Grandmother Hawkridge bustling about, ironing bed linens, pulling fresh bread from the oven, dumping another bun on my plate as she insisted I was getting too skinny. She would often pause to brush a stray curl from my brow, just as my own mother used to do. The recollection brought a lump to my throat. Mal was not the only one who missed his grandmother.

I took another swallow of tea as Mal popped open a tin and offered me a gingerbread man. I regarded the treat with suspicion and surprise. But the little cake men neither looked moldy nor hard as rocks. I accepted one and cautiously bit off a leg. It was delicious.

As I chewed, slowly savoring the morsel, I mumbled, "You have been baking?"

"Silly girl. Of course not. These were a gift from the witch next door."

I choked and spat out what remained of the leg onto my plate. Mal laughed and said, "Relax, Ella. It really is just gingerbread, not something that will give you warts or place you under a sleeping spell."

"How can you be so sure?" I muttered, washing my mouth out with tea. Unlike Mal's inept spells, I have heard it rumored that Delphine possessed considerable skill when it came to the arcane arts.

"Delphine would never serve me such a trick," Mal said. "Despite her obnoxious cat, she and I get on quite well. I believe Delphine is a bit smitten with me." As though to convince me, Mal scooped up a gingerbread man and bit off its head, chewing and swallowing with great relish. "She often trades me cakes or pies for some of my herbs, although the gingerbread was a gift. I do have a birthday coming up which I daresay you have forgotten about."

"How could I possibly forget your birthday?" I retorted with a wry smile. "You would never let me. So have you decided yet what you want?"

Mal crammed the rest of the gingerbread into his mouth but still managed to mumble, "I may just possibly have thought of something."

He settled back into his chair, a mysterious smile on his lips. He clearly wanted me to coax it out of him. I refused to oblige, knowing he would tell me soon enough.

Mal and I have never bought birthday gifts for each other. Instead, we have traded favors. It was a tradition that started back years ago, during the annual Festival of the Flowers. This was celebrated every spring with a parade, dancing and feasting in the streets and the awarding of prizes for the best gardens. There were also foot races, archery contests and even jousts in the town square. Because what demonstrates the joy of spring better than one great lummox trying to knock another lummox off his horse?

The highlight of this festival was the pageant for young girls in which one simpering miss was chosen to be crowned Princess Rosebud and preside over all these celebrations. Imelda once proudly bore the title and she was determined that at least one of her daughters should achieve this dubious honor. When I turned ten, the age of entry, I was selected to become Imelda's first victim.

In vain did I plead, trying to convince her I was not the stuff of which princesses were made. Even if I had been, I could not have hoped to compete with any of the young ladies from the Heights with their poise, their jewels, and costly gowns. No Midtown girl had ever been crowned Princess Rosebud, I told my stepmother, but Imelda insisted I would be the first.

I was groomed, primped, frizzed, and curled. I was subjected to endless lessons on how to walk, sit and smile, skills that I thought I had performed quite adequately most of my life. I had to endure endless fittings in a frothy taffeta gown that made me itch and was so restrictive I could not bend or raise my arms.

As the day for the pageant approached, I felt ill with apprehension, imagining making a total fool of myself by tripping on the hem of that ridiculous dress or by sneezing, belching, or farting when I paraded before the judges. I dreaded the hoots of the obnoxious boys whose parents forced them to attend the event and the superior sneers of the Heights girls.

I knew there was no hope of appealing to my father for rescue. He would only say what he always did, *Obey your stepmother, Ella. She knows far more about raising a daughter than I do.* If I was going to be spared this ordeal, I needed to find a way to save myself, and on the eve of the pageant, I came up with a simple but brilliant plan.

I asked Mal to punch me in the eye as hard as he could. Horrified by my request, Mal adamantly refused, but I reminded him that it was almost my birthday, and this was all I wanted from him. If he would comply, I would do anything he wanted on his birthday. I begged, badgered, goaded, and gave Mal no peace, but it was not until I threatened to hit myself in the face with a hammer that he finally gave in. He drew back his fist and popped me a good one.

Mal was so distressed by what he had done, he cried, but I was elated because the results were spectacular. My eye swelled shut and my cheek sported the most glorious greenish- purple bruise. Imelda took one look at me and shrieked in horror, castigating me as the most wicked, ungrateful hoyden of a girl who ever lived. But never again did she attempt to make a Princess Rosebud out of me.

Thus, the tradition of the birthday favor was born, although Mal made me promise there would never again be any wishes that involved him hurting me. Most of my requests over the years had been quite mild. This year, when my birthday came, I intended to ask Mal to help me unstop the library chimney.

As for Mal, he had never asked anything that extreme of me either, although he did enjoy making me guess what he wanted.

But as he continued to sip his tea in silence, I realized he was not just being coy. He really did seem reluctant to tell me what he wanted.

I finally grew impatient. "Come, Mal, whatever it is, you know I would do anything for you. Just tell me."

He fortified himself with another gulp of tea. Holding his breath like a swimmer about to plunge into an icy lake, he blurted out, "Iwantyoutogototheroyalball."

"What?"

"I want you to go to the royal ball," he said, enunciating each word more clearly.

I still couldn't believe I had heard him right. I must have borne a close resemblance to the village idiot as I sat there, gaping at him. Had Mal entirely lost his wits? He wanted to escort me to the ball as though he was my suitor or my betrothed?

There had never been any question of anything like that between me and Mal. There had been that time when we were twelve and had experimented with kissing. It had been such an awkward business, involving bumping of noses and banging of teeth, that we had never been tempted to repeat it. We had always been content to remain close friends— or so I had thought.

I reflected uncomfortably about some of the remarks Mal had made this afternoon, about me being beautiful, about being madly in love with me. He had been jesting, hadn't he? Bad enough that the stern Commander Crushington harbored some foolish fancy for me, but if Mal was about to confess to such a thing, I could not endure it. Not my just-like-a-brother, dearest friend Mal! It was unthinkable.

I remained silent for so long, Mal gave an uneasy laugh. "It is not that outrageous of a request, Ella. Do say something."

"I don't know what to say. I never dreamed you would— seriously, Mal, you wish to take me to the ball?"

Mal blinked. "Take you to the ball? Oh, frap no. A thousand

fiery dragons could not force me to attend such a mutton-headed event."

So, this was all just another of Mal's jests. I expelled a breath, torn by relief and a strong desire to kill him.

He continued, "I couldn't go to the ball even if I wanted to. After that business between my grandfather and the king, all Hawkridges were banned from coming anywhere within a league of the royal palace. You ought to remember that, Ella."

Mal was right. I should have remembered. Even though this had all occurred before either Mal or I were born, we had both heard the story often enough from Grandmother Hawkridge.

Mal's grandfather had been a mage of great power. Fully licensed, a member in highest standing of the Sorcery Guild, Hiram Hawkridge had often been consulted by the king until the unfortunate occasion of the king's tenth jubilee.

Every year, the king celebrated the anniversary of his ascension to the throne with a grand parade to the town square where he would modestly accept a gift from the good citizens of Midtown and then deliver an address to his loyal subjects.

The king prided himself on being a brilliant orator, which meant he knew how to smile, flatter, and lie shamelessly to his subjects with the greatest sincerity. He always fortified himself with a cup of claret before mounting to the podium. That particular year he had several cups.

The king's speech began well until he started to slur his words and reel on his feet. He lost his place several times and finally meandered into a diatribe of disastrous honesty in which he sneered and said he regarded all the people of Midtown as a "fat, greasy bunch of porkers who needed to be fleeced." And if Midtown did not come up with a better present than some paltry golden candlesticks next year for his jubilee, he would puff and blow the entire town to bits like a gale force earthquake. It was difficult to say which affronted his audience the most; the insults, the threats, or the way the king mixed his metaphors.

Many assumed the king had been drunk, but it was later discovered that his claret had been laced with Truth Elixir and the culprit was none other than the king's grand ducal wizard, Hiram Hawkridge. When brought before the king, Mal's grandfather had at first denied responsibility and then declared it had all been an unfortunate accident. He had been experimenting with a potion designed to make the king's voice more golden and had added the Truth Elixir to the wine by mistake.

It was a feeble excuse, but Hiram was a great favorite of the king, so he might have escaped retribution if he had not been imprudent enough to add that surely little harm had been done, because no one ever really listened to the king's speeches anyway. Some suspected Hiram might have been dipping into his own Truth Elixir, but Grandmother Hawkridge stated bitterly that it was because her husband never knew when to keep his mouth shut.

Whatever the reason, Hiram's flippant remark sealed his fate. He was convicted of practicing malicious and deleterious magic against the Crown, which should have resulted in a swift visit to the Lord High Garroter or at least a lifetime of incarceration in the Dismal Dungeons. Perhaps our king had been more mellow in his youth or perhaps he was a bit afraid of Hiram's magical abilities.

Instead of meeting his doom, Hiram was stripped of all his high offices and membership in the sorcerer's guild, forbidden to practice magic or come within a league of the palace ever again. Grandmother Hawkridge always concluded her story of these long-ago events by sternly reminding Mal that both bans applied to Hiram's heirs as well. While Mal ignored the ban about practicing magic, to the best of my knowledge, he had never defied the edict regarding the royal castle.

As I took another sip of my tea, I said, "I ought to have remembered you are not allowed near the palace before I allowed you to tease me with the notion you wanted to escort me to the ball.

Considering how distressed I already am about this stupid ball; I think it very mean of you."

"I wasn't teasing you, Ella. You merely misunderstood me. What I said was I want you to go to the ball. And you needn't worry about the cost of it. I will pay for your ticket, your gown, your carriage, everything."

I was certain he still had to be joking. I could usually tell when Mal was teasing me. I tried to probe his eyes as he reached for another cookie from the tin. I found no sign of duplicity, but I sensed he was not being entirely forthcoming either.

"Why?" I asked. "Why would you want me to go to this wretched ball?"

"Because I think it would be good for you," he mumbled around another mouthful of gingerbread.

"Good for me! To display myself before that dolt Prince Florian, like some heifer brought to market—"

"You don't need to worry about the prince," Mal interrupted. "If I thought you were likely to be troubled by him, I would never send you to the ball. But there is not the least chance Florian would ever choose you for his bride."

I had no desire to wed the prince, but Mal's remark nettled me all the same. "Truly? Am I so repulsive then? And after you just assured me how beautiful I am."

"You are beautiful. Dazzlingly so. The problem would come when you opened your mouth."

"Oh? There is something wrong with my voice then?" I huffed.

"Not your voice, Ella. It's your tongue. It's sharper than my shaving razor."

"I suppose you are still miffed with me because of those remarks I made about your hair. I have already said I am sorry."

"It's nothing to do with my hair," Mal said, raking his hand back through his pompadour and then looking in disgust at the strands that came loose. He brushed them off on his breeches as he continued, "You have a habit of making sarcastic quips, sometimes downright caustic. You never used to be that way. When you were younger, you were so sweet... well, you were never exactly sweet. But you were much softer, less cynical, and more hopeful. You still believed in magic, dreams, and romance, or so I thought. Have you never even considered the possibility of falling in love?"

I did not answer immediately. Mal was my closest friend. But I had never told him about my trysts with Harper. Mal had been away that bittersweet summer I had fallen so desperately in love with my bard. By the time Mal had returned, it was all over, and I was finished weeping into my pillow. My memories were still far too raw and painful to share, even with Mal.

Something, either in my hesitation or my face alerted Mal. He leaned forward in his chair and said half-teasingly, "You have been entertaining thoughts of romance. Who is it? Never tell me you are harboring tender feelings for the Crusher?"

"No! Don't be ridiculous."

"For whom then?"

"For no one," I snapped.

An odd smile played about Mal's mouth. If he sensed I was keeping any sort of a secret, he could be worse than a ferret shredding the lawn digging for rabbits. I made haste to change the subject.

"Back to the matter of this royal ball, I still do not understand why you are so eager for me to attend an event that I despise as much as you do. It would be dreadful of me to sally off to the ball when my poor Amy and Netta are positively breaking their hearts to do so. I could not be so cruel as to go without them." I paused, eyeing Mal speculatively. "Unless you might also afford to include them—"

"I could, but I won't," Mal said. "The ugly stepsisters must simply learn to accept their disappointment."

"Don't call them that! Amy and Netta are darling, lovely girls."

"They are spoiled brats, and your wicked stepmother is even

more selfish. Do you know why your father even married her? My gran always said it was because he saw Imelda in the park, cooing over her girls and got this fool notion she would make you a good mother."

"And do you know why Imelda married my father? She saw him as a knight in shining armor coming to carry her off to his castle where she would live happily ever after. So, they were both doomed to unhappiness and—" I heard my voice starting to rise and checked it.

Mal had nothing but contempt for Imelda and my stepsisters. It was one of the few things we ever quarreled about, and I had no wish to do so again.

An uncomfortable silence fell between us. Mal finally said, "I am sorry, Ella, but the problem is if your stepsisters accompany you to the ball, they might get in your way."

"In the way of my what?"

"Of you doing what I need you to do," Mal replied vaguely. The way he avoided meeting my eyes roused all my former suspicions that he was keeping something back.

"Enough, Mal, what is the real reason you want me to attend the ball? This is supposed to be your birthday favor, something that will benefit you. So, what is it?"

Mal pulled a rueful face. "I would have had to tell you eventually. But perhaps we should have some more tea first."

"No more tea," I said, moving the pot out of his reach. "Quit stalling, Mal, and just tell me."

"Oh, very well. It has been brought to my attention recently— never mind how or by whom," he added hastily. "That's not important, but someone has informed me that the king has a crystal orb that he keeps locked up in his treasure chamber. That orb belonged to my grandfather, and I want it back."

"I still don't understand what that has to do with me attending..." My words trailed off as comprehension smacked me over the head. "Oh, no, no, no!" I said, vigorously shaking my head.

"Oh, yes." Mal gave me his most charming and wolfish grin. "You must admit the ball will be the perfect distraction for you to slip into the treasury chamber and retrieve the orb."

It was fortunate I was no longer holding my teacup, or I would have bounced it off Mal's head, and I thought my aim was every bit as good as Granny Hawkridge's. Instead, I gasped, "Have you completely lost your mind? That's why you are so eager for me to attend the ball? You want to steal from the king?"

"It is not stealing. That orb was my grandfather's, so by right, it belongs to me."

"I doubt the king will see it that way when I am caught."

"You won't be caught. I have planned the whole thing out carefully, a way for you to slip easily past the guards and unlock the chamber. The orb is so small, you can easily hide it in your reticule."

"Ladies don't carry reticules to a ball," I said.

"Then we'll have a special pocket sewn into your ball gown. It will be easy, Ella. You will be in and out of there in five minutes."

"And on my way to the Dismal Dungeons."

"That won't happen, I tell you. Do you think I would ever ask you to do anything that would put you in danger? I have devised an enchantment that will afford you extra protection."

"Another one of your enchantments? I might as well choke myself and save the Lord High Garroter the bother."

"Thank you very much." Mal's face suffused with annoyance. "You are as bad as my grandfather was. Neither of you have any faith in my magical abilities."

"I wonder why that would be," I said as another clump of Mal's hair fell out and hit the table.

Mal swept it impatiently onto the floor. "Do you know, Ella, I thought you might show a spark of enthusiasm. You used to enjoy taking risks. You had such a sense of adventure—"

"Stop." I groaned. "I am so tired of everyone pointing out that I am not the girl I once was, how I am not as romantic or as fun or daring as I used to be. Pardon me for growing up, but I have responsibilities now."

"Your stepmother and stepsisters! Do you intend to saddle yourself with their care forever?"

"They are my family and I love them. I cannot do anything that would place them in danger. I do not expect you to understand. You are quite free to be as reckless as you please. You have no one."

Mal fell silent. Then he said in a taut voice, "You are right. I have no family left, but I always thought I had you, Ella."

"Oh, Mal, you do." I reached across the table to take his hand. "You are my dearest friend, and I would do anything for you. Anything but this. Is retrieving that orb so very important to you? What does it do?"

"The orb can find something that has been lost. I am not even sure I would know how to use it, but it was my grandfather's. That alone makes it important enough to me. I have very little left to remember him by. The royal government confiscated nearly everything he owned when he died and I for one am mighty sick of our cursed king seizing all that we have."

A rare bitterness crept into Mal's voice, and it made me uncomfortable. I had heard rumors there might be people wishing to depose the king. Whispers had circulated for years that only Queen Anthea's son and daughter-in-law had died of the plague. Her grandson had survived. The old queen had feared for the infant's life when King Cuthbert had invaded to claim the throne and so she had hidden the babe away. The legend claimed that one day a descendant of good Queen Anthea would appear to lead an uprising to save Arcady from the Helavalerians tyrannical rule. A foolish tale. If there was a missing heir, surely, he would have been discovered decades ago.

I could not believe that Mal, even as reckless as he was, would ever be part of such an insane plot, which could only end in disaster. It was considered treason to even criticize the king as angrily as

Mal had done. King August was protected by his grand ducal wizard, Mercato, and it was said that the powerful magician had his spies everywhere.

I could not help glancing nervously over my shoulder. Mal and I were quite alone and there was no one to hear, but the witch's cat lurking on a tree limb outside the window.

"I wish I could help you retrieve the orb, Mal," I said. "Truly I do, but I am sorry. I just can't—"

"Never mind," he said, withdrawing his hand from mine. "There is no need to apologize. If you feel you cannot, then you cannot. I'll find another way to get the orb."

"But how?"

"You needn't worry about that."

I did worry. I knew that if Mal had made up his mind to have that orb, he would go to any dangerous lengths to get it. But I could not allow him to use my fear for his safety to goad me into doing anything rash.

"I am sorry," I repeated miserably. "I have never had to refuse any of your birthday favors before."

Mal shrugged. "I daresay we have outgrown this childish nonsense of doing each other birthday favors. You should just bake me a little cake or knit me a pair of socks or something."

"It will have to be the cake," I said. "We broke the only knitting needles I ever owned, the time we used to play at jousting, remember?"

Mal gave a wry smile and nodded. No more was said about birthday favors or the king's ball. We spoke of indifferent matters until it was time for me to go. Our parting was cheerful enough on the surface, but I sensed that I had deeply disappointed Mal and I hated it.

I had hoped my visit to Mal would cheer me up and take my mind off this wretched ball and all my other cares. I left his shop, feeling worse than when I had arrived. As I emerged onto the street, I once more had the eerie feeling of being watched.

I thought it might prove to be the witch's cat again, but this time it was the witch herself. Delphine lingered upon the stoop of her crooked house; arms folded across her bosom. I raised my hand in a halfhearted greeting she ignored. I have no idea what I might have ever done to offend the woman, but for some reason, Delphine did not like me any better than her cat did.

When I had expressed my concern about this to Mal, he had said that Delphine did not get on well with any other women. The witch much preferred the company of men. If I was ever worried about where I stood with her, I had only to glance at Delphine's hair which had the curious property of changing color according to her moods.

When her wild mane waxed golden orange, it indicated Delphine was feeling happy. Bright red, she was excited or passionate: green, she was envious or perhaps coming down with something. Deep blue, the witch was sad, and purple... Mal had never been able to figure out what purple hair meant. If I ever saw Delphine's tangled tresses turn black, Mal had warned me I had better keep my distance and be right quick about it.

As Delphine studied me from the shadows of her doorway, her hair darkened from green to a hue as black as pitch, the look in her eyes pure malevolence. I shivered and hurried on my way.

Five

The next two weeks passed by with grinding slowness. "Grinding" being a very apt word because I had begun to feel like a millstone being worn down by a steady deluge of water, the water in this case being my stepsisters' tears. Any hope I had that Amy and Netta would grow more resigned to my decision about the ball was put to rout. As the days passed, their beseeching only waxed more desperate. Add my stepmother's pleas into the mix and I felt driven to distraction.

Everywhere I turned in my own home, I encountered pleading looks, melancholy sighs, and morose silences. Netta plucked out sad tunes on her harp that could have reduced to tears even the laughing loons that flew over the Conger River. Amy's latest campaign consisted of drawing sketches of languishing maidens with visibly broken hearts and leaving them for me to find pressed between the pages of my book, at the bottom of my marketing basket or tucked inside my favorite shoes.

As I entered the kitchen that morning to bake bread, I found Amy's latest effort pinned to the flour bag. It was a watercolor of two dark-haired young women contorted into paroxysms of grief as they stood, locked outside the gates of the castle. I had to suppress a chuckle. Amy was not good at drawing people. Her sorrowful maidens resembled a pair of stiff necked, miserable trolls.

My stepsister did have a genius for depicting buildings. She had accurately captured the royal castle with its gleaming white walls and proud towers. The softness of her sky, the wisps of clouds infused the palace with a fairylike beauty, a place of dreams and the promise of romance.

Although I smiled at Amy's drawing, I sighed as well. Mal had insisted the girls would recover from their disappointment. But it still pained me to see them so deeply unhappy. If I was ever tempted to grow impatient with their histrionics, I reminded myself it was not their fault.

I had been raised on stories of Queen Anthea, the Magnificently Wise. Amy and Netta had grown up with stories of princesses being rescued by bold heroes and carried away on white chargers to a beautiful palace where they all lived happily ever after.

My stepmother would often tell such tales at bedtime. Imelda was a gifted storyteller and even I got caught up in the sagas she wove, although I rewrote them a bit in my mind, so sometimes I was the one rescuing my prince or at least fighting beside him.

But at the age of seventeen, I had been just like Amy and Netta in one respect, longing to find my hero and fall in love. My heart was open and eager when I first clapped eyes on my handsome bard. I was smitten at first sight, although I convinced myself I was not like the other silly girls, captivated by Harper's golden hair, sky blue eyes and charming voice.

I was not merely infatuated, as my father had insisted. I was genuinely in love with Harper, valuing his intelligence, his talent, his sense of humor and above all else, his honesty and sincerity. When my bard proved false, he did far more than break my heart. He completely shattered my confidence in my own judgment.

I caught myself about to sigh again and sternly suppressed it. I do not know why I had been thinking so much about Harper of late and once again feeling all the old pain and longing. Perhaps because the entire female population of Midtown was so giddy over the prospect of this ball. Nothing else was spoken of except romance and finding true love, hopefully in the arms of a handsome prince. I wondered how many of those starry-eyed young women would someday end up as disenchanted as I was.

I could have endured all this royal ball madness much better if I had Mal to turn to, but I had seen nothing of him for the past two weeks. When I tried to visit him, the Hawk's Nest was closed. No one answered my knock, although sometimes I suspected Mal was in there. I might have been desperate enough to inquire after Mal at the witch's house next door, but there was never any sign of Delphine or her horrid cat either. I finally gave up going to Misty Bottoms, but I keenly missed my friend's sharp wit and sense of humor, which would have helped me keep all this royal ball nonsense in perspective. Although I knew my refusal of his birthday favor had disappointed Mal, it hurt that he could shut me out this way.

I also worried that the reason for his absence was that he was neck deep in some insane plot he did not want me to know about. My nights were tormented with hideous dreams of Mal being caught trying to steal that orb and being strangled with the Lord High Garroter's noose.

Between lack of sleep and the daily barrage of misery from my family, I was being worn down. Two more weeks, I tried to comfort myself as I set Amy's drawing aside. Two more weeks and this wretched ball would be over. Perhaps it would take another week or two for my stepmother, Amy and Netta to realize the world had not ended and return to a semblance of their usual cheerful selves. In the meantime, there was bread that needed baking.

I was just tying my apron strings when the kitchen door burst open. Glancing around, I was startled to see my stepmother. Imelda was not an early riser. She was seldom out of bed at this hour of day, let alone out of the house. But there she stood in her best pelisse and velvet hat, the one trimmed with the most dashing ostrich feather.

Although she was approaching fifty, my stepmother looked years younger than her age. She was a beautiful woman, her hair still a lustrous shade of black with not a hint of grey, her face remarkably smooth and unlined. Perhaps this was because, despite the tragic loss of her first husband and her subsequent unhappy union with my father, Imelda had managed to retain her optimism and a youthful outlook on life. I envied her for that. I shuddered to think how haggard I would look when I reached her age.

This morning, Imelda looked every one of her forty-eight years. Her features were pale and drawn and instead of her normal graceful carriage, her shoulders slumped. Even her ostrich feather drooped.

Alarmed, I hurried over to her. "What is wrong? Are you ill?"

She looked up at me, her eyes brimming with tears. "Oh, Ella, I have done s-something very foolish."

"What?" I cried. "What did you do?"

She began to weep so hard, I could barely understand her, but two words stood out disastrously clear... borrow money.

"You didn't!" I began, but my stepmother was in no fit state to be scolded. She was trembling so much; I feared her knees might give way beneath her.

I guided her over to the kitchen table and eased her down onto one of the chairs. "There, there," I soothed as I removed her hat and her pelisse as though she were a distraught child. "I am sure you have done nothing that cannot be set right."

Imelda hiccupped on another sob. I dug inside her reticule and found her handkerchief. While Imelda dabbed at her eyes, I gave her a brisk hug and settled into the chair opposite her. I waited until her weeping had subsided before saying gently, "You know whatever money you received, you will have to take back. We have discussed this before. We cannot afford to borrow what we can never repay."

Imelda sniffed and blew her nose. "N-nothing to worry about. No money. I was r-refused."

"Oh." I heaved a great breath of relief although it was obvious that being denied the loan had left my stepmother devastated. "Who did you approach with your request?"

"Madam Dearling."

"That woman? Oh, Em, whatever possessed you to go that spiteful shrew for money?"

I already knew the answer to that. The ball. The frapping ball.

"I know you don't like her, but Matilda is my closest friend!" Imelda said but another tear rolled down her cheek. "My only friend, or so I thought. She is certainly rich enough to have lent me such a sum and I was feeling desperate. You have not been able to find a way for us to buy the tickets. Not that I blame you in the least, Ella dear."

My stepmother reached out to pat my hand. "I know that you would if you could. And after all, I am the mama. I am the one who should be looking out for the interests of you girls. When I explained to Matilda why I needed the money, I felt sure she would sympathize. It is not as if she has daughters of her own to worry about, so she could not consider you and your sisters as rivals. I assured Matilda, I would be able to repay the debt very quickly, because I know one of you can secure the affections of a wealthy nobleman if we can just attend that ball.

"Amy and Netta are such darling girls and you, Ella. If you could just learn not to speak your mind so freely around the gentlemen, you are so dazzlingly beautiful, I am sure you could be the one to win the heart of Prince Florian."

"The fairies forbid," I muttered. Although I could well guess what had happened next, I asked, "How did Madam Dearling respond to your request?"

Imelda's lip quivered. "She laughed at me and said I needed to get my head out of the clouds, that you girls could consider your-selves fortunate if you were able to wed some honest tradesmen.

And really, it was too bad of me to place her in such an awkward position by coming to her and groveling for money."

Imelda's cheeks flushed pink. "I didn't grovel, Ella. I swear I didn't."

Mentally I called the Dearling woman a name that would have shocked my stepmother. Aloud I said, "I am sure you did not. You are far too proud and elegant for that."

My assurance comforted Imelda a little. She continued, "All the same I apologized to Matilda for distressing her with my request."

"Apologized? You should have just spit in her teacup and stalked out."

"My behaving in such vulgar fashion would not have improved the situation, Ella dear. Indeed, Matilda was quite gracious about accepting my apology."

I barely suppressed a snort.

"She said we need not ever mention my humiliating request ever again." Imelda sighed. "But she kept talking about the ball and how every eligible young lady in Midtown was going. It was almost as if Matilda wanted to rub salt in my wounds, as if she was taking great pleasure in the fact, I could not afford to send my girls to the ball." Imelda's eyes clouded with distress and confusion. "But I don't understand why she would."

Because Matilda Dearling was a sour woman with a cramped soul and shriveled up heart whose only source of enjoyment was the misery of others. Imelda would never be able to understand that.

I was not blind to my stepmother's faults. Imelda could be vain, shallow, and even foolish at times. But she did not have a single mean fiber in her very sentimental heart. Consequently, this left her quite vulnerable to the spite and cruelty of others. That was why from a young age, I felt protective of my stepmother, although I was unkind enough myself when she first married my father.

I wasted little time informing her she was never going to replace my mother. I would never call her "Mama" and I thought Imelda was a stupid name. If I spoke to her at all, I would call her "madam" just as my father did; only I infused the word with all a seven-year-old girl's scorn. I was astonished when Imelda started to cry. I had never realized before that a child could reduce an adult woman to tears.

It made me squirm with discomfort, but I still refused to retract my words or apologize. Perhaps because I felt guilty for being so mean to my stepmother, I resented it when anyone else did so. As I have said before, when Imelda's first husband brought her into disgrace, she was shunned by all her former friends from the Heights. The Countess of Pangbourne took a particular delight in Imelda's downfall and she sought out every available opportunity to snub my stepmother in the most public and humiliating manner possible.

I had not wanted Imelda as a stepmother, but like it or not, she was part of my family now and I seethed over these insults that sent Imelda weeping into her pillow every time she returned from town. I knew my father could not be counted upon to redress this wrong, so I resolved to seek retribution upon the countess myself.

Mal had never liked my stepmother from the first, but he entered my scheme for vengeance with great enthusiasm. One afternoon, we hid behind some hedgerows and lay in wait for the countess's carriage to pass by. This was long before she ever came up with her absurd design for the cucumber carriage. Her coach in those days was an ordinary box-shaped vehicle with rather large windows enabling Her Ladyship to gaze haughtily down upon the peasantry as she rattled by.

Thus, it was an easy matter for two enterprising children with good aim to launch a pair of large and excessively repulsive toads through the coach windows. The shrieks that came from the interior of the carriage were spectacularly loud and gratifying. It was a fortunate thing that the coach was not traveling at any great speed when the door was flung open, and the countess leapt out to tumble in the road.

Miraculously, the countess was not hurt. The only harm was to her dignity as she fell facedown into a mud-filled rut, but years later, my conscience continued to plague me about this incident. I still feel bad about what Mal and I did to those poor toads.

As the countess dragged herself out of the mud, looking like some sort of swamp troll, Mal and I erupted into such giggles, we did not make our escape as stealthily as we should have done. Despite the mud water dripping into her eyes, the countess had no difficulty identifying us as the culprits.

That same afternoon, Her Ladyship called upon my stepmother in a state of high dudgeon, declaring that I was the most evil, monstrous child she had ever encountered and demanding that I be whipped. I expected Imelda to cringe before this harridan as she usually did. Maybe she would even hand me over to the countess for punishment.

To my delight and astonishment, she stood up to the countess with a ferocity that would have done credit to Queen Anthea leading her army of women onto the battlefield.

"How dare you!" Imelda had cried in such furious accents, as the countess took a wary step back. "How dare you accuse my daughter of such a thing! Ella is the sweetest, most darling little girl you could wish for. A perfect young lady who would never dream of behaving in such an awful way."

By this time, my mouth was gaping as wide as the countess's. If Imelda had not mentioned me by name, I would have had no idea whom she was talking about. I folded my hands in front of me, doing my best to look all innocent and demure.

My stepmother concluded by ordering the countess to leave her house at once and consult her doctor. "Because if you think my dear little Ella was the one tossing toads at you, it is clear Your Ladyship needs spectacles."

The countess regarded me with suspicion, but she no longer

looked so sure of herself. She had no choice but to leave with what dignity remained to her. I am ashamed to say I was feeling quite gleeful about escaping the consequences of my mischief unscathed. I thrust my tongue out at the countess's retreating back.

The countess did not see it, but unfortunately Imelda did. As my stepmother rounded on me, I realized I had not fooled her at all. Hands on her hips, she eyed me sternly.

"How could you, Prunella! I do not know what I am ever going to do with you. You truly are a horribly wicked little girl and—"

Imelda's voice broke and I cringed thinking I was about to make my stepmother cry again. Instead, I was dumbfounded when she burst out laughing and enveloped me in a hug and for the first time, I tentatively hugged her back.

That day marked the beginning of a curious kind of friendship with my stepmother. Although I could never call her "Mama," I dubbed her "Em," a term I used with greatest affection.

As I bustled about the kitchen, making Imelda a cup of tea, I continued to fume about Madam Dearling's treatment of her.

"Just wait until the next time I see that shrew," I growled.

"Oh, Ella, no!" my stepmother cried in alarm. "Please promise me you will do nothing to avenge me."

When I remained stubbornly silent, she clutched at my sleeve. "Promise!" she insisted. Gazing down at her anxious face, I finally said, "Very well. I promise. No toads."

My wry remark coaxed a smile from her, but it quickly faded. She looked somber and pensive as I placed the steaming cup of tea before her, fixed just the way she liked it, with an extra dollop of honey even though our supply was running low.

She made no move to taste it, her brow knit in a heavy frown that was rare for Imelda.

"Matilda was right about one thing."

"She confessed she is really a troll in disguise?"

Leveling a stern look at me, Imelda continued, "I do need to start being more sensible about securing a comfortable future for my girls. I was thinking about it the entire way home." She fetched a deep sigh. "I believe Mr. Bafton will do for Amy."

"Do what for her?"

"Make her a good husband."

"Fortescue Bafton?" I scoffed. "He is a complete idiot."

"Amy seems to like him."

"Amy would like any young man who brought her flowers and chocolates. She is hardly old enough to worry about marriage."

"She is sixteen, Ella. Many girls are wed by that age and even have children."

I shook my head, unable to think of Amy as anyone's wife or mother. She was still my little sister who dreamed of castles and princes, who loved her sweets and braiding her ponies' manes.

"Mr. Bafton is the son of a prosperous tailor. If Amy married him, she would never want for anything. I am sure she would be quite happy," Imelda said, although she sounded as though she were trying to convince herself as much as me. She looked even more forlorn as she continued, "Finding Netta a proper husband may prove more difficult. She is so shy and awkward. But Mr. Hackersmith has expressed an admiration for her."

"Hackersmith! The frap merchant?"

"Ella!" My stepmother regarded me reproachfully. "My dear, what have I told you about using that vulgarity? Hackersmith owns the manufactory that refines the... er... waste products of the mating mountain elks. As such he is a man of wealth and position and Netta would certainly never want for fuel to stoke her hearth. You know how your sister gets cold so much easier than the rest of us."

"But Hackersmith must be at least thirty years older than Netta and he always smells like fr— like mountain elk droppings."

"I agree he is not an ideal candidate. Perhaps we can think of someone else." Imelda emitted another deep sigh. "And then of course there is you."

I stiffened, dreading to hear who Imelda might have settled upon as my prospective spouse.

She fidgeted with her spoon. Not looking at me, she said, "Commander Crushington has become very fond of you."

I gaped at her. "You know about that?"

"My dear Ella, everyone in Midtown knows about that."

Everyone but me apparently. Ever since the day that Crushington had confessed he "really liked" me, I had been doing my best to avoid the man. I was dismayed when my stepmother added, "I met the commander on my way home and he inquired after you so civilly I— I—" Imelda stole a nervous look at me. "I invited him to call upon us."

I sank down into the chair opposite her, groaning. "Oh, Em, you didn't."

"The commander does appear to be a very stern man. I confess I find him a little alarming, but you have always been so much braver than the rest of us. Even such a grim husband would be better than you running off to marry that horrid young man. You cannot know how much I have worried that you would do that."

"You need not be. I have not seen Harper for years. I have no idea—"

"Not the bard," Imelda interrupted. "I am talking about that Hawkridge villain."

If Mal despised my stepmother, the feeling was more than mutual. Imelda had always regarded Mal as a hobgoblin's spawn. She considered him an evil influence on me. The day the Hawkridge family moved to Misty Bottoms, I believe Imelda performed a little jig in the garden and my stepmother never indulged in such undignified displays.

It distressed me that two people I cared about so much should regard each other with such loathing. But trying to defend one to the other was nothing but a waste of my breath. Instead, I reassured my stepmother, "You know I would never run off and wed Mal. We are just good friends, that is all."

"So, you always insist, my dear." The look Imelda directed at me was skeptical.

"I insist because it is true. I daresay I will never marry anyone. I will likely end up as one of those eccentric old women who live alone and keep a dozen cats."

"I fear that even more than you marrying that horrible Malcolm. Such a great waste of all your wit and beauty." Imelda's eyes filled with tears again.

I reached across the table and squeezed her hand. "I was only teasing. I don't even particularly like cats."

"I know." Imelda blinked back her tears. "It is just that— oh, Ella, I had such dreams, such hopes for you girls. If only we could go to that ball. You cannot imagine how wonderful it would be. After all these years, I still remember my first time attending a royal ball."

"I am sure you must have been the most beautiful girl there, Em."

My stepmother's lips curved in a misty smile. "I do not know about that, but I managed to turn a few heads. I still recall the gown I wore. It was the loveliest confection of white satin and pink ribbons and lace. The great hall of the castle was ablaze with hundreds of candles, the air perfumed with the flower garlands that decorated the arches. And the music! All those violins and silver horns and harps. My Netta would be in ecstasies."

"I am sure she would," I murmured. "But there is no sense even thinking of—"

"My heart was beating so hard," Imelda continued, pressing her hand to her bosom. "You cannot fancy how nervous I was when I was announced. After all, I was only the daughter of a mere knight. Among such a brilliant assemblage, I dreaded that I might be ignored and become one of those maidens left languishing for a dance partner. But no sooner had I descended the grand stair than I found myself surrounded by so many handsome young men clamoring to be the first to lead me onto the floor."

Lost in her memories of long ago, Imelda closed her eyes, a dreamy expression on her face. "Every young girl should have one night like that, to feel beautiful and admired, her entire future shining before her with so many magic possibilities."

Imelda opened her eyes. She did not weep again, but there was such a depth of sadness in them. "That is all I have ever wanted for my daughters. Especially you, Ella."

"Why me in particular?"

"Because you need it so badly. I have noticed the changes in you over these past years and it hurts my heart."

"I am not as sweet as I used to be?" I jested, trying to lighten her mood.

"You were never sweet, but you were so bright and lively. And you believed in dreams, Ella. You believed in love. I wish I could give that back to you."

"I don't want such delusions back. Far better that I learned to think with my head instead of my heart."

"Is it?" Imelda asked forlornly. "I suppose I must do likewise, but being practical all the time seems such a dreary prospect. You girls need to be settled in good marriages, but I also long for you to experience that happily forever after love, the kind of wedded bliss that I shared with your father."

I tried not to cringe. It always discomfited me when Imelda spoke like this about my father. Besides her unquenchable optimism, my stepmother also had the ability to cloak harsh reality beneath the soft mantle of illusion, especially regarding the past.

She never mentioned the tragic downfall of her first husband. It was as though Albert Wendover never even existed, as though there had never been anyone except my father, the gallant hero who had rescued Imelda and her daughters from poverty and disgrace. She seemed to have entirely forgotten the number of occasions when my father had reduced her to tears.

Not that he was ever unkind to her. My father treated Imelda with the greatest respect and civility, always addressing her as "madam." But polite indifference to a loving heart could be as cruel in its own way as harsh words. I could not remember my father ever calling my mother by her first name either. He always referred to her as "my lady," but never had two words been infused with such tenderness.

The truth was that my father had never loved anyone as he did my mother. I often wondered how much he had even cared for me. Sometimes I grew impatient with Imelda's romantic notions, but I could never bring myself to disillusion her. That would have been as cruel as my father's neglect of her.

I was relieved when Imelda did not pursue her rose-tinted reminiscences any further.

"Ah, well," she said. "It is no good dwelling on the past. We must be sensible and look to the future. All this practicality is very fatiguing. It has quite given me a headache."

"You should go upstairs and have a lie down."

Imelda rose to her feet, rubbing her brow. She cast a guilty look at the bowls, spoons and pans I had set out for baking.

"I really ought to help you."

"No, no," I said hastily, guiding her toward the door. "You just go take care of yourself."

It took a little more persuading, but I shooed her out of the kitchen, much to my relief. Mal had often complained that my stepmother and sisters were lazy creatures, leaving all the work to me.

This was more my fault than theirs. When I realized we could no longer afford to keep a maid, Imelda and the girls had been fully prepared to roll up their sleeves and pitch in. Netta was a tad clumsy and tended to break things. Amy whisked through chores leaving half the dust behind or just swept the dirt under the rug. Imelda was so easily distracted; she spent more time chattering to me than working so that neither of us accomplished anything.

I discovered early on if I wanted a task completed to my satisfaction, it was far easier and quicker if I did it myself. But after my conversation with Imelda, I was not as focused as usual. My stepmother was the third person to remark on how sadly I had changed. As much as these comments distressed me, I had to admit the truth of them.

After that summer when Harper abandoned me and I lost my father, I bade farewell to my girlhood as I assumed the burden of taking charge of my family. My heart broken and laden with guilt over that final quarrel with my father, it was easier to block my feelings and concentrate on maintaining our household.

I was so focused on surviving day to day; I gave little thought to the future. My discussion with Imelda had jolted me into realizing that I had to think of it, if not for myself, then at least for Netta and Amy.

Whether I liked to contemplate the prospect or not; my little birds had grown up and were ready to take wing to homes of their own. Yet it pained me to think of them marrying men like the tailor's son and the frap merchant, merely for the sake of security.

We could not continue as we had done indefinitely, not with our financial resources dwindling. One of us at least was going to have to marry well and being the practical one, I supposed it should be me. Would it really be such a sacrifice to wed a man like Commander Crushington?

He was an honorable man who would certainly do his duty by me and my family. But all I could picture was an endless succession of monosyllabic suppers, of him staring at me blankly every time I made a joke. Long evenings of helping him to polish his boots and manacles, trying not to think of the latest unfortunate person he had clapped up in jail for some trivial offense. And what would I ever do if the day came when Crushington arrested Mal? Bash my own husband over the head and steal his keys?

No, there had to be someone else out there for me. He would not need to be rich, but astute when it came to managing money, well able to support a family. Someone who would share my sense of humor and pleasure in books, someone who would understand my affection for my stepmother and sisters and come to love them as much as I did. Someone kind and wise, steady, and true, someone I could hold in high esteem, perhaps even come to love one day. But considering that most of my ventures out of the house involved trips to the greengrocers or the fish market, where was I apt to meet such a man? Over a tank of eels as I selected one for our supper? Highly unlikely.

If only we could go to the ball... Imelda's wistful voice echoed through my mind. I tried to shut it out, refusing to allow myself to be swept up in this royal ball insanity, the belief that it could somehow prove the magical solution to everything.

But once I allowed the idea to take root in my head, I could not stop thinking about it, so much so that I kept losing track of the amount of flour I had sifted into the bowl. After I had measured it out six times, I finally gave up and left off to tackle other chores.

I could not seem to settle to anything else either, wandering listlessly about the house until I ended up in my room, standing in front of my old dollhouse. I lifted the attic lid and stared down at my treasure box.

I hesitated for a long time, chewing my bottom lip almost raw, before delving into the chest and digging out my mother's earrings. I cradled the sparkling emeralds in the palm of my hand. I suppose I had always known the day would come when I would have to sell them. They would likely fetch a tidy sum. There were so many practical things I needed to spend that money on. Could I really sacrifice such a treasured possession in pursuit of a dream, a wild gamble on one night?

Every young girl should have one night like that, to feel beautiful and admired, her entire future shining before her with so many magic possibilities.

I blocked out the memory of Imelda's voice, trying to think of what my own mother would have recommended that I do. I could no longer recall how ill and wasted she had looked on her deathbed, perhaps because I did not choose to remember her that way. But my mother's last words came to me now with startling clarity.

Look after your papa, my little Ella. He will need your love more than ever. And promise me you will never lose your belief in magic.

I promise, Mama, I had intoned solemnly.

I had not kept the first part of my pledge, but perhaps there was still time to redeem the second. I clutched the emeralds tight in my hand, fretting over the decision for moments longer. Then I bundled them up in a handkerchief and hurried to fetch my shawl before I had a chance to change my mind.

Six

Mal had often warned me to stay out of Misty Bottoms on days when the fog rolled in. But I was in such haste to reach Master Fugitate's shop before I lost my resolve that I paid little heed to the fingers of mist curling about me. Not until those fingers thickened into a suffocating embrace.

I halted in midstep, groping my way. I tried to peer through the haze to regain my bearings. The fog had grown so heavy that if I stretched my arm too far in front of me, I could barely see my own hand. I thought of turning back, but I had as good a chance of becoming lost in the twisted lanes behind me as I did if I continued onward toward the river. Besides, it had taken a great deal of determination to get me this far. If I slunk back home, I feared I would change my mind and lock my mother's earrings back in the chest.

I pressed onward, trying to rely on my other senses. The fog muted everything, trapping me in a silent dreamlike world, the only thing solid and real being the ground beneath my feet. Although it was only midafternoon, I met no one. Other people could have been passing within yards of me and I would never have known it.

Eventually I blundered into a rickety fence. I could just make out the bulk of a cottage beyond, but the wretched hovels of Misty Bottoms looked so much alike, even if I could have seen it more clearly, it would not have helped me figure out where I was. I considered knocking at the cottage and asking for directions. But if anyone bothered to answer the door, Bottoms dwellers are not known for their cordiality to Midtown folk. At best, the owner would snarl at me to be gone. At worst, I might end up with frap flung at me.

Instead, I kept close to the fence, using it as a blind man might have clutched his cane for guidance. When I came to the end of it, I realized I was at a crossroads. A sudden burst of noise startled me. Coarse laughter mingled with the screech of a fiddle and rough voices raised in some raucous drunken song.

The fog distorted my hearing, but the sounds seemed alarmingly nearby. My heart skipped a beat. I had blundered too near the Winking Goblin, that den of villainy and debauchery Mal had told me to avoid at all costs. I stumbled in what I hoped was the opposite direction, the lane that would lead me down toward the river.

To my relief, the sounds of the tavern grew fainter. I believed I could even hear the distant lap of water. I inched along, proceeding more cautiously. I did not want to find myself ankle deep in muck and reeds, or worse still actually fall into the chilly waters of the Conger River.

A wooden sign loomed in front of me, and my heart lifted at the sight of a landmark I recognized.

These signs were posted at all the borders of our realm, proclaiming in cheery red letters, WELCOME TO ARCADY, THE KINGDOM OF HAPPILY EVER AFTER. Only on this welcome post, some wag had carved an n before the e, so it read HAPPILY NEVER AFTER.

Only someone from Misty Bottoms would dare to deface one of the royal signposts. I wondered if it might have been Mal. The n slanted in that peculiar way he had of forming his letters and he was certainly reckless enough to mock the king in this fashion.

Thanks to the signpost, I had a clearer idea where I was. If I pressed forward, I would come to the bridge near the tall stone tower that housed the riverside border patrol. By veering off to the left, I should eventually reach the area where the eel sellers plied their trade.

My nose informed me that I was groping my way in the right direction. The heavy fog might hide everything else, but nothing could disguise the reek from barrels of eels pickled in brine. Right next to the Snigglery, I located Fugitate's establishment.

The curio shop was little more than a shack with small dingy windows. A creaking sign on rusted chains hung over the door. FUGITATE'S FANCIES. WITHYPOLE FUGITATE, PROPRIETOR. I hesitated on the threshold, seized by an attack of nerves. I had never visited Fugitate's shop on my own before. Mal had always accompanied me whenever I wanted to sell something, and he had been the one to handle all the negotiations. It was a tricky and difficult business, striking a good bargain with Withypole Fugitate.

Even if I could have found Mal in his shop this afternoon and explained what I wanted to do, he would have flatly refused to help me. He would have been furious at the idea of me selling my mother's earrings to get Imelda and my stepsisters tickets to the ball. I was entirely on my own.

I wiped my moist palms on the inside of my cloak and entered the shop. The little bell suspended above the doorway announced my arrival with a discordant jangle. Fugitate's shop was a murky place on the sunniest days owing to the small grimy windows. With the fog pressing on the glass, the interior was swathed in shadow. I had to give my eyes time to adjust before I could pick my way forward.

The tables and shelves of the shop were laden with merchandise stacked up in haphazard fashion. Silver plates, blue patterned china and copper pots crowded next to ivory-hilted daggers, jewel boxes and sewing chests. Embroidered footstools, settee cushions and fireplace screens battled for space alongside stacks of oil paintings and piles of dust covered books.

A rack of old-fashioned clothing, full skirted satin gowns, velvet doublets and moth-eaten wool cloaks took up far too much room. I had to ease past it, taking care not to dislodge any of the porcelain vases and delicate figurines crammed on the opposite shelf. A feeling of melancholy washed over me as it always did when I entered Fugitate's shop. I could not help wondering about the people who had owned all this, the desperation that had driven them to sell off their belongings.

Had they crept in here as I had often done, placing their small treasures on the counter and anxiously waiting for Fugitate's valuation and the coins he would count into their trembling hands? Then like me, did they rush from the murky shop, clutching their purses, glad to be back out in the sunlight, a relief tempered by regret and a sense of shame?

I could not decide what depressed me more, the porcelain dolls leaning forlornly against one another, their curls disheveled from the last time they had been hugged by a little girl or the box of toy soldiers, their general still sticky from marmalade-covered boyish fingers. Or perhaps it was the piles of musical instruments, tin whistles, pipes, tambours, and the lutes that reminded me of Harper.

His lute had a letter etched near the frets. Harper had said that it was from a jealous rival who had seized his lute, cut the strings, and tried to scratch the word "plunker," a slur upon Harper's musical abilities. This rival had only got as far as the letter p before Harper had stopped him.

Although I told myself I did not care, I could not help wondering. What if Harper had fallen upon hard times and been obliged to sell his lute? I started to examine the stringed instruments more closely, only to stop, disgusted with myself. I did not care, and Harper had not been seen in Arcady for years. It was idiotic to imagine I might find Harper's lute abandoned here. Discarding me had been easy, but Harper would have perished of starvation before parting with his beloved lute.

As I squeezed my way toward the counter, the shop was choked with more wares than the last time I had visited. Yet Master Fugitate rarely seemed to have customers or sell much of his merchandise. What could he possibly want with all this stuff?

Most fairies had no use for human possessions, although they did have a penchant for sparkling gemstones. At least they did according to one of the volumes in my father's library, *The Quaint Customs and Ways of the Fey Folk*. The book filled me with wonder when I was a child and I had longed to make the acquaintance of a fairy.

At one time, the Red Grove Forest had been full of them, but the king's edicts restricting the use of magic and his exorbitant wing tax had driven most of the fey from our kingdom before I was ever born. Withypole Fugitate was the only one I knew of, and this was based on Mal's belief that Fugitate was a fairy in disguise, a suspicion neither of us had ever confirmed. The dour shopkeeper was nothing like the fiercely proud, beautiful creatures my father's book had depicted.

Usually, the jangle of the bell would bring Master Fugitate scurrying from the back room to glower at anyone who had entered, as though he suspected you had come to steal from him. I waited at the counter for what seemed a considerable length of time and there was no sign of Fugitate's scowling features.

At last, I called out, "Hallo! Mr. Fugitate?"

When I received no response, I began to feel uneasy. The shop appeared to be deserted but I could not imagine Withypole going away and leaving the premises unlocked, his merchandise unprotected.

I called again and louder. When there was still no answer, I skirted around the counter. The shop was separated from the back by a doorway hung with a musty purple velvet curtain trimmed with golden tassels. Above the door, a sign proclaimed in huge black letters: ABSOLUTELY NO CUSTOMERS BEYOND THIS POINT! OR ELSE!!!

Or else what? I had often wondered, but never had I risked finding out. Nervously, I plucked back a corner of the heavy drapery and peered through the crack.

I was astonished to discover Fugitate's shop was larger than it appeared from the front. A narrow corridor opened before me with four closed doors, two on either side. The hallway ended at a fifth room with the door ajar, a glimmer of light coming from inside.

"Mr. Fugitate?" I called. Only silence greeted me, and my unease deepened. Mindful of the sign menacing me with its vague threat, I started to draw back. What lay beyond that curtain had to be Withypole's private quarters. I had no right to intrude and Fugitate was not known for his kindly disposition.

But what if he had been attacked or had fallen so ill, he could not cry out for help? I could not just leave the shop without making some effort to see if Withypole was all right.

Mustering my courage, I ducked past the curtain and headed down the corridor toward the room where the light beckoned. I eased the door open and peeked inside to find a modest bedchamber with a small bed that was little more than a cot. A battered night table stood next to it, bearing a chipped vase of wilting daisies.

The only ostentatious piece of furniture in the room was a full-length cheval glass set in an intricately carved oak frame with sconces for candles. Fugitate posed before this mirror. He was bared to the waist, his wings exposed.

My breath caught. Fully unfurled, his gossamer wings spanned outward, nearly touching the walls on both sides, a distance of at least eight feet. The light that had drawn me did not come from the candles on either side of the mirror. They were not even lit. It was the wings. They shimmered with an intensity that reflected the alabaster whiteness of the fairy's skin, the frosty sheen of his thick waves of hair. Fugitate looked tall and proud as he studied his image in the mirror. His face was beautiful with finely chiseled cheekbones and delicate brows arched over his eyes. It was little wonder that he had not heard the bell or me calling him. He appeared lost in another world, a realm of poignant memory and untold sorrow. A single crystal tear escaped and cascaded down his cheek.

I averted my gaze, realizing I had witnessed a private moment no human had a right to see. I tried to tiptoe away, but I had the misfortune to stumble over a loose floorboard. As I flung my hand out to keep from falling, I inadvertently pushed the door all the way open. The knob hit the wall with a loud crack.

Fugitate whipped around, staring at me with a horror that swiftly turned to anger.

"What are you doing here? Are you spying on me?"

"N-no." I shrank back as he stalked closer, his brows crashing together, his wings flattening behind him. "I called out for you but when no one answered, I feared—"

"Get out!"

"I never meant to— I am so sorry."

His face loomed within inches of mine. His eyes flashed golden fire. "I said GET OUT!"

I fled, my heart racing ahead of me. I tore down the corridor, past the curtain and through the shop, knocking over books, paintings, and drums in my scramble to escape. A gnome tumbled off the shelf and shattered, but I did not stop until I reached the door. I fumbled with the knob, glancing over my shoulder, terrified I would find Fugitate in vengeful pursuit.

He was not. I did not see or hear anything except for a peculiar noise I could not place. I listened intently, my eyes widening at the realization. The fairy was weeping, harsh wracking sobs that tore at my heart.

Still shaking from the fright Withypole had given me, I longed to go and comfort him, but I did not dare. Any solace from me would not be welcome and I dreaded provoking his wrath again, although I suspected that his fury masked his own fear. He must be terrified that I would go straight to the royal authorities and expose him. Penalties for fairies attempting to disguise their identity and avoid the wing tax were especially harsh. I had heard horrible rumors about punishments that involved stone presses and crushed wings, although I was not sure I believed them. Could even King August be that cruel?

Withypole must have believed it, hence the depth of his despair. I wondered why he had chosen to remain here in Arcady, especially in Misty Bottoms, the most wretched corner of our land. Why had he not gone with the rest of his people, traveling to a far-off kingdom where he could be free and safe?

Whatever his reason for staying, I could not leave his shop without trying to apologize and promise that his secret was safe with me. I came away from the door and waited although it was difficult to listen to those heavy sobs and do nothing. Eventually they faded to a soft snuffling and then there was silence.

I was picking up the pieces of the shattered gnome when Withypole appeared from behind the curtain. Gone was the magnificent creature I had caught a glimpse of earlier. His beautiful wings were crushed beneath his brown woolen shirt. He looked like the stooped, hunchbacked shopkeeper I was accustomed to seeing. The fury was gone from his eyes as he regarded me. They had turned dull amber and were red rimmed from his weeping.

"You still here?" he muttered.

I approached him timidly. "Yes, I am sorry. I broke your gnome." I laid the pieces on the counter. "I'll pay for it."

Withypole jerked his head to one side. It was an odd gesture I had seen him make before, but I had finally puzzled out what it meant. With his wings so cramped, it likely hurt him to hunch his shoulders. The head jerk was Withypole's version of a shrug.

Mumbling something about gnomes being stupid, irritating creatures, Withypole swept the pieces off the counter and bent to drop them into a waste basket. When he straightened, I took a deep breath and plunged in, "I also want to apologize again for invading your privacy. When you didn't answer the bell or my shouts, I feared something might have happened to you and I just wanted to check."

"I was busy thinking, wasn't I? And I locked the shop door. What did you do, pick the lock?"

"No, of course not. You must have forgotten to lock up or else the spring didn't catch. But it doesn't matter because I promise you, I would never ever betray you or tell anyone about your wings."

"Wings?" he snapped. "What wings?"

"Why, yours. It must be so hard for you to keep them hidden away all the time. They are so dazzlingly beautiful but so delicate. Can you really fly? What does it feel like?"

"I have no idea what you are talking about, Miss Upton." He scowled at me. "Are you one of those as likes to sniff pixie dust? If that is what you are after, you should take yourself off to the Winking Goblin. I don't deal in anything like that here."

"I am not a pixie sniffer," I began indignantly and then faltered as I realized what Fugitate wanted to do: pretend that this incident had never happened. Upon reflection, I decided it might be best if I did likewise, although it was difficult to swallow the rest of my assurances, to say nothing of my curiosity about his wings.

"Sometimes I do let my imagination get away from me and I have not eaten much today. I was probably feeling a little giddy and — and—"

"No doubt," he interrupted. "So did you have some reason for coming to my shop today, other than poking your nose where it didn't belong?"

I had been so upset that I had allowed myself to forget why I had come. My spirits plummeted as I replied, "I need to sell something."

I dug inside my reticule to retrieve the knotted handkerchief cushioning my mother's earrings. I had never imagined parting with these beloved treasures was going to be easy, but I had not expected how hard it would be until the moment was upon me. I clutched the handkerchief, hesitating for so long, Withypole grew impatient. "Let's see what you've brought then."

I laid the handkerchief on the counter, struggling with the knot until it gave way. The emeralds sparkled against the white linen, looking as bright and entrancing as the last time my mother had worn them. I tried to tell myself they were only earrings. It was not as if I was selling my memories, the last fragments of my mother I had left.

All the same, I stepped back from the counter to keep from snatching up the earrings. I shifted from foot to foot, waiting for Fugitate's valuation of the emeralds' worth and dreading it.

I expected him to take up his jeweler's glass and examine them more closely. Instead, he just stared at the emeralds before finally saying in an odd voice, "You really want to sell these twinkles?"

"These what?" I asked, startled by the fairy's use of my childhood term for my mother's earrings. How could Fugitate possibly know about that?

"Twinkles. It is what my people— er, ah... what the fey call gems. Or so I have heard," he added hastily. "These are the green twinkles Julius acquired for his good lady."

"Julius?" I echoed.

"Julius Upton," the shopkeeper replied irritably. "Your father."

"I know who my father was. But how did you know him?"

Withypole's gaze shifted away from me. "I am sure lots of folks did, him being such a notable advocate, pleading cases before the king."

"You have my father mixed up with someone else. He was never any sort of advocate."

"He gave it up before you were born. Had to, didn't he, after defending too many of the wrong sort of people."

"What do you mean the wrong sort of people? Are you trying to tell me my father defended villains?"

"No, I mean representing the kind of people that the king didn't want defended. Such clients do not make for a successful career as an advocate. Your father was better off out of it."

My mind reeled from what Fugitate was telling me. I could hardly bring myself to believe it. My father had been such a quiet, reclusive man. I could not imagine him speaking before the king to defend anyone, let alone a person who had offended his majesty. It would have been such a defiant thing to do, and my passive father had never seemed the sort of man to take such risks. And yet I was troubled by my memory of him refusing to comply with the law that our auras be registered.

Could Withypole be speaking the truth? He sounded as though he had been well acquainted with my father, enough so that he referred to him as Julius and he recognized my mother's emeralds. Had my father bought the earrings from Withypole? Was that how they knew each other? When my father had read to me out of the book of fairy lore, why had he never told me that he had met a real one?

I was bursting with questions, but Fugitate clammed up, refusing to tell me anything more.

"That's all I know about your father," he grumbled. "Now are you going to waste my entire afternoon or are we going to get down to business? How much would you want for these twink— these emeralds?"

I seethed with frustration, but it was clear I was not going to glean any more information from Withypole.

"I need at least eighty gold pieces." I said.

"Eighty! What do you need such a sum as that for?"

I had been in Fugitate's shop many times selling things. The transactions had all been brisk and businesslike. Never had he once given me a hint whether he had known my father or shown any interest in what I intended to do with my money. I was so taken aback by his demand that I answered him.

"I want to attend the royal ball."

"You and every other silly girl." He made an odd chuffing sound. "I would've thought Julius Upton's daughter would have better sense. A royal ball to win the heart of Prince Florian? Bah! You would not want to win that prince, Miss Upton. Better to forget about the ball, better to stay away from the palace altogether."

Only that morning, I would have heartily agreed with him. But that had been before my conversation with Imelda had forced me to reconsider.

"Nonetheless, I still need to buy those ball tickets, although it is more for my sisters than myself. As much as I appreciate your advice, Master Fugitate, it is not your concern how I spend my money. So how much will give me for the earrings?"

Withypole's lower lip jutted out. He squirmed, but he reached for his jeweler's glass to inspect the emeralds more closely. "I could perhaps offer you fifteen."

"Fifteen! I won't take a penny less than seventy-five."

"Those earrings are very old-fashioned. I'll probably have to take them apart and reset the gems to have any hope of selling them."

The thought of my mother's cherished earrings being broken apart made me ill. "You have never seemed to worry overmuch about making sales before," I retorted.

"Times are hard, not enough customers these days. That is why I cannot afford to be too generous. I can maybe go as high as twenty."

"They are worth at least seventy and you know it."

"Twenty-five. Best I can do."

"Sixty-five," I snapped.

Back and forth we went, with me trying to press him as hard as Mal would have done, but this bargaining felt different from those previous negotiations. Withypole wanted those earrings. There was an acquisitive gleam in his eye when he looked at the emeralds and yet he seemed reluctant to buy them. He would start to reach for them, only to clamp his fingers about his own wrist and draw his hand back.

"Forty-five, final offer," he said and then moaned. "No, I shouldn't. I can't—"

"Done!" The word burst out of me before I had time to reflect. The effect was very similar to dropping a large rock into an empty well. A loud thunk followed by a hollow silence.

Withypole and I stared at each other and for a moment, I thought I saw my own dismay mirrored in his eyes. Then he ducked behind the curtain to fetch the money from the back. I had never seen where Fugitate kept his strongbox. He was quite naturally very secretive about it.

While he was gone, I had to fight the urge to grab the earrings and flee. What had I just done? Sacrificed my mother's earrings for far too little, certainly not enough to buy four tickets to the ball. Yet I had sensed that if I had not snapped up Withypole's last offer, he would have been about to refuse to buy the emeralds at any price. Although why that should be, I had no idea.

The fairy returned and carefully counted out the coins. I felt numb as I scooped them into my purse. I could not even bring myself to look at my mother's earrings one final time. When the last coin had been collected, I tugged the drawstrings closed and rushed out of the shop, not even bidding Fugitate goodbye.

I felt like I wanted to retch. I had to swallow hard as I wondered if the fairy really would pick the earrings apart to make something new. It might have been just as well if he did. I had heard that wealthy Midtown women and even ladies from the Heights would sneak into Fugitate's shop in search of a bargain, although none of them would ever admit to buying anything secondhand. I would have found it unbearable to see my mother's cherished earrings become the property of some smug merchant's wife or a haughty countess. If the jewels were reset, I would never have to know, although anytime I saw emeralds sparkling in a lady's ears, I feared that I would wonder.

The heavy fog had dispersed somewhat as I began my trudge homeward. I could find my way better although I should have continued to be wary of my surroundings. My head was too full of all that had transpired within the curio shop: my first glimpse of fairy wings, Withypole's surprising revelations about my father, the woefully poor bargain I had struck.

With such thoughts consuming me, I never noticed the hulking figure that stepped in front of me until it was too late. I nearly walked straight into the ugliest brute of a man I had ever seen, so large and ugly it was enough to make one suspect he might have a drop of goblin blood in him.

His egg-shaped head was bald except for a tuft of pepper-colored hair set between his enormous ears. His grizzled jaw was as coarse as a warthog's bristles. His eyes were of a similar porcine nature, his bulbous nose mapped with red lines that indicated a heavy drinker. He did indeed stink of stale beer, combined with the odor of rancid fish and garlic. I had to resist the urge to plug my nose.

"Afternoon, miss," he said. His tone was respectful enough, but his grin was nasty, thick lips peeling back to expose yellowed teeth.

Concealing my alarm, I responded with a cool nod and attempted to skirt around him, but he moved to block my path.

"Where you off to in such a great hurry, m'lovely darling?"

"That is no concern of yours."

"Aww, no need to get snippy. I call that bad manners when I

just want to be helpful. You could get along much faster if you let me lighten that heavy purse a bit."

I backed away from him, clutching the sack of precious coins closer, cursing myself for a fool. I should have been more alert and kept the purse hidden beneath my shawl, not parading through these lanes with my head up my bottom.

My heart thudding, I retreated even farther. When he lumbered after me, I cried, "Don't you take a step closer, or I will scream loud enough to bring all of Misty Bottoms running."

He guffawed. "Folk hereabouts tend to mind their own business, m'darling. Who do you think will come? Just another charming rogue like m'self and I'm in no mood to share. So just hand over that purse and we can part ways all amiable-like."

I tightened my grip on the pouch, my gaze darting wildly about me, assessing my options. If only I had some sort of weapon like a dagger or a rock, but the brute would likely have taken it from me with one swipe of his meaty paw. I wished the fog had not dispersed. I could have lost him in the thick mist with little trouble.

The only advantage I had was speed. If I could make it down to the waterfront where the guard tower stood, surely one of the Border Scutcheons would come to my aid.

Whirling about, I tore off at full tilt. I have always been a fast runner. Even Mal could never beat me in a race. But the great oaf behind me was far swifter.

I did not manage to get far before he tackled me, dragging me to the ground. The fall jarred me, but I rolled over, trying to regain my feet. He pinned me down, grabbing the purse. I hung on to it with all my strength. Using my head like a battering ram, I smashed my skull into his face, hoping to break his nose. It was like dashing my brain against a concrete wall. My head throbbed with pain and all it did was make him angry.

"Witch," he snarled, twisting my hand savagely to loosen my grip on the purse. My wrist felt about to snap, and I screamed. He clamped his dirty fingers over my mouth, his hand so huge it covered my nose as well.

I bucked and struggled as hard as I could, but to no avail. I was suffocating, my lungs tortured for want of air. As webs of darkness spun before my eyes, I could feel my grip on the purse going slack. My despairing thought was it had all been for nothing— the sacrifice of my mother's beautiful earrings. I silently cursed the ugly thief, consigning him to the deepest, blackest pit of the demon bogs.

Then as though seized by some dark unseen force, the brute was wrenched away from me. It was like my curse had been granted. I gasped, gulping in great lungs full of air. My vision cleared. Although I still felt dazed, I struggled up onto my elbows, trying to figure out what happened.

I saw my attacker wrestling to get free of the large arm locked about his neck. The thief's opponent appeared to be a man of equal size and strength, although leaner and far more muscular. Yet I felt no joy at the sight of a rescuer. As the thief had predicted, all my scream had done was draw the attention of another villain, this one even more sinister, cloaked as he was all in black, the hood concealing his face.

I felt battered and groggy, but I could not afford to sprawl in the road, waiting to see which rogue won. I groped for my purse and experienced a moment of alarm when I could not find it. To my relief, I discovered it lying nearby, but the drawstring had pulled open during the struggle, my precious coins scattered in the dirt. I shifted onto my hands and knees, frantically scooping up the gold, all the while aware of the desperate contest taking place but yards away.

I heard curses, grunts, and the thud of blows, followed by the sound of running feet. I crawled about, trying to hurry. I was reaching for the last coin when my fingers struck up against a thick black boot. I gazed fearfully upward to find the victor of the battle looming over me, the villain in the black hood.

I gave a piteous moan. I had no more fight left in me. As he bent over me, I did not even have the strength to shrink away. I cowered before him, expecting the worst. He swept back his hood, and I gazed up at surprisingly familiar features, a harsh countenance with a full dark beard.

"Miss Upton," Commander Crushington said, his eyes softened by concern. "Are you all right?"

Seven

He could not be real. I had to be having some bizarre dream about wandering in a fog, being frightened by an angry fairy, losing my mother's earrings, and then getting attacked by a goblin man. Now, of all unlikely things, I was being rescued by Commander Horatio Crushington.

He hunkered down beside me, demanding, "Miss Upton, are you hurt?"

"No." I continued to gawk at him. I had never seen the commander without his uniform. His military tan and blue always seemed molded to him like a second skin.

"I thought you must sleep in it," I said.

"I beg your pardon?"

"Your uniform. I imagined that you even wore it to bed."

"Er— no, I don't wear anything at all. Ella, are you sure you are all right?"

He was real. Even in my strangest dream, I would never have conjured up the stern commander of the Midtown garrison informing me that he slept naked. My mind was assailed by a picture of a bare chest, muscular shoulders and arms, hard thighs and— I have always possessed far too good of an imagination. I shook my head to dispel the embarrassing vision.

Crushington once more started to ask if I was hurt, but I cut him off. "I am fine, truly."

To prove it, I clutched my purse and struggled to stand. The commander hooked his arm about my waist to help me. I needed it. Now that the assault was over, my body reacted, and I started to shake. I saw something move out of the corner of my eye and I jumped. It was only a cat slinking past a nearby cottage. It looked like Delphine's obnoxious feline, Ebony, but it was gone in a streak.

Misinterpreting my start, Crushington reassured me, "You need not be frightened. That varlet who attacked you is gone. He got away from me, but I promise you, I will hunt him down."

"It does not matter. I am unharmed and more important; my gold is safe." I hugged the precious pouch tightly to my bosom.

Crushington frowned. "You appear to have acquired a great deal of money."

"I did not steal it, if that is what you are thinking."

"That never occurred to me for a moment, but I fear you must have paid another visit to the gleaner."

"The what?"

"Mr. Fugitate's establishment."

I had never heard Fugitate called that before and yet the term "gleaner" was not unknown to me. I had heard it somewhere long ago, but I was too rattled to recall.

Crushington continued sternly, "What were you thinking, woman? To be wandering about in this part of town alone and on such a murky afternoon! What was so urgent to bring you down here?"

I already knew how stupid and rash I had been. I did not need the Midtown commander interrogating me in that scolding tone as though I was a wayward child.

I tried to compress my lips in a mutinous line, but I was trembling too much.

"I had to sell a pair of emerald earrings. They belonged to my mother, and they were very p-precious to me." I would have never expected to confide such a thing to Crushington or that I would burst into tears.

It was just another response to all these distressing events, but I hated to cry in front of anyone, let alone the commander of the Midtown garrison. He patted himself as though searching for a handkerchief and came up empty. Using the rough pads of his thumbs, he tried to stem my flow of tears, but they were coming too freely.

"Miss Upton... Ella. Please don't. I did not mean to make you cry. I am sorry you had to part with something you valued so much. Are you in some sort of financial difficulty?"

"N-no. I j-just needed money for tickets. T-to the ball."

"But you told me you didn't want to go."

"I d-didn't, but now I do. B-because every girl should have a night of magic and— and I must think of the future. Because my little s-sisters are growing up and— and I don't want Fortescue Bafton for a brother-in-law."

"No, I should not like that either."

There was something about the solemn way that Crushington agreed with me that caused me to erupt into laughter. He stared at me in dismay. The poor man probably thought I was going mad.

I hiccupped on a combination giggle-sob and strove to regain control of myself.

"S-sorry," I gasped. "This has just been an unsettling afternoon."

"It is all over now," he said, wiping away the last of my tears with a gentleness I would never have imagined him capable of.

"Y-yes, thank you. I am fortunate you were around to come to my rescue, although you alarmed me, wearing that black cloak. I have never seen you dressed in such a fashion." I was still puzzled by the absence of his uniform. "Are you taking a day of leave from your duties?"

"I never take leave, Miss Upton. I am sorry if I frightened you, but I have discovered it is better to dress this way when I am obliged to travel across the river."

"There is nothing across the river, but the fenlands. Why would you ever have to go there?"

"Reconnaissance," he replied. The clipped way he said it warned me that was all the answer he intended to give. His tone softened as he added, "I was just riding back from the ferry when I heard your cry, and you will never know how glad I am of that. If anything were to happen to you—" He checked himself, shaking his head at me. "You have had such a narrow escape. I told you to stay out of Misty Bottoms."

I sniffed. "So, are you going to arrest me?"

"I wish I could for no other reason than to keep you out of trouble. But ignoring my advice is not against the law." His mouth tipped upward in a reluctant half-smile. "However, I must insist upon escorting you home."

Any other time, I would have proudly refused, but I was still shaken from the attack. "Thank you," I said meekly. "I would be most grateful."

Crushington bent down to retrieve my shawl, which had come off during the struggle. He tried to brush away some dirt from the fringe. "I am afraid your shawl has become soiled and torn."

"It doesn't matter. It is an old one and already stained from my younger sister borrowing it."

He draped it awkwardly about my shoulders and then startled me by placing his fingers in his mouth and emitting a loud whistle. I was astonished when his horse ambled toward us out of the mist. It was a sign of how dazed I was that I had not realized the massive roan had been standing patiently within earshot.

"Does your horse always just wait for you like that?" I asked. "He never wanders off?"

"Not when I order him to stay. Loyal is very well trained."

"You named your horse Loyal?"

"That was his name when I bought him. It suits him and he likes it," Crushington said, patting the roan's neck.

"Does he? How obliging of him to tell you," I teased him, although I should not have. I knew the man had no sense of humor.

Crushington reddened and said gruffly, "What I mean is that he responds to 'Loyal,' and I have far more important things to do other than think up new names for horses."

It was rather adorable how flustered the formidable commander looked as he swung himself up onto the saddle. Adorable? Now there was a word I never thought I would use to describe Crushington. I must have hit my head against the goblin man's jaw harder than I realized.

The commander stretched his hand down to me and said simply, "Come."

I paused to fasten my purse to my belt before reaching up to him. He hauled me onto the saddle in front of him as easily as if I weighed no more than one of the roses in my garden. With his arms banded around me, he urged his mount forward.

I have never been the sort of woman to swoon at the thought of a knight in shining armor swooping me up on his charger. But I did appreciate the feeling of the commander's protective arms surrounding me. After my harrowing ordeal, I could not help melting a little against the solid security of his chest.

I had not expressed my gratitude enough for his rescue. But when I tried to do so, Crushington would have none of it.

"It is I who am grateful to have been of service, Miss—" He paused before asking diffidently. "May I call you Ella?"

"You have already done so without my permission," I pointed out. "But you saved my life to say nothing of my money, so the answer is yes. You may call me whatever you wish, except for Prunella."

"And you must call me Horatio."

"Oh no, must I?" I blurted out before I could stop myself. "Don't you have some sort of nickname? What do your friends call you?"

"A Scutcheon commander does not have the luxury of friendship."

"Oh." I found that truly sad. It had never occurred to me what a lonely man Crushington must be.

"If you do not care for Horatio," he continued, "I have other names to choose from. My full name is Horatio Alexander Samuel Edward Crushington."

"Goodness! Your parents were excessively generous when they christened you."

"Every time I am obliged to sign a document, I wish they had been a bit more frugal."

His tone was solemn, but when I glanced up at him, I caught a glimmer of amusement in his eyes. Was it possible the commander had a sense of humor after all? What a day of astonishing revelations this was turning out to be. He smiled at me, a genuine smile, not his usual quirk of the lips. I smiled in return, and we rode onward in silence, but it was not an uncomfortable one. The commander was not the sort of person given to idle chatter and neither was I.

He kept his horse to a very sedate pace. I wondered if this was to prolong his time with me. I was aware Crushington liked me, but I could not be vain enough to imagine he would dawdle just to hold me close, not a man so devoted to the pursuit of his duties. Most likely he lingered because the Bottoms were still hazy and the lanes rough and full of ruts. He would not want to risk Loyal stumbling and straining a fetlock.

Whatever his reason, our slow progress suited me. I was not eager to reach home. My one consolation for selling my mother's earrings had been imagining my family's jubilation when I announced we could all go to the ball. How deliriously happy

Imelda, Amy and Netta would be! Now I dreaded their reaction when I had to tell them I had only acquired enough money for two tickets. My stepsisters were too young and inexperienced to navigate the royal court without a chaperone and I certainly did not feel qualified to act in that role. The elite society of the Heights had once been Imelda's world, so she must have one of the tickets. I had never had any desire to attend the ball, so Em would have to decide which of her daughters to take.

Netta was the oldest and she had the sylphlike loveliness that was the current fashion. Amy was only sixteen, short and buxom. But she was much livelier than Netta and far more comfortable meeting strangers. What a difficult choice for a mother to make.

But I knew my tenderhearted stepmother too well. Imelda would never be able to choose between her girls. She would turn helplessly to me, and I would be the one obliged to decide. So, which one of my sister's dreams would I have to shatter? Netta's or Amy's?

I sagged against Commander Crushington. With the prospect of such an impossible decision looming before me, I felt weighted down by a sense of failure. I should have pressed Master Fugitate much harder, not only for more money, but for more information about my father.

When I was young, my parents were simply that— my mother and father. It never occurred to me that they might have had lives beyond me, their own memories, their own histories, perhaps even their own secrets. By the time I had grown mature enough to ask questions, it had been far too late.

I did know that my mother, Cecily, had been the only child of the royal forest warder. Her position in society had not been as high as Imelda's as the daughter of a knight, but my mother would have been considered of a better class than the trade people of Midtown. I believed my father had been the only son of a prosperous wine merchant. How my parents had ever chanced to meet and fall in love, I had no idea.

I had only been six years old when my mother died, but I had many warm memories of her. Although I had had twelve more years to become acquainted with my father, he was a shadow man to me, the quiet recluse who had haunted the library. My best memories of him were those times I snuggled on his lap while he read to me and my mother. Even then my recollections centered more on all those wonderful stories and not the man himself.

The blow to my head seemed to have jarred something loose in my brain. I suddenly recalled where I had learned the fairy word for jewels. My father had taught me to call my mother's emeralds "twinkles." This recollection was succeeded by one more startling and vivid.

It must have been days after my mother's funeral. I was too young to understand the final nature of death. Mal's grandmother had told me my mother had traveled to some beautiful kingdom high among the stars where she would be well and happy and watch over me forever. I did not believe it. How could my mama be happy so far away from me?

I trailed after my father demanding that he climb up to the stars and fetch my mother home right now. I must have driven the poor man to distraction, consumed as he was by his own grief. He engaged a nanny to look after me. I could not recall her name only that she had been a dour, unsmiling woman. She had insisted I start acting like a big girl and accept my loss. My mother was never coming back.

I had kicked her in the shins, and she retaliated with a sharp smack. My father had heard and seen it all and he was furious. How could I have forgotten that? It was the one time in my life I could ever recall him losing his temper. He had dismissed the nanny, roaring at her to leave his house. She had been so frightened of him, she had run. My father's anger had evaporated as he realized he was left to cope with a hysterical, sobbing child. He scooped me up in his arms, seeking to comfort me in the only way he knew how.

The twisting lanes of Misty Bottoms, the ambling movement of the horse, the creak of the leather saddle, even the feel of the commander's arms around me faded before the blur of memory.

I was back in the library, curled up on my father's lap, shuddering from the last of my sobs. My father's voice was a soothing drone as he read to me the final chapter of *The Quaint Customs and Ways of the Fey Folk*.

"And it came to pass that King Zanthypod had to depart from the High Forest for he had become a gleaner and the fey would no longer have him for their king."

"What's a gleaner, Papa?" I asked.

My father kept on reading as though he had not heard me. I placed my hand upon his bristly unshaven cheek, obliging him to look at me as I repeated my question.

"What is a gleaner?"

My father's brow furrowed. It was usually my mother who answered my questions, reducing difficult words into terms a child could understand. He expelled a deep breath as he struggled to explain.

"A gleaner is a fairy who is an outcast, a stranger to his people because he becomes obsessed, greedy to acquire the things humans value, like furniture, fancy clothes and china. That is anathema to the fairy way of life... er, they don't like it and so they wanted their king to go away."

I frowned as I turned this over in my mind. "So why didn't the king just stop doing it?"

"I don't think he could help it. Grief can make a fairy behave in a way he knows he shouldn't, but he cannot seem to stop himself because his heart hurts too much." My father paused to swallow. "Fairies only turn into gleaners when something really bad happens to them or they lose someone they loved very much."

"Like their mama?" I quavered.

"Yes."

My lower lip wobbled. "But I don't want to become a gleaner, Papa."

"You won't," my father said, gathering me closer. "You are not a fairy, Ella. You are a wise little girl."

"Magnificently wise?"

"Yes," he said hoarsely, burying his face against the top of my head and I could feel the splash of his tears...

My own eyes stung as the memory faded and I recollected where I was and who I was with. I had already disconcerted Commander Crushington enough by weeping. I could not do so again, so I blinked hard to stem my tears although the resurrected memory of my father touched me deeply.

I understood now what I had not as a child. My father had not just been trying to explain the effect grief could have on fairies, but on a man as well. The death of my mother had turned him into a gleaner of books, seeking to bury his aching heart within their pages.

I now felt anxious to return home. I wanted to find *The Quaint Customs and Ways of the Fey Folk* and read it again, as though by doing so I could forge a connection with my father and find answers to my questions. If not about Julius Upton, then at least about Withypole Fugitate.

Yet I suspected many of the things my father had known about fairies had not come from the book, but from Withypole himself. Withypole had seemed quite familiar with my father's history. Had my father likewise been acquainted with Withypole's past, whatever tragedy had turned the fairy into an outcast? At the very least, my father must have known enough to recognize Fugitate for what he was, a gleaner.

My father was not the only one to do so. I tensed as I recalled the words that had provided the spark to my recovered memory.

I fear you must have paid another visit to the gleaner, Crushington had said.

I sat bolt upright, twisting around to stare at him. "You know!"

The commander must have thought I was in danger of falling because he tightened his arms around me. "I beg your pardon, Ella. I know what?"

"About Mr. Fugitate. You called him a gleaner."

"Did I? I don't recall saying—"

"You did! You know you did! Just as you know Withypole is a fairy."

"And it would seem, so do you. The reckless fool! I warned him to be careful about concealing his identity."

"You warned him? But aren't you obliged to arrest him for being an unregistered fairy or wing tax evasion?"

"Yes, well, ordinarily that would be true. But there are times when enforcing a minor law can be overlooked. Fugitate is of far more use to me where he is than locked up in a cell."

"What use could that poor fairy possibly be—" I gasped as the realization hit me square between the eyes. "Fugitate is your informant. You are using him as a spy, aren't you?"

"I have already said more than I should, Ella," the commander replied. "You need to be still. You are making Loyal uneasy."

It was not the horse I was making uncomfortable. It was his master. I lowered my voice as I continued, "How did you persuade Fugitate to spy for you? Are you paying him? Or is he simply too terrified of being arrested to refuse?"

Crushington compressed his lips, not answering me. He did not have to, not when I remembered how terrified the fairy had been when he realized I knew his secret. I imagined that his deal with the commander hinged upon Withypole never exposing his identity.

"How can you!" I choked. "How can you bully that poor creature this way? Do you have any idea how miserable Withypole is already, having to keep his beautiful wings compressed and hidden? It must be heartbreaking enough for him to be cast out from his own people."

"That is none of my doing," Crushington said tersely. "I am not responsible for Fugitate becoming a gleaner."

"But you are certainly taking advantage of his plight."

"The Bottoms are a lawless place. I must gather information however I can. Now, I am sorry, but I cannot discuss my arrangement with Master Fugitate any further."

Crushington's voice was stern, with perhaps even a hint of warning. I should have held my tongue, but I could not, especially when something else struck me.

"You said that you feared I had paid another visit to the gleaner. You must know about the previous times I was at Fugitate's shop. Are you keeping some sort of record of my activities?" I demanded.

"Not yours."

"Then whose?" But I already knew the answer to that.

"Mal," I said softly. "You are using Fugitate to gather information about Mal."

"Among others. I did warn you that Malcolm Hawkridge's activities are of great interest to me when I advised you to stay away from him."

"Mal is my dearest friend and I have no intention of avoiding him."

"That man is no friend to you, Ella. Why was he not with you today? How could he allow you to take such a risk, venturing into this part of town alone?"

"I am an independent woman. I don't need Mal's permission or that of any other man. Mal has been so occupied with his business of late, I did not even ask him to accompany me."

"Exactly what business would that be?"

Merely a little smuggling, practicing illegal magic and plotting to break into the royal palace to steal back his grandfather's orb.

I replied, "Why, what else but the business of brewing medicine. After all, Mal is an apothecary."

"An apothecary who has been gone from his shop frequently these past two weeks." Crushington's hard grey eyes probed mine. "Do you have any idea where Hawkridge has been?"

"He has probably been off gathering herbs or paying calls upon customers too old or ill to visit his shop."

"How noble of him," Crushington said. There was such a bitter edge to his voice that for a moment I wondered if he could be jealous of Mal. That was surely absurd.

"Mal can be quite noble and generous," I said. "Your time would be much better employed hunting down a real villain like the man who attacked me."

"I intend to."

"Good! Then you can arrest someone who actually deserves it. What a refreshing change that would be."

I winced as soon as I said it, cursing my wayward tongue. But I was tired. I was bruised. I was angry and upset that Crushington was so relentlessly determined to prove Mal guilty of something. Still, it was not wise of me to antagonize the commander.

Crushington looked more frustrated than angry as he began, "Ella—"

"Miss Upton," I corrected, turning my back to him. I sat rigid in the saddle, trying to keep as much distance between us as possible.

I heard the commander heave a deep sigh, and he fell silent. Not a comfortable one this time.

I fumed quietly, disgusted with myself. I could not believe that I had been relaxed in Crushington's arms or even started to like him. His rescue of me had caused me to forget who he was: The Royal Scutcheon commander, the king's ruthless enforcer of his crushing laws. A man whose rigid sense of duty allowed him to exploit a miserable creature like Withypole and to pose a great threat to my closest friend.

All I wanted was to get away from Crushington as soon as possible. The commander must have felt the same because he urged Loyal into a trot. Perhaps he no longer really liked me quite so much.

As we left the Bottoms behind and clattered through the town square, we attracted a great deal of attention. Some of Crushington's men, loitering near their barracks, pointed at us and grinned. Citizens on their way to conduct official business at Quad Hall paused to stare and smirk.

My cheeks flamed as I realized everyone must be thinking that I had finally decided to welcome the commander's courtship. It was even worse when Crushington was obliged to slow his horse as we passed through the marketing area. Housewives tittered and whispered behind their hands, although others were not so subtle. Some of the remarks were carried to me with disastrous clarity.

"I never knew a man to be so slow."

"It looks like the commander has finally gotten around to some serious wooing."

"Ha! More likely he is arresting her."

I recognized this last snide voice as belonging to my stepmother's false friend, Matilda Dearling. As we trotted past, I shot her a venomous look. Despite the promise I had made Imelda, I would have given anything to have a large ugly toad in my pocket.

I wondered if Crushington was finding all this speculation as humiliating as I did. I risked a glance back at him. He stared rigidly ahead; his mouth set in the familiar stern line.

When we reached my house, he reined Loyal to a halt and dismounted. I did not wait for him to lift me from the saddle. I leapt down, but my heels struck the pavement hard, and I staggered. I would have fallen if Crushington had not caught me. For a moment, I was close to him, cradled in his embrace. As soon as I recovered my balance, I thrust him away.

I backed up a step and dropped a stiff curtsy.

"Thank you, Commander. For everything."

Not pausing for his reply, I whirled about, hurrying toward my front gate.

"Ella! Miss Upton, wait!" he commanded.

The gate creaked as I hurled through it and slammed it behind me.

"Miss Upton. Please..."

I turned around reluctantly. I waited as the commander approached, but I kept the gate between us. My expression could not have been encouraging. He was silent for a moment as though struggling for words.

"I wish there was some way to make you understand. These are dangerous times for our kingdom, far more dangerous than you realize. When I became a Scutcheon commander, I swore that I would give my life to protect Arcady and uphold its laws. I did not make such a pledge lightly."

"I never doubted you are a man of duty and honor," I said.

"No, what you doubt is that I could be a good man. You think of me as hard and unfeeling, perhaps even cruel. I wish that you might not judge me too harshly until we become better acquainted."

He added tentatively, "Your stepmother has been kind enough to say that I might call upon you some afternoon."

I had forgotten all about that. I grimaced.

"Of course, I would never do so if you do not wish it." When I said nothing, his face fell.

He backed away from the gate, clicked his heels in a rigid bow. As he turned to go, my conscience pricked me. I could not forget how deeply I was indebted to him. I would likely be sprawled dead in the lanes of Misty Bottoms if not for the commander.

But if I permitted Crushington to call upon me, it would only encourage him to hope I would one day return his regard and that was quite impossible. Still, he looked completely disheartened as he reached for the reins of his horse. So strangely vulnerable and alone, this man who thought of friendship as a luxury he could not afford.

One half hour visit, a cup of tea, a few cakes... would it really cost me so much to allow him that? I was probably going to regret this, but I opened the gate and hurried after him.

"Commander Crushington."

He was about to vault into the saddle, but he paused at the sound of my voice. Although there was little hope in his eyes, he regarded me questioningly.

I drew in a deep breath. "I was unkind to you just now and it was very wrong of me when I owe you so much."

"You owe me nothing, Miss Upton. I do not want your gratitude."

"You have it all the same. I cannot tell my family what happened this afternoon without greatly distressing them. But if they knew how you had rescued me, they would be grateful as well. What I am trying to say is... if you did wish to call upon us some afternoon, you would be welcome."

I was aware that I sounded more reluctant than cordial. I sought to make up for it by offering him my hand. When he eagerly accepted it, I gasped at the sudden throb of pain in my wrist.

Crushington released me at once. "Ella, I am sorry—" He stopped and frowned. Taking my hand more gently, he upended my palm and exclaimed, "You were hurt by that brute."

I stared down at the bruises darkening my skin. My wrist was even starting to swell a little.

"It's nothing," I said. "I will apply a cold compress to my wrist. It will be fine."

I tried to ease away from him, but he cradled my hand in his grasp. "When I was a wee lad and got injured, my mother had her own remedy for my pain."

I had difficulty picturing the formidable commander as ever having been "wee" or for that matter, even having a mother. I stiffened as he raised my hand to his lips, thinking he intended to kiss my hurt away as my own mother would have done.

Instead, he blew softly against my wrist. His lips never even grazed my skin and yet the contact felt so— so intimate, I shivered.

"Better?" he asked.

I nodded, too astonished to even reclaim my hand. When he released me, I hugged my hand close to my bosom.

"I have many duties that require my attention, but if you truly do not mind, I will call upon you early next week?"

"Next week would be fine."

He mounted his horse and smiled down at me. "Until next week then."

I nodded, stepping back out of the way as the commander urged his horse into motion. As Crushington wheeled Loyal about, heading toward town, I stared after him. What an extraordinary gesture for a man as stiff as Crushington, blowing on my wrist that way. What stunned me the most was my reaction. As I headed toward the house, my skin still tingled from the warmth of his breath.

All thoughts of the commander flew out of my head as my front door burst open. My two stepsisters rushed toward me, squealing, "Oh, Ella! Ella, thank the fairies, you are home at last!"

I stopped in midstep, tensing with alarm. "What is it? What's wrong?"

I barely got the words out before Amy and Netta launched themselves at me, flinging their arms about my neck. The fact that they were giggling eased my fear, but I gasped, "Girls, please," as I tried to pull free of their strangling hugs.

It was not that I did not appreciate such a welcome home. My stepsisters had hardly been speaking to me when I left the house earlier. But my body was too bruised to endure this much exuberance.

They released me, but they were still bouncing around with such excitement, I had to take a step back to spare my toes.

"Ella, you have been gone forever," Amy cried.

"We have been waiting and waiting for you," Netta chimed in.

"We have just been about to burst," Amy said.

"Let me tell her," Netta insisted.

But Amy thrust her aside, shrieking, "We are so happy! Now we can all go to the ball!"

I stared with incomprehension. Had Amy have been snooping in my room again? If she had picked the lock on my treasure chest and noticed the emeralds were gone, my stepsisters might have leapt to conclusions, guessing that I planned to sell the earrings to buy the tickets. It was an unlikely surmise, but the only explanation I could find to explain all this wild excitement.

The girls linked hands and began a joyous dance around me.

"Amy! Netta! Please stop," I said. I felt sick at the idea of informing them I had not acquired enough money and that one of them was going to be weeping soon.

When they ignored me, I spoke more forcefully. "Stop." Because there was no easy way to say it, I just blurted out, "We cannot all go to the ball because we can only buy two tickets."

The girls stumbled to a halt, but they were still smiling, unfazed by my announcement. Amy chortled. "Silly Ella! What are you talking about? We already have the four tickets."

"How is that even possible? Did Madam Dearling decide to loan Em the money after all?"

"That horrible woman? Of course not," Amy scoffed. "Now you really are being silly, Ella."

"Then how?" I demanded.

The girls exchanged a grin and cried in unison, "We have a fairy godfather."

"What!"

They both giggled and assured me that I would see for myself. I could not get another sensible word out of either of them as they dragged me into the house. I tried to curb my impatience with all this air of mystery as they hustled me through the drawing room and out the double doors leading to the rear garden.

Like most of the homes in Midtown, we had a modest-sized back lawn, not even half an acre. Ours was surrounded by a picket fence badly in need of painting. Next to the small stable that housed Amy's beloved ponies was my forlorn attempt at a vegetable garden, badly in need of weeding. The most charming feature of our yard was a pergola where we sometimes had afternoon tea. The latticework covering supplied shelter for a wrought-iron table, a bench, and some dainty carved chairs.

I could see my stepmother hovering over someone as she handed her guest a cup of tea. But it was not until Imelda resumed her seat that I obtained a clear view of her visitor. That was when I received my final shock of the day.

The person lounging upon the bench was Mal.

"Here he is." Amy tittered as she propelled me toward the pergola. "Our fairy godfather!"

Eight

Never had a man looked less like anyone's idea of a fairy godfather than Malcolm Hawkridge. He was dressed in his usual fashion, high black boots, tight breeches, and a loose-fitting white shirt open at the neck. Whatever he had been doing the last fortnight, Mal had acquired a deeper tan and shed the last of that ridiculous black hair he had tried to grow. He had lost what remained of his own hair as well and was now completely bald. It suited him, enhancing his virility, making him look dangerously seductive. I was astonished that Em had allowed him to cross the threshold, let alone served him tea on her best china.

Her reason for doing so rested next to the sugar bowl on the table; four, gilt-edged, creamy vellum tickets to the ball. My stepsisters had not been talking utter nonsense.

Imelda sprang to her feet, appearing considerably relieved to see me. "Ella, dear, here you are at last. We have all been waiting for you." Imelda's hands fluttered in that way she had when she was nervous. "Only look who surprised us with a visit in your absence, your friend, Mr. Hawkridge."

"That is not all he surprised us with." Netta scooped up a ticket and pressed it into my hand.

"Mal has made it possible for us all to go to the ball," Amy trilled. "Can you believe it?"

"No, I can't." As I stared at the ticket, my first thought was that I need not have hazarded my life, selling my beloved mother's earrings after all. My second thought was far more disturbing. What was Mal up to now?

I lifted my gaze from the ticket, directing a sharp glance at him. Mal dabbed his mouth with a napkin. He set his teacup aside before rising leisurely from the bench.

"Hallo, Ella." He smiled at me as though we had parted company just yesterday and he had not disappeared for two weeks, leaving me to worry and wonder about his absence.

I wanted to hug him. I wanted to strangle him. I wanted to barrage him with questions, but I could do none of those things in my family's presence.

I sank down into the nearest chair, waving the ticket. "This is indeed a surprise. I hardly know what to say."

Mal shrugged. "A simple 'thank you' will suffice."

As he resumed his seat, my stepsisters jostled each other to secure the place on the bench next to him. Amy won, casting Mal a coy smile. Netta emitted a tiny sigh, settling onto the nearest chair. If even I had noticed how wickedly attractive Mal looked, I should not have been surprised by the effect he was having on my sisters. There was far more than gratitude in the way they regarded their "fairy godfather."

Netta twirled one of her curls while peeping at him through the thickness of her lashes. Amy's cheeks were stained with a rosy blush. Mal treated their flirtatiousness with a wry amusement. My poor Em appeared on the verge of having a spasm, despite the ball tickets.

She fluttered as she poured me a cup of tea. "Of course, you were not here for me to consult, Ella. I did worry it was not quite proper to accept such a costly gift from a single gentleman, even if he is your friend."

"But then Mal explained that he won the tickets," Amy put in.

"Mr. Hawkridge, dear," Imelda reproved gently.

I frowned at Mal. "You won them? How?"

"Shooting dice with Waldo and Long Louie at the Winking Goblin."

"Oh, dear," Imelda said. "You did not mention that. How—how extraordinary."

"Isn't it just," I said dryly. "I would not have expected the sort of rapscallions who frequent the Winking Goblin to have ball tickets to wager."

"Why not? Rapscallions have daughters too," Mal said. "As a matter of fact, the person I won the tickets from, Waldo the Wharf Rat, has four charming girls."

Imelda fanned herself with a napkin. "Waldo the Wharf Rat? Oh my! What an unusual name."

"How fortunate for us that he is not lucky at dice," Amy chortled, but my tenderhearted Netta cast Mal a stricken look.

"But that means that Mr. Wharf Rat's poor daughters cannot go to the ball because we have their tickets." Netta's face fell, and she appeared ready to cry.

Mal paused in the act of adding another lump of sugar to his tea, clearly surprised by Netta's reaction. He made a swift recovery. "Don't worry about that. Waldo's girls won't mind."

"How could any girl not mind being deprived of the ball?"

"Because they have no interest in wedding a prince. Er... they are already happily married. Quite recently they all up and eloped so Waldo no longer needed those ball tickets."

"All four of his daughters eloped at once?" Imelda exclaimed.

"How romantic!" Amy sighed.

Netta brightened. "They must have found their true loves. That's wonderful."

No, it was a load of frap. I could not believe that even my stepsisters could be naive enough to credit such an outlandish tale. But Mal always has had the ability to tell the most blatant lies while contriving to look as guileless as a newborn babe. He enjoyed testing to see how much nonsense he could get a person to swallow. As his gaze met mine across the table, I saw the mischief dancing in his eyes.

When I thought no one was looking, I mouthed silently, I am going to kill you.

Mal grinned and mouthed back. I love you too.

Blast the man. He knew that I could not challenge his ridiculous story any further, not without upsetting Imelda, who was already struggling with the proprietary of accepting the tickets. Mal was obviously determined that she do so. But why?

When he had offered to send me to the ball, he had made it abundantly clear he would not advance a penny toward tickets for my family. What had caused him to change his mind? Unfortunately, there was only one reason I could think of. Mal must have been unable to find another way to break into the royal palace. By supplying tickets for my entire family, he knew I would be obliged to attend the ball. Very likely, he hoped he could still persuade me to steal the orb for him. I knew Mal could be devious when it came to achieving his ends, but I felt hurt and angry that he would seek to manipulate me in this ruthless fashion.

I could not confront him with my suspicions until we were alone. All I could do was fume in silence until an unexpected opportunity presented itself in the form of Mrs. Biddlesworth.

I could just see the top of her straw bonnet and her eyes as she spied upon us over the garden fence. The woman had been doing that more often of late. No doubt she hoped to catch me conjuring up another exotic plant using illegal magic. Usually, I would tease her by squinting and mumbling nonsense words as though I really was casting a spell. A silly and reckless thing to do, I knew. One of these days, I probably would provoke her into filing a complaint against me. I wondered if Commander Crushington would be the one to arrest me, looking all sad and rueful, but clapping me in irons all the same.

I astonished both Mrs. Biddlesworth and my family by waving and calling out cheerily, "Hello, Mrs. B!"

Mrs. Biddlesworth was obliged to straighten from her hiding spot behind the fence. She made a halfhearted gesture of greeting, her face flushed as red as her peonies.

"That woman! Always snooping," my stepmother huffed. "You should not encourage her, Ella."

"Oh, Em, you can hardly blame Mrs. B for being curious about why we are all making so merry. I should go tell her our good news."

"No, please, let me," Netta cried. "I am just bursting to tell someone."

"No, I shall tell her," Amy said.

Just as I had known they would, my sisters leapt up, rattling the table.

"Girls, really!" Imelda protested. "I will not have you indulging that woman's vulgar curiosity."

Amy and Netta were already racing across the yard, eager to be the first one to share the glad tidings. I laid one hand soothingly on Imelda's arm.

"I think someone should offer Mrs. B an explanation. After all this time, I doubt she recognizes Mal. She is probably wondering why we are entertaining a man who looks rather like a river pirate. One would hate for any unsavory rumors to get started..."

I did not even have to finish the thought before Imelda leapt to her feet and rushed after the girls. Mal had been smothering his laughter into his napkin during this entire exchange. His mirth abruptly ceased when I whipped around the table and pounced, seizing him by the ear.

"All right, Hawkridge. What by all the fairies are you up to?"

"Ow! Ow! Ow! Let go!" He pried my fingers away and regarded me reproachfully. "Is this any way to treat your fairy godfather?"

"This is one fairy godfather who is about to get his wings

clipped if he doesn't start talking. Where have you been all this time? What mischief have you been plotting? Where did you acquire those tickets?"

Mal rubbed his ear. "Could I have one question at a time, please?"

I plunked down on the bench beside him so hard the wood creaked. "Let's start with those tickets. I don't want to hear any more frap about you winning them at the Winking Goblin. The palace might claim everyone is welcome at the ball, but I highly doubt the king sent a herald to pole down the river to deliver an invitation to Waldo the Wharf Rat."

"His Majesty might have done."

"But he didn't. Any more than the Wharf Rat has daughters."

"That is where you are wrong, Ella. Waldo does have four girls, although—" Mal chuckled, "his daughters are more into swordplay than waltzing, and if he had so much as suggested they deck themselves out in frills to attend that ball, they would have chucked their father into the river."

"Then why did you tease my poor stepmother with such an absurd story?"

"Because if I told her the truth, that I had bribed a herald to give me an invitation so I could buy the tickets, Imelda would have refused to take them. She appears to have some ridiculous scruple about accepting expensive gifts from a man outside of the family." He added teasingly, "Of course, I could have told her we had become betrothed."

"Only if you wanted to give my poor Em heart failure. Why did you go to such pains to acquire the tickets and get Imelda to accept them? If you think by sending us all to the ball, you will be able to maneuver me into stealing that orb for you—"

"I thought nothing of the kind. The tickets are a gift, Ella. Pure and simple, no conditions attached."

"Then I truly do not understand. I know how much you

despise my stepmother and sisters. Why would you give them such an expensive gift?"

"Because I hated the way we parted that day in my shop. I felt ashamed for the way I tried to pressure you into stealing the orb and sulked when you refused. It seemed important to you that your stepmother and sisters go to the ball. I guess that makes it important to me too."

Mal shifted to face me. "I can be a genuine ass sometimes, but I really would do anything for you, Ella. I hoped you would realize that by now."

I studied his countenance. Mal could be an ass. He could be so thoughtless, provoking, and evasive that I wanted to throttle him. There were also those rare times when he let down his guard and was completely open, his sincerity shining through.

This was one of those moments.

"Oh, Mal," I murmured, reaching for his hand.

"And I do mean anything, including wasting money on tickets for your spoiled, foolish stepsisters and—"

"No, don't ruin it," I said. "Just stop at the part where you would do anything for me."

Mal's lips tipped in a rueful smile, and I smiled back at him. He entwined his fingers through mine.

"How I have missed you, Ella."

"And I, you. So where have you been and what were you doing all this time that you could not even spare a moment for me?"

"I am sorry I have been so preoccupied."

"With what?"

"I have been kept busy brewing my Elixir of Love. Word has spread and you would not believe the demand for it. I have sold at least ten dozen bottles so far."

"Wonderful," I grumbled. "That makes me feel so much better, hearing your illegal potion is such a great success."

Mal only laughed. As worried as I was about the conse-quences of him peddling that fake potion, I was more afraid of what else Mal might have been up to during the past fort-night, such as plotting to steal back that orb. The return of Imelda and the girls prevented me from questioning him further.

I could well imagine how distressed Imelda would be to find me sitting so close to Mal and holding his hand. I untwined my fingers from his and put a prim distance between us. When Amy realized she had lost her seat beside Mal, she pouted, but not for long.

Both of my sisters were in a state of euphoria because of the ball tickets. Informing our neighbor of our good fortune had only increased their exuberance. Even Imelda was beaming.

"I had no idea Mrs. Biddlesworth could be so amiable. She was full of good wishes for all of us."

"Especially you, Ella," Netta said. "She seemed quite eager for the prince to sweep you off to his castle."

"I'll wager she is." Mal was quite aware of how matters stood between Mrs. Biddlesworth and me. "Mrs. B is so kind and neigh-borly, I am sure she would even help Ella pack."

I had to choke back a laugh as I replied, "Such assistance will not be necessary. I think it highly unlikely I shall be the one to marry the prince."

"Whyever not, my dear?" Imelda asked. "You are lovely enough to win the heart of any worthy man."

"Or even some unworthy ones," Mal murmured, provocatively draping his arm behind me along the back of the bench.

I saw the alarm in my stepmother's eyes. I shifted farther away from Mal, casting him an admonishing glance. The gift of those ball tickets could mark a new era of... if not goodwill, at least of tolerance between my stepmother and my closest friend, which would make life far more agreeable for me. If only Mal could be induced to behave himself!

Netta's face clouded over. "It is wonderful that we have the tickets to the ball, but how are we to manage the rest of it? Ella said we cannot afford new ball gowns or the hire of a carriage and horses."

Amy batted her eyelashes at Mal. "I'll wager Mr. Hawkridge could manage to conjure something for us."

"Amethyst!" my stepmother cried.

"What, Mama? He said he is our fairy godfather."

Mal looked amused by Amy's audacity, but her mother was horrified. Before Imelda could scold Amy, I made haste to intervene. "We do not need to rely upon a fairy godfather, Amy. I can provide all that we will need."

When everyone regarded me questioningly, I realized the time had come to reveal what I had done. As I fumbled with the ties that fastened my purse to my belt, I dreaded Mal's response. He was going to be thoroughly vexed with me for selling my mother's earrings. But I experienced satisfaction that my sacrifice would not be in vain after all. Grateful as I was to Mal, it piqued my pride that I had not been able to provide my family with the tickets. But I would be the one to make sure they attended the ball in fitting style.

It was with a small flourish of triumph that I upended my purse, spilling the pile of galoons onto the table. The gasps from my stepmother and sisters were quite gratifying.

"Ella!" Netta gasped.

"It's a fortune," Amy squealed.

"My dear, however did you acquire so much money?" Imelda asked.

"Obviously she sold something." Mal scowled at me. "What was it this time?"

I shrugged. "Just my emeralds."

Mal flushed with anger. "You confounded little idiot!"

"Mr. Hawkridge, really!" My stepmother protested, but Mal ignored her.

"I can't believe you parted with your mother's earrings and

worse still, you went off and did it alone when I warned you never to—"

I gave Mal a sharp kick to silence him. My stepmother realized I had sold things in the past, but she had only the vaguest notion how I went about it, believing that I dealt with some respectable merchant in Midtown. She knew nothing of my ventures into Misty Bottoms and I preferred her to remain in ignorance.

I followed up the kick with a warning shake of my head. Mal swallowed the rest of his blistering rebuke, but I could tell it was difficult for him. He looked daggers at me and drummed his fingers on the arm of the bench. I hated to imagine his reaction when I told him I had been nearly robbed and killed. Perhaps it would be better if I kept that part of the story to myself.

My stepmother regarded me gravely. "My dear child, I wish you would have consulted me first. I would have never allowed you to make such a sacrifice."

Netta's eyes filled with tears. "I am so sorry, Ella."

Even Amy looked somber, although she could not refrain from pointing out, "But it is not as though Ella ever actually wore the earrings."

"Amy!" Netta cried.

I forced a smile to my lips. "Amy is right and although I did experience a pang when I sold them, it is nothing to the joy I will feel when I see my two little sisters transformed into the most dazzling belles that ever graced a royal ballroom."

"Oh, Ella!" Both of my stepsisters leapt up and descended upon me. They obliged Mal to retreat to the very end of the bench to avoid being smothered in skirts. Netta and Amy embraced me, declaring that I was the most wonderful, amazing sister in the entire world.

"Certainly, she is the stupidest one," Mal muttered.

"What Ella did was not stupid," my stepmother said sharply. "It was noble and kind and an investment in her future as well."

When Amy and Netta resumed their seats, Imelda also came to

embrace me. She wrapped her arm about my shoulders and squeezed. I allowed my head to rest against her as she dropped a kiss upon my hair and cooed, "My darling girl, you shall be transformed as well and have the most magical evening of your life. You believe your heart was completely broken, but when you are waltzing in the arms of the prince, I think you are going to be very glad you never married that wretched young musician and— oh!"

Imelda clapped her hand to her mouth as though she could recapture her impulsive utterance. It was far too late for that. Amy and Netta gaped at me. As for Mal, he could not have appeared more stunned if the pergola's roof had crashed down on his head.

My stepsisters had been far too young at the time to be aware of my infatuation with Harper and I had been quite secretive about the trysts with my bard. Now they were both on the edge of their seats, agog to hear all the details of my tragic romance. They assailed me with questions.

"You were going to marry a musician, Ella? But he broke your heart? Was he handsome? What was his name?"

"Never mind, girls," my stepmother interrupted as she returned to her chair.

"But Mama—"

"I said never mind. Ella's unfortunate romance happened a long time ago and I should never have mentioned it. We will forget about it and speak of more important things such as all that we must do to get ready for the ball. We have only two weeks."

The girls subsided with disappointed sighs. But their excitement over the upcoming ball would cause any secrets I harbored to dwindle in significance. While my stepmother might have been able to curb my sisters' curiosity, I knew Mal would not be so easily distracted. At the moment, he was stunned into silence. When I risked a glance at him, his eyes were full of hurt and questions I wished I did not have to answer.

Mal stood up rather abruptly, announcing that he had to leave. Imelda's sigh of relief was audible, although she was gracious, thanking him once more for the tickets and politely saying she hoped he would call again. The invitation was warmly seconded by my stepsisters.

Mal barely acknowledged them, his gaze focused on me. "Will you walk me to the gate, Ella?"

The coward in me longed to refuse. But I could not avoid forever what was sure to be an unpleasant conversation.

"Of course," I murmured.

Bidding farewell to my family, Mal offered me his arm. I rested my hand on the crook of his elbow as we left the garden. Imelda looked far from happy with this arrangement, but there was little she could say.

Mal and I made our way back through the house, neither of us speaking. I had often taken strolls with my friend in this companionable fashion, but never had his arm felt so stiff beneath my touch or the silence so heavy.

As we passed through the front door and down the garden walkway, I started to chatter as though I could delay the inevitable.

"...and although Amy has never been good at housework, you would not believe what prodigious care she takes of her ponies. When she was a little girl, whether she had happy or sad tidings, she would always rush to tell Pookie and Pippa everything."

"Ella..." Mal began.

"I am sure that is what she is doing right now, telling her ponies about the ball tickets. But you must not mention that to anyone. Amy would be so mortified if anyone knew."

"Ella!" Mal said more sharply. He came to an abrupt halt in the middle of the garden path, demanding, "So who was he? This musician who supposedly broke your heart?"

"No one." I withdrew my arm from his. "I mean he is no longer of any importance. Just let it go, Mal, please."

But of course, he was not about to do that. He took hold of my shoulders, obliging me to face him. "You fancied yourself in love with someone and you never told me? When was this?"

"It happened a long time ago when I was seventeen and you were not around to tell. It was that summer after your grandmother died and you were grieving so much you took off on that trip upriver."

"But I came back, and you still never breathed a word to me. Not once in all these years." Mal looked far more than hurt. He appeared devastated. "I sensed there was something different about you when I returned from that trip. But I always attributed it to your father's dying and leaving you with so much responsibility heaped on your shoulders. I never imagined there could be any other cause for your sorrow. Why, Ella? Why did you never tell me?"

"There are some emotions that are too private for me to share, even with you, Mal. And it doesn't matter now, whatever I thought I felt for this young man, because it all came to nothing."

"Why not tell me then? Who was he, Ella? This nothing that you fell in love with?"

I sighed, more than ever regretting my stepmother's slip of the tongue. I knew Mal would give me no peace until I confessed everything to him. "He was a traveling minstrel. His name was Harper."

"A traveling minstrel who called himself Harper! Thundering fairies, Ella! How naive could you be? You realize that likely wasn't even his real name."

"And you wonder why I never told you any of this."

"Sorry," he muttered. "But I know what these wandering musicians are like even if you don't. He probably had some girl besotted with him in every town, maybe even a wife and children tucked away somewhere in another kingdom."

"He didn't," I snapped. "He could hardly have asked me to marry him if he was already wed—" I stopped, wondering why I was still so heatedly defending the man who had broken my heart. The bitter truth was I had known so little about Harper, Mal could possibly be right.

"Maybe he was married," I conceded. "That would certainly explain why he never turned up the night we were supposed to elope."

"Elope! You intended to run off with this villain without even telling me goodbye?"

"You weren't here! I was going to send you a note."

"A note? Oh, well that would have made everything just great, wouldn't it?" Mal said bitterly. "I would have come home to find that my dearest friend had disappeared with some itinerant lute player, but it's all fine because she left me a frapping note!"

"I am sorry," I cried. "So will you kindly stop berating me for something I didn't do years ago?"

"Apparently the only reason you didn't run off was because he deserted you. Frap, Ella! How could you be so cruel?"

"I don't know," I replied miserably. "When I was with Harper, it was as though the rest of the world disappeared. All I could think about was him. I adored him so much."

"No doubt you did if you were willing to abandon everything for him. You were never a lukewarm girl, Ella. I always knew if you ever fell in love, you would surrender completely to the man lucky enough to win your heart." Mal swallowed. "But I always hoped it would be me."

"Don't, Mal." I pressed my fingers to his lips to silence him. "Please don't say anything we will both regret."

Mal shifted my fingers aside. "What you mean is, don't say anything you don't want to hear." He gave me a look so rife with longing and despair, it made my heart ache.

"All right, I won't," he conceded with a sigh. "At least not, for now."

I sighed, feeling grateful for the reprieve, even if it was only temporary. Mal had never been the sort of man easily discouraged when it came to getting what he wanted. I valued our friendship beyond anything, but I could never feel anything deeper for Mal than that. He had grown to be a mightily attractive man, but a part of me would always see him as the boy who used to swing on my garden gate, calling, "Ella! Come out and play." Someday, I would have to force Mal to accept that. When that day came, I wondered what would become of our friendship.

I realized that he was still holding my hand, but not with any amorous intent. He had discovered the bruises on my wrist and was frowning. "What happened here?"

I withdrew my hand, so eager to shift the conversation away from any further discussion of Harper that I told Mal about the attack in Misty Bottoms and how Commander Crushington had rescued me. I expected another eruption from Mal, but perhaps by this time his anger was spent.

He merely scowled and lightly rapped the top of my head. "Idiot! What were you thinking? Wandering around Misty Bottoms alone in the fog and laden with a sack full of coins? I never thought the day would come when I would say this, but thank the fairies for Commander Crushington!"

"His arrival on the scene was indeed timely."

"What did this brute that attacked you look like?"

I described the hulking creature, from his egg-shaped head and bulbous nose to his enormous feet. "He had an odd way of talking, trying to sound mockingly affable while giving me a nasty grin and he stank of garlic and fish."

"That sounds like Burt Iggy. He has a habit of lurking about Fugitate's shop, hoping to waylay unwary customers."

"Then that should not make it too difficult for Crushington to find him. The commander has promised me to arrest the villain."

Mal bared his teeth in a grim smile. "Not if I find old Iggy first."

"Mal, please do not do anything that could bring more trouble to your doorstep. The commander's attention is already far too focused on you. Do you realize that he has even coerced poor Withypole into acting as his spy?"

I expected Mal to be as shocked and outraged to hear this as I had been. Mal only laughed and shook his head. "You clearly do not know enough about fairies if you think they can be that easily intimidated. They are not sweet, gentle creatures, Ella, especially not one as cantankerous as Withypole Fugitate."

"But Commander Crushington told me this himself. Withypole is his informant."

"I have no doubt that he is. But according to what I have heard, Fugitate sought the commander out and volunteered his services."

"That makes no sense. Fugitate's life has been made utterly miserable by the royal taxes and laws. Why would he volunteer to spy for one of the king's commanders?"

Mal hunched his shoulders and spread his hands wide. "Who knows what goes on in the mind of a fairy? But I've had my information from a good authority, Long Louie, who manages the Midtown livery stables."

"Long Louie," I scoffed. "I am sure he is as reliable as your other chum, Waldo the Dock Rat."

"That's Wharf Rat and Long Louie is by far more reliable. There is not much that goes on in Midtown or the Bottoms that escapes Louie's notice."

As Mal and I wended our way toward the gate, I fretted my lower lip. "If what Louie told you is true, I owe Commander Crushington an apology. I thoroughly berated him when I thought he bullied poor Withypole."

"I would not lose any sleep over that." Mal's lips tipped in a smug smile. "I wonder how the Crusher enjoyed his morning out in the swamp, listening to the frogs croak and fending off the mosquitoes."

"How did you know where—" I glared at Mal accusingly. "You fed Withypole some sort of misinformation to pass on to Crushington, didn't you?"

"I may have just let slip I had something sinister planned, and I was meeting up with smugglers out in the fens."

"Mal! How could you play such a trick on the commander? Crushington may be unrelenting in his sense of duty, but he is an honest man, simply trying to do his best to uphold the law and—"

"Whoa!" Mal interrupted, raising his brows. "Since when did you become his champion? It was bad enough falling in love with that lute player, but if you are becoming smitten with the Crusher, I might as well fling myself off the nearest bridge and be done with it."

"Don't be idiotic. I am not smitten with anyone, but I am very grateful to the commander."

"So am I. The next time I meet him in town, I will make it a point to shake his hand and thank him for rescuing you."

"No! You stay away from him and stop drawing attention to yourself. What were you up to when you sent the commander off on this wild toad chase?"

"Nothing." Mal leaned up against the garden gate and grinned. "I was only having a bit of fun with your solemn suitor."

"He is not my suitor." I heaved an exasperated sigh. "You were upset because I didn't tell you about Harper, but you are forever keeping secrets from me, Mal."

"Perhaps because you have made it abundantly plain you prefer to remain in ignorance of my more clandestine activities. As it happens, I was quite innocently engaged for the most part of this morning, purchasing ball tickets."

"What about the other part?"

"I might also have snuck into the maps and ordinance office at Quad Hall and been searching for a way to break into the palace grounds to recover my orb."

"You have not yet found a way to do so?"

Mal shook his head. His smile faded, replaced by a look of extreme frustration. "It has become more difficult than ever to get past the gates. The king has recently doubled the number of guards."

"Perhaps because of the upcoming ball?" I suggested.

"More likely because our king has made himself so unpopular, he is afraid one of his loyal subjects will be tempted to assassinate him. I have learned that Sidney Greenleaf has even trained these huge beasts to patrol the palace grounds." Mal grimaced. "Supposedly these enormous cats are able to detect the auras of persons forbidden to approach the castle, such as anyone of Hawkridge descent."

"Who is this Sidney Greenleaf?" I asked.

"The king's grand ducal wizard."

"I thought that was the Great Mercato."

"Louie learned that Greenleaf is Mercato's real name. If you are seeking to convince everyone you are the most formidable wizard the kingdom has ever known, calling yourself the Great Sidney just doesn't have the same clout," Mal said contemptuously.

Ordinarily I would have been amused by Sidney Greenleaf's pretentiousness. But hearing of these extreme measures the king had taken to guard the palace only made me more anxious for Mal.

I pleaded with him. "Can you not just forget about that orb, Mal? I know it belonged to your grandfather, but I am sure he wouldn't have wanted you to risk your life to recover it. You will always have memories of your grandfather. Even the king cannot take those from you."

Mal's face darkened. "Ah, yes. My treasured memories of the man who regarded me with complete contempt."

"No, Mal. I am sure your grandfather loved you."

"All right then, affectionate contempt. If I allow the king to keep that orb, my grandfather would have said it was typical of me: feckless, irresponsible, too much of a clown to ever accomplish anything of importance."

"Your grandfather is gone. You no longer have anything to prove to him."

"No, only to myself." Mal's lips thinned in that obdurate,

determined look I knew all too well. "I mean to have that orb, Ella, no matter what it takes."

Even if you die in the attempt? I thought but did not voice the question aloud. Mal would simply shrug off my fear as he always did. My shoulders slumped. It had already been such an overwhelming and emotionally draining day. All I wanted to do was retreat to my bed and pull the covers over my head.

I felt completely worn down. Perhaps that was why I surrendered to the inevitable, conceding with a sigh. "Fine. I will do it."

"Do what?"

"Steal the orb for you. Since I am obliged to attend the ball anyway, I might as well not waste my entire evening."

"Don't be absurd, Ella," Mal said. "That is not the reason I gave you the tickets. I told you there were no conditions attached."

"I believe you. But I want to help you. You know I will find the ball rather boring. Stealing the orb will liven things up for me. You were right when you accused me of becoming too stodgy. I am longing to have a bit of excitement again. Besides what else will I give you for your birthday? We both know my cakes never turn out that well."

Mal folded his arms, regarding me skeptically. "Are you sure you aren't agreeing to do this because you believe I will do something stupid and get myself killed?"

"No, although I confess, I would find your death very inconvenient. You see I have already thought of what I want you to do on my next birthday."

I managed to coax a smile from him, but it took some more convincing before Mal relented, hugging me with a grateful sigh. "Thank you, my dearest friend. You will not regret this."

I ducked my head so that he could not see that I already did. As I drew away from him, he clasped both of my hands, his face lighting up. "This will be just like the old days. The two of us scheming together, plotting some daring adventure."

"Just not too adventurous, I hope," I murmured.

"I would never let you do this if I thought I was putting you in any real danger. I will map it all out with great care and devise protections to ensure your complete safety."

"Protections like what? A full suit of armor?"

Mal chuckled. "I don't think chain mail is in fashion among the ladies. But I will supply you with the most beautiful gown ever seen."

"You are going to design a dress for me?"

"Not me personally. But I do know a very good seamstress whose discretion I can trust. Your gown will need to have a hidden pocket to conceal the orb."

"I am skilled enough with a needle that I could manage to do that myself," I said.

"I am sure you will be kept busy enough fashioning gowns for your stepsisters. Leave your attire to me. I will supply everything, the gown, the gloves, the dancing slippers."

"No, thank you. You know how particular I am about my shoes. I will choose my own dancing slippers."

Mal squeezed my hands. "Ella, you need to trust me on this. The dancing shoes I have in mind for you will be something special." His eyes twinkled. "You are going to be completely enchanted by them."

Nine

No general could have worked harder to martial the troops than my stepmother did during the ensuing days. She insisted that we be drilled in deportment, dancing, and court etiquette, practicing curtsies until our knees ached. She laced poor Netta into a back brace to force her to stand up straight and placed Amy on a strict diet. Although Imelda pronounced my figure perfect, she said I needed to work on developing a more pleasing attitude and practice my smile. When I retorted that I had been smiling since I was an infant, Imelda had sighed and said, "Yes, dear, but a smirk is not quite the same thing."

Between the dancing and etiquette lessons, we all sewed frantically on ball gowns until our fingers were sore. I could not afford to engage a seamstress to help us. The cost of the silk fabric for three dresses had been exorbitant, taking a huge gulp out of my precious store of coins. I had not known how I would be able to hire a coach and horses. The livery stables, like the Silk Emporium and all the other greedy merchants in Midtown, had greatly inflated their prices. But Mal had insisted that he would arrange for our conveyance. With the help of his friend Long Louie, Mal assured me we would travel to the ball in grand style. I had decided not to tell my stepmother any of this. Em was already distressed enough over the fact that Mal was providing me with a gown.

Although I was left exhausted by all these ball preparations, part of me was glad to be so occupied. It left me little time to dwell on the rash offer I had made to steal that orb. Unfortunately, my busy days also afforded me little time to pursue the mystery of my father's past. It did little good to ask Imelda any questions. To her, my father was the hero who had rescued her and her daughters from disgrace and poverty. Her image of Julius Upton was too colored in the rainbow hues of romance to be of any help to me.

I tried to think of someone else who might be able to provide me with information, but as far as I knew, we had no extended family, aunts, uncles, or cousins. Nor did I recall either of my parents having any close friends beyond our acquaintance with Mal's grandparents. I had never thought much about it before, but it startled me to realize what a secluded life the three of us had led, my father, my mother and I, inhabiting our own charmed little world until my mother had died.

There appeared to be only one person who could give me answers, the one who had started me questioning in the first place — Withypole Fugitate. But when I would find the time or the courage to approach the fairy again, I did not know.

I did finally manage to steal into the library. Closing the door firmly behind me, I stood still for long moments as I breathed in the wonderful musty scent of old books and ran my fingers over the worn fabric of my father's chair. As if by doing so, I could somehow recapture his presence, the aura of a man I had never really known.

All I felt was the melancholy weight of incomplete memories and lost opportunities to ever speak to my father again and under-stand him. My father had left no personal papers or letters behind. The only words he had bequeathed me were between the pages of his beloved books. I roved along the shelves, seeking one, *The Quaint Customs and Ways of the Fey Folk.*

I had not read the book since I was a child, so I had difficulty finding it. Toward the end of his life, my father had collected so many books, he had had to shelve them two deep. I finally found the one I wanted tucked behind *A Brief History of the Kingdom of Arcady.*

As I opened the book of fairy lore, I was assailed by a recollection of my father's long, fingers turning the pages and the deep timbre of his voice as he read aloud to me. The memory was so vivid, it was as though his spirit had risen beside me, but like a ghost, the memory quickly slipped away.

I had to blink the moisture from my eyes before I could study the book's illustrations that had fascinated me as a child. The little girl in me was still enchanted by the sketches of sweet, lovely creatures with delicate wings. After my glimpse of Withypole with his wings unfurled, I realized how inaccurate the fairy drawings were. Breathtakingly beautiful? Of a certainty that described Withypole Fugitate. But there had been nothing sweet or gentle in his features. His beauty was of an austere kind, full of pride and pain.

I wondered what other inaccuracies *The Quaint Customs and Ways of the Fey Folk* contained, but it did not matter. There was nothing in the book that could help me solve the riddle of my father's past.

I started to close the book when I realized there was something inscribed on the flyleaf. I had never noticed it before, because I had been so impatient for my father to flip to the drawings and the text of the book itself. The writing was faded and done in such a spidery hand; I could barely read it. I carried it over to the library window. Even with the sun spilling over the page, I had to squint to decipher the words.

Julius,

I thought this little tome might amuse you, especially considering our friend. But you ought to be warned that fairies are not... You will never know how much I regret that...

Try as I might, I could not make out the sections that had been blurred. I could discern nothing of the writer's signature beyond the capitalized letter S.

Who was the friend referred to in the inscription? Withypole? What had the warning about fairies been? What had the giver of the book regretted? Who was *S*?

I vented a frustrated sigh. No answers, just more questions.

"Ella?" After a brief rap at the door, Amy thrust her head inside the room. "Oh, there you are."

Her face flushed with excitement, she squealed, "You must make haste. It is almost time. He's coming! The prince is coming!"

"What? Again?" I groaned.

Netta crowded forward to join Amy in the doorway. "Hurry, Ella. Or we will miss him."

"What a tragedy that would be," I muttered.

But I knew my sisters would give me no peace unless I joined them. My brief time to myself was over. I shelved the book with its puzzling inscription and reluctantly followed my sisters from the library.

I was clearly not moving fast enough to suit them. They seized my hands and dragged me out of the house, down the pathway and out the gate. The roadside was thronged with other people, mostly women.

Aside from Mrs. Biddlesworth, I never took much heed of my neighbors. I was surprised to note how many young females of marriageable age lived on our lane. Just like my sisters, they were all fussing with their hair and fidgeting with eagerness, all eyes turned toward the cavalcade approaching down the hill from the Heights.

We seldom caught a glimpse of royalty in Midtown, but for the past several days, Prince Florian had made a point of taking his morning ride directly through the heart of town, thrilling the female populace.

Cynic that I was, I suspected the king had ordered the prince to do so just in case there was anybody still balking at the cost of the ball. Each appearance by Florian resulted in more disgruntled fathers trudging into Exchequer Tower to purchase tickets.

A blare of trumpets sounded as the prince drew nearer. Even that combined with the clatter of horses' hooves was not enough to drown out the sound of sighs from all the women.

During the past week, my sisters had emerged from their seclusion of misery. Now that they were going to the ball, Amy and Netta enjoyed the company of their friends again, subjecting me to an overabundance of excited feminine chatter. My sisters and these other girls rattled on and on about how many handsome, eligible men would attend the ball. They declared that they would be quite content if they could but win the heart of a knight, a lord, a duke or perhaps one of the prince's four younger brothers.

They were all lying, of course. I could tell that from all the rapt expressions as they waited for Florian to pass by. Every young woman in Midtown (except for me) wanted *that* prince.

As he rode into our midst, Florian slowed his horse to a walk, obliging his entourage to do the same. Mounted on a snowy-white steed, the prince stood out from his two equerries, riding their sorrel mares. But his magnificent horse was not the only reason that all eyes were drawn to the prince.

Grudgingly, I had to admit he was handsome enough, with his fine chiseled features and flowing mane of white-gold hair. The scarlet cape he wore emphasized the breadth of his shoulders. As the crowd erupted into cheers, he acknowledged their adulation with a gracious wave of one gauntleted hand, flashing his teeth in a blinding smile.

All around me, ladies dropped curtsies and fluttered their handkerchiefs to attract the prince's attention. I was the only one who stood, arms folded, wearing my not-impressed face. I doubt the prince noticed because in their eagerness, my sisters pushed in front of me.

One of our neighbors from across the lane, the eldest Miss Hanson, rushed out into the road, tossing rose petals. In her enthusiasm, the foolish chit strayed directly into the path of the prince's steed. Florian quickly drew rein, raising one hand to halt his entourage. Myrtle Hanson gazed adoringly up at him before swooning and collapsing in the street.

Her younger sister, Ivy, shrieked and rushed to Miss Hanson's aide, but the prince got there first. With a swirl of his cape, Florian leapt from his horse. Kneeling, he gathered the stricken girl into his arms.

"Oh!" All the other girls cooed, their cries echoing along the lane.

The younger Miss Hanson stumbled toward the prince. Her knees buckled and she likewise sank down into a faint. To my astonishment, Florian managed to catch her with his other arm, breaking her fall. One did have to admire his dexterity.

As though a contagion had spread, soon other young ladies collapsed into graceful faints until our street began to resemble a satirical canvas by the fey artist Peccano, a painting that could have been titled The Massacre of the Maidens.

Amy moaned. "Oh, I am feeling a little weak myself." She started to sag, but I prevented her by catching her around the waist. I administered a sharp pinch, growling in her ear, "Don't you dare!"

Amy rubbed her arm and looked at me reproachfully, but she made no further effort to join in this ridiculous display.

His arms already full of the Misses Hanson, Prince Florian regarded the other fallen young women with a look of such comical dismay, I started to laugh. I couldn't help it— even though my chortles drew outraged stares from those in the crowd still standing.

"Ella!" Both my sisters rebuked me in horrified whispers.

Fortunately, the prince's equerries dismounted and came to his rescue. They relieved Florian of his swooning burdens and the prince backed away toward his horse. Drawn by the sound of my chuckles, his head turned in my direction, his eyes meeting mine. I doubted that our prince was the sort of man to tolerate being laughed at. I clapped my hand to my mouth to stifle my mirth.

He stared at me for a moment. He slowly smiled and then... Did I imagine it or had His Highness winked at me? With another twirl of his cape, he leapt back onto his steed and wheeled the horse about in the direction he had come. It was usually his custom to continue his ride through the center of town, but today he preferred to gallop back to the safety of his castle walls.

As the prince vanished from view, it was as though a sleeping curse had been broken. The Misses Hanson straightened, indignantly thrusting away the prince's servants, leaving them free to remount and follow their master. The other swooning girls struggled to their feet, looking disappointed as they dusted off their skirts.

With the excitement over, I shepherded my sisters back toward the house. As I closed the garden gate, I was dismayed to notice Amy's eyes shimmering with tears.

"What is the matter, Amy?" I asked. "I hope I did not hurt your feelings when I prevented you from swooning. Truly, my dear, you would not want to attract the prince's attention in such a foolish way. All those other girls did was make themselves appear ridiculous."

"I will never be able to attract the attention of the prince or any man so magnificent." Tears trickled down my sister's cheeks. "Because I am so fat!"

"Amy," I groaned.

Netta also began to cry. "At least you can work on becoming slimmer. There is nothing I can do about my height. I am as tall as Ella's wretched weed."

"I can't get any slimmer," Amy wailed. "I have tried so h-hard, but— but I like food too much."

"And I can never shrink," Netta sobbed.

"Oh, my dears." I spread my arms wide and gathered them to me. With a sister weeping on each shoulder, I understood how the prince must have felt when he had been beleaguered by the swooning Misses Hanson.

Imelda was a loving mother, but in her zeal for the success of her daughters, she had no idea how damaging her criticisms could be. I wracked my brain for words of wisdom and comfort.

"No girl is ever satisfied with her reflection when she regards herself in the mirror," I said. "I believe it is a failing of our sex that we always search for flaws and are sure to find them because no woman is perfect."

"You are, Ella," Netta sniffed.

"Yes, p-perfectly beautiful," Amy added.

"No, I am not. My feet are too large and apparently my attitude requires adjusting, along with my smile." I squinted my eyes and twisted my mouth into a horrible grimace that elicited reluctant chuckles from them. As usual, I did not have a handkerchief on me. Using the hem of my apron to dry their tears, I continued, "My friend Mal says that a woman's true power lies not in the perfection of her features, but in her confidence, how much she believes in herself."

"Yes, that is what he told me as well," Netta confided shyly. "He said a real man would not be in the least troubled if his lady was a bit taller than him."

Amy nodded. "And Mal told me that men greatly prefer women who are as buxom as me."

"Truly?" I stared at my sisters in astonishment. "When did Mal tell you all of this?"

"Two days ago, the last time he came to call," Amy said. "The day he brought us the chocolates and Mama said I should not have any." Her lips tipped in a sheepish smile. "When Mama wasn't looking, Mal swiped a chocolate out of the box and popped it into my mouth."

Amy giggled. "Mal whispered in my ear that surreptitious chocolates are not as fattening as the regular kind."

I laughed as well. Since the day he had brought the ball tickets, Mal had been coming to call upon my family almost every day, mostly to snatch time alone with me to further our plans for stealing the orb. One afternoon he needed to take my measurements for the ball gown. Em would simply die if she knew that. She would be even more outraged to learn Mal had been feeding Amy chocolates and complimenting her on the size of her bosom.

I was pleased to discover Mal had been kind to Amy and Netta. Indeed, when we had last parted, Mal had conceded, "Maybe the silly stepsisters are not as bad as I thought. At least the younger one appears to have some spirit."

"You may certainly trust Mal's opinions," I told my sisters. "I believe he has had more than a bit of experience with women. Now we have wasted enough of the morning gawking at the prince and being lachrymose. Time to return to plying our needles. Those ball gowns are not going to sew themselves."

Both of my sisters groaned.

"I wish they would," Amy said. "I wish we could enchant Pookie and Pippa to do the sewing for us."

"Or perhaps some obliging field mice," Netta suggested. "They would be so clever at it with their little paws."

I joined in their laughter at the picture that was created. Their spirits restored; my sisters returned to the house. I started to follow them when someone cried out, "Hey! You there! Lady!"

Looking about for the source of the sharp little voice, I spied an urchin hovering outside of the garden gate. When I regarded him with puzzlement, he beckoned to me imperiously. "Yes, you, the lady with the yaller hair. C'mere."

I approached him cautiously. He was a grubby lad with a thatch of unruly brown hair tumbling into his eyes. His scrawny arms and legs jutted out from his coarse woolen garb. I could not gauge his age, perhaps nine or ten, judging from his size. Yet there seemed something much older about the shrewd eyes that peered at me through his thicket of hair.

A beggar, I thought with a pang. I stole an anxious glance up and down the lane, fearful of what could happen to this boy if he were caught. He and his entire family, if he had one, would be exiled, driven into the wild fenlands across the Conger River.

Leaning over the gate, I whispered, "It would be better if you sneak around back by the kitchen door. I'll be able to slip you some bread and a little coin with no one the wiser."

The boy reared back on his heels, glaring at me. "Eh? What you take me for? I'm no beggar. I'm a man of means with reg'lar employment."

He puffed out his thin chest. "Just so happens, I'm the trustiest deliverer you can find in all the Misty Bottoms and the Midtown if it comes to that. My service is in great demand, and I am well paid for it."

"I do beg your pardon," I said, biting back a smile. "What do you deliver?"

"You have to answer my question first." He swept back his hair to peer at me more closely. "Be you Miss Ella Upton?"

"Yes."

"You swear to that? If you be lying, may the fairies curse you and goblins eat your liver."

"Indeed, I am Ella Upton."

"You have to swear."

I sighed and held up my right hand. "I do hereby swear and affirm that I am Ella Upton. If I am lying, may the fairies cover me in boils and goblins cook my liver. Satisfied?"

He stared at me fiercely for another moment before nodding. "Then this be for you," he said, producing a small brown paper–wrapped parcel from beneath his tunic.

I blinked in surprise as he handed it to me. "What is this?"

The boy rolled his eyes. "Well, it's a package, ain't it?"

"I can see that. But where did it come from? Who sent it?"

"Can't tell you that. My only 'structions were to deliver the box."

"But who instructed you?"

"Nope. I'm mum." The boy motioned with his fingers as though sewing his lips closed. "I get paid extra for my 'scretion. Now if you'll 'scuse me, I got other affairs to tend."

He made a quaint bow and then tore off running back down the lane. I stared after in bemusement before turning my attention to the parcel. I peeled away the paper wrapping to reveal a small, plain wooden box. When I lifted the lid, my breath caught in my throat. There, nestled against the silk lining, were my mother's emeralds.

Recovering from my shock, I bolted out the garden gate, hoping to summon the pert lad back and oblige him to answer my questions. The urchin had already vanished down the lane. Upon reflection, I decided it did not matter. There was only one person who would have employed such a messenger and returned my earrings in this anonymous fashion. Mal.

He would have been aware if he had proposed buying the earrings from Withypole, my pride would have prevented me from accepting his offer. I worried about how much coin and effort he'd had to spend to redeem the emeralds. It could not have been easy or cheap to persuade the fairy to surrender the "twinkles" he had so obviously coveted.

I would have ordered Mal not to do it, but I was so grateful that he had. Deeply moved by his gesture, my eyes filled with tears. The man was a complete rogue, but how I did love him. Malcolm Hawkridge was truly the best friend a woman could ever have. As I wended my way back to the house, clutching my precious parcel, for the first time, I allowed myself to wonder.

Was it possible for friendship to develop into something warmer?

After all the excitement of the morning, I had difficulty getting Amy and Netta to settle down to the task of working on the gowns. Neither of my sisters was fond of sewing. Netta could set a neat enough stitch, but Amy was so restless and inattentive that her seams often had to be picked out and redone.

As a girl, I had never had much patience for needlework either, but necessity had obliged me to master the art. Making clothes for my family had turned me into an accomplished seamstress and now I rather enjoyed the task.

At least I did when I was allowed to stitch in peace and quiet, absorbed by my thoughts as my needle dove in and out of the fabric in a soothing repetitious rhythm. Alas, such was not the case with all four of us crowded into the parlor. Imelda had returned from a morning visit to Madam Dearling, the woman's previous unkindness forgotten. My stepmother tended to forgive easily so the two were fast friends again. Consequently, Em was full of the latest gossip and my sisters were no less eager to discuss the prince's morning ride.

All the chatter and the state of the parlor grated on my nerves. I preferred to work in a tidy, organized space and our sitting room was a total disaster, sewing boxes, scissors, stray spools of thread and bits of fabric scattered everywhere. Netta's green silk and Imelda's mauve brocade were still in pieces, the garments slowly taking shape. Amy's pink gown was nearly done, or it would have been if I had not had to pick out her gnarled stitches from the hemline.

The conversation shifted from the prince to his brothers. I only half paid attention as I struggled to pick out the knots without damaging the delicate silk.

"Florence Bafton says the reason that Prince Florian's brothers never visit Midtown is because they are far too snobbish," Amy said. While waiting for me to undo the mess she had made, she played annoying games with thimbles, clacking them together on her fingers.

"I do hope not," Imelda replied. "I remember them as being such sweet little boys, well except for the twins who could be a bit naughty."

"I have heard that the next oldest brother, Kendrick, is very sweet and charming," Netta said. "Never disagreeing with anyone, never cross, always smiling."

"That could get really tedious," I grumbled as a stubborn knot refused to yield. The silk was fraying from my efforts. Likely, the entire hem would have to come out and be redone. I hunted for my scissors and discovered Amy had appropriated them again. As I retrieved my shears, I plucked the thimbles from her fingers and dropped them back in the sewing basket. In too good of a humor to pout, she playfully thrust her tongue out at me.

"I was told that the twins, Dahl and Dashiel are the charming ones," Amy said. "Full of fun and mischief. They like to fool people by pretending to be each other."

"Surely they are too old for such childish pranks," I said as I resumed my seat.

Amy continued, "And then there is Prince Ryland who is reputed to be so brave, going on quests and slaying dragons."

"What did some poor dragon ever do to him?" I muttered.

"Ella!"

I looked up from threading my needle to find my stepmother frowning at me.

"Attitude, my dear," Imelda reminded me gently.

I donned a simpering smile, which caused Amy and Netta to giggle and Imelda to heave a long-suffering sigh. As the conversation resumed, I tried to listen without offering acid remarks.

Conspiring with Mal had caused me to forget the true purpose of the ball. Like my sisters, I would be expected to look over the field of men in search of a future husband, a prospect I found more daunting than the theft of the orb.

Imelda had gone off into rhapsodies again, assuring us all what a magical night the ball would be when a knock sounded at the front door.

"I'll get it," Amy cried, leaping up with such alacrity, she knocked over her sewing basket. Glad of any diversion that would get her away from the needlework, she rushed from the parlor before my stepmother could protest.

While Netta and I righted Amy's basket and set about gathering up pin cushions, thimbles and stray spools of thread, Imelda fretted. "Oh dear! I do hope that is not your friend Mr. Hawkridge calling again with more gifts of chocolates."

Despite his gift of the tickets, Imelda remained uneasy about Mal, and we had had quite a heated discussion about the propriety of him providing me with a gown. Mal had insisted it was nothing, merely an early birthday gift for an old friend. According to Imelda, proper gentlemen did not give young ladies anything as intimate as clothing, no matter how long they had been acquainted.

That is why I had said nothing about the return of my mother's earrings. Imelda would be delighted that I had them back, but she would be distressed to learn that Mal had been lavishing more money on me.

Netta spoke up timidly. "But, Mama, we all enjoy Mr. Hawkridge's visits. He is so kind and amusing and I am sure we should all be grateful enough to welcome him at any time."

"So I am," Imelda replied. "I concede that he is vastly entertaining. But the sad truth is, my dears," she added with a pointed look at me, "no matter how charming, rogues do not make good husbands."

"How fortunate it is then, that none of us are planning to marry him," I said as I returned to my chair and resumed my work on the hem.

Imelda said nothing, merely regarding me with sorrowful skepticism. I wished I could have told her that the reason for Mal's frequent visits had far more to do with plotting larceny than romance, but I doubted that would have afforded Em much comfort either.

Amy returned, looking flushed, her eyes dancing with suppressed merriment. Before she could speak, Imelda said, "If that is Mr. Hawkridge, dear, you must inform him that we are far too occupied—"

"It is not Mal. It is another gentleman come to call upon Ella." Amy giggled. "Commander Crushington."

I was so startled, I jabbed myself with the needle. Beyond the parlor door, I could see the tall shadow of Horatio Crushington looming in the vestibule. For one panicked moment, I thought, he knows. Somehow the commander had found out what Mal and I were plotting, and he had come to arrest me. I calmed myself, remembering that I had given the commander permission to call. I had been so occupied with preparations for the ball; the invitation had completely slipped my mind.

Imelda sprang to her feet with a dismayed glance at the parlor's disorder. I leapt up as well, feeling equally flustered and conscious of my own disarray. I was wearing one of my oldest frocks, my hair scooped back from my face by a scarf knotted around my head.

I had an urge to fly to the nearest mirror, yank off the scarf and try to finger-comb my unruly tresses. I brought myself up short. Since when have I ever fussed over my appearance? Not since the days I used to steal away for trysts with Harper.

Amy grinned. "Shall I show the commander in?"

"Yes," I said.

"No!" Imelda exclaimed. "Oh, what is that man doing here?"

"I invited him to take tea with us some afternoon," I said.

"Why ever did you that, Ella?"

I regarded my stepmother indignantly. "It was you who first invited him, when you suggested the commander to me as a possible suitor, remember?"

"But that was before— before—"

"Before we had tickets to the ball and now you no longer think the commander good enough? For shame, Em!"

Imelda reddened. "It is true that I hope you will have better prospects, but that is not my only reason. The commander harbors a dreadful secret. Matilda Dearling warned me only this morning."

My stepmother clasped her hands together and announced dramatically, "Commander Crushington is a foundling."

My sisters gasped and even I was momentarily taken aback. It was considered enough of a stigma to be born out of wedlock, but it was far worse to have absolutely no idea of one's parentage. Any woman desperate enough to abandon her infant along the roadside must have done something truly wicked like mating with a monster or other non-human creature. According to popular belief, such a child would inherit their sire's evil tendencies.

Netta dropped her voice to an excited whisper. "Commander Crushington is a foundling? Who would have thought it?"

"He is a very large and alarming man," Amy said. "Perhaps he has a drop of goblin or bad fairy blood in him."

"Madam Dearling thinks he could be part ogre," Imelda added in a hushed tone.

"Nonsense," I said. "Why do you listen to that nasty woman, Em? If anyone has hobgoblin blood, it is probably her. I happen to know that the commander has parents. I have heard him speak of them."

"Then where are his mother and father? Why has no one in Midtown ever met them?" Imelda asked.

"Most likely because they live elsewhere. There are other more distant parts of this kingdom. Besides you know that most foundlings are doomed to labor in the silver mines. One would never be given such a prestigious appointment as commander of the Midtown garrison."

Imelda frowned. "I had not thought of that."

My sisters heaved disappointed sighs. They had clearly been intrigued by the idea that Crushington might be part ogre. As for Imelda, she still looked unconvinced that he was not. One of these days, I thought, I am going to strangle that Dearling woman.

"Are we going to leave the poor man waiting in the hall forever?" I demanded irritably. "Amy, please show the commander into the parlor."

My stepmother made no further protest, but she appeared quite uneasy. As Amy left to fetch Crushington, Netta and I scrambled to clear away some of the sewing debris. I had just retrieved a pin cushion from beneath the settee when Amy returned with the commander in tow.

Ten

Horatio Crushington could be an intimidating figure when riding through Midtown, his piercing gaze fixed on the populace. He was even more formidable as he snapped to attention, the blue jacket and dun-colored pantaloons of his uniform starched to crisp perfection. I had always realized that he was a large man, tall and broad shouldered. Never had he appeared more overwhelmingly masculine than he did when surrounded by our dainty parlor furniture.

He doffed his black beret and bent in a stiff bow. "Good afternoon, ladies."

My stepmother murmured a greeting. My sisters curtsied and ogled the commander with an interest they had never shown before. Whether it was because they were still hoping to discover he was part ogre or simply because it was a novelty for me to have a prospective suitor, I could not tell.

I held out my hand and smiled, trying to look glad to see him and not like someone plotting to rob the king. "Good afternoon, Commander. How kind of you to call."

"Kind of you to receive me," he said gruffly. His large hand engulfed mine. His steady grey eyes drank me in as though it had been twelve months since we parted, and he had been parched for the sight of me. The man seemed oblivious to my disordered curls or worn frock.

When moments passed and Crushington continued to hold my hand, muffled giggles escaped from my stepsisters. The commander reddened and released me at once. I cast a quelling frown at the girls before saying, "Please do be seated, sir."

Crushington cast a dubious look at one of the delicate armchairs. He lowered himself gingerly onto the silk cushion. The rest of us settled into our seats and an awkward silence descended.

Crushington cleared his throat. "I trust I have not called at an inopportune moment."

"As a matter of fact—" Imelda began.

"Not at all," I said hastily. "We needed a rest from our sewing. May I offer you some tea, Commander?"

"No, I thank you, but I would not put you to any trouble."

"It would not be any trouble," Netta spoke up. "Ella makes excellent tea and biscuits. She is quite the best cook and seamstress in all of Midtown."

I winced as I realized what my sister was doing. Scenting the possibility of a romance between me and Crushington, she was attempting to help by singing my praises. She often did the same for Amy. Much as I loved Netta for it, I wanted to clap my hand over her mouth as she continued enthusiastically, "Ella quite excels at everything."

"Indeed," Amy said, slanting a mischievous look at me. "You will quite adore her— I mean her strawberry jam."

Forget using my hand, I thought as heat flooded my cheeks. I needed pillows to stifle my sisters.

Crushington smiled and said, "I am sure Miss Ella's jam is excellent, but I really only stopped by to see if she is entirely recovered from—"

I cut him off with a shake of my head, trying to warn him I did not want my assault mentioned before my family. Taking the hint, he subsided, but my stepmother demanded, "Recovered from what?"

Crushington appeared at a loss. Obviously, the man was not as adept at inventing instant fiction as I was.

"My headache," I filled in quickly.

"But, Ella, you never have headaches," Amy protested.

"That day I did, but yes, as a rule, I am seldom ill."

"Besides being so beautiful, Ella is the healthiest girl," Netta said eagerly. I stifled a groan.

"Indeed, Miss Ella always appears quite—" Crushington floundered beneath the weight of my sisters' anticipatory stares. "Quite robust," he finished.

More smothered titters issued from my sisters. If I had been sitting closer, I would have poked them. Crushington kneaded his beret, looking uncomfortable and embarrassed.

My stepmother had been unusually quiet since the commander entered the parlor. When she began to question Crushington, I heartily wished she had remained that way.

"What about you, Commander? Have you been well?" she asked.

"Yes, thank you, madam."

"And what about your family?"

I shot Imelda a warning glance, but she ignored me. "Is your father in good health?"

"Er— no. Actually, he's dead."

"I am so sorry," I said.

Crushington gave me a melancholy smile. "Thank you, Miss Ella, but I lost him many years ago."

"What about your mother?" Imelda asked.

"She died not long after my father."

"How sad," Netta cried.

"Do you have any other relatives?" Em pursued. "Any brothers or sisters?"

Crushington shook his head. "Only a distant cousin who looks after the property that my parents left me."

"Oh, you inherited an estate?" Em brightened a little at that.

"Er- no. Just a small farm."

"And where exactly would that be—" Imelda began, but I startled everyone by leaping to my feet to put an end to this embarrassing inquisition.

"Commander Crushington, would you care to take a stroll about the back lawn with me?" I asked in a tone of breathless desperation. "I have been simply perishing to show you— er— something."

Crushington stood, looking relieved at my suggestion, but my stepmother also rose and protested, "Where are your manners, Ella? We truly should serve our guest some tea."

"He already said he doesn't need any tea." I all but propelled the commander in the direction of the French doors. "He doesn't want tea. I don't believe he even likes tea."

"Well, it isn't that I—" Crushington tried to interrupt.

"In fact, I think he hates tea." Yanking open the door, I thrust the commander outside. When my stepmother and sisters gathered as though preparing to join us in the back garden, I stopped them with a glare.

"I believe you all have sewing to do."

"But, Ella," my stepmother whispered, "do you really think you should be alone with that man?"

"What do you think he's going to do, Em?" I hissed back. "Devour me?"

"He might try to steal a kiss." Netta sighed.

"The commander is so bashful, Ella will likely have to kiss him," Amy said.

They dissolved into giggles again and Imelda regarded me imploringly. I gave them all one last exasperated scowl before stepping outside and slamming the door closed.

I leaned up against it, fearful they might try to follow me.

When moments elapsed and the door handle did not rattle, I released a deep breath. As I came away from the door, I realized that the stiff set of the commander's shoulders had relaxed. He stopped crushing his beret and tucked it inside his belt.

I summoned up a rueful smile as I approached him. "You are well versed in the law, sir. Tell me. Is it illegal to drop any of one's relatives down a very deep well?"

Crushington's lips twitched, but he replied solemnly, "I fear that the law does discourage such actions, although perhaps allowances might be made for extenuating circumstances."

I laughed. "Do not mistake me, sir. Although my stepmother and sisters can at times be a bit..."

"Solicitous?"

"I was going to say as aggravating as mud fleas, but I do still love them dearly."

"I am sure they are all as charming as you are, Ella."

"They are usually a great deal nicer. I am not known for the sweetness of my disposition."

Crushington looked as though he would have liked to argue that point, but all he said was, "I believe you wished to show me something?"

"What? Oh. Yes, that." I had already forgotten my foolish excuse for dragging Crushington out of the parlor. My gaze swept across the lawn from my struggling vegetable patch to the ivy-choked pergola. I finally settled on the old stables.

"I thought you might like to see my sister's ponies."

"Indeed, I would," he agreed.

It occurred to me that the man would have been just as pleased if I had offered to show him the algae floating on the surface of the bird bath, anything to spend time in my company. I cringed with guilt. I had only invited him to call upon me out of gratitude, not to encourage his suit. Perhaps being alone with him in the stables was not the best idea. But glancing back, I could see my stepmother's and sisters' faces plastered against the windows.

I sighed and led the commander away from the house. Our carriage house had once been an impressive structure for Midtown. Many of the local people did not bother stabling horses or owning a carriage. Everything in town was within walking distance and one could easily hire a conveyance from the Midtown livery stables if a journey into the countryside was contemplated.

Although our coach house was nothing as grand as the stables on the great estates in the Heights, it boasted a broad set of double doors with a round window on the upper floor where the groom's quarters had been. Once colored a rustic red, the paint had started to crack and peel, the doors beginning to sag.

As I struggled to open one, Crushington moved to help me. I murmured apologetically, "I fear the stables have become rather neglected. Besides a fresh coat of paint, these doors need replacing."

Crushington tested the movement of the door, inspecting the hinges. "I think you only need to replace this section here where the wood has begun to rot." He paused and added diffidently, "I could do that for you if you wished."

"You could?" I asked, unable to conceal my astonishment. "You do carpentry work?"

"I do possess a few skills, Miss Ella. Beyond clapping innocent citizens in irons and intimidating informants," he added wryly.

I winced, recalling that I owed the commander an apology for the accusations I had made the day that he rescued me. I drew in a deep breath.

"Commander, I have needed to speak to you ever since the morning you saved my life. I want to tell you how sorry I am."

"For what?" Dried paint flaked off and fell on his uniform sleeve. He paused in his inspection of the door to brush them off.

"For all the dreadful things I said to you, the harsh way I accused you of bullying Withypole. I have since discovered how wrong I was, that Master Fugitate volunteered to spy for you."

Crushington frowned at me. "Where did you learn that?"

"I don't really remember," I replied, avoiding his eyes. I could hardly tell him that my source was Long Louie, Mal's friend from the livery stable. Not without betraying the fact that Mal was aware of the commander's arrangement with Withypole and using it to his own advantage.

I continued, "The point is that I wronged you with my accusations and I am sorry. It never occurred to me that Withypole would be willing to act as your informant. I still cannot understand why a fairy—"

"Ella, please stop. I have already explained to you that I cannot discuss Withypole Fugitate."

I heard the ring of finality in his voice, but I rushed on, "There must be something more that you can tell me about Fugitate. This is very important to me." I hesitated before adding, "That morning I sold him the emeralds, he told me the most extraordinary thing about my father."

Crushington's brow furrowed. But his expression was encouraging enough that I related everything about how Fugitate had recognized my mother's emeralds, how at one time he might have been friends with my father. I even told the commander about my book of fairy lore and the strange, blurred inscription on the flyleaf.

I had no idea what impelled me to blurt this out to Crushington, things that I had not even yet confided to Mal. Perhaps it was because these questions niggled at the back of my mind. I needed to talk to someone and there was something solid and steady about Crushington.

"Withypole claims that my father had once been a royal court advocate, passionate and brave, defending people who were wrongfully accused, even in defiance of the king," I said. "But that sounds so unlike the quiet, reclusive man I knew. Or at least, I thought I did."

I bit down hard upon my lower lip before admitting, "My father and I were not on good terms near the end of his life. If only

I had not been so foolish and stubborn, I could have mended the breach before he died. There is so much I wish I could say to him, so much I need to ask, and it is all far too late. If I could learn more of his past, at least, I might come to understand who Julius Upton truly was."

"I am sorry, Ella," Crushington said. "I wish I could help you, but I never knew your father. By the time I assumed my command here in Midtown, your father was already deceased."

"But you do know something about Withypole. Perhaps learning of his past might help me discover more about my father."

"I know little of Fugitate's past and I have never pressed him to learn more. All men and even fairies are entitled to keep their secrets."

"I thought that was part of your duties, to uncover and expose secrets."

"Only regarding lawbreakers, but I don't think there is anything criminal in Fugitate's past, only deep pain and sorrow. If he does not wish to share his tragic history with the world, that is his choice."

I nodded in understanding, but much as I admired the commander for his reticence, part of me wished the man did not have to be so frapping honorable.

"There is information from Fugitate that I can share with you," Crushington said. "He was able to identify the brute who attacked you. His name is Burt Iggy. I have crossed paths with him before, a man of most villainous reputation although I have never been able to prove anything against him. Unfortunately, it is never easy to track miscreants in Misty Bottoms. I have checked all the varlet's usual haunts and been unable to find him. It is as though he has vanished into the fog."

Vanished? I felt the color drain from my face as I recalled Mal's grim reaction when I had told him of Crushington's pledge to hunt down my attacker and arrest him.

Not if I find him first.

Crushington must have misunderstood the reason for my dismay because he placed his hands reassuringly on my shoulders. "Don't worry, Ella. You will be safe. That villain shall never come near you again. I will find him."

I smiled weakly, hoping that Iggy wouldn't be found floating face down in the Conger River. How far would Mal go in his zeal to avenge me? Even I was not sure.

Suddenly I was aware of how close I stood to Crushington. I could feel the warmth of his palms through the worn fabric of my gown and experienced that same curious tingle as I had when he had blown on my wrist. His deep grey eyes seemed to turn to smoke. I sensed how badly he wanted to kiss me even though I had little experience of such things.

There was my experiment with Mal when we were twelve, an awkward and uncomfortable experience for both of us that involved more bumping of noses than actual lip contact. Other than that, there had only been my trysts with Harper, all those sweet, stolen kisses that had caused me to believe I would never want to feel any other man's arms around me but his.

I could not help wondering what it would be like to kiss Horatio Crushington. But curiosity is not a good excuse for toying with a man's feelings.

I eased away from the commander, murmuring, "The ponies are down here in the last stall."

I thought I heard him give a faint sigh as I ducked past him into the stables. The interior was shadowy and cool, the air redolent with the scent of sweet hay and the earthier aroma of horse-flesh and dung. There were four stalls, two of them empty. We had had to sell off our horses and the gig a long time ago.

As I led Crushington down the length of the barn, I could already hear Pookie and Pippa whickering and stamping their hooves with impatience, expecting it to be Amy bringing them a treat.

When I first bought the miniature ponies for my sister on her tenth birthday, she had wanted to share her bedchamber with them. It had taken much persuasion to convince her they would be happier in the stables. I had hired an itinerant carpenter to knock down the wall between two of the stalls and replace one of the doors with wooden slats.

As we approached, Pookie and Pippa poked their shaggy heads over the topmost rail, their glossy coats the color of chocolate. I had never fully appreciated how small the ponies were until Crushington loomed over them. They barely came up to his kneecap.

Many horsemen would have regarded Amy's pets with indulgent contempt, but the commander's eyes lit up with delight.

When Crushington hunkered down to pet the ponies, I warned him, "Be careful. They only like Amy and they tend to bite. Hard."

Pookie's and Pippa's ears flattened back as they bared their teeth in ominous fashion. But the commander murmured something low and soothing. As he slowly extended his fingers toward them, an astonishing thing happened. The ponies whickered, their ears coming forward. They jostled each other in their eagerness to nuzzle Crushington's hand.

He stroked them each in turn, rubbing behind their ears, reducing the ponies to a state of equine bliss. It was as though the man had magic in his fingertips.

"That's amazing," I said. "I have never seen them respond that way to anyone but Amy."

Crushington shrugged. "I have always been better with horses than people. Even as a small boy, I..." He trailed off.

I waited for him to continue, but his eyes had clouded over. He straightened so abruptly; he startled me. Turning to face me, he burst out, "Ella, there is something I need to say to you."

My heart missed a beat. Surely, he did not mean to declare himself so soon and here in the stables. Dismayed, I stepped back from him. My first instinct was to stop him, but if the commander intended to propose, it was better to have done with it. I could gently refuse him and that would be the end of the matter.

Yet Crushington did not look a man about to avow his love. His eyes darkened with some inner torment as though he wrestled with a difficult decision.

Finally, he said, "I overheard the remarks your stepmother made earlier. About me being a foundling."

That was all he wanted to discuss with me? I let out a sigh of relief and said, "Pray forgive her. Imelda is far too credulous, believing every nonsensical bit of gossip she hears."

"It is not nonsense," Crushington said quietly. "It's true."

"Oh," was all I could think to say at first, then I protested, "But what of the parents you spoke of, the ones who christened you with all those names, the mother who taught you to blow the pain away?"

"The Crushingtons adopted me when I was seven. I have no idea who or what my real parents were. As an infant, I was abandoned in the Red Grove Forest. I would likely have perished if I had not been found by a hermit."

"And this hermit took care of you?"

"No. Do you not know what is done with abandoned children, Ella?"

I was rather ashamed to admit that I did not. "I assume they are taken to an orphanage somewhere."

"The Royal Foundling Asylum is located high in the hills beyond the forest. It is a grim place, more like a fortress because it is considered necessary that foundlings be kept well away from all decent society. The conditions there were not pleasant."

"I am sorry," I said. "But then you were adopted by the Crushingtons?"

"I was one of the rare, few fortunate ones. Most foundling children are trained for a life of servitude in the silver mines. It was obvious I would grow to be too large for that. I most likely would have ended up indentured to a pig farmer or a goat herder on one of the remote farms near the northern border. But then one day I was noticed by Lieutenant Benjamin Crushington."

The commander's tale was interrupted by the ponies. Irritated by his lack of attention, they tried to nip at his pant leg. He bent down to pat them absently and then paced farther away from their stall. As I followed, he continued, "The lieutenant was a Border Scutcheon, assigned to the northern outpost. One of his assigned duties was to inspect the asylum. He rode a black stallion, and I remember how I used to wait for his visits. I would hide in the stables even though I knew it was forbidden and I would be beaten if I was found. It was worth the risk for me to obtain just a glimpse of that magnificent horse.

"One afternoon, I grew bold enough to creep from my hiding place and stroke its mane. The lieutenant caught me, and I trembled in fear before him. He was a large, fierce-looking man so I braced myself for the blow that was sure to follow.

"But he simply stared at me for the longest time as though he was seeing a ghost. I was stunned when his eyes welled up with tears. The next thing I knew the lieutenant was counting out coin into the warder's hand and I was ordered to ready myself to leave with him."

"The lieutenant bought you?" I gasped.

"All foundlings are eventually sold into servitude, although usually at an older age. Such was our fate and I never questioned it."

"But you were only seven years old! Surely you must have been frightened to be handed over to a stranger in that callous fashion."

"Frankly, I was more excited at the prospect of riding in front of the lieutenant on that incredible horse. I did not think much beyond that. If I did, it was only to suppose I would be set to some kind of labor when we arrived at our destination. I even dared to dream I might be employed cleaning his stables."

Crushington was so matter of fact about all of this, minimizing what he must have suffered as a boy. Nothing could have painted a clearer picture of his bleak childhood than the fact that mucking out horse stalls had been the pinnacle of his dreams.

He did not appear in need of my comfort, but I longed to press his hand. But he had locked them behind his back, his stance rigid as he went on. "When we reached the lieutenant's home, nothing went as I had expected. I confess I was frightened when he prepared me to meet his wife. My only experience with women was those toothless, grey-haired crones hired to clean the asylum and make sure none of the orphans were overfed. They might even have been witches."

If Crushington thought that was what a witch looked like, he had never met Mal's friend Delphine. But I said nothing, not wanting to interrupt.

"When I was presented to Sara Crushington, she was the most beautiful thing I had ever seen, as frail and delicate as a fairy princess. Her reaction to me was even stronger than her husband's had been. She took one look and burst into tears. She caught me up in a fierce embrace, her thin arms trembling. I had never been hugged before and I am sorry to say that I jerked away from her, as wary as a cornered wild thing."

The commander's eyes clouded at the memory. "That was when I learned why the lieutenant had bought me. The Crushingtons had recently lost their only child, a boy named Horatio. They had both been devastated, but Sara Crushington had nearly died from her grief. Apparently, I bore a remarkable resemblance to Horatio. His clothes even fit as though they had been sewn just for me."

"That was why they wanted you? As a replacement for their dead child?" I was unable to conceal how appalled I was. "But that — that was—"

"The most fortunate thing that could have ever happened to me."

"But you were forced to become someone else, your own identity stolen."

"What identity, Ella?" Crushington gave a sad laugh. "Who was I? Merely another foundling with no past and even less future. I didn't even have a name. The warder called me Clodpole because of my clumsiness and size.

"With the Crushingtons, for the first time I had a bed to sleep in, warm clothes to wear and enough to eat. I had a real home and more names than I knew what to do with."

The commander drew himself up proudly. "Horatio Alexander Samuel Edward Crushington. I didn't care that it was only a borrowed name, or I had to walk in a dead boy's shoes. I would have been anything or anyone the Crushingtons wanted of me. They gave me everything, Ella, an education, and a future. With the passage of time, the Crushingtons forgot that I was not their trueborn son and I forgot as well."

I nodded. "I understand what a blessing it must have been to be adopted, but have you never wondered about the woman who bore you or the man who sired you? Have you never wanted to know who they were?"

"Why would I? I cannot bear to think what sort of depraved creatures could abandon their child to die. I prefer not to ever know how much of their darkness I might carry in my blood. There is a good reason very few foundlings are ever adopted, because of the fear of what evil might be lodged in their hearts. The Crushingtons were quite brave to risk it and I will love and honor them forever for that.

"But I never intended to go on at such length about my past. I just felt that you needed to know the truth about me. If you should decide that you do not ever wish me to call upon you again, I will understand."

He was offering me an out, a way to end his attentions to me, something I had thought I desired. But all I could think of was driving the self-doubt and sorrow from his eyes.

"Don't be such a great fool, Horatio Alexander Samuel

Edward Crushington." I placed my hand flat on the center of his chest. I could feel his heartbeat quicken.

"What are you doing?" he asked.

"Hush." I furrowed my brow as though deep in concentration. I finally pronounced, "I don't sense anything evil in there. Only honor, courage, determination, seriousness and perhaps a tiny streak of obstinacy."

The commander gave a dubious half-smile. "You can sense all that, can you?"

"Just one of my gifts." I lowered my lashes, feigning a simper of false modesty. "I may not be sweet, but I am exceedingly clever. Far too clever to place any stock in these nonsensical beliefs about foundlings."

He did smile then, completely, and unreservedly as he rarely did. His eyes shone with such gratitude it brought a lump to my throat. He covered my hand with his own and then raised it to his lips, brushing a soft kiss on my fingertips.

Again, I experienced that strange tingle, warmer and stronger this time. I shivered. Mistaking my response, Crushington released me. "I am sorry. Was that too bold of me?"

"No, no. It is only..." I sought for a way to explain my unaccountable reaction. "Your whiskers tickled me. I am not fond of beards." I flushed and added hastily, "Although yours is— is quite—"

"Tolerable?" he asked dryly, arching one brow.

"Yes." I gave a sheepish laugh.

We stood for long moments smiling shyly at each other before I gave myself a brisk mental shake.

"I really should be getting back before my stepmother comes in search of me," I said. "There is still a great deal of sewing to be done on the ball gowns and we only have another week."

"So, you are all going to the ball?" he asked.

I pulled a face. "Yes, may all the fairies help me."

The commander fell into step beside me as we left the stables. I led Crushington toward the back gate by the kitchens, to spare him having to run the gauntlet of my family again. He stopped abruptly and cleared his throat. "I also plan to attend the ball."

"You do?" I glanced up at him in surprise.

"Yes, the Scutcheon commanders have always been invited, but I have never had the slightest inclination to go before. However, this year is different with nearly all of Midtown going. As the head of the garrison, I feel I should put in an appearance." Even as he offered this excuse, I sensed it was my attendance that had influenced his decision.

"Of course, I have been ordered not to stand about like a stone pillar and look as though I am policing the crowd. I will be obliged to take part in the dancing, so I was wondering..." He paused for a deep breath. "I wondered if you might grant me a dance, although I perfectly understand if you do not wish to do so. I know you will be besieged with so many other offers, knights, and lords. I am sure even the prince will want to—"

"Horatio!" I laughed, stopping him. "Yes. I will dance with you."

His face suffused with pleasure. "Thank you. That will be most kind of you."

"The kindness is all on your side. I only ever wanted to attend the ball because my stepmother and sisters wished it so badly. I dread the prospect of meeting so many strangers, especially all those aristocrats from the Heights. It will be good to find a familiar face in the crowd."

"I feel the same way. Especially if it is yours."

I smiled and offered my hand. "Then consider it a pact. My first dance shall be yours."

He beamed at me and started to raise my hand to his lips. Recalling my earlier objection to his beard, he gave my hand an awkward shake instead.

I cannot explain or excuse the mad impulse that came over me.

I stood on tiptoe and kissed the tip of his nose. As I rocked back on my heels, Crushington looked surprised but pleased.

He fumbled with his beret, dropped it twice before he managed to get it settled on his head. The man was so flustered, I had to help him unlatch the garden gate.

"Until next week then," he said. He bowed and bid me farewell several times before striding on his way.

I laughed softly as I locked the gate behind him, thinking that perhaps attending the ball would not prove to be such an ordeal after all. It was only after the commander was gone that I came back to earth with a thud. My foolish grin faded.

What in the name of all the fairies was wrong with me? I had behaved as though as I was some ordinary girl looking forward to waltzing the night away in the arms of a handsome man, not who I was, a desperate brigand, plotting to pilfer the king's treasury. Idiot that I was, I had promised to dance with the one man sharp enough to guess what I was up to and seek to prevent me.

Once I had been sure if the commander ever caught me breaking the law, he would arrest me without compunction. Now that I knew him better, I was not as certain. What would Horatio do if ever forced to choose between his duty and me? I did not know but I never wanted to put him in that position.

I sank down upon the kitchen stoop and buried my face in my hands. Why did my life always have to be so frapping complicated? Imelda kept insisting what a magical night the ball would be. All I had to do was look out for my younger sisters, ensure they had a good time, meet Imelda's expectations by attracting a wealthy suitor, dance with Horatio, try not to arouse his suspicions and steal the orb for Mal.

I heaved a deep sigh. I did not know how magical the night would turn out to be, but it was certainly going to be a very busy one.

Eleven

The day of the ball dawned at last or far too soon, depending upon one's point of view. I veered between both emotions, trembling with a mixture of anticipation and dread. Mal had yet to arrive with my gown. I was still clad in my cotton dressing robe as the sun set. I paced to my bedchamber window and peered down the lane. Across the street, I could see the Misses Hanson rustle out of their house in their silk gowns. They headed eagerly toward the waiting barouche, as though determined to be the first to arrive at the palace as soon as the gates opened.

I smiled as I wondered if the young ladies had thought to bring a cushion to land upon should they venture to swoon again. One could not always depend upon the gallantry of a prince as the other silly girls had discovered on that day I had come to think of as the Maiden Massacre.

My smirk faded as the barouche disappeared up the hill and there was still no sign of Mal. The moon had risen like a silver-white queen presiding over a brilliant court of stars. It would be a beautiful night filled with the promise of romance and adventure or total disaster. I was leaning toward the latter. If Mal did not get here soon, I would be attending the ball in my chemise. Where was the wretched man?

Imelda had been in a state of near panic when she had helped me to style my hair earlier. Her nervous fluttering had only increased my own anxiety. I had shooed her out of my bedchamber to go tend to the girls. But as carriage after carriage lumbered past our house, I began to feel rather panicky myself.

As I came away from the window, I was heartened by the sight of the small nosegay of white roses resting upon my dressing table. It had been delivered earlier by an earnest young Scutcheon corporal who had snapped off a sharp bow. He had handed me the bouquet with "the commander's best wishes and compliments, milady."

Settling onto the stool in front of my dressing table, I picked up the roses and breathed in their sweet fragrance. Once again, I examined the card that had accompanied them.

Ella,

I know you have much finer blooms in your own garden, but I hope you will find my humble offering acceptable.

Yours, Horatio

An involuntary smile curved my lips. If anyone had told me even a week ago that I would look forward to dancing with Commander Crushington at the ball, I would have declared that person as mad as a Red Grove hermit. But after hearing all that Horatio had overcome in his youth, I was intrigued and wanted to know him better. I was even willing to consider the possibility something romantic could develop between us— if he did not arrest me first.

As for Mal, the only thing that prevented me from wanting to kill my dear friend was the small wooden box resting next to my hairbrush. I opened the box and drew out the precious emeralds that Mal had restored to me. I had not yet been able to thank him, and I resolved to do so while I was choking him to death.

I had to brush my hair back to fasten the emeralds in my ears. I had no idea if they would match my dress. Mal had been so infernally mysterious, he had refused to tell me anything about the gown's design, fabric or even the color. He had insisted I would just have to trust him.

I was trying to do so, but as the minutes ticked by and he still did not arrive, it grew increasingly more difficult. At least, wearing my mother's earrings afforded me some comfort. It did not matter if they would complement my gown or not. Imelda had arranged my hair in a soft cascade of curls tumbling over my shoulders. The earrings would not be visible, but I would know they were there, as though this evening I would carry a small part of my mother with me.

As much as I loved Imelda, I could not help wishing that my own mother was here tonight. I tried to imagine what it would have been like, the shared laughter and excitement, the way she would have smiled as she insisted, I borrow her "twinkles," fastening them on me herself, the look of pride in her eyes as she hugged me. My throat swelled with emotion, and it was with relief that I heard the distant knock on the front door. I leapt up and bolted out into the hall, crying, "I'll get it!"

I tore down the stairs, nearly tripping over the hem of my dressing robe. When I reached the front door, I flung it open. "Mal! Where have you been—"

I broke off in dismay because it was not my friend. Instead of Mal, I was greeted by the blast of the royal herald's trumpet. Rhufawn Smythe obviously recalled what had happened on his last visit because he stood well out of my reach so I could not snatch the instrument from him. I had to endure the rest of his fanfare. Leaning up against the doorjamb, I folded my arms and glowered until he finished. As soon as he lowered the trumpet, I demanded, "Now what?"

Ignoring my hostile tone, the herald tossed his red curls as he said, "A message from the royal palace, one of the greatest importance—"

"Don't tell me. Let me guess. The royal ball has been cancelled and regretfully His Majesty is unable to refund the price of our tickets."

"Of course not, Miss Upton. You truly are the most cynical and suspicious young lady I have ever met."

"Then you claim to bring me more good news from the palace?" I asked.

"Er— not precisely. It will depend upon how much stamina you possess."

"What!"

Rhufawn ventured closer, although he eyed me warily. He drew forth a scroll and unfurled it. Clearing his throat, he used the light spilling from the house as he read, "His Supreme Highness King August the first of that name, ruler of the great kingdom of Arcady, descendent of the noble house of Helavalerian, declares that henceforth swooning in the presence of royalty is strictly forbidden. Any person caught fainting in the vicinity of the king or any of the noble princes, Florian, Kendrick, Ryland, Dahl, or Dashiel will be subject to a heavy fine and an afternoon confined in the Yoke of Shame."

As the herald finished reading the decree, I did not know whether to laugh or roll my eyes. Someone must have reported the absurd episode that had taken place on our lane to His Majesty. While I was glad that there would not be a repetition of the Maiden Massacre at the ball, I was vexed with the king for using it as an excuse to enact another petty law.

"I do hope you read this decree to the Hansons before they left for the ball," I said.

"No." Rhufawn squirmed, managing to look both guilty and defiant. "They were gone before I got there, as were many of the other families on this street. But it is not as though I dawdled. What is a poor herald to do when he is handed a decree to announce at the very last moment?"

"I am sure you did your best, but the king had better be

prepared to increase his supply of yokes," I said. "What if a girl faints because she is genuinely ill? Will allowances be made for that?"

Rhufawn squinted at the document. "There do not appear to be any exceptions, miss."

"Oh? What about coughing or sneezing in the presence of the king? Has that also been banned?"

"I see no mention of that, so I suppose it is permissible if done discreetly."

"What about puking?"

"Well, I would hardly think that—" Rhufawn looked up from the document and realized I was merely giving him a hard time. He eyed me reproachfully. "Why must you always be so difficult, Miss Upton? I am only a poor herald, striving to earn an honest living and—"

He broke off as a magnificent carriage lumbered down the lane. Unlike the others that had swept on by, this one drew to a halt before my house. Rhufawn's jaw dropped and mine did as well because the equipage looked as though royalty had come to call, or at the very least a grand duke. Moonlight spilled over a team of snowy white horses sporting golden plumes. They were a perfect match for the coach, which was all ivory and gold, even the wheels picked out with gilt trimming. The carriage boasted no less than four running lamps, a bewigged coachman, and a footman in blue livery riding on the back.

The footman scrambled from his perch, but the coach door was already opening. The herald and I watched breathlessly, but there was more of the pirate than prince about the man who appeared. Mal leapt down, not waiting for the footman to lower the steps. Clad all in black, he would have blended with the night except for the gleam of the running lamps.

Whistling a jaunty tune, Mal opened the garden gate and sauntered down the path. Relieved as I was to see him, I wanted to clout him upside the head for the anxiety he had caused me. Before

I could utter a word of reproach, Mal greeted the herald with a cheerful grin.

"Hallo, Ruffy."

Rhufawn flushed as red as his hair. The little man stammered something incoherent and slunk away as quickly as his plump legs would carry him.

"You know the herald?" I asked.

"Of course. Who do you think I bribed to get an invitation so I could buy the tickets? The little weasel charged me five galoons."

"No wonder he looked guilty. So much for all his whining about being just a poor, honest herald," I said. My indignation veered in Mal's direction. "Where have you been, Hawkridge? You should have been here hours ago."

"I know I am sorry, but I had a last-minute disagreement with Delphine about where the hidden pocket on the gown should go. She had stitched it inside the sleeve, but I told her that would never do because what if one of your dancing partners—"

"Wait!" I exclaimed. "What do you mean about Delphine? She is the one who helped you with my gown?"

"Perhaps just a bit."

"How much of a *bit*?"

"Well, actually she designed and sewed all of it."

"And you are just telling me this now?"

"I had a feeling you wouldn't be happy about it, but truly, Ella you are going to be thrilled with the gown. Delphine is a brilliant seamstress."

"She is also a witch who despises me! I believe she has trained that evil cat of hers to hiss and spit at me, so who knows what she might have done to that gown? Am I going to break out into boils or explode into flames when I put it on?"

"Of course not. I admit that Delphine does not much care for you, but she adores me, and she knows how important it is for you to acquire that orb for me." Mal rested his hands on my shoulders and gave me a coaxing smile. "Take a deep breath and relax, Ella. Everything is going to be fine."

I thrust his hands away, but before I could retort, the footman approached, toting several bandboxes and a large linen garment carrier. The man was so short, I could only make out his tricorne hat and his eyes peering over the top of the bag. When the stack wobbled, I hastily stepped aside, allowing him to enter the vestibule. Mal followed, performing introductions as he helped the little man set down his burden.

"Ella, this is Long Louie. Louie, this is Ella."

The little man doffed his tricorne, beaming at me from beneath his powdered white wig. He was a plain-featured man, but he had a charming gap-toothed smile.

"Truly a pleasure, Miss Ella." He bowed to me before turning to Mal. "Shall I have Harry take the carriage around the town square a time or two? It appears to me that Miss Upton might be awhile, and you know how Harry hates to keep his horses standing."

Mal nodded. "Better give Ella ten minutes."

"Ten minutes!" I squawked.

"Fifteen then."

Before I could protest further, Long Louie swept another elaborate bow before he backed out of the door and was gone. Mal turned to me, wearing an expression of deep satisfaction.

"Didn't I tell you I would send you off to the ball in grand style? Louie makes a most excellent footman."

"Yes, although he is rather short. Why do you call him Long Louie?"

"I didn't give him the nickname." Mal hemmed and hawed a bit before continuing, "It was bestowed upon him by some of his — er— lady admirers. The 'long' doesn't refer to his height but to — um—"

"Stop!" I flung up one hand. "That is much more information than I needed."

"You did ask."

"And I should have known better."

"What do you think of the coach?" Mal asked.

"It's a bit overwhelming."

When Mal appeared crestfallen, I hastened to add, "I worry how much you must have spent acquiring such a regal equipage."

"I didn't buy it, Ella. The coach and horses are hired for the evening, and I was able to strike up a bargain because the carriage is rather old-fashioned. You know the rage these days is all for those pumpkin vehicles. Although..." Mal's lips quirked mischievously. "I could have gotten a great deal on a slightly used cucumber. But I imagined your reaction if I had turned up with that and I have far too much regard for my own skin."

"Occasionally you do display some small sign of wisdom, Mr. Hawkridge," I said with a wry smile. "Thank you. The coach is wonderful. Netta and Amy will be in ecstasies when they see it. They truly are going to believe you are their fairy godfather."

"The fairy godfather needs to hasten things along a bit." He gathered up two of the bandboxes and the linen garment carrier. "Grab that last small box and follow me."

"Follow you where?" I demanded as Mal strode toward the stairs.

He paused on the first riser to glance back at me. "Up to your room. Thanks to Delphine, we are running late. I have some important instructions for you, and we can save time if I explain those while you are getting dressed."

I locked my arms across my bosom. "I think not, sir!"

Mal heaved an impatient sigh. "What is the problem, Ella? I have often been in your bedchamber."

"When we were children! My poor stepmother is already having spasms, fearing you were not going to show up with my gown. If she catches you in my room while I am dressing, Imelda will dissolve into complete hysterics."

"Then we had better be really quiet," Mal said in a stage whisper. He headed the rest of the way up the stairs before I could stop him.

I swore, but I had no choice but to grab the last box and follow him. By the time I arrived on the landing, Mal had disappeared inside my bedchamber. I paused to listen and was relieved to hear Imelda's voice coming from the direction of Amy's room. I darted after Mal, closing the door behind me and feeling strangely nervous as I locked the bolt.

Perhaps I was being foolish. Mal had often been in my room before. But there was little trace of the mischievous boy who had climbed through my bedchamber window, hauling his sack of toy soldiers and cannons to lay siege to my dollhouse. Watching him pile the boxes and garment bag on the bed, I was far too aware of Mal as a man and a seductive one at that.

His black garb and bronzed skin made a marked contrast to the feminine unicorn-embroidered silk of my bed curtains. As he bent down to undo the ties on the garment bag, his shirt strained against the musculature of his back. I had never fully realized how much his movements possessed a sensual catlike grace. I knew many other women had always found him attractive. He was lean, he was dangerous, and his wicked eyes seemed to hint of forbidden pleasures.

Closeted with him in the intimacy of my bedchamber, I was dismayed by how flushed and discomfited I was. How I longed to turn back time to the days when my feelings toward Mal had been far less complicated, when I had been able to see him only as a brother and friend.

Mal undid the last tie on the garment bag. Casting a look at me over his shoulder, he grinned. "Are you ready for this?"

"No." I sighed.

He laughed. As he removed the gown from the linen bag, I braced myself, hardly knowing what to expect of a gown designed by a rogue like Mal and a witch who detested me.

Mal turned and held up the gown for my inspection. For a

moment, I think I stopped breathing. It was truly the most beautiful dress I had ever seen although the style was simple enough. The bodice was cut on modest lines, tapering to a V at the waistline, the sleeves short, fashioned into two puffed tiers. The skirt was full, attached to the bodice with a gathering of tiny pleats.

What made the gown so extraordinary was the fabric, dyed a golden hue. Or so I thought until I drew close enough to caress the cool silk. The fabric shimmered and changed with my slightest touch, shifting with the light, one minute shining gold, then iridescent silver, then glistening ivory.

"Oh, Mal! What is this material?"

"It's called river silk, rather rare in these parts. It's woven from threads obtained from the cocoons of prism butterflies only found on the Isle of Altoria. I was quite fortunate to buy so many yards of it from one of the fen smugglers. Let's see how it looks on you."

I took the gown from him. "All right, but you have to turn around."

Mal arched one brow. "Seriously?"

"Yes!" I pointed toward the corner opposite my bed. "Go! And keep your face to the wall until I say you can look."

Mal rolled his eyes, but he complied. Folding his arms, he stood with his back to me. I kept a wary eye on him as I undid the buttons on my dressing gown. I would have completely trusted Horatio not to peek, but the commander was far too honorable to have barged into my bedchamber in the first place.

I shrugged out of my dressing gown, stripping down to my stays, drawers, and stockings. I carefully pulled my chemise over my head, taking care not to disarrange my hair. Then I fastened a cage hoop skirt about my waist. The hoop was modest compared to the broad kind women wore in my mother's day. I was glad that the fashion now was for dresses cut upon straight, simpler lines. But for all formal occasions at court such as the ball, hoops were still required.

As I donned the final layer of petticoat, Mal complained, "Aren't you ready yet?"

"No, as I have often explained to you, it takes women longer to dress because we wear more."

"A fact I have always lamented," Mal murmured wickedly.

At last, I slipped into the gown, and it was like plunging into a waterfall of silk. The cool fabric whispered against my skin as I worked my arms into the sleeves.

"You can turn around now—" I began, but then realized at some point Mal had already done so. He leaned against the wall, studying me through the thickness of his lashes, the hint of a smile on his face.

I refused to let him make me blush, merely shaking my head at him in an admonishing fashion. Turning my back to him, I ordered him to close the gown. He proceeded to do so with alacrity, demonstrating that he was far too familiar with the fastenings of a woman's garment.

As he deftly worked the tiny hooks and eyes, I had to sweep my hair out of the way. When he reached the top rows of fastenings, his fingers brushed against the skin of my upper back. I experienced an odd flutter in the pit of my stomach, and I heard Mal catch his breath.

Desperately seeking to ignore both of our reactions, I fanned out my skirts, admiring the way the color shifted between light and shadow, like the sun shimmering on a flowing stream. "The gown is truly enchanting," I said. "But I thought the idea was for me not to attract any attention."

Mal chuckled, although his fingers were no longer quite as steady as he fumbled with the last hook. "The only way you would ever escape notice is if that lovely face of yours was masked. Your best disguise tonight is to appear as a carefree beauty come to the ball to steal hearts, not a magic orb. Now let's have a good look at you."

I turned around slowly. Mal stepped back to study me. He was silent for so long, I grew nervous. I thought I was good at reading his expressions, but never had I seen such a stillness come into his eyes.

"What is it?" I asked. "Is something wrong? Does the gown not fit right?"

"See for yourself."

He took my arm and positioned me in front of the full-length cheval glass next to my wardrobe. I froze, for one stunned moment thinking my mother's spirit had risen before me. I reached out to her. When my image in the mirror reached back to me, I noticed the subtle differences. My mother's eyes had been green. The stranger in the looking glass had deep blue eyes, the same color as my father's. Her features were not as gentle as Mama's, the mirror woman's cheekbones more sharply defined, but the cascade of golden hair was the same.

I stared, pressing my hand to my lips and my image did likewise, her eyes soft with wonder. Could that lovely, fey creature trapped within the glass truly be me? I have never set great value upon my appearance, but I stammered, "I don't wish to sound vain, but I suppose I am rather... rather..."

"Beautiful," Mal said hoarsely as he stepped alongside me. He slipped his arm about my waist. "I would give my life to be going with you tonight."

"I daresay you would enjoy all the intrigue of stealing the orb far more than I will."

"I wasn't thinking of the orb." His eyes met mine in the glass. "I wish I could be the man at your side, the one who will lead you into your first dance."

"Oh." I lowered my gaze, feeling strangely guilty. I could not bring myself to tell Mal that man was going to be Horatio Crushington. Instead, I forced a laugh. "You would hate all the flummery that goes along with a royal ball, the etiquette, the idle chatter, the bowing, and curtsying. After five minutes, you would be as bored with it as Waldo the Wharf Rat's daughters."

"I fear you are right." His hand fell away from my waist. "But sometimes I wish I was a very different kind of man."

"What kind of man would that be?"

His expression waxed pensive, almost sad. "Someone more noble and heroic, the kind of man who—"

"Who what?"

"I don't know. I am talking utter nonsense." He tried to smile but could not quite manage it.

I regarded him with surprise. This sort of brooding introspection was so unlike Mal. Usually the man brimmed over with bravado and self-confidence.

"I happen to like you just fine the way you are," I said. "In fact, I quite adore you. Especially because of this."

I held up my hair on one side to reveal the emerald glittering in my ear. "Recovering my mother's emeralds was the sweetest, most wonderful thing you have ever done for me. I was so surprised when your young messenger turned up at my gate. I thought he was a beggar at first.

"I am afraid I insulted him. He wasted little time informing me that he was a 'man of means with reg'lar employment.'" I chuckled as I imitated the boy's indignant voice.

"That was Tom Piper. Quite an enterprising young rogue. It wouldn't surprise me if he ended up as the wealthiest man in the kingdom one day."

I closed the distance between Mal and me, draping my arms around his neck. "I should scold you for lavishing so much money on me, but I am far too grateful. I hardly know how to thank you."

I expected Mal to come back with some sort of wicked suggestion, perhaps even try to steal a kiss. He patted my back awkwardly and eased me away from him.

"That is quite all right, my dear. But time is wasting," he said. "We need to return to the enterprise at hand."

I blinked in astonishment, thinking he truly had fallen into a strange humor. Perhaps he was merely tense about the success of our plot. That thought did nothing to ease my own anxieties. He strode over to the bed and began pulling covers off the bandboxes, revealing a gossamer pelisse, an ivory fan, and a pair of long white gloves. As I struggled into them, I was surprised to see Mal donning a pair of much shorter ones. I realized why when he drew forth an object from the smallest box. He held up a small glass ball.

"Here is the imitation orb that you will switch for the real one."

He handed it to me, and I cradled it in the palm of my glove.

"It's much smaller and lighter than I expected it would be," I said.

"It is an exact replica of the real one or as close as I could make it. Now do we need to go over the plan again, the route you will take through the palace to get down to the king's private treasure room?"

I shook my head. "We have been over it so many times, I feel like I have been walking those corridors in my sleep. If you are sure the information you have given me is correct?"

"It is. I told you that my contact in the palace was a very clever young footman. He might have been able to help me get the orb except that—" Mal broke off, busying himself by closing the boxes.

"Except what?" I prompted.

"His spying activities aroused suspicion and he had to flee for his life."

When I groaned, Mal added hastily, "Nothing like that is going to happen to you. Once you have the orbs switched, no one will even notice the real one has gone missing. If eventually someone does, it still will not matter because nothing can be traced back to either of us. Your aura is unregistered, thanks to your father. I wish my grandfather had been as wise, but I have taken great care not to touch the fake orb. Now tuck that thing away in your hidden pocket."

Delphine had done such a clever job of disguising the pocket in the folds of the silk, I had to grope along the skirt of my gown to find it. I found it on the left side and slipped the false orb inside. It was so light I could hardly detect it was there, but I still expelled an uneasy sigh.

"Stop fretting," Mal said. "This plan really is beautifully simple. It will all go as smooth as silk."

"Oh, don't say that. Do you have any idea how easily silk unravels?"

"The only difficult and dangerous part of this scheme is getting you in and out of the treasure chamber unseen and as I promised I have something that will help with that." With a mysterious smile, Mal tore the lid from the last box. "You thought the dress was enchanting, but now let me show you the real magic."

With a triumphant flourish, Mal produced the strangest looking pair of shoes I had ever seen.

"Your dancing slippers, milady," he said, presenting them to me with a deep bow.

I crept closer to inspect them. The shoes had a bit more of a heel than I was accustomed to, but that was not the disconcerting aspect. The slippers were completely transparent, appearing spun from fine crystal.

Cautiously, I tapped my fingernail against the heel. It pinged. "Mal, are these actually made of—"

"Glass." He beamed at me. "Are they not extraordinary?"

"They certainly are quite beautiful, but is there any reason my shoes could not have been made of a nice soft, comfortable kid?"

"Do you have any idea how difficult it is to enchant leather?"

"And you are claiming that these shoes are—"

"Magic, yes. Didn't I say so? Guess what they can do."

"Give me blisters on my heels the size of the orb?"

"No! These shoes will" —Mal paused for dramatic effect— "render you invisible."

"Oh." I cocked one eyebrow, unable to conceal my skepticism. "Truly?"

Mal heaved a vexed sigh. I could tell my reaction was not the awe that he had hoped for. "Yes, all you must do is slip the glass slippers on, click your toes together three times and you will completely vanish. When you want to reappear, just take off the shoes and the magic will end until the next time you don the slippers and click your toes again. The important thing to remember is that although you will be completely invisible, you will still be corporeal, so you will need to take care not to bump into anyone or brush up against... and I can tell from the look on your face you don't believe a word I am saying."

"Slippers made of glass possessing the power to turn you invisible? Even you must realize how mad that sounds." I hated to disappoint Mal or hurt his feelings by reminding him that the last bit of magic he had tried to perform resulted in him becoming completely bald. Invisibility shoes struck me as being an impossible feat for a man who could not even produce a successful hair-growth potion.

Mal thrust the shoes at me. "I will prove to you the shoes are magic. Just try them on."

I reached for them when a brisk rap at the door startled me. I nearly dropped the shoes, but Mal caught them just in time.

"Careful," he said. "The slippers are sturdier than you might think, but they are not unbreakable."

"Ella?" my stepmother called out as she knocked again.

I held my finger to my lips, cautioning Mal to silence as I replied, "Yes?"

"I thought I heard Mr. Hawkridge's voice. Did he finally arrive with your gown? Is he still here?"

"Er— no, he had to leave, but he did bring the gown."

"Oh, let me see it!" The doorknob turned and then rattled. "Ella, why is your door locked? Please let me in, dear."

I cast Mal a panicked look. He merely gave a fatalistic shrug. "I suppose you had better let her in."

"Are you insane?" I hissed. "Do you ever want to be allowed across the threshold of this house again?"

"What do you expect me to do? Hide under the bed?"

"Don't be ridiculous. You'd never fit." I looked about frantically for another hiding spot, but there was none, even my wardrobe was too small.

The doorknob rattled again. "Ella?"

"Coming, Em," I sang out as I propelled Mal across the room. I whispered to him, "You'll have to climb out the window."

Mal balked. "What? Do you want me to break my neck?"

"You used to manage well enough when you were a boy."

"I was much lighter then. Do you think those vines will still hold me?"

"Yes! There are a lot more of them now." I eased up the sash as quietly as I could and pointed outward. "Go."

Mal gave me a disgruntled look, but he said, "Fine! I need to be going anyway."

He handed me the glass slippers again and this time I clutched them to my bosom.

"Just don't forget to test the shoes until you are certain you know how to work them."

I nodded as Imelda's voice sounded even more anxious. "Ella? Is someone in there with you?"

"No, just me, Em."

"Then is everything all right? Why won't you open the door?"

"I am just finishing... um... scrubbing my teeth. I will be right there," I called.

Mal swung one leg over the sill and paused. "Now you do remember where and when you are supposed to meet me to give me the orb?"

"Yes, yes! Go through the back gate in the palace gardens and head toward the abandoned cottage at the edge of the woods."

"Midnight. Do not forget. If you are not there at the rendezvous, I will assume something has gone wrong and come looking for you."

"And walk straight into the arms of the palace guard? Don't be ridiculous, Mal. Just be patient and wait for me. I will be there."

Mal wriggled the rest of his body through the window. "And, Ella?"

"Yes?"

"Try to enjoy yourself tonight." He grinned.

I glared at him. I swear I would have given him a shove if he had not already found purchase among the vines and started his scramble downward. I hurried away from the window and set the shoes down carefully beside the bed. I took a deep breath to compose myself before I unlocked the door and opened it.

Imelda burst over the threshold, her satin ball gown rustling as she darted suspicious glances about the room. "Tell me that you never allowed that wicked young man to—" My stepmother broke off as she got her first good look at me.

Her stern demeanor melted at once. "Oh, Ella!" she breathed.

I fanned out my skirts, displaying the shimmering fabric.

"Oh, Ella!" She squeaked again, clapping her hands together in an expression of wonder and delight.

"Then you approve of the gown Mal gave me?"

"Approve? Oh, Ella! That wicked young man. That wonderful wicked young man!" Imelda inspected me from every angle. "The gown is stunning. You are stunning."

She pressed her fingers to her lips, her eyes welling with sentimental tears. "You are every bit as beautiful as I imagined you would be."

Imelda flew at me, and I thought she meant to embrace me in a huge hug. She contented herself with touching my cheek and then carefully smoothed out a stray curl. "You will break hearts tonight. I know you will."

"I suppose it will be better if I break hearts instead of my shoes," I muttered.

"What?"

"Nothing." I smiled at her. "I only remarked how beautiful you look, Em. You will put all of us in the shade."

"Oh, well." Imelda preened a bit, patting the feathered headdress that confined her dark hair. "You must not talk nonsense, dear. My day is long past," she added somewhat wistfully. "Tonight is all for my three lovely daughters."

"Are the girls ready yet?"

"Almost."

"You had better hurry them along, Em. I believe our coach will arrive at any moment."

Imelda nodded, took one more look at me, sighed and kissed me on the cheek. As soon as she had bustled out of the room, I closed the door. I was relieved that Imelda had been so distracted by my gown, she had never thought to ask how I had managed to do up the hooks and eyes by myself. Explaining that would have required more ingenuity than even I possessed.

I crossed the room and stared down at my glass slippers. I regarded them dubiously for a moment. Clutching the bedpost for support, I eased my feet into them. They were about as stiff and uncomfortable as one would expect shoes spun from glass to be. I wobbled a little as I accustomed myself to them.

I minced over to the mirror.

"Well, here goes," I said as I clicked the toes together three times. I held my breath, waiting. My image in the mirror did not even waver. Had I rightly recalled what Mal had told me to do? I was certain that I had, his instructions were simple and clear.

All you must do is slip the glass slippers on, click your toes together three times and you will completely vanish.

I braced myself, this time making each tap slower and more deliberate. Still nothing. I tried clicking very fast and then slower again. I tried tapping softly, then harder, and finally so forcefully I feared the shoes would crack.

Throughout each attempt, my reflection peered stubbornly

back at me, a look of disgust on her face as though she wondered how big of an idiot I could be.

"Oh, Mal," I groaned. His magic shoes did not work. Had I ever truly believed that they would? A foolish part of me had hoped that for once Mal might have succeeded with one of his enchantments. If I could have turned invisible, it would have made the daunting task that lay ahead of me so much easier. Now I would have to rely on my own wits.

I lifted the hem of my gown, peering glumly down at the shoes. I had to admit the glass slippers made the perfect complement to my extraordinary gown, but they were so transparent, I could see the hole in the toe of my left stocking.

I tried to imagine dancing in them, but I had this dreadful vision of Horatio making a misstep and treading down hard on my toes. The horrible crunch, the warm spurt of blood, my pain-filled shriek as shards of glass embedded in the tender skin of my foot.

I shuddered and removed the shoes. I carried the glass slippers over to my wardrobe. Shoving clothes aside, I hid them at the far back of the wardrobe. Then I located my old dancing slippers. They were more scuffed than I remembered but considering the length of my gown's hem and how crowded the ballroom would be, I doubted anyone would notice.

I eased into my old shoes, reveling in the feel of soft, well-worn leather embracing my feet. "Ah," I breathed. At least now, I would be able to move quickly, even outrun the palace guards if it became necessary.

A commotion outside my window, the clatter of wheels and horses' hooves on the street below alerted me that Long Louie had returned with the carriage. I grabbed up my fan and cloak and bolted from my bedchamber to herd my stepmother and sisters downstairs to the waiting coach.

Twelve

⌘

Our coach lumbered through the night, creaking, and lurching whenever we hit a rut. The old carriage was not as well-sprung as newer vehicles, the blue velvet cushions a little faded. But the interior was spacious, allowing Imelda and I to sit comfortably side by side without crushing voluminous gowns billowing over hoops. Amy and Netta were seated opposite us, both girls unusually silent, a fact that surprised me. I had expected to be inundated by breathless chatter during the entire ride to the palace. Even Imelda said little beyond admonishing Netta to sit up straight and ordering Amy not to dare nibble at her nails.

Moonlight filtered through the coach windows and revealed my sisters' faces flushed with a mixture of excitement and nervousness. Imelda looked subdued as she stared out the window at the changing landscape as we left Midtown far behind.

Our modest lanes disappeared, widening into the broad boulevards of the Heights. The district was lit by glowing streetlamps, as ornately carved as the wrought iron gates and fences that enclosed the great estates. Beyond stately elms and oak trees, we caught glimpses of imposing manors the size of small palaces.

My sisters gaped and uttered awed exclamations. Even I was impressed. But there was a wistfulness clouding Imelda's eyes. Although she spoke little of her life before she married my father, I realized how familiar all of this must be to my stepmother.

The Heights had been her world before her first husband's fall from grace. Imelda would have passed her girlhood here among this grandeur, fallen in love, married, given birth to her two daughters, and been widowed. I wondered which one of these great houses might have been hers, before her property had been seized by the king. Could one of these gates we passed have been where Imelda had been turned out to fend for herself, with her two small daughters and a few modest belongings?

Amy and Netta would have been far too young to remember much of this, but Imelda must be flooded with painful and poignant memories. When I noticed her eyes well with tears, I reached across the seat and quietly pressed her hand.

She dragged her gaze from the window and squeezed my fingers, her mouth crooked in a sad smile. She released me abruptly, sitting upright. Her gaze homed in upon her daughters.

"Amy, what was that?"

Amy stiffened. "What was what, Mama?" she replied in that airy voice she used when she was trying too hard to appear innocent.

"That thing I just saw you pass to Netta."

"I am sure I don't know what you mean, Mama."

"Yes, you do, Amethyst! It looked like some sort of flask. Garnet, hand it over at once."

Amy gave her sister a warning nudge. I am sure she would have tried to brazen it out. Stricken with guilt, Netta meekly handed a small blue bottle to her mother.

I sucked in my breath sharply because I recognized what it was at once.

Blast you, Malcolm Hawkridge, I thought.

Imelda looked puzzled as she inspected the bottle and then she scowled. "You girls have sought to steady your nerves by imbibing spirits? Never did I think to see the day when a daughter of mine would—"

"It is not spirits, Mama," Netta interrupted. "It is a magic potion."

"A what?"

"I believe it is called the Elixir of Love," I said with a disgruntled sigh.

Imelda gave me an astonished look. "You knew about this?"

"I certainly did not, or I would have put a stop to it. Mal has been peddling this elixir all over Midtown, but I never dreamed he would sell a bottle to my own sisters."

"No! He gave it to us," Netta said.

"Because he is our fairy godfather and he promised us if we drank this, we would be the belles of the ball," Amy added.

"What utter nonsense," Imelda said sternly. "I am not at all pleased that Mr. Hawkridge should practice such deception upon you girls."

"It is not nonsense, Mama," Amy said. "Mal's grandfather was a brilliant mage. At one time he was even the chief wizard to the king and Mal has inherited all his grandpapa's magical abilities."

Imelda turned uncertainly toward me. "Is that true?"

"Er... well," I stalled as I struggled with my answer. I did not wish to lie to my stepmother, but on the other hand, I hated exposing Mal's failures. I recollected what he had told me about his potion. He admitted himself that it was a harmless concoction, designed merely to enhance a woman's belief in her own charms. My nervous young sisters clearly needed a large dose of confidence. Mal had probably thought he was doing Amy and Netta a favor, but I still wished he had consulted me before giving them the potion.

I finally temporized, "Yes, it is true that Mal's grandfather Hiram was indeed a great wizard."

The carriage hit a rut, jarring all of us. When the vehicle

resumed its steady motion, Imelda uncorked the bottle and took a cautious sniff. "What exactly does Mr. Hawkridge's potion do?"

"It renders a woman so completely desirable that any man, even a prince, will be dazzled by her charms and fall helplessly in love with her," Amy recited.

I was certain that she was directly quoting Mal. "You and Netta are both lovely, charming girls. Neither of you have need of a love potion."

My sisters stared blankly back at me, clearly unconvinced. I expected Imelda to second my opinion and dispose of the elixir at once. To my utter shock, she raised the bottle and took a swig.

"It tastes rather… flowery," she pronounced.

"That would be Mal's secret ingredient, the magical blue rose hips," Amy said.

"Can't be much of a secret if Mal told you," I replied dryly.

Amy pulled a face at me. Looking a trifle sheepish, Imelda offered the bottle to me, but before I could decline, Amy snatched the bottle away.

"Ella certainly has no need of this." She took another swallow and passed the elixir to Netta. Netta took a sip and handed it back to Amy who tipped the bottle up and chugged.

She hiccupped and leaned back against the coach's velvet cushions. "Ah, I think I can feel the elixir working already."

"I can't." Netta looked disconsolate as she upended the empty bottle. "You had far more than me, Amy, you greedy thing. You drank it all."

Amy's only response to her sister's complaint was a beatific smile that made me uneasy. I wondered what else Mal might have put in that potion of his besides rose hips. I heard Imelda draw breath to scold Amy but before she could do so, the coach lurched to a halt.

"Goodness!" my stepmother said. "Surely we cannot have arrived already."

We all scooted across the seat to peer out our respective

windows. I could ascertain little beyond the fact that we had stopped behind a pumpkin styled carriage. I lowered the glass and leaned out as far as I could. By craning my neck, I could see we had joined a queue of coaches wending their way up the hill toward the palace gates. The carriages' running lamps made it look like an orderly procession of fireflies on the march.

Imelda tugged at my skirt. "Do come back inside and close the window, Ella, before you disarrange your hair."

I did as she asked and settled back against the cushions. While Em fussed over me, smoothing out my hair, I noticed my sisters perched on the edge of their seat.

"You may as well relax, girls. It may be a while before we are able to alight. The entire kingdom appears to be on their way to the ball."

"Oh, dear," Imelda said. "It is quite vulgar to be the first to arrive, but I hope we shall not be the last either."

"Don't worry, Em. I'll tackle whoever is in front and you and the girls can scramble over their bodies."

Amy and Netta giggled, but my stepmother gave me a long-suffering look.

"I believe we discussed this, Prunella. You need to mind your tongue tonight and not blurt out some of the inappropriate thoughts that flit through your head."

"I will try," I promised.

"Try very hard, dear."

We traveled the rest of the way to the palace in a series of fits and starts until even I grew impatient. I thought we could have arrived much faster if we had disembarked and walked.

Finally, our coach door swung open and Long Louie let down the steps. He bowed and stretched out his hand to help my stepmother down, but Imelda froze in the doorway.

"This cannot be right," she said. "We have stopped by the gates. Tell the coachman he must follow the drive so that we may alight by the palace steps."

"I am sorry, milady," Louie replied. "But it appears that the king has forbidden it."

"Nonsense! Why should His Majesty do such a thing?"

"I believe it is for reasons of security. The king does not wish any undesirable sort of persons sneaking into the ball."

Undesirable? Such as people who had not paid for their tickets or prospective thieves like me? I wondered.

My stepmother, who is not a good walker, protested, "But it must be at least a half mile to the castle. There was never such an order given before. How very strange and disagreeable!"

I tugged at Imelda's sleeve to gain her attention. "Please, Em. Clearly, we have no choice, and it is a very pleasant evening for a stroll."

Imelda looked far from pleased, but she made no further demur, allowing Louie to help her alight. My stepsisters came next, Amy nearly shoving her sister aside in her eagerness.

I studied Amy, looking anxiously for any sign that Mal's potion might have had some strange effect on her. She seemed a little flushed and her eyes glittered with excitement, but I supposed that was to be expected.

As soon as my sisters had disembarked, I followed, clinging to Louie's hand until I arrived safely on the pavement. After what Mal had told me about him, I was embarrassed to admit I had difficulty keeping my eyes from straying to his crotch.

"We will be stabling the coach in the mews behind the palace," Louie said. "If for any reason you should wish to depart early, you only need to send a page to fetch me." He added in a lower tone meant for my ears alone, "Good luck, miss."

I gave him a startled look and he smiled reassuringly. It was obvious that Mal had trusted Louie with the secret of my mission tonight. I hoped Mal had been right to do so, but I was given little time to worry about that.

Louis climbed back up onto his perch and our carriage lumbered off to make room for the next guests to alight. Gathering up the hem of my gown, I followed Imelda and my sisters. Moonlight glinted off the gleaming white walls that surrounded the royal park, the massive golden gates flung open in welcoming fashion.

Imelda had exaggerated the distance to the palace. It appeared to be a quarter of a mile at most. Even from here, I could see the sweeping stairs that led up to a wide veranda. The palace beyond glowed with light, a romantic confection of towers and balustrades etched against the starry sky.

The palace grounds sprawled before us, an endless maze of topiary bushes, lush gardens and burbling fountains. Lit by the moon and dozens of flaming torches, it was all as magical as my stepmother had promised. Or it would have been if not for the gauntlet of sentries lined up on both sides of the drive leading to the palace steps.

They were all garbed in crisp red uniforms with brass buttons. Tall black shakos framed faces with stony countenances as they stood to attention, staring rigidly ahead. A few of them closest to the gates held chains fastened to the collars of aura beasts.

I had heard about these creatures from Mal but had never had the misfortune to see one until now. Larger than Amy's ponies, these furless cats were so pale, the veins throbbing beneath their skin were visible. With small, flattened back ears and narrowed eyes, the beasts stood as motionless as their handlers, but I shuddered, easily able to imagine how one of these cats could shred a person to ribbons at the slightest command.

My stepmother halted just outside the gate, murmuring, "Oh dear. This is very different from what I remember."

I reflected that it likely had been very different when Imelda had attended royal balls in her youth. That would have been before our king's tyrannical and greedy behavior had made him so many enemies that he had learned to be suspicious and fearful of his own subjects. Mal had warned me that security at the palace had tightened, but I had not expected anything like this. How had he ever imagined that I would be able to steal that orb and escape undetected?

I knew the answer to that. Mal relied far too much on the fact that I had an unregistered aura and that those absurd glass shoes of his would render me invisible. Confronted by the army of sentries and those eerie cats, I seriously doubted my ability to keep my promise to Mal.

I was not the only one daunted by the reception awaiting us beyond those gates. Imelda paled and my stepsisters clung to each other, even Amy's eagerness dissipating. The other arriving guests were equally dismayed, their excited chatter fading to nervous murmurs. Everyone hung back, milling outside the gates despite a sentry's gruff command for us to keep moving.

I found myself leading the way. Plucking up my skirts and my courage, I marched down the drive. I had not taken many steps when a man with shoulder-length, silver-streaked black hair loomed before me. His gaunt frame was engulfed in a flowing dark robe with wide sleeves, the satin fabric glittering with mysterious symbols. In his right hand he clutched a strange object that was a cross between a wand and a scepter.

I caught the whisper of someone in the crowd behind me. "The Great Mercato."

So, this was the king's chief wizard, the infamous mage who had designed the Aura Chamber to capture all our auras. He did indeed appear formidable with his pointed beard and cold narrow eyes, but I was not intimidated. I found his garb as outlandish as the way he dramatically pointed his scepter in the direction of the uneasy guests. It was as though he was trying too hard to convince everyone how powerful and important he was. I even had to bite back a smile when I recalled what Mal had told me of his true name.

I suppressed the urge to greet him with a cheerful, "Good evening, Sidney." I had promised Imelda to mind my tongue tonight and whatever Sidney Greenleaf chose to call himself, it was unwise to trifle with such a man.

A tall young sentry stood by his side, trying hard to look just as stone-faced, but his countenance was far too sweet and boyish for him to maintain such a stern demeanor.

"Tickets, please, miss," he said in clipped accents.

Imelda had insisted upon taking charge of the tickets herself. I glanced around for her, hoping she had not forgotten to bring them. My stepmother crept forward; trembling as she handed the costly vouchers to the young guard.

While he inspected them, Mercato's ice-chip eyes remained fixed on me. I stared back, summoning up my sweetest smile. Suddenly the stone on the end of his scepter flashed bright blue. Mercato reared back. He leveled an accusing finger and thundered, "Witch!"

My heart thudded as I started to stammer, "No, I assure you I —" I broke off when I realized he was not pointing at me, but at someone beyond my shoulder. I turned around to discover the crowd of guests behind me shrinking away from the strange woman who was the focus of Mercato's angry gesture.

Delphine.

I blinked in astonished recognition. The witch's slender neck hardly seemed capable of supporting the elaborate mountain of orange-red hair piled on top of her head. Whatever exquisite taste Delphine had employed when fashioning my gown had not carried over to her own attire. A scarlet gown that consisted of tiers and tiers of ruffles cut low across her bosom, leaving her shoulders completely bare.

Mercato shoved me out of the way as he cried out again, "Witch! Guards, seize that woman."

Sentries sprang to life, the aura beasts setting up a fearsome growl. The guests closest to Delphine cried out in fear, scrambling to get out of the way of the advancing soldiers. The only one unperturbed was the witch herself.

"Oh frap," Delphine muttered and flung something at the ground. Suddenly we were enveloped in a blinding white cloud thicker than any fog I had ever experienced in Misty Bottoms.

Guests screamed, the cats snarled and Mercato cursed. Above this chaos of sound, I heard my sisters' frightened cries and I tried to grope my way toward them. But I felt my wrist seized in an iron grip. Suddenly I was standing nose to nose with Delphine.

"Listen," she hissed. "I thought I might be of use if I could get past Mercato, but obviously I can't. You are on your own, girlie. Mal is counting on you, so don't fail him. Or else!"

"Or else what?" I asked, wrenching away from her.

I watched in alarm as her hair darkened to an ominous shade of black. Her face darkened as well, gradually becoming... furry? My jaw dropped as Delphine sprouted whiskers, her head getting smaller and smaller. She appeared to dwindle and disappear before my astonished eyes.

As the thick white cloud began to dissipate, I gaped at the witch's discarded gown pooling at my feet. The scarlet ruffles stirred, and Ebony emerged. The cat glared at me for a second before streaking off with a flit of her tail.

My mind reeled, unable to accept what I had just witnessed. I bent down to pick up the gown, shaking it as though I still expected to find some trace of Delphine. Besides the scarlet gown, nothing remained but a heap of petticoats and a pair of red dancing slippers. Not even a pair of drawers, a chemise or stays, I was scandalized to discover and— What was wrong with me? I had just watched a woman transform herself into a cat and I was shocked to realize she did not wear undergarments?

I gave my befuddled head a shake to clear it. As the last of the mist disappeared, Mercato bore down upon me and snatched the gown from my hands.

"Where is she? Where did she go?" he demanded.

"I-I don't know," I stammered because I truly did not. It

would sound completely mad to say Delphine had turned into a cat. Perhaps the strange mist had wreaked havoc with my mind.

"I just found her gown discarded there," I said. "As though she just vanished."

Mercato glowered at me as though he suspected I was lying. "No one can simply disappear, young woman. Not even the most powerful—"

"Sir!"

Mercato whipped around to glare at the burly sentry who had dared interrupt him. As the guard struggled to keep his aura beast under control, he blurted out, "Sir, the cat has picked up the trace of the witch's aura. I think she escaped out the gates."

"Get after her then," Mercato growled.

The aura cat snarled its agreement, so eager to take up the pursuit, it nearly yanked the guard's arm from his socket. Still the guard hung back, casting a dubious look at the gown clutched in Mercato's hands.

"How will we find her, sir, even with the aid of the aura beasts? Has she turned invisible?"

"No! Don't be a frapping idiot! No one can do that!"

I thought someone should have informed Mal of that before he wasted his time fashioning useless glass shoes.

The guard gulped. "Then the witch is running through the Heights... er... unclad?"

Mercato scowled at the discarded red gown. "It would seem so. The creature must be completely demented, but that is of no consequence. Track down her mad, bare arse and arrest her."

The sentry looked less than enthusiastic about hunting for a naked witch, but he had no choice but to obey. He summoned another aura cat handler and several more guards to accompany him. Newly arriving guests shoved each other to get out of the way as the search party raced out of the gates.

I experienced a moment of alarm for Delphine, but upon reflection, I figured that any woman who could produce a blinding mist and transform herself into a cat would have no trouble eluding a handful of sentries and a couple of aura beasts.

Backing away from Mercato, I went in search of my family. The drive leading to the castle was still in a state of chaos, ladies weeping or fanning themselves, gentlemen retrieving hats that had been lost in the panic, alarmed guards milling about. One young girl had fainted (although thankfully not in the presence of royalty) and was being revived by her anxious mama.

I spotted Imelda and Amy trying to soothe Netta who was sobbing. "This is all horrid and f-frightening, n-nothing like you said it would be, Mama. Where is Ella? I just w-want to go home."

As I hastened toward them, I was in complete agreement with Netta's sentiments. Stealing the orb struck me as a hopeless proposition. Mal would surely understand if I could not do it.

Perhaps Mal would, but what about Delphine?

Mal is counting on you, so don't fail him. Or else!

I shivered as I recalled Delphine's fierce threat, wondering exactly what she meant by that. I had this horrible vision of her turning me into a mouse and gleefully pursuing me in her guise as Ebony. I could almost feel the stab of her claws and her sharp teeth chomping down on my poor little tail.

Mal would not allow her to harm me, but I wondered if he had any idea of the full range of Delphine's abilities. Considering the number of times he had allowed Ebony to curl up on his lap, I suspected he had been unaware it was Delphine he was petting. I could not wait to see the expression on Mal's face when I told him.

By the time I reached Netta, she had stopped crying. She was being comforted by the fresh-faced young guard who had taken our tickets.

"I am so sorry, miss. I know that witch was terribly unsettling, but she is gone now, so there is nothing to be frightened of. Everything will be better once you have entered the palace, and the ball begins. Truly, you are going to have a wonderful time."

"T-thank you." Netta sniffed. Glancing up at the young guard, she froze. Perhaps it was merely the novelty of finding a man tall enough that she had to tip back her head to look at him or she was struck by the kindness in his eyes. The sentry appeared equally struck, staring at Netta with such a dazed look, I started to wonder if Mal's potion worked after all.

More likely it was because Netta was one of those rare females who did not come over all blotchy when she had been crying. If anything, she looked even prettier, her eyes luminous, moisture still clinging to the tips of her long lashes.

I have no idea how long the two of them might have remained drinking each other in, but the tender moment was disrupted by Mercato snarling at the sentry.

"Sergeant Wharton! Return to your post at once. Ladies! Be on your way to the palace."

The sergeant snapped to obey, and we all did likewise, although as we moved down the drive, Netta kept turning her head for another look back.

Imelda took Netta firmly in hand, propelling her forward. I am sure it did not figure in her plans for one of her daughters to become smitten with a handsome castle guard. As we mounted the stairs to the veranda, I could not resist murmuring to my stepmother, "Well, Em, you did promise that this would be a magical evening."

Imelda grimaced. "Witches and impertinent young sentries were not what I had in mind. I pray there are no more surprises in store for us."

I heartily agreed with her. As we approached the palace doors, it was a relief to find no more stony-faced guards or ferocious aura beasts blocking our way. Two bewigged footmen bowed and bid us welcome as they swept the doors open.

Even Netta beamed with delight as we entered the ballroom. It was just as Em had promised it would be, the glittering chandeliers, the garland draped marble pillars, and the scrape of violins as the royal musicians tuned their instruments.

The ballroom was so crowded, I did not know how we were going to move, let alone dance. I was doubly glad I had not worn those glass slippers because my toes were stepped upon more than once. My unusual gown did not attract the attention that I feared it would. I noticed many of the aristocratic ladies from the Heights were also wearing the costly river silk in varying hues. Unlike me, they were dripping with jewels, which detracted from the beauty of their gowns. The dresses I had sewn for Netta, Amy and Imelda were just as elegant if not more so because of their simplicity. I could not help noting with pride that my two sisters were among the loveliest girls present.

Here and there among the crowd, I spotted a few familiar faces from Midtown; the Misses Hanson, Fortescue Bafton and his sister. As I craned my neck, scanning the room, there was only one face I was looking for. Where was Commander Crushington?

I wished I could circulate about the chamber, but that was impossible since we had arrived just in time for the grand entrance of the king. A herald blasted a fanfare on his trumpet and the royal majordomo, clad in a plain grey uniform, stepped forward. He was a nondescript man of medium height, a little on the thin side, with a halo of white hair ringing his bald pate. Despite his mild appearance, his voice rang out high and clear as he announced, "His Supreme Highness King August Adolphus of the royal house of Helavalerian, supreme ruler of the great kingdom of Arcady."

Everyone sank into a deep obeisance as the king appeared. A hush fell over the crowd, the only sound, the tap of the king's cane as he hobbled forward. Everyone around me stood with lowered eyes, but I could not help staring.

I had seen the king once before when he made his annual speech in the town square, but this was my first opportunity to study up close the tyrant who had made our lives so difficult. His portly frame was attired in a scarlet uniform with enormous epaulettes on his plump shoulders. A golden sash cut across his barrel chest, the satin fabric bejeweled with badges of honor and medals the king had never done anything to earn.

King August was reputed to have been a very handsome man in his youth. I saw little sign of that in a countenance ravaged by years of overindulgence. He smiled graciously as he worked his way down the line of his subjects, but the genial expression looked forced and unnatural. Our king was so fearful of assassination; it surprised me that he was not flanked by guards.

Perhaps he felt safe enough within the palace walls, owing to Mercato's protective measures. The only one who trailed after the king was the majordomo, the quiet man appearing unobtrusive, but ready to leap forward at the king's slightest command. Here and there, King August paused to murmur a word of greeting, but these marks of attention were reserved exclusively for aristocrats or the wealthy citizens of the Heights. The king bestowed no such royal favor upon anyone from Midtown. Why would he? I thought cynically. He had already fleeced them out of their hard-earned money for the ball tickets.

As the king drew nearer to where my family stood, I heard Imelda hitch her breath. I glanced at my stepmother and saw her pale. I could only imagine what my poor Em must be feeling, being so near to the man who had condemned her first husband to death and obliged her and her daughters to leave the Heights in disgrace.

Perhaps Em feared that even after all these years, the king would still heap angry reproaches upon her for the late Albert Wendover's misdeeds. I tensed, ready to spring to Imelda's defense should the king utter so much as one cross word.

He limped past my stepmother without even a glance at Em. It was clear he did not recognize her. I should not have been surprised. The king had ruined so many innocent people over the years, he could hardly be troubled to remember them all.

I heard Em breathe easier as the king moved past her. I had to lower my gaze lest he see the resentment simmering in my eyes. I froze when His Majesty came to a halt in front of me. I could almost see my reflection as I stared down at his glossy shoes.

"And who is this lovely young woman?" the king demanded.

Was he referring to me? Was I expected to answer him? What could I say?

I am no one, Your Grace. Only the woman who is hoping to plunder your treasure room tonight.

This was not good. Out of all the people from Midtown, what had I done to merit the king's notice? Me, the one person who least desired such royal attention. Were my larcenous intentions in some way obvious? I ducked my head lower, wishing that those glass slippers had worked, so I could click my toes and disappear.

The majordomo stepped closer, gently prodding me. "Your name, miss? The king would like to know your name."

I suppressed my guilt and looked up, staring defiantly into the king's hard blue eyes.

"My name is Upton, Your Grace. Ella Upton."

The effect of this simple statement upon the king was astonishing. His mouth went slack, and it appeared as though he could not breathe. He stared at my face, devouring me with his eyes.

"Cecily," he mumbled at last. "You are Cecily Farringdale's daughter."

"Yes. You knew my mother?"

"She was my royal forest warder's daughter."

"I am aware of that, Your Grace. But you seem as if you knew and remember her well. How is that possible?"

Em emitted a horrified gasp, and she gave me a sharp nudge to remind me this was no way to address a king. I ignored her, intently studying the king's face.

I was stunned to see his cold eyes misty.

"When I was out hunting, I often stopped by the warder's house." King August sighed. "Your mother was the loveliest, most enchanting woman I have ever known."

The king seized my hand. "You look so very much like her."

Still clutching my hand, he appealed eagerly to his servant, "Is that not true, Majordomo? Is not this girl Cecily's very image?"

"Indeed, she is, sire." The majordomo agreed, but his gaze rested thoughtfully upon me as he added, "Except for her eyes. I do believe she has her father's eyes."

The king's head whipped back toward me. He stared hard into my eyes and the strangest look crossed his face. If it did not seem so ridiculous, I would have said it was one of fear. The king abruptly released my hand as though he had discovered he was grasping a snake. Without another word, he turned and limped away from me. The majordomo followed, giving me a nod and a smile. It was a strange smile, almost as if he was trying to convey a warning.

My mind teemed with questions, and I trembled with the urge to rush after the king and demand explanations.

Em must have sensed my impulse because she laid a restraining hand on my arm. "Let it go, Ella," she murmured.

"But, Em!" I whispered. "You heard the king. He spoke of my mother as though— as though he was once in love with her. Did you notice how strangely he acted when the majordomo mentioned my father? What was that all about?"

"I have no idea, but I learned a long time ago it is wiser and safer not to dwell on the past." She patted my arm. "Better that you keep your distance from the king and just try to have a good time tonight."

I knew Em was right, but I kept getting these tantalizing hints about my father's mysterious past. First, Withypole letting slip that my father had once been a passionate advocate of the downtrodden, even daring to defy the royal justice council. Then discovering that strange inscription in my father's book of fairy lore, signed by some unknown person whose initial was *S*. And now this odd behavior of the king. Always more questions and never any answers.

I seethed with frustration, but I was obliged to suppress it. Not long after the king's encounter with me, he appeared to grow weary of greeting his subjects. He retreated toward the end of the hall where his throne awaited him, the majordomo trotting after him like a faithful hound.

As the king eased himself down onto the velvet cushion, Mercato joined him upon the dais. The sleeve of the sorcerer's robe fell back as he rested one long elegant hand along the back of the throne. Any foolish hope I entertained about daring to approach the king was put to rest by his sinister magician hovering by his side.

Another trumpet sounded and the majordomo announced it was time for the presentation of the royal princes. The crowd surged forward to mill about the foot of an enormous staircase sweeping up to the balcony overlooking the ballroom. Ladies behaved with an unbecoming lack of decorum, shoving, and pushing in their efforts to get to the front. Somehow, I became separated from Em and my stepsisters, perhaps because I was distracted.

I spied an arch half hidden behind the banners hanging near the throne. It had to be the door that Mal had described to me, the one that would lead down to the restricted part of the palace and the king's treasure room. What Mal had failed to mention was that the archway would be guarded by two fierce soldiers.

How in the world had Mal ever thought I would be able to sneak past not only the king on his throne, but also the watchful eyes of his wizard and two burly Scutcheons armed with halberds? I knew exactly how. Those glass slippers. Mal had truly expected their magic to work.

Now I would have to rely on my own ingenuity to get past that arch, but I had not the slightest idea how. The prospect of success appeared utterly hopeless. I was roused from my despairing thoughts by the sound of the majordomo announcing, "His Royal Highness, the Prince Kendrick."

I dragged my attention from the door to the blond youth standing at the top of the stairs. He was clad in a white uniform with gold buttons and a sash cutting diagonally across his chest. The assembly bowed and curtsied as the prince descended the stairs. Kendrick beamed and acknowledged their greetings with nods to either side. I recollected that he was noted for being the charming one and I could only marvel at how he could maintain that constant smile.

Another blast of the herald's trumpet and the servant intoned, "His Royal Highness, the Prince Dashiel."

Clad in the same white uniform as Kendrick, another blond prince descended the stairs.

"And His Royal Highness, the Prince Dahl."

The next prince bounded down the stairs in an undignified manner. Dahl was almost an exact copy of his brother Dashiel except for one small detail. I was amused to note that Prince Dahl's fingernails appeared ragged. The boy was obviously a nail biter. The king leaned forward to growl at the young prince. Dahl hastily drew forth the gloves he had shoved inside his trouser pockets and put them on.

The crowd dutifully paid their respects to the twin princes, but I could sense the anticipation building, the impatience for the arrival of Prince Florian. I finally espied Commander Crushington near the foot of the stairs. I almost did not recognize him because he had shaved off his beard. Had he done that for me?

If he had, I heartily approved. I had never fully appreciated what a handsome man he was, the candlelight giving a blue-black sheen to his hair. With his upright military bearing, he appeared far more regal than any of these insipid blond boys.

Horatio also spotted me, and his face lit up. I confess my heart missed a beat and he seemed to draw me toward him with the sheer force of his gaze.

The trumpet sounded again, and His Royal Highness Prince Ryland was announced. I paid little heed as I wriggled my way through the crowd, heading toward the commander. I finally emerged into the clearing at the bottom of the staircase. Focused upon reaching Horatio, I blundered straight into the path of the oncoming prince.

I nearly lost my balance, but Prince Ryland's gloved hand caught my elbow to steady me. I could hear titters of laughter from the crowd, and I blushed with embarrassment. But the prince kindly inquired, "Are you all right, miss?"

His voice sent a strange shiver down my spine. My gaze traveled slowly up the prince's sash, the gilt buttons of his uniform until I reached his face.

The entire world stopped as I stared into the eyes of Harper, my long-lost bard.

Thirteen

I could not speak. I could not move. I was barely breathing as I stared at the faithless lover I had never expected to see again. I could feel the blood draining from my face. Harper appeared equally stricken, his countenance just as pale. I do not know how long Harper and I might have stood there, blocking the stairs. He was the first to recover, bowing stiffly and walking away. I still did not seem able to move, but Crushington was there, gently leading me out of the way.

"Ella, what is wrong? Are you all right?" Horatio bent down to murmur in my ear.

"No," I whispered. "You are going to have to arrest me."

"What!" He reared back, startled. "Why?"

"I think I may be about to faint."

Indeed, I did feel my knees start to wobble, but the commander slipped his arm about my waist, holding me upright. I did not know how Horatio managed it, but he got me through the crowd gathered by the stairs and found a chair. He eased me onto it, snapping out an order to a footman to fetch a glass of wine.

I sat there, feeling dazed. It was as though Delphine's strange mist had seeped into my head, fogging my brain, plunging me into a never- land where women could turn into cats and bards into princes.

Harper and Prince Ryland were one and the same. How was that even possible? Surely this would turn out to be some bizarre dream and I would awaken soon. The only thing that seemed solid and real was Horatio. He bent down, pressing a glass to my lips.

"Here," he ordered. "Drink this."

I obeyed, taking a few sips. I pushed the glass away, pulling a face at the potent, cheap wine. Little of the ball ticket money our king had raked in had been wasted on refreshments. Somehow that cynical thought helped me recover. Feeling more like myself, I was able to breathe again.

Horatio hunkered down in front of me, his grey eyes clouded with worry.

"Are you feeling any better?" he asked.

I managed to nod. "Yes, thank you. I just had a momentary attack of— of—"

Harper.

"The vapors," I said and winced. I had no idea what the vapors were. It was merely a complaint that I had heard used by other women.

Horatio arched one brow, eyeing me dubiously. I wondered how much of my strange reaction to Prince Ryland he had noticed. Very little escaped the commander's keen grey eyes, but he did not seek to question me for which I was grateful.

I studied Horatio's face, the clean strong line of his jaw. The absence of his beard made him look younger and somehow more vulnerable. I touched his smooth cheek.

"You shaved," I said.

"Er— yes," he replied, looking self-conscious.

"I like it."

His mouth tipped in his half-smile. When I started to rise, he protested, "Are you sure you are feeling well enough? You still look pale. Is there nothing else I can do?"

I shook my head. "I am fine. Just give me your hand."

Horatio straightened, his fingers closing over mine. I clung to him, his hand the only thing that felt strong and steady in a world that had been tilted off balance by the appearance of Harper.

As we rejoined the crowd around the stairs, I thought Em would be scandalized if she saw me holding hands with the commander. I was rather surprised that she had not come in search of me before now. Amidst all these voluminous gowns, feathered headdresses and broad shoulders, I could not even see where I had left my family.

Another fanfare sounded, a longer and more impressive one, and the majordomo announced, "His Royal Highness, heir to the kingdom of Arcady, the most noble Prince Florian."

The crowd erupted into applause, many of the young ladies forgetting their dignity enough to squeal with delight as Florian strode down the stairs, his blond mane of hair tied back with a golden ribbon. He looked handsome and impressive in a uniform like his brothers except for the epaulettes adorning his shoulders.

I spared him no more than a cursory glance. I craned my neck to see what had become of Prince Ryland. He stood near the throne, lined up with his other brothers who appeared rather sullen now that Florian had arrived to claim all the attention. Even Prince Kendrick, the endlessly cheerful one, looked dour. Only Ryland seemed unaffected. He stood to attention, staring rigidly at nothing.

Clutching Horatio's hand, I studied the man I had once known as Harper, thinking perhaps I was mistaken, that my long-lost bard only bore an uncanny resemblance to the prince. Harper's hair had been a shade lighter, his countenance far livelier than this stone-faced man.

But there was no denying it, no forgetting the face of the

young man who had haunted my dreams for the past seven years. Harper was Prince Ryland, even though he had behaved as though he had entirely forgotten me. Perhaps he had. It still seemed incredible to me that during all these years, Harper could have been dwelling mere miles from me and our paths had never crossed. But I recalled Amy saying that Ryland was known as the questing prince, often absent from the kingdom, hunting dragons.

I marveled that he could have carried out such a deception that long ago summer, passing himself off as a traveling minstrel. Granted I had been a starry-eyed little fool, but surely someone in Midtown must have recognized him... except that other than the king and Prince Florian, the rest of the royal family was never seen outside of the Heights.

Looking back on our days together, I only remembered one time that Harper had ever played his lute in the village square and that had been when we had first met. After that, he sang his songs for me alone. It had ever been he and I, lost in a magical world of our own making. Well, one of us had been lost, the other as calculating as any predator, a prince amusing himself with an idle dalliance.

I should have been furious with him, but all I felt was that familiar hollow ache, even deeper and more acute as I realized my lost love had never existed. All had been false, all illusion.

I became aware of Prince Florian moving among the guests, dismissing all the bowing, and curtsying with a wave of his hand. "No more of all this stiff protocol. Majordomo, command the royal musicians to strike up a lively tune." He smiled, holding his arms wide as he surveyed the crowd. "Now which of you lovely ladies shall I have the honor of leading into the first dance?"

Was the man completely mad? I expected at any moment to see the prince crushed beneath a herd of rampaging petticoats and wondered if the king would be compelled to enact a new law against stampeding royalty.

Most of the maidens present blushed and fluttered their fans to catch the prince's eye. Only a few were brazen enough to push forward, among them my own sister. Amy edged her way to the front of the pack, tripping up one competitor, subtly elbowing another in the stomach.

As she boldly presented herself to the prince, holding out her hand, I worried that Mal's potion had given my sister too much confidence. I held my breath, wondering how Prince Florian would react and feared that Amy might be publicly humiliated if he snubbed her. I was preparing to rush to her side when the prince grinned and with a gallant bow, accepted Amy's hand.

The crowd fell back as the prince led my little sister onto the dance floor. No matter how I felt about the heir to the throne, I could not help experiencing a rush of pride. I was beaming as I turned to Crushington.

When Horatio smiled back at me, the discovery of Harper's duplicity seemed of little importance. He offered me his arm. "Shall we, my lady?"

"Indeed, we shall," I said. I rested my hand through his arm, and we moved to take our place among the other couples forming sets. We had scarcely taken two steps when Prince Ryland blocked our path.

The prince accorded me a stiff bow. "Miss, will you grant me the honor of this dance?"

"Why, I— I—" I stammered. I thought I had recovered from the shock of seeing Harper but once again, I felt as though I had been punched, driving the breath from my body.

After our first encounter, I had supposed he would ignore me for the rest of the evening. His request to dance with me completely took me aback. I did not know how to respond. I expected Horatio to inform the prince that my hand had been claimed.

But the commander drew away from me. When I looked up at

him, he regarded me gravely and I realized Horatio was leaving the choice to me. As I glanced helplessly between the two men, Ryland decided the issue by taking my hand and leading me away.

I should have pulled away from him and returned to Horatio, but I allowed the prince to guide me onto the dance floor.

Fourteen

⮑◦⮐

My stepmother had promised me that attending the ball would be like a dream come true. It felt more like a nightmare in which a spell had been cast over my handsome, charming Harper transforming him into this stiff, unsmiling prince. As we moved through the opening steps of the dance, I stole glances up at him, trying to find some trace of the warm gentle lover I had once known.

There was none because I had not known the real Harper at all. He did not even exist. There was only Prince Ryland, a man who looked wearied of the world and everything in it, including me. The royal gallop was supposed to be a lively dance in which young men often lifted their partners and spun them about exuberantly.

Ryland behaved as a bored older courtier would do, resting one hand lightly upon my waist to guide me in a circle. It was as though he could not bear to touch me, even with those thick ornate gloves he wore. He went through the motions with me in complete silence, avoiding my gaze until I wondered why he had bothered asking me to dance at all.

I was so miserable I could hardly bear it, but somewhere in the ashes he had made of my heart, I could feel the embers of anger begin to burn. As we circled again, I said loudly, "What? What was that you said, Your Highness? I'm afraid I could not hear you above the music."

"I have not said anything," he replied, staring straight ahead.

"So I have noticed."

He winced at my tart rebuke. Although it appeared to cost him great effort, he asked, "Are you enjoying the ball?"

"No, I am sorry to say I am not. I have just realized I am not appropriately dressed."

My remark startled him into flicking an unwilling glance at me. "But you look quite— quite— beautiful," he concluded weakly.

"Thank you, Your Highness, but I wish someone had warned me this was to be a masquerade."

"But it is not."

"Truly?" I feigned astonishment as we clasped hands, stepped together and then back again. "But your costume is so perfect. A bard disguising himself as a prince. Or am I merely confused, thinking of something that happened long ago, a prince masquerading as a bard."

I had the satisfaction of seeing his rigid composure crack. "Ella..."

"Oh, so you do remember who I am."

"Of course, I do," he burst out. "How could you believe I would ever forget you?"

"Very easily, because that is exactly what you did."

"Never! I—" He stumbled, nearly treading on the hem of my gown. As he regained his footing in the dance, he struggled to regain command of himself as well. I thought he meant to lapse back into his morose silence, but after a moment, he said, "How have you been?"

Seriously? He had the gall to ask me that? I glared at him, torn between the urge to blister him with reproaches and the equally strong desire to appear icily indifferent.

"Wonderful," I said, baring my teeth in a smile. "Just wonderful."

"Good." He ventured a tentative smile in return. "You appear in excellent health."

"Oh, I am. Well enough except—"

"Except for what?"

"I don't seem to have ever recovered from the chill I took the night I spent on a hillside. All alone in the dark, waiting and waiting for someone who never came, who never sent one word of apology or explanation, who made me believe he loved me and then just abandoned me."

So much for icy indifference. I checked myself before my voice rose loud enough to attract the attention of the other dancers. I became aware that Harper and I— I mean, the prince and I were already drawing some curious looks.

Ryland only made matters worse when he came to an abrupt halt, clasping my hand. "Ella, I never wanted to hurt you. I could never make you understand how sorry I am."

"You never even tried! You couldn't even be bothered to send me a note. You just disappeared. You could have been dead for all I knew. Then I started hearing these rumors about a minstrel traveling through other kingdoms seducing young maidens with his beautiful voice."

"That was not me, Ella."

"Oh no, of course it wasn't. I forgot. You are Ryland, the brave questing prince. You have spent the last seven years slaying dragons." I sneered. "Dragons! What a load of frap! The only thing you have been assailing are the hearts of other gullible, trusting fools like me."

"That is not true. There has never been anyone but you. I have not even touched my lute since I last saw you. When I had to leave you, all the music died."

I gave an outraged gasp. How dare he claim that? How dare this perfidious prince stand there looking at me with Harper's eyes, all sad and sincere?

I wrenched away from him. In another moment, I was either going to burst into tears or punch him. Considering it was now a crime to faint in front of a prince, I could not imagine how severe the punishment would be for giving one a bloody nose.

Ignoring the startled looks of the other dancers, I fought my way across the floor, treading on toes and blundering into people. I realized I was drawing the exact kind of attention I had wanted to avoid, not good for someone who later hoped to slip away unnoticed to plunder the king's treasury. I didn't care. I rushed onward, seeking any avenue of escape.

I found it in a set of imposing glass-paned double doors that led out onto a small balcony. I hurled myself through them, grateful to find the refuge deserted. I pulled the door firmly closed behind me, shutting out the noisy hum of voices and music emanating from the ballroom. Annoyed to discover that I was trembling, I rested my hands on the stone balustrade. I drew in deep breaths of the warm night air, seeking to calm myself.

The balcony overlooked the rear gardens of the palace, and I would have found the lush floral arrangements and the burbling fountains soothing to my turbulent emotions. But several of the palace guards prowled the moonlit paths with those eerie aura beasts straining at their leashes.

I wondered if they were still searching for Delphine and hoped that she was far away from here by now, more for my sake than hers. I dreaded the thought that she might yet find a way inside the castle and appear at my side to hiss more threats.

When someone crept up behind me to rest a hand on my shoulder, I nearly leapt over the balustrade. My heart hammering, I whirled around, only to discover that Ryland had been foolish enough to follow me.

"Ella are you all right?" he asked me in that tender tone I remembered all too well.

Was I all right? I wanted to shriek. Did this man have no sense of self-preservation? Obviously, he did not if he had spent the last seven years hunting dragons.

"Go away." I shrugged his hand off my shoulder.

He regarded me mournfully. "I can't do that."

"Why not? You managed perfectly well seven years ago."

"And you will never know how much I regretted that, how strong I had to be to abandon you. It was like cutting out my own heart. I— oh, Ella!" He gave an agonized groan.

Before I could prevent him, he wrapped his arm around my waist and kissed me. I went rigid with shock, but his embrace stirred far too many bittersweet memories and longings in me. Harper's kisses had always been wonderful, as warm and tender as the ballads he composed. I could not help it. I threaded my fingers through his hair, melting into his embrace until a familiar deep voice brought me back to my senses.

"Ella?"

I broke off the kiss, horrified to realize that Horatio had come in search of me. I thrust Prince Ryland away from me, but it was already too late. Horatio froze in the open doorway, a myriad of emotions playing across his face, shock, hurt, disappointment. My cheeks flamed and I foolishly pressed my hand to my mouth as though I could somehow hide that kiss. Ryland looked equally embarrassed and disconcerted.

Horatio recovered, masking his emotions beneath his usual grave expression. "Miss Upton, forgive me. I saw you rush from the ballroom, and I thought that you were... that you might need... and well, obviously I was wrong.

"I do beg your pardon for the intrusion. Miss Upton. Your Highness." He snapped off a rigid bow to each of us. Before I could get a word out, Horatio pivoted on his heel and was gone.

I took a step forward, my first impulse to rush after him and explain, but I had no idea what I would say. How could I make Horatio comprehend the madness that had just come over me when I did not understand it myself? I cringed when I imagined what Horatio must be thinking of me— that after declaring I had no interest in becoming a royal bride, I was fickle and shallow, as ready to chase after a prince as any of those other silly girls in the village.

There was a time when I would not have cared what Commander Crushington thought of me. Now I was stunned to realize how much his good opinion mattered. It mattered very much indeed.

I rounded on Prince Ryland. "You stupid, frapping idiot!" I growled although I was not sure who I was more furious with, the prince or myself.

Ryland winced. "I know. I am sorry, Ella. But that man— he is the commander of Midtown garrison?"

"Yes, Commander Horatio Crushington."

"And he is a particular friend of yours?" Ryland asked hesitantly.

"That is no concern of yours."

"No, of course not. But is he a man of discretion? Will he be likely to relate to others what he saw?"

I shot Ryland a look of utter disgust. "Horatio Crushington is a man of complete integrity, nobility and gallantry, traits you could not begin to understand. So, the answer is no. He would never stoop to spreading idle gossip." I added with scorn, "Your reputation is quite safe, Your Royal Highness."

Ryland flushed. "I am more worried about yours, Ella. I always swore that if I ever saw you again, I could contain myself. What a foolish delusion that was. One look into your eyes, one whisper of your voice and—" He raked his hand back through his hair and groaned. "Oh, why did you have to come here tonight?"

"You could have just ignored me. Why did you have to ask me to dance?"

"Why did you accept?"

"What choice did I have? How does one refuse a request from a prince?"

"The Ella I knew would have had no trouble doing so."

"The Ella you knew is dead!"

We were both becoming more agitated, fairly shouting at each other until we ran the danger of our voices carrying back to the ballroom. I turned away from him. Bracing my hands on the balustrade, I continued in a constrained tone, "That Ella perished long ago on a dark windy hillside waiting for a lover who never came. Do you have any idea what that night's folly cost me? When my father discovered the note I had left, saying I had run off with you, he fell into a fit, paralyzed from the shock. He never recovered. A week later he was dead."

My throat constricted. "I killed my own father and for what? My infatuation with a worthless wretch like you."

Ryland joined me at the balustrade. He started to place his gloved hand over mine, but wisely thought better of it. "I heard about what happened to your father. I was so sorry."

"And you still did not have the decency to send me one word of apology or explanation!"

"I convinced myself it was better for you if I did not, far better that you just forget me and learn to hate me. But I am such a weak man. Now that I see how much you despise me, I find it unbearable."

"You flatter yourself. One must care enough to hate, and I do not. I might think you are a miserable sniveling, lying little slug worm, but I certainly don't hate you."

My words provoked a reluctant sad smile from him. "Perhaps I was wrong. I should have tried to explain my callous behavior. If I may—"

"You may not. You are years too late, and I don't want to hear it." I locked my arms across my bosom and stared haughtily into the distance. I ruined the entire effect by adding, "What excuse could you possibly have to offer?"

"To begin with, you must understand that I never meant to hurt you."

"Thank the fairies for that," I said. "I cannot imagine how devastated I would have been if you had actually intended me harm."

"That summer I met you, all I was seeking was a brief escape from this castle. I have no words to tell you how miserable my existence here had become."

"Oh, poor little prince! Forced to live in a palace with all the luxuries you could desire while so many people in this kingdom are grateful for a crust of stale bread and to be spared being driven into exile merely for the crime of being poor."

He flinched but continued, "I believe you are wise enough to understand, Ella, that there are many kinds of prisons and no matter how luxurious, a cage is still a cage. From the time I was a small child, music has been the great passion and consolation of my life, especially after my mother died. My only happiness came during those hours I practiced my lute and even dared to compose my own songs.

"But my love of music was scorned by my father and my brothers, especially Florian. Lute playing is not deemed manly enough for a prince of the royal house of Helavalerian. I was ordered to forget my music and spend more time practicing with my sword and lance. I had to hide my lute to prevent it from being destroyed. Florian would have been too happy to do so. He mocked my musical abilities, said it was a good thing that I was not obliged to make my living as a minstrel. I would either starve or be stoned to death for inflicting such an assault upon people's ears."

Ryland sighed. "I knew I could not defy my father forever and Florian had shaken my confidence in my music. When I disguised myself as Harper and stole into town that day, all I was seeking was an audience. I needed to know if Florian was right or if I did possess the ability to share the magic of all those notes that played in my head, if somehow, I could touch other hearts, even just a little with what beat so strong in mine."

"You could. You touched mine," I admitted before I could

stop myself. I amended, "That is— you were very good. I enjoyed your performance. So did everyone else in the village square that day."

"I didn't care about everyone else. From the moment I looked across that square and your eyes met mine, I played for you alone. I wanted to spend the rest of my days singing only for you."

"Stop! Just stop!" I flung up one hand to fend off these protestations that I found both false and painful.

Ryland ignored me and rushed on, "I loved you so much, Ella, enough to cherish this romantic dream that we could just run away and share a life together. But word carried back to my father about me sneaking out of the palace to woo some Midtown girl. I was warned in no uncertain terms to stay away from you, that there would be dire consequences if the king ever discovered your identity. My father would never tolerate one of his sons marrying a commoner—"

"Wait," I interrupted. "Do you mean the same father who is giving this lavish ball so that his son and heir to the kingdom might select a bride from among any of his subjects?"

Ryland bent closer to me, speaking in low and urgent tones. "You are surely far too clever to believe that nonsense, Ella. You must see this ball for the sham that it is. My father would never permit his beloved heir to marry anyone less than a wealthy princess or aristocrat and may the fairies help whatever poor woman ends up with my brother as her bridegroom. There is so much that you do not know about Florian, Ella. He—"

"Ah, brother, there you are." The silky voice cut Ryland off in mid-sentence. We sprang apart as we were joined by the very man he warned me against.

Ryland paled although there was nothing alarming in Prince Florian's aspect. I could not tell how much he might have overheard what Ryland had been saying, but Florian's smile was affable, almost tender as he regarded his younger brother.

"Father wondered where you had gone and sent me to find you and check if you were all right."

"You have done so, and you can see I am fine," Ryland said. "You can go report back to Father and leave me alone."

"My dear brother—"

"I am not your dear brother," Ryland growled.

Florian heaved a pained sigh. "Father and I both hoped you would endeavor to enjoy yourself this evening and not hide away as you usually do. You need to mingle with our guests, and no matter how bewitching this young lady is"— Florian directed a smile toward me— "you should not be keeping her out here on this drafty balcony when I am sure she would rather be dancing."

Prince Florian accorded me a graceful bow. "My lady, would you honor me with the next—"

"No!"

The vehemence of Ryland's outburst startled both Florian and me.

"My dear brother, you must allow the young lady to speak for herself—" Florian began but he was cut off by Ryland's snarl.

"I already told you no. You just stay away from her. Do you hear me?"

Florian shook his head, giving his brother a patronizing smile. "Tsk, tsk. This display of jealousy is most unbecoming, Ry. I only want one dance with the lady. I am not intending to steal her away forever. Unless the lady wishes it?"

Florian held out his hand to me, raising one eyebrow in a teasing fashion.

Before I could react, Ryland charged his brother. I had never known the man I had thought of as Harper to behave in a jealous or possessive fashion. He had never been anything but kind and gentle. I watched, stunned, as Ryland tried to hurl Florian away from me.

Florian was a full head taller and stronger. I suspected he could have easily knocked Ryland down. Instead, he sought to restrain

Ryland by seizing his wrists. Somehow in the scuffle, one of Ryland's embroidered gauntlets came off.

Not just his glove, but his entire right hand!

I gasped at the sight of the gauntlet that Florian still clutched. A carved wooden hand protruded from the end of the velvet cuff, the leather straps that had attached the device to Ryland's arm now dangling free. I caught a glimpse of an ugly stump before Ryland shook down the sleeve of his frock coat to conceal it.

Ryland turned to me with stricken eyes. My face has always been too transparent. I could not conceal the horror I felt. Ryland emitted a choked cry. He snatched his false hand away from his brother, shoved his way past Florian and fled.

The merry lilt of the music, the sound of happy voices drifted from the ballroom, made a mockery of the dreadful revelation I had just witnessed. Now I understood the reason for Ryland's awkwardness during our dance, why he had not lifted me off my feet.

I sagged back against the balustrade, numb with shock. Florian approached me with an apologetic look on his face. "I am so sorry you had to see that, my lady. My brother is very sensitive about his injury. It hurts and mortifies him deeply to have it revealed to anyone. I could kick myself for my clumsiness. I never intended to expose him so cruelly."

"But... but his hand," I faltered. "What happened to him?"

"Alas, he lost his right hand during one of his dragon-hunting quests. My brother is a gentle soul. I never understood his need to prove himself in such a reckless fashion. He should never have attempted to challenge a dragon. He is no warrior."

No, the man I had known as Harper was not. His folly infuriated me, chasing after dragons when he should have found the courage to stand by me if he loved me as much as he claimed. I tried to harden my heart against his dreadful injury. So, what if he had lost his hand! It served him right. But when I recalled the sweet music, he had made, the magic in his fingers as he strummed his lute, I wanted to weep.

My eyes filled with tears, and I had to blink hard to contain them. I started when Prince Florian touched my cheek. I had not even noticed how close he had drawn to me. Even though he was regarding me with an expression of great concern, I felt strangely uncomfortable. I inched away from him, but he caught my hand.

"My lady, I can see how distressing all of this has been for you. Please allow me to make amends by escorting you back to the ballroom and leading you into the next dance."

Easing my hand away, I shook my head. "I thank you for the honor, Your Highness, but I am still a bit overcome. I do not feel equal to any more dancing."

"I perfectly understand, but I beg you to make the effort." A slight frown creased his brow. "I do not know what passed between you and my brother. Ryland has many excellent traits, but he can be rather impetuous and thoughtless at times. When you fled from him and he followed you to the balcony, I am afraid that caused a bit of a stir. I should hate for any of his careless actions to subject a lovely lady such as yourself to any unpleasant speculation or scandal. As his eldest brother, I feel it my duty to prevent that."

"And you think that my dancing with you will fix everything?" I asked.

"I believe it will. I know that must sound ridiculously arrogant, but because I am the heir to the throne, many people set a foolish value upon my opinion, whether I merit it or not. My dancing with you will display to everyone that you are a lady worthy of respect and admiration and no will dare speak a word against you."

I could not fault his logic, especially when he expressed himself in such a self-deprecating manner. I did not care what anyone here tonight might think of me. But any negative gossip about me might reflect badly on my entire family, spoiling Amy's and Netta's chances as well.

"I would be pleased to dance with Your Highness." I said reluctantly.

He gave me a warm smile. Tucking my hand in the crook of his arm, he escorted me back to the ballroom.

The assembled company drew back respectfully as Florian led me to the center of the dance floor, but I was already regretting this decision. I might have done better to try to sneak back into the ballroom unnoticed. I was keenly aware of the curious looks cast in my direction; the whispers exchanged behind fans.

Although my face burned bright red, I forced myself to hold my head up high. I scanned the sea of faces, looking for Horatio, wishing that he would step forward to claim the dance that should have already been his. If he was lost somewhere in that crowd, watching me, he must think that I had run completely prince-mad, kissing one royal brother, and now pursuing the heir himself.

My heart sank even further when the orchestra struck up the strains of a waltz. It was such an intimate dance. My heart gave a nervous skitter as Prince Florian drew me closer. Ryland had been on the verge of warning me about his brother. I wondered what he had intended to say, and yet could I ever again believe anything he might tell me?

Florian seemed to be the epitome of everything a prince should be, handsome, tall, and broad shouldered. I always thought his long mane of hair a little ridiculous on a man, but I had to admit the golden sheen of his hair was rather pleasing when bound neatly back in a queue. With his hair drawn away from his face, it made his chiseled features appear more striking.

He twirled me about the floor, one strong hand resting lightly upon my waist, the other firmly clasping mine. I was keenly aware of the envious stares directed at me by the other ladies who ignored their own partners as they ogled the prince. Those women would believe me mad if they knew what I was thinking: that I would rather be at home digging slug worms out of my garden.

Florian smiled down at me, his blue eyes inviting me to melt in his arms, but in some odd way, that only made me tense. I stumbled along awkwardly, trying to keep pace with Florian's graceful steps. I was doubly glad that I had not worn those ridiculous glass slippers Mal had given me. It was bad enough that I kept stepping on the prince's toes with my soft, well-worn shoes. When I tried to apologize, Florian would have none of it.

"Nonsense. You are as graceful as you are beautiful."

I pulled a wry face before I could stop myself. Unfortunately, the prince noticed.

"Ah," he said, "you are one of those rare ladies who does not care for compliments."

"I like them well enough when they are sincere." I winced as the words fell out of my mouth. Mind your tongue, Ella, I could almost hear my stepmother admonishing me.

I hastened to add, "Your Highness is very gallant, but I know I am not a graceful dancer."

"But you surely cannot deny that you are beautiful."

"I would rather be thought intelligent or brave, Your Highness. Beauty is far too fleeting, and I have nothing but contempt for those vain creatures that spend hours admiring their reflection in the mirror."

"Such as you have been told that I am wont to do?"

"Yes— I mean no, Your Highness!"

It is impossible to mind one's tongue and one's dance steps at the same time. I was not succeeding well with either.

"I have never heard anything but praise of Your Highness," I lied.

Florian chuckled. "Oh, come now. I wager that Ryland has told you many less than flattering things about me. He is fond of regaling anyone who will listen with tales about how vain and arrogant I am. I am sorry to say it, but my younger brother has always been jealous of me. Unfortunately, you saw that for yourself. Look at the unreasonable way he flew at me just because I asked to dance with you. The poor boy has never been the same since his tragic encounter with the dragon." Florian gave a heavy sigh. "I will admit Ryland may be right. I can be rather vain. I like to admire myself in the surface of a pond as I trot past. A hazardous occupation, I know. I might well fall out of the saddle, but my horse always slows down, because he likes to admire his reflection too. He is rather vain as well."

Florian spoke solemnly enough, but when I glanced up at him, there was a teasing twinkle in his eye that coaxed a smile from me.

"Now there! I like that so much better than your serious face. Your smile is enchanting, but I suppose I should not compliment you on that either."

"Unfortunately, Your Highness has already done so," I pointed out. I added quickly, "Thank you. Your Highness is very kind."

"I would find you much kinder if you would relax and stop saying Your Highness."

I silently congratulated myself as I made it through the next twirl without tripping. "I can hardly call you Florian. That would be most improper and—" I stopped just short of adding that the king had probably enacted some sort of petty law against it.

The prince smiled. "I cannot blame you for not wanting to use my name. I have never liked it myself."

"I positively loathe mine, but happily my family has always called me Ella."

"Bella. Yes, I like that. It suits you."

I realized that because of the noise in the ballroom, the prince had misheard me, but I did not trouble to correct him.

"Alas, my family has a nickname for me as well. My younger brothers are fond of calling me Florrie."

"And you allow them to do that without cracking their heads?"

The prince looked startled and then he flung back his head and laughed. "I can see you possess a bit of a violent streak, Bella. I like that in a girl," he murmured, drawing me a little closer.

Although I smiled, I experienced a twinge of unease. Florian was more amusing and charming than I had ever expected him to be. Too charming perhaps? There were moments when I caught a look of calculation in his eyes, as though he was assessing his impact on me.

I try to be fair when judging anyone. I was aware that much of my bad opinion of Florian originated from stories Ryland had told me in his guise as Harper. I no longer trusted Ryland. But I didn't really trust Florian either. I strongly suspected that all these Helavalerian princes were well versed in the arts of charming deceit.

When the last strains of the waltz sounded, I suppressed a sigh of relief as I peeled myself from Florian's embrace. He seemed reluctant to release me.

"I can see why my brother wanted to keep you all to himself," Florian said. "But I must not be as selfish as Ryland. Alas, as the heir to throne, I am far too burdened by my sense of duty. I cannot neglect my other guests no matter how badly I yearn to remain at your side." The prince bowed and raised my hand, looking intently into my eyes as he kissed my fingertips.

Any other girl in my position would have been thrilled by the gesture. I could only wonder how many times Florian had practiced it.

"Until we meet again, my lovely Bella," he murmured.

Yes, when fairyland freezes over, I thought. I gave him a noncommittal smile, managing not to roll my eyes until after he had gone.

I wriggled my toes inside my slippers and winced. My comfortable dancing shoes had grown perhaps a little too well worn. They were more stretched and looser than I remembered. The left one was starting to rub a blister on my heel. I could have happily spent the rest of the ball not dancing with anyone unless it was Commander Crushington.

But the prince had hardly left my side when I was besieged by at least a dozen men clamoring to lead me into the next dance.

Unfortunately, not one of them was the man I longed to see. Where was Horatio? He had intimated to me that his main reason for attending the ball was because I would be there. Had I disappointed him so much that he had left? That might be for the best. I had worried about my ability to slip away and steal the orb under his watchful gaze.

If he was gone, that might make my daunting task somewhat easier. But the thought that he might have given up on me and gone home caused my heart to sink. I gritted my teeth in a polite smile as I tried to fend off this pack of eager gentlemen. What I really wanted to do was seize one of the ornamental swords from the wall and drive them back.

Prince Florian had not exaggerated the effect his dancing with me would have. He might as well have taken the royal seal and stamped "approved" on my forehead. When I caught a glimpse of Amy, I saw that her dance with the prince had had a similar effect. The difference was that my sister was enjoying her surge of popularity.

I was dismayed to note that Amy appeared flushed with her success and far too animated. She swilled a glass of wine as if it was water, then flirted excessively, fluttering her fan at her court of admirers. Or rather I should say my fan. Amy had clearly been in my room, borrowing things without my permission again. I was far more concerned about her present behavior. She had removed the lace from her bodice, exposing an alarming amount of décolletage much to the delight of the twin princes, who were admiring the view.

The young princes crowded close to Amy. Dahl— or was it Dashiel— stealing his arm about her waist while the other twin whispered something into my sister's ear that caused her to giggle loudly.

Where was Em? She usually chaperoned her daughters with great care. Why was my stepmother not doing something to curb

Amy's impetuous behavior? I looked around, but I could not find Imelda anywhere.

Escaping from my own pack of admirers, I headed in Amy's direction. But I was too late. By the time I reached her, one of the twins had escorted her into the set forming for the next dance. I could hardly snatch my sister from the prince and drag her aside for a stern lecture without causing a scene.

I was so frustrated and distracted that I accepted an offer to dance without thinking. The man who claimed my hand was yet another of the royal brothers, the persistently cheerful Prince Kendrick. As he led me to find a place in one of the sets, I finally spotted Horatio. He had not gone home after all.

My spirits lifted only to plummet when I realized he was leading a girl forward to dance. I could not blame him for that. After I had proved to be so unreliable, he had every right to dance with someone else. I still would have been jealous except for the partner Horatio had chosen.

I thought I recognized her. The girl was from Midtown, one of the butcher's daughters, I believed. Her mustard-colored gown was truly hideous and only accented the flaws of her plump, pear-shaped figure. Carrot-red hair framed a youthful face suffering from an attack of blotchy red spots.

I had little doubt that this poor girl would have spent the entire ball huddled in a chair in the corner, wistfully watching everyone else dance and feeling miserable. Certainly not one of these so-called charming princes would have ever bothered to ask for her hand.

I knew Horatio well enough to guess how carefully he would have framed his invitation. He would not have made her feel as though he was merely being kind or pitied her. No, he would have been solemnly gallant, convincing her that she was favoring him.

Small wonder that shy girl was gazing up at Horatio so adoringly. I tried to steer Prince Kendrick toward the same set. If I could not dance with Horatio myself, as we circled through the movements and changed partners, I might at least be able to touch his hand. Maybe I could even find a moment to whisper how sorry I was, try to explain away that foolish kiss.

But Horatio's set already had eight couples. The other sets were filling rapidly as well. Prince Kendrick and I did not find an opening until we were completely on the opposite side of the ballroom.

The prince and I faced each other as the orchestra struck up the music. He bowed and I curtsied. The promenade was a slow and formal dance. It consisted of a lot of stepping forward, stepping back, holding hands, circling, switching partners with the couple next to you, more circling, returning to your own partner, repeating the same steps all over again as you moved farther down the line. A simple dance, it did not require much by way of concentration, but it was interminably long, lasting nearly twenty minutes.

Although Prince Kendrick seemed to be an amiable young man, he was not a scintillating conversationalist, most of his remarks either dealing with the fine spring weather or how splendid the ball was. He continued to beam at me throughout the dance. When someone smiles at you that much, you feel peculiarly obliged to smile back. We were not even halfway through the dance before my face muscles began to ache and I could feel the blister on my left heel getting worse.

I could not run away from another prince, but I was seriously considering faking a sprained ankle when it occurred to me that I might be wasting an opportunity to learn more about the royal family. Kendrick was far too young to know anything about the king and his dealings with my parents, but he could provide me with a different perspective regarding his brothers.

The next time the movement of the dance drew us closer, I said, "I had the honor of dancing the waltz with your oldest brother."

"Oh yes, Florian. He's a very good dancer." Kendrick grinned. "All the girls are quite mad for him."

I sashayed forward and back. "And I had the privilege of dancing with your brother Ryland as well."

"Oh yes, indeed! Good old Ry. He is a very fine fellow."

As we joined hands and circled, I leaned closer and said in lowered voice, "I was so shocked to learn about his injury."

"Injury?" Kendrick started but managed to keep his smile fixed in place. "What injury?"

"His missing hand?"

"Oh, that." Kendrick's smile finally dimmed. "I am surprised Ry told you about that. He does not like anyone outside the family to know of it."

"I discovered it by accident, but I assure you the prince's secret is safe with me. I was just so saddened to learn of his loss."

"Yes, yes, indeed. Terrible beasts, dragons. It was all so very sad." Kendrick gulped, but then rallied, recovering his beaming smile. "But that was a long time ago. Ry has completely recovered. He's fine now."

We were separated again as we switched partners. As I went through the motions with a bored-looking baronet, I gave up the idea of getting more information from Kendrick. There was no breaking through his barrier of impenetrable cheerfulness.

When the dance brought us back together, I was therefore astonished to see his face completely clouded over. Tears welled in his eyes as he confessed to me, "My brother is not fine. Ry will never be fine again. Losing his hand devastated him. Y-you see, he loved music. He used to p-play the lute so b-b-beautifully."

To my horror, two fat droplets escaped and rolled down the prince's cheeks. He moaned, "Oh, this is far too painful. I cannot talk about this."

"No, no, of course not," I said hastily, aware that we were drawing odd looks from the other couples in our set. "Please.

Please don't cry. We will change the subject and speak of something less mournful."

He gave a heroic nod, but once he started to cry, Prince Kendrick seemed unable to stop. I made soothing noises, tried to jest with him, but to no avail. Although he attempted to smile, his tears continued to flow. As usual, I had forgotten to bring a handkerchief and he did not have one either. A few of the other dancers cast accusing glares at me, but most of them just averted their gaze in embarrassment, trying to ignore the weeping prince. That was all but impossible as we danced down the line. Kendrick sniffed loudly to keep snot from dripping onto the collar of his uniform. He still managed to curve his lips upward. It disconcerted me; this ability to smile and cry at the same time. Besides a penchant for deception, I wondered if there was also a strain of madness in the Helavalerian family.

When the dance finally ended, Kendrick wiped his nose on the back of his glove. His eyes were raw and red, but he appeared to have finally regained control of himself as he bowed over my hand.

"Thank you for the dance, miss. It has been a great p-pleasure." His voice broke with a sob, and he started crying all over again. He was still weeping as he staggered away from me. I became aware of the other dancers giving me a wide berth as though I had contracted the plague. The staring, the pointing and the whispers started up all over again.

So much for my reputation. By this time tomorrow, I would be known throughout the kingdom as the woman who had run away from one prince and reduced another one to tears.

I consoled myself with the thought that at least I would not be pestered by more offers to dance, but I soon discovered I was mistaken. Perhaps for some men, infamy only adds to a woman's allure. I was still pursued by a few intrepid souls. Two noblemen, Lord Ludlow and Sir Eustace, were especially persistent.

I finally discouraged them by declaring loudly that I had twisted my ankle and needed to rest. Because of my sore heel, I was able to produce a very creditable limp. My two admirers withdrew and left me in peace, or at least as much peace as I was likely to find at this infernal ball.

I did a quick scan of the room and was dismayed to discover that I had once more lost sight of Horatio. More alarming still, Amy had also disappeared, and it occurred to me that I had not seen Netta or my stepmother since the presentation of the princes. Adding to these worries was the fact that I was no nearer to figuring out a way to get past those guards to steal the orb.

This night was becoming a total disaster. I should have followed my first instincts about this ball and remained at home, blissfully tucked up with a good book. I needed a moment to collect myself. When I spied an alcove just beyond one of the pillars, I limped in that direction.

Unfortunately, the nook was occupied. My jaw dropped open at the sight of Imelda ensconced on a settee with a grey-haired gentleman sporting mutton chop whiskers. Neither of them noticed me because this scarecrow of a man was gazing fondly at Em and holding her hands.

I froze, uncertain whether to retreat or march forward and demand that this stranger release my stepmother at once. Before I could decide, Imelda caught sight of me and snatched her hands away. She did not appear in the least abashed as she sprang to her feet and called out to me. "Oh, Ella, do come here. I wish to introduce you to an acquaintance of mine, Lord Charles Redmond."

The gentleman rose in more leisurely fashion, bending down to whisper loudly to Em, "Only an acquaintance, my dear?"

Em blushed and groped for her fan. "Chuffy, this is my darling stepdaughter, Ella."

Chuffy?

I cast Em an astonished look. She avoided my eyes as I stepped closer.

His Lordship was a tall, gangly man, clad in the sort of ornate gilt-trimmed frock coat still favored by the older generation. The stiff satin fabric crackled as he sketched a courtly bow.

"Charmed, my dear, charmed."

I curtsied. "Your Lordship."

"Oh, no need for such formality, my dear. You must call me Chuffy as your stepmother does."

"Then you have known Em for a long time?"

"Oh, my yes." Imelda cooed, fluttering her fan. "Chuffy was one of my friends back when I was a mere slip of a girl. Such a long, long time ago."

"Not that long ago," His Lordship insisted. "And I was far more than a friend. I was Imelda's most ardent suitor. It devastated me when she married that other chap. Just devastated."

"Oh, pooh." Imelda simpered.

Chuffy clapped one hand dramatically to his chest. "This enchanting lady stole my heart away and she never gave it back to me."

"Old fool." Imelda rapped him with her fan, but she appeared quite pleased with his flattery.

I was delighted that Em was enjoying herself with this old beau of hers. I wished I could leave her to her flirtation. It had certainly never been my way to bear tales about my sisters. I usually tried to handle everything myself, but after all the revelations and disconcerting turns this night had taken, I was feeling tired and overwhelmed.

I tried to keep the anxiety out of my voice as I said, "Em, I have been looking for you everywhere. I have not seen Netta since the ball began and now Amy has disappeared."

"Oh, it is difficult to find anyone in this crowd." Em dismissed my worries with an airy wave of her hand. "I am sure your sisters are off dancing somewhere."

"But you need to speak to Amy. She has been behaving a bit too exuberantly."

"Why shouldn't she? She was the first one Prince Florian chose for a dance partner." Em smiled at me. "And you have not been doing so badly either. I saw you led away by Prince Ryland. I was so proud of you both."

"But not at all surprised," Chuffy put in. "Such pretty girls. Those Helavalerian men are no fools. They've always had an eye for beauty. That's why I've been trying to keep your stepmother tucked away here. Now that I have found her again, I don't want one of those rapscallion princes snatching her away from me."

"Oh, you silly man." Imelda gave a girlish giggle.

I stared at her in dismay. Granted Imelda has never been what one could call a sensible woman, but tonight she was acting as if she was a bit pixified. Uneasily, I recalled Imelda and the girls sharing the contents of that flask in the carriage and I wondered exactly what Mal had brewed into his elixir besides rose hips. If I survived this wretched ball, I intended to have a sharp word with him about that.

I made another attempt to bring up Amy's impulsive behavior, but Em interrupted. "Stop worrying so much, Ella. Your sister is merely enjoying herself which is what you should be doing."

"Indeed, you should, my dear," Chuffy said. "If I am not mistaken, I see an eager young chap heading this way, no doubt in hopes of dancing with you."

I groaned. "It better not be another frapping prince."

"Ella!" my stepmother squealed, and His Lordship's eyes popped.

I turned around, wishing with all my heart that it might be Horatio, finally coming to claim his dance. My hopes were dashed when I saw Fortescue Bafton sauntering toward me.

The tailor's son swept me a deep bow, trying to put some swagger into it. "Miss Ella Upton, may I have the great honor of leading you into the next dance?"

"No, you may not."

His swagger vanished in an instant. He looked so deflated that I hastened to add, "I am sorry. I am finished with dancing this evening, but I am sure there are many other ladies here eager to stand up with you."

"No, there are not. No one wants to dance with me."

He looked almost ready to cry. I sighed, unable to handle the prospect of reducing another man to tears.

"Oh, very well," I said. Realizing this was not the most gracious acceptance, I added, "I would be honored to dance with you, Mr. Bafton."

Fortescue's mouth tipped upward in a broad smile. I thought Em might have tried to raise some objection to me dancing with the tailor's son, but she was so enraptured with Lord Redmond's attentions, she hardly seemed to notice Fortescue leading me away.

I grimaced when I realized the next dance was to be another waltz. Fortescue took me woodenly in his arms. He had no ability to keep time with the music and we did far more swaying than twirling.

As we danced past that tantalizing arch, I noticed that the king was no longer ensconced upon his throne. But the two formidable guards had not shifted an inch from their positions. One of them smothered a yawn, both men looking mightily bored with their sentry duty. Nonetheless, they remained at their posts.

There was no way I would ever be able to retrieve that orb for Mal. He was going to be dreadfully disappointed, but I knew he would not reproach me for my failure. Delphine, on the other hand, would likely enact some horrible retribution, either cursing me with boils or turning me into a slug worm.

I felt too despondent to care. I moved halfheartedly through the steps of the waltz, but it did not matter because Fortescue was not dancing with much enthusiasm either. I doubted anyone could have found a more miserable couple in the entire ballroom than the pair of us.

We danced in silence until I finally ventured, "So you are not enjoying the ball?"

"Not at all," he replied. "It has turned out nothing like I expected."

"Tell me about it," I muttered.

He took my wry comment as an invitation to air his complaints. "All of these grand ladies from the Heights are so conceited and arrogant. They sneered at me when I approached them to dance. Some of them even behaved as though my mere asking was an insult."

"Pay no heed to any of those affected snobs," I began but was cut off when another couple bumped into us.

We were sadly in the way of the more graceful couples. I managed to take the lead and guide Fortescue to the fringes of the ballroom before I continued, "I am sure there are plenty of girls here from Midtown who would be flattered by your attentions."

"Usually they would be, but not tonight. They are all too busy chasing after lords and knights and princes to have any time for me. But do you know what, Miss Ella? I don't even care," Fortescue declared stoutly. "Because I realized something important. There is only one girl in the world that I will ever love and that is your sister Amy.

"Oh, I know what you must be thinking," he rushed on before I could reply. "That I am not good enough for that divine creature and you would be right. After all, I am a bit of an ass."

I winced when Fortescue trod on my toe. Although I entirely agreed with him, I tried to demur. "Mr. Bafton, I am sure that—"

"No, you need not attempt to be kind. I am not an intelligent man. I always blurt out the first thought that comes into my head and it is always something foolish. You know it. I know it. Everyone knows it, including Amy, but this is the wonderful thing about your sister. Amy has never minded me being an ass. She liked me anyway. I believe I was her favorite beau until this cursed ball."

Fortescue emitted a heavy sigh as he twirled me in a circle that nearly caused us both to stumble. "Now all these handsome, clever wealthy men have clapped eyes on my lovely Amy and realized how amazing she is. Even several of the princes are smitten with her. No doubt she will end up a princess, and I have lost my chance with her forever."

I refrained from telling him that there never had been any chance of him wedding Amy. My stepmother would not have allowed it, not unless our family had become completely destitute and faced with the prospect of moving to Misty Bottoms. I had never been keen on the notion of Fortescue Bafton as a brother-in-law either.

But the poor man looked so downcast, I could not help feeling sorry for him. I was struggling to come up with some sort of consoling remark when Prince Florian waltzed past us with the youngest Miss Hanson clasped in his arms. I could tell the prince was subjecting her to the full barrage of his charms just as he had done with me, only Ivy was lapping it up. She did not appear under the prince's spell enough to remain unaware of the envy of other ladies who had been obliged to settle for less noble partners. She directed a particularly smug smile at her older sister, Myrtle, who was without a partner and watching wistfully from the sidelines.

As Fortescue and I shuffled past Myrtle, I saw her face flush bright red. I could have sworn she gnashed her teeth with jealousy and the most calculating look transformed her face. Myrtle pressed one hand dramatically to her brow and it was as if I could read her mind. She had gained the prince's attention once before by swooning. Why not try it again?

I recalled that the herald had not reached the Hanson household before they set out for the ball. Myrtle could not be aware of the king's new edict against swooning in the presence of royalty. I tried to call out a warning, but Fortescue and I danced out of range of her hearing.

Caught up in his own misery, Fortescue was oblivious to his surroundings. He almost tripped over me when I came to an abrupt halt. I pulled away from him, my intent being to stop Myrtle, but I was already too late.

Myrtle staggered out onto the dance floor, directly in front of Prince Florian. She gave a pitiful moan and sank down into a graceful swoon. Unable to check his steps, the prince tripped over the recumbent girl and fell, taking the startled Ivy with him. Several other couples followed suit and tumbled into the flurry of tangled petticoats and flailing legs. I managed to avoid the collision by shoving Fortescue out of the way.

The music came to an abrupt halt. The dancers disentangled themselves and regained their footing. Some of them laughed, amused by the incident, while others cursed, rubbing sore knees and elbows. Florian was one of the last to rise. His queue had come undone, his long blond hair tumbling about his face and there was a boot print on the sleeve of his pristine white uniform.

Despite all the chaos she had caused, Myrtle maintained the pretense of her swoon, much to my amazement (although I did notice her furtively adjusting her body to a more comfortable angle on the floor). If she expected the prince to sweep her up in his arms as he had done that day in the lane, the girl was to be disappointed.

Attempting to brush the dirt from his uniform, the prince scowled at her. A tense silence fell over the ballroom. Before Florian could say anything, Mercato thrust his way through the crowd, his wizard's robes flapping. He was flanked by two burly palace Scutcheons.

Mercato pointed at Myrtle and bellowed, "Arrest that young woman!"

Myrtle's eyes flew open, and she screamed as the two guards surged toward her. Seizing the girl by her arms, they gave her no chance to stand, dragging her across the floor.

"I say!" Fortescue sputtered.

Thrusting him out of the way, I rushed toward Mercato. "Please, stop. Myrtle meant no harm. She didn't know about the new law. If I could but speak to the king, I—"

"The king has retired for the evening." The wizard stared haughtily down the length of his long nose at me. "But I am sure His Majesty would agree with me that ignorance is no excuse. The law is the law, and you would do well to stay out of this."

I turned from him to appeal to Prince Florian. "Your Highness, please."

The prince waved me away with an irritated gesture. He was too absorbed in trying to bind back his hair to concern himself with Myrtle's plight.

By this time, the guards had hauled her to her feet and the girl was sobbing. I looked desperately around for another source of royal help to contravene Mercato's authority. But I had not seen Ryland since he fled from me. The tenderhearted Prince Kendrick might have been persuaded to intervene but there was no sign of him either or any of his brothers. I bit my lip in vexation. Earlier I had been practically tripping over unwanted princes. Now when I needed one, there was none to be found.

Then, better than any prince, I saw Commander Crushington forcing his way through the gawking crowd. I hurled myself at him, pressing my hands against his chest.

I have no idea how distraught I must have looked, but Horatio regarded me with alarm. His hands came up to cover mine. "Ella, what is going on? What's wrong?"

"It's Myrtle Hanson," I gasped."The foolish girl feigned a swoon in front of Prince Florian. She didn't know about the new law and Mercato is having her arrested and it isn't fair. Please, can you not do something?"

Even as I pleaded, I realized I was asking a great deal of Horatio. The commander had his strict code about upholding the king's laws and I was begging him to set aside his duty. Horatio's dark grey eyes looked deep into mine for a long moment. A troubled frown creased his brows as his gaze traveled from me toward Myrtle.

The guards would likely have already hauled the weeping girl away, but her sister was also wailing. Ivy clung to Myrtle, trying to yank her free from her captors. One of the guards shoved Ivy roughly to the floor.

I heard the sharp intake of Horatio's breath. He set me aside and marched forward. "Stop! Release that girl at once."

He did not shout. He did not have to. His voice carried a ring of authority that caused the entire room to snap to attention. As he helped Ivy to her feet, my heart swelled with such relief and pride in him, I could have kissed the man.

I was astonished when the guards did not instantly obey him. I certainly would have. They kept their grip on Myrtle, but they hesitated, looking uncertainly at Mercato.

The wizard flapped toward Horatio, shaking his finger at him. "This is a matter for the Royal Guard, Commander Crushington. It does not fall within your purview."

"Respectfully, sir, I believe that it does." Horatio accorded the king's sorcerer a stiff bow. "Miss Hanson is from Midtown."

"But she dared to commit her offense right here in His Majesty's palace."

Horatio stepped closer as he tried to reason with Mercato. Aside from the snuffling of the Hanson sisters, the entire room was silent, straining to hear and breathlessly awaiting the result of the commander's bold intervention.

I inched as close as I dared. I could only pick up snippets of Horatio's low, terse arguments.

"...girl made a mistake... her arrest bound to cause resentment. Surely the king would not wish... ball to be spoiled over such a trivial matter. If I could only speak to..."

Mercato locked his arms across his chest. He was frowning, but he was listening. I believed that Horatio might have prevailed. Unfortunately, word of what was going on must have spread to the farthest corners of the ballroom and reached the ears of Myrtle's brothers.

The two Hanson boys burst through the crowd. Although

they were known to be a bit rowdy, Payton and Toland were usually respectful of authority. But their flushed countenances suggested that they had consumed too much of the king's cheap wine.

Toland's voice was slurred as he yelled, "Get shur hands off my sishter, you bashtard!"

"Oh no," I groaned as Payton, the hot-tempered Hanson brother tackled one of the guards. He wrestled the man to the floor. Toland took a wild swing at the second guard and missed. The Scutcheon let go of Myrtle and socked Toland in the jaw.

Myrtle shrieked. Mercato sputtered with outrage and Horatio swore. He dove at Payton and pulled him off the guard. He pinioned the young man's arms. Toland, recovering from his blow, came at Horatio from behind.

I cried out a warning. I leapt forward and tried to grab Toland's arm. He thrust me backward. As I staggered to keep my balance, Horatio released Payton. He felled Toland with one sharp jab.

I gasped as Horatio seized me by the waist and lifted me off my feet. He plunked me down a safe distance away and ordered, "Stay out of this, Ella."

He whirled back to where the Hanson boys traded blows with the two guards.

"Stop," he roared, getting Payton in a headlock.

Most of the crowd gasped and gaped, trying to keep out of the way. But the drunken Lord Ludlow staggered forward, growling something about "Midtown ruffians." Beckoning to his inebriated friend Sir Eustace, the two aristocrats set upon the Hanson brothers.

This prompted several of the Midtown lads to rush to the aid of their friends. To my astonishment, Fortescue Bafton was among them. I would never have thought the tailor's son had it in him as he went after Lord Ludlow.

Under other circumstances, I might have found it amusing,

watching the two dandies dance around each other, taking ineffectual swipes. But the melee spread to an alarming degree, fists flying, curses roaring and ladies shrieking. I shrank back farther to avoid being knocked down.

I lost sight of Horatio in the uproar, but I saw Ivy trying to hustle her weeping sister to safety. Mercato blocked their path.

The wizard grabbed Myrtle by the arm to prevent her escape. Ivy shrieked and pummeled the wizard. When he did not release her sister, Ivy seized his beard, giving it a savage yank. Mercato howled in pain, screaming for more guards.

Two more Scutcheons rushed past me, jamming me against the pillar. I straightened, rubbing my bruised shoulder. I bit back a curse, but my breath caught in my throat at the realization.

They were the two bored soldiers posted by the arch. I stole a glance behind me and saw that the forbidden doorway was left unguarded. My pulse skittered. This was the opportunity I had waited for all evening— if I was bold enough to seize it.

As I took a step closer to the arch, I stole a nervous look around to make sure my actions were unobserved. Anyone not fighting was either dodging or gawking at the combatants. No one was paying the slightest attention to me.

I felt guilty at the thought of abandoning Horatio to this chaos, especially since I was the one who had persuaded him to intervene. One glance in his direction assured me the commander was more than capable of holding his own. He separated a Midtown boy from Sir Eustace by collaring both. He cracked their heads together with a force that made me wince.

Even as he fought, Horatio issued terse orders. Under his command, the palace guards would soon have this situation under control and my chance would be gone. Yet I felt immobilized by fear, unable to take another step.

I had to remind myself that Mal would not rest until he recovered that orb. If I failed in stealing it for him, he would make some reckless attempt himself and end up arrested or killed.

My heart pounded harder, the ballroom blurring before my eyes as I willed my trembling legs to move. It was now or never. I drew in a deep breath. Plucking up my skirts, along with my courage, I darted through the forbidden arch.

Fifteen

I ran down the flight of stone steps so fast, one of my shoes flew off. Swearing under my breath, I had to hop back a few steps to retrieve it. It was as well that I was obliged to pause. I needed to proceed with more caution until I took stock of my surroundings.

The wide hall that stretched ahead of me was exactly as Mal had said it would be. The walls were crammed with an assorted collection of weapons from ages past, axes, pikes, halberds, and heavy swords. Blunter and clumsier than the rapiers now in use, the ancient swords were still lethal looking.

After the brilliance of the ballroom, the hall seemed dark and forbidding. The way ahead of me was lit only by flaming torches embedded in the stone walls. As I bent to pick up my dancing slipper, I stole an anxious glance back the way I had come. There was no sign of any pursuit, no harsh voice calling out a command for me to halt. The noise and safety of the ballroom already seemed far away.

I was quite alone here in what was part of the oldest part of the palace. That did not mean that I was not in danger of being discovered. I could stumble upon a stray guard or servant at any moment. I needed to keep moving, carefully, but quickly.

I cringed at the thought of forcing my sore heel back into my loose slipper. Instead, I opted to remove my other shoe as well. Carrying my dancing slippers in one hand, I tiptoed past suits of armor lined up on both sides of the hall like soldiers awaiting inspection. The torchlight flickered over these eerie, silent sentinels.

I am not usually given to flights of fantasy, but I could not help imagining hostile eyes watching me through the slits of those visors. At any moment one of those iron gauntlets could reach out to seize me and—

"Stop it," I scolded myself. "Concentrate."

I needed to control my racing pulse and remember the directions Mal had given me.

Just traverse the length of the old War Hall.

Mal had made it sound so easy, but what he had neglected to tell me was how long that hall would be. The frapping chamber went on forever, but perhaps it just seemed that way to me with my nerves wound so tight.

I breathed a faint sigh of relief as I neared the end of the hall. I silently congratulated myself on having made it this far undetected. Then I heard it. The sound of a footfall. I froze, listening, and realized that someone was approaching from the corridor ahead that branched off to the left.

I panicked, unable to move for a split second. Then I dove for the only hiding place available, a niche behind the last suit of armor. I flattened myself back against the rough stonework as far as I could. It was a poor place of concealment. In this dim light, the sheen of my golden gown would stand out like a beacon. I tried to gather up my skirts and hug them as close to my body as I could, but it was impossible. Even if I had not been holding my shoes, my hoop and layers of petticoats thwarted my efforts.

As the footsteps drew nearer, I tried to come up with an excuse should I be discovered. I was terrified by the fight in the ballroom, and I ran down here to get out of the way. No, that sounded ridiculous. What about… I was knocked down during the fight and I was so dazed, I didn't know where I was going. There was an edict that forbade swooning, but surely there was no law against being dazed, was there?

I had no time to come up with anything better before a man entered the hall. I caught a ghostly glimpse of white and recognized it for a uniform like all the princes wore. As he drew nearer, I saw that it was indeed one of the royal brothers, Kendrick, in fact.

I held my breath as he ambled past where I hid behind the suit of armor. One glance in my direction and he was bound to spot me. But Kendrick behaved in a manner as furtive as me.

He stole a look behind him, and then craned his neck to peer ahead. Appearing satisfied that he was alone, he crept over to a suit of armor positioned along the wall opposite from where I hid.

He lifted the visor and thrust his hand inside the helmet. He groped about for a few seconds and pulled out a small pouch. I watched mystified as he loosened the drawstring and poured what looked like a silvery powder in the palm of his hand.

Kendrick raised his cupped fingers to his nose and inhaled so deeply that he sneezed violently. He gave a deep sigh, "Ah!"

As a beatific smile spread over his face, I realized the strange silvery substance had to be pixie dust. The most noble Prince Kendrick was a pixie sniffer! As he hid the pouch back inside the suit of armor, my tension eased. Kendrick drifted in the direction of the stairs leading up to the ballroom.

When I was sure he was gone, I crept out from my hiding place and continued to the end of the hall. Corridors branched out in both directions. I took the one to the right, hurrying past a succession of heavy wooden doors until I came to an enormous portrait that stretched from the floor almost to the ceiling.

The painting depicted a young man in full royal regalia, an ermine trimmed purple robe draped about his broad shoulders. A jeweled crown encircled his head and in his right hand, he clutched a golden scepter. His long blond hair and features were not unlike Prince Florian's, but from what Mal had told me this was a portrait of King August at his coronation.

If the artist had been true to his subject and not seeking to flatter, our king would have been a handsome youth. I was arrested by the expression in his eyes. They were almost shining; the eyes of a young man gazing into a future bright with promise. Not a hint of the miserable old tyrant he had become. I could have pitied him, if August's cruelty and avarice had not brought so much suffering to our kingdom.

I shifted my gaze from the portrait, focusing on the ornate frame instead. The gilded wood was carved with an elaborate design of vines and intertwining roses. Running my fingers along the right side of the frame, I counted. One, two, three, four, five roses up from the bottom. My heart hammered. I looked around me, fearing some guard would come running to stop me.

None did. I pressed in on the center of the flower and heard a faint click. I leapt back as the portrait slowly swung forward, revealing it to be a door. With one final anxious glance down the corridor, I slipped through the opening. There was a handle on the back of the painting. I pulled on it, closing the door.

I rested my forehead against the wooden panel, clutching my dancing slippers to my breast. I exhaled a deep breath, unable to believe I had made it. I was in the king's private treasury. Granted I still had to find the orb and steal back to the ballroom undetected. I had succeeded in getting this far. I had to believe that I would manage the rest.

I came about slowly, trying to adjust my eyes to the darkness. The chamber was windowless and would have been pitch black if not for a small lamp mounted near the doorway. Its glow did not offer much by way of illumination, just enough for me to gape at my surroundings.

I do not know exactly what I had expected to find in the king's treasure room, but certainly not this utter chaos. The chamber was heaped with coin chests, jewel boxes, stacks of paintings and porcelain statues to such a degree, it appeared impossible to find a path between all these stacks.

It reminded me of Withypole Fugitate's shop and I wondered if it was possible that a king, just like a fairy, could become a gleaner. A fairy's compulsive hoarding had its roots in a broken heart. I was sure that King August's acquisitiveness was inspired by greed. My heart swelled with anger as I thought of how many of his subjects he must have persecuted and defrauded to amass all this treasure.

I had little hope of finding the orb in all this mess, at least not in this dim light. I spotted a silver branch of candlesticks amidst the piles. Setting my shoes down atop a large chest, I carried the candelabrum over to the lamp and removed the globe. The flame was the oddest that I had ever seen. The wick burned brightly but I could detect no source of fuel, neither wax nor oil.

This had to be some sort of magic that the wizard Mercato had devised. I tentatively touched the wick of one of the candles to the strange flame. Nothing happened. I wondered if the candles were too ordinary to ignite by the wizard's lamp. Suddenly the flame crackled, and the wick caught.

I lit the other two wicks and the candles burned with an astonishing brightness that illuminated the entire room. I could see what lay hidden in shadow. I held the branch of candles aloft and stared straight into the eyes of the dragon looming over me.

I shrieked and stumbled back, nearly dropping the candles. Hot wax spattered my hand, and I could feel the burn even through my glove. Trembling, I wielded the candlestick as though it was a sword, hoping I could make it to the door before the beast snapped me up in its terrible jaws.

I was astonished that the dragon had not tried to do so already. Then I realized why. The alarming creature was no more than a stuffed head mounted on the wall. I took a deep breath, feeling foolish for having panicked.

Whoever had preserved the dragon's head had done an incredible job. Recovering from my fright, I examined the fearsome beast more closely. Judging from the size of its head, the dragon must have been huge. I imagined that the ground would tremble beneath its mighty feet. Its golden scales appeared iridescent beneath the glow of the candles. No sharp horns sprouted from its brow, but rather a tall crest the color of flame. Its deep-set eyes must have been mesmerizing when the creature was alive. Now they regarded me with a vacant glassy stare.

I had heard that dragons were not aggressive creatures unless challenged by some vainglorious knight out to enhance his reputation as a warrior. That struck me as a more apt description of Prince Florian than his younger brother Ryland.

Yet Ryland was the one known for his quests to slay dragons. Was this the very beast that had devoured his hand? Despite what had happened to Ryland, I mourned for the dragon. Such a magnificent creature deserved better than to become a trophy on the king's wall. The gentle lover I had known as Harper would have agreed with me. But that boy was gone, as dead to me as this dragon.

I stretched up on tiptoe to caress the poor beast's snout, offering up a silent apology. I withdrew my hand at once, frowning in puzzlement. I do not know how I expected the scaly skin of a dragon to feel, certainly not like stiff painted leather. I rapped against the dragon's nose and produced a hollow, wooden echo.

The dragon's head was fake, nothing more than a clever reproduction. It was as false as everything else about the Helavalerian family. I rocked back on my heels, relieved that the dragon was not real and yet at the same time, seething with indignation.

I wondered if there had ever been an actual dragon or if the story about Ryland going on such a quest was nothing but more lies. If there was no dragon, how had Ryland come to lose his hand? Why did I even care?

I needed to forget about Ryland and concentrate upon my reason for being here. I backed away from the dragon's head, directing the glow of my candles toward the rest of the chamber. As the light flickered over all those endless stacks of confiscated treasure, I felt overwhelmed. If the orb was buried in one of the chests, it would take me all night to find it.

According to Mal's source, the orb was supposed to be somewhere prominently displayed beneath a glass dome, easy to access. I skirted through the piles of trunks, paintings, and statuary, doing my best not to knock anything down. My aim was to find the orb and replace it without leaving a trace of my presence. The fact that I had an unregistered aura would help, but that advantage would be lost if I dislodged too many items during my search.

I did not know how anyone could tell if anything had been shifted in all this mess. But Mal's apothecary shop was also a mass of clutter, and yet Mal would know at once if someone had moved a bottle so much as an inch. I suspected that our king might be equally sharp-eyed when it came to protecting his treasures.

I crept about the chamber, examining every nook and crowded shelf with a sense of increasing desperation. I saw no sign of anything resembling a glass dome crammed amongst all the figurines, old books, and music boxes. Only one small ledge remained uncluttered in all this chaos.

The carved, half-circle shelf boasted no more than a single miniature portrait. I needed to keep searching for the orb, but my curiosity was roused. Whose image did our tyrant king cherish so much that he would give it pride of place above all the other treasure in this room?

I expected that it would turn out to be a painting of the king's most beloved son and heir, Prince Florian. As I drew nearer, I saw that it was a miniature of a lovely young woman with soft golden tresses. My breath hitched in my throat as I recognized her gentle features, that warm, sweet smile.

It was my mother.

I picked up the small oval painting to examine it. It was so like the miniature of my mother that belonged to my father, I felt a flash of rage, wondering when and how the king had managed to steal it.

But I realized that was impossible. My father's portrait of Mama was locked away in the bottom drawer of his desk. I had seen it only recently when I had been searching for a fresh bottle of ink.

As I studied the miniature, I perceived subtle differences between it and my father's portrait. My mother looked younger in this one and there was a blue ribbon threaded through her hair. How did the king come to have such a thing? This cameo was the sort of token a young woman would only bestow upon someone that she cared for deeply. I could not believe that any sort of affection had ever existed between my mother and a man as selfish and cruel as King August. And yet...

I recalled King August's strange reaction to me earlier during the reception, the way his eyes had misted as he stared at me. *Your mother was the loveliest, most enchanting woman I have ever known. And you... you look so very much like her. Is that not true, Major-domo? Is not this girl Cecily's very image?*

Except for her eyes, the king's quiet little servant had replied. I do believe she has her father's eyes.

The king had recoiled from me as though I had transformed into a hissing snake.

I cradled the portrait in the palm of my hand and wondered. Was it possible that the king had fancied himself in love with my mother and ordered this portrait to be painted? Was that the original source of the enmity that had existed between King August and my father— the fact that my father had been the one to win my mother's heart?

The king could never have had any serious intentions toward my mother, a mere forest warder's daughter. August had been wed and widowed three times, once to a princess and then to two grand duchesses. These royal brides had all shared two traits; they were blonde, and they were wealthy, bringing a hefty dowry to fill the Helavalerian coffers. Any tender sentiment the king might have cherished for my mother would have been overcome by his avarice.

Of course, this was all speculation on my part. I had no way of knowing what had happened between the king and my mother and father all those years ago, just more of the mystery that surrounded my parents' past.

All the same, I loathed the idea of the king owning this miniature of my mother. When he stole into this chamber to gloat over his treasure; did he sigh over Mama's portrait, perhaps even fondle it with his fat, sweaty fingers? The thought sickened me. My own fingers tightened about the miniature. I longed to shove it into my hidden pocket and carry it away with me, but I dared not.

Of all the objects in this room, the portrait would be missed, alerting the king that an intruder had been here. Despite my undetectable aura, the theft of my mother's portrait would be a crime that could be traced back to me. I forced myself to return the miniature to its shelf.

Having to abandon Mama's portrait disheartened me. I continued to search for the orb, but it felt hopeless. I had no idea how much time had lapsed since I had first entered the room, but this was taking me much too long. Beads of sweat gathered on my brow, in part due to the closeness of the chamber, but mainly owing to my mounting anxiety.

Order could have been restored to the ballroom by now. Those two bored young guards might be back at their posts. How would I ever get back through the arch without drawing attention to myself? What if Horatio had noticed my absence and instituted a search?

If I was caught in the treasure room itself, there would be no plausible excuse I could offer. I would be clapped in irons and hauled off immediately to the deepest dungeon in the King's Royal Prison. Not even Horatio would be able to save me and perhaps he would be so disgusted to discover I was a thief; he would not even try.

I hated to give up, after the risk I had already taken. But I did not see that I had much choice. I started to make my way toward the door, when the light of my candles reflected off the top of something that could have been glass.

The object was shoved to the very back of a shelf, hidden behind a plethora of beautiful figurines depicting fairies. My heart quickened with hope. I set the branch of candles down atop of stack of heavy leather-bound books that looked like a stack of ledgers.

Carefully, I shifted the figurines, clearing a path through the fairy folk. There it was at last. The orb nestled upon a blue velvet cushion set beneath a glass dome coated with a fine film of dust.

At one time, perhaps the orb had been prominently displayed, just as the footman had told Mal. As the king had acquired new treasures, the glass dome must have been relegated to the back of the shelf. Just another possession to the king, but one that meant the world to Mal, a cherished memento of his wizard grandfather.

My throat thickened with emotion as I imagined Mal's joy when I restored the orb to him. But I could not give myself up to feelings of relief just yet, not until the orb was safely in my pocket and I had managed to sneak back into the ballroom undetected.

I drew the glass dome closer to me, my palms damp with perspiration inside my gloves. I wished I could have removed them, but even with an unregistered aura, it would be unwise to leave finger marks all over the glass.

I lifted the dome off carefully lest I drop it, shattering glass everywhere. Despite my slippery gloves, I succeeded in removing the dome from its base. Setting it aside, I delved into my pocket and produced the fake orb. Mal had pulled off an astonishing feat, producing an exact copy. I certainly could not discern any difference between them. I switched the orbs, tucking the real one into my hidden pocket. I replaced the glass dome and nudged it to the rear of the shelf. I arranged the fairy figurines in front of it, trying to put them back in the same positions I had found them.

I was dismayed to realize that I had dislodged the layers of dust, but hopefully, a new coating would settle before the king noticed anything amiss. Blowing out a deep breath, I allowed myself a moment of relief.

"There, Malcolm Hawkridge," I murmured. "Never say I don't keep my birthday promises."

Snatching up the candlestick, I headed for the door. As I passed beneath the dragon head, the light glinted strangely off the creature's glassy eyes. The back of my neck prickled and for a moment, I had the eeriest sensation the dragon was staring at me. I shook off the ridiculous notion as I snuffed out the wicks on the candelabrum and put it back where I had found it.

I groped for the door handle in the dim light of the wizard's lantern. I started to ease it open when I drew up short, realizing I was on the verge of forgetting my shoes. That would have been a disastrous and costly mistake.

I grabbed up my dancing slippers. Inching the door open, I took a cautious peek down the corridor. It was as deserted as before. I stepped through the opening and quietly closed the door behind me. The king's portrait settled back into place. No one looking at it would ever guess that there was a treasure room hidden behind it or that I had been in there.

Despite my tension, I felt an odd thrill course through me. I recognized it for what it was, the excitement I had experienced whenever Mal and I had succeeded in pulling off some outrageous bit of mischief. I kept insisting to him that the reckless, adventurous girl I had once been gone. Perhaps a trace of the old, daring Ella remained, I thought with a grin. I set off down the corridor with a spring in my step. All caution was forgotten as I whipped around the corner into the main hall.

And walked head on into Horatio Crushington.

Sixteen

My shoes dropped from my nerveless fingers to the floor. I could not breathe, could not move, as though if I remained still enough Horatio would not notice me. A rather irrational notion since my nose was flattened against his chest.

I stumbled back a step as I gazed, stricken, up at him. My lips parted but no words came. My brain seemed to have shut down as well. Despite being immobilized by sheer panic, one realization penetrated my frozen mind. Horatio looked nearly as shocked as me.

"Ella," he gasped. "What are you doing here?"

"Well, I— I—" I babbled. I noticed the bruise darkening his eye and momentarily forgot all else. "Oh, you have been hurt."

I reached up to caress his cheek.

"It's nothing," he said. He closed his eyes, sighing at my touch. Then he removed my hand from his face and eyed me sternly. "You did not answer my question. What are you doing in this part of the palace? Don't you know it is forbidden?"

"Is it?" I widened my eyes, trying to look both innocent and appalled. I have never been as glib a liar as Mal. I had to moisten my dry lips before I went on. "Well, ah— you did order me to stay out of the way of the fighting."

"The fight is over, and I never meant for you to come here."

"But the entryway was not guarded, so how should I know I was not allowed to come this way? I was so alarmed and confused that I blundered beneath the arch to hide and... and then I saw all these suits of armor and was intrigued by them, so I thought there was no harm in doing a little exploring and... and..."

I trailed off. I saw by the skeptical arch of his eyebrows that Horatio did not believe a word I was saying. Seeking to distract him from questioning me further, I asked, "If this area is off-limits, why are you here?"

"I am a garrison commander, one of the king's loyal Scutcheons. Unlike you, I am allowed to be here."

"So, you came looking for me?"

"No, I had no idea where you had vanished. I was looking for Sidney Greenleaf."

"Mercato?" I cast a panicked look around me. The thought that I could have blundered into the king's formidable wizard instead of Horatio chilled me to the bone. "Mercato is lurking somewhere near here?"

"I doubt that he is 'lurking,'" Horatio replied drily. "But yes, I saw Greenleaf come this way and I urgently need to speak to him."

Greenleaf? That was the second time Horatio had dared to call Mercato by his real name. Was he on such intimate terms with the king's powerful wizard? I found the idea a little disturbing.

"Why were you looking for Mercato?" I asked.

"I need to speak with him. Because of that foolishness in the ballroom, the entire Hanson family and a few other Midtown citizens have been arrested by the palace guard. Besides the king, the wizard is the only one with the power to contravene that order. If I cannot convince Sidney—" Horatio caught himself this time and amended, "Mercato, to release the prisoners into my custody, their punishment could end up being dire indeed."

I shuddered, afraid to imagine what would happen to Myrtle and her family if they were hauled off to the Dismal Dungeons. And Fortescue! Had he been arrested as well?

"Do you think you will be able to persuade Mercato?" I asked anxiously.

"I believe so. Mercato can be reasonable at times."

Considering the wizard's hysterical rage that I had witnessed, I doubted this was going to be one of those times, but I nodded in agreement.

"Then it is urgent that you should find him as soon as possible. I must not detain you." I tried to slip past Horatio, but he was not about to let me escape so easily.

Stealing his arm about my waist, he pulled me gently but firmly back in front of him. "We still have not settled the matter of you being here in this restricted area."

"Haven't we?" I gave a nervous laugh. "Goodness! I hope you are not planning to arrest me."

The stern set of his mouth softened with a slight smile. "No, of course not, but—"

"I am so glad that you found me," I rushed on. "I have been looking for you all evening."

"You have been?" Again, that skeptical lift of his brows.

"Indeed, I have. We were supposed to dance, remember?"

"I did not forget," he replied gravely.

"But you thought that I did. I am so sorry, Horatio. I never intended to forsake you to dance with Prince Ryland."

"It is all right, Ella. You need not explain. I understood. A garrison commander is of little consequence next to a prince."

"Perhaps to most women, but not to me. Prince Ryland caught me entirely by surprise."

Horatio studied my face. "Yes, I observed that His Highness appeared to have a powerful impact on you."

I was unable to meet Horatio's questioning gaze. I had no wish to trot out the entire pathetic tale of my youthful folly with the boy I had known as Harper. I settled on a partial truth.

"The prince merely reminded me of someone I knew a long time ago."

"It must have been someone you cared about a great deal, considering the way you kissed him," Horatio said with a rare edge to his voice.

When I flushed, he immediately apologized. "Forgive me, Ella. I have no right to mention that. It is none of my concern—"

"No, please, I want to explain to you about that."

"You don't have to explain anything."

"Yes, I do," I insisted. "I would hate to have you believe that I am some royalty-mad doxy ready to fling herself into the embrace of the nearest prince."

"I never believed that of you."

"Good! As I said, it was only that Harper— I mean, Prince Ryland touched upon some memory from my girlhood, and before I even knew how it happened, he was kissing me. But I assure you that it meant—" I hesitated, recalling the brief rush of emotion I had experienced, that stirring of embers I had believed long burned to ash.

"That kiss meant nothing to me," I said firmly. "And I promise you, when I came here tonight, there was only one man I wanted to dance with."

I smiled up at Horatio. I am still at a loss to explain what I did next. Perhaps I merely wanted to keep Horatio distracted from returning to the subject of me wandering through the forbidden corridor. Perhaps I wanted to prove to him and myself how little Ryland's kiss had mattered. Or perhaps it was something in the way Horatio smiled back at me, the warmth in the depths of his deep grey eyes.

I wrapped my arms around his neck. Stretching upward, I boldly touched my lips to his. Horatio's eyes widened for a moment. Then he drew me close, enfolding me in his embrace and returning my kiss. Kissing me in a way that I had never been kissed before. The kind of kiss that begins at your lips and curls all the way through you down to your toes.

When he finally released me, I was breathless and even a trifle giddy.

"Oh!" I sighed. "That was… was…"

"Yes, it was," Horatio agreed. His gaze was tender as he looked down at me, but surprisingly sad as he continued, "And now, Ella, perhaps you'll tell me what you have really been doing here."

Still melting from his kiss, I had a mad urge to confess everything. Then I stiffened, wondering exactly who had been distracting whom. Or perhaps "seducing" was a better word.

Horatio was so upright and honorable; I could hardly accuse him of that and yet whoever would have imagined that the stern commander could kiss a girl senseless like that? Regretfully, I pulled out of his arms, trying to decide if I should stick to my original story or come up with a more plausible reason for invading the forbidden part of the palace.

"Well, I… actually, I was… um… looking for… for…"

I was spared the necessity of finishing my answer when a door at the end of the corridor opened. I tensed, dreading that it heralded the arrival of Mercato. Instead, my sister sauntered out, or perhaps staggered might have been a more apt description.

If I thought Amy had seemed a bit too convivial before, my sister appeared to have reached that state Mal would have described as thoroughly pickled. She had lost all the pins and the ribbon binding up her hair and it fell about her face in a disorderly tangle. The bodice of her gown was half-slipping off her shoulder and her nose was lit up like a lighthouse beacon.

She reeled back when she saw me, but then her lips curled upward in a silly grin. "Why, hullo, Ella."

I stared at her in shock, which quickly turned to consternation when I saw the frown settling over Horatio's face. Bad enough I needed to excuse why I had been caught in forbidden territory, but now I would need to account for my sister as well. Exactly what was Amy doing here?

I moved to interpose myself between the commander and my sister. "Amy!" I exclaimed with forced brightness. "There you are! I have been looking everywhere for you."

I leaned closer, hissing. "What are you doing wandering alone down here?"

She blinked owlishly at me. "I'm not alone. I'm with my prinsh."

"Prinsh? I mean what prince?"

"Why, my beloved Dashy." Amy made a vague gesture to the empty space beside her. Her lips puckered into a frown as she looked right and then left. She tottered around in a complete circle. "Oh! I've lost him."

She tipped back her head and bellowed. "Dashy! Where are you, sweetie?"

"Hush!" I said, casting a mortified glance back at Horatio, but my sister continued to shout.

"Dashy! Dashy?"

"Coming, darling," a voice echoed back.

One of the royal twins stumbled out of the same doorway from which Amy had appeared. He grinned. "Amy, you little minx. Look what you forgot down in Papa's wine cellar."

To my complete outrage, the young prince dangled one of my sister's garters. "We'd both be in for it if my father knew we'd been sampling his private..."

The prince's words trailed off, his grin disappearing as he caught sight of me and Horatio. He whipped the garter behind his back, trying to finger comb the disorderly waves of his blond hair. As disconcerted as he was, years of royal training came to the young rascal's rescue. He managed a very creditable bow.

"Good evening, my lady. Commander."

Amy giggled. "Thash no lady. Thash my older sishter."

"Oh, frap!" the prince muttered, but did his best to offer me a charming smile.

I had no idea what Horatio might be thinking, but he was more equal to the situation than I was.

"Your Royal Highness." He returned the prince's bow with a stiff one of his own.

What exactly was the protocol when one catches a prince trifling with one's little sister? I suppose I should have curtsied instead of stalking toward the prince. Some of my more murderous thoughts must have shown on my face because he stumbled back from me.

"This is not at all what it looks like, my lady. I— I mean, Miss Upton."

"Oh, is it not? Prince Dahl!" I snapped, staring pointedly at his bitten fingernails.

The prince curled his fingers into a fist to hide the ragged cuticles. "No, you are quite mistaken. I am Prince Dashiel."

"Then you must have been rechristened since you entered the ballroom."

"Don't be shilly, Ella." Amy hiccupped. "That is my Prinsh Dashy. Think I don't know my own beloved?"

"I think you would be fortunate to know your own name. All thanks to this young villain."

"Ella..." Horatio laid his hand on my arm in calming fashion, but I shook him off.

"Madam, I-I assure you," the young prince stammered, "your sister and I have done nothing wrong. Upon my honor."

"Your honor, Prince Dahl?" I snapped. "Do you or any of your brothers have any? If you have done nothing wrong, exactly what are you hiding behind your back?"

"I have no idea what you are talking about." The prince's lofty tone was ruined when his voice cracked.

I seized his arm, trying to drag his hand from behind his back, but Horatio intervened.

"Ella, that's enough!" Horatio pulled me away from the prince. "Your Highness?" The commander held out his palm in demanding fashion.

Red-faced, the prince produced my sister's garter and dropped it in the palm of Horatio's hand.

"Her garter broke," the prince mumbled. "And her stocking fell. I was just trying to help."

"Oh, I'll just bet you were," I began, but Horatio cut me off.

"I think it would be best if Your Highness returned to the ballroom and your other guests," he said.

"What? No!" I protested.

Grateful for the chance to escape, Prince Dahl seized upon Horatio's suggestion. He dodged past me. Without even pausing to say goodbye to my sister, he bolted down the corridor.

"Dashy! Don't go," Amy wailed.

I snatched my sister's broken garter from Horatio and shoved it into my hidden pocket with the orb. I started to charge after the prince, intending to haul the young wretch back here and force him to account for his actions, but Horatio restrained me.

"Let him go, Ella."

With Horatio's strong arm about my waist, I fumed, watching the prince disappear. As soon as Horatio released me, I rounded on him. "How could you let that rapscallion saunter on his way after he lured my innocent sister down to his wine cellar so he could have his way with her?"

"He didn't!" Amy cried, her eyes filling with tears. "You are ruining everything, Ella. Oh, Dashy!"

Horatio and I ignored her as he tried to reason with me. "You must not fling out such reckless accusations. You do not know exactly what happened between the prince and your sister."

"And now I have no way of finding out because you just let him go!"

"No good could come of forcing a confrontation with Prince Dahl. Surely you must see that."

"Why? Because that nail-biting little weasel would just lie his arse off?" I huffed an angry sigh. "No doubt you are right. What I need to do is demand an audience with the king and inform him of his son's iniquitous behavior."

"That would be an even worse idea. Prince Dahl might find a way to blame whatever happened here on your sister and the king would of course side with his son."

"And as the king's loyal Scutcheon, whose side would you be on, Commander?"

"Your sister's," Horatio said quietly. "My main concern and yours should be to protect her reputation."

"There's nothing wrong with my reputashion." Amy sniffed. "Don't you be scolding me, Ella. What have you been up to with your commander, running around all barefoot?" She swayed on her feet as she pointed accusingly at my discarded shoes.

Much to my annoyance, I felt a telltale rush of heat to my cheeks. "We are not discussing my behavior, but yours. How could you be so wantonly reckless, Amy?"

"You think I have been w-wicked but I haven't been and neither has Dashy. He loves me. He's going to marry me. I'm going to be a princhess." Amy hiccupped and placed an unsteady finger against her lips. "Shh! It's got to be a shecret for now."

"Oh, Amy!" I groaned at my sister's gullibility in believing she was beloved by a young man who had not even been honest enough to give her his true name. But I could hardly fault Amy for that, not when I had once been as big of a fool, taken in by Prince Ryland's deception.

My sister swayed dangerously. When Horatio steadied her, she blinked up at him. "Didn't know you were twins, Commander."

Horatio looked startled. "I'm not."

"Then why are there two of you?"

Amy went cross-eyed and she moaned. "Oh, I think I need to shit— sit down." She backed away from Horatio and slowly slid to the floor. As she plunked down on her bottom, she knocked against one of the suits of armor.

Amy gazed blearily up at it. "Oh, pardon me. Didn't see you there." Leaning her head against the wall, she sighed and closed her eyes.

Even when she was not drunk, Amy had the enviable ability to doze off anywhere and in the most uncomfortable positions. The way her head drooped to one side reminded me of all those times when she had been a little girl and I had found her asleep in her ponies' stall, nestled against a bale of hay.

She looked so young and innocent, I felt a lump form in my throat. Prince or no prince, if Dahl Helavalerian had done anything to hurt my little sister, I silently vowed to kill him. Bending down, I shook her shoulder gently.

"Amy? Amy, please, dearest. You've got to wake up and come with me."

Amy roused enough to push my hand away. "Just five more minutes, Ella," she mumbled.

I expelled a frustrated sigh. After the way I had snapped at Horatio, I was ashamed to appeal to him for help, but I did not need to do so. He was already hunkering down beside me.

"If you would allow me?" he asked diffidently.

I gave him a grateful nod and scooted out of his way, so he could scoop Amy up in his arms. My sister's eyes flew open.

"Whoa!" she cried, stiffening.

"Your pardon, Miss Amy. I need to get you and your sister away from here."

"You need to start calling me 'Your Highness,'" she insisted groggily. "But we give you permisshun to carry us."

Horatio's lips twitched but he replied gravely, "Thank you."

He exchanged a wry glance with me as Amy burrowed her head against his shoulder. Glad as I was to have Horatio take charge of my sister, I could not help asking anxiously, "How are we going to explain what happened to her? If anyone should imagine that she has fainted…"

I let the rest of the thought trail off, but Horatio understood me well enough. He grimaced.

"I already have enough difficulties to deal with because of swooning women. Fortunately, we need not go through the ballroom. I know a back way where no one need see your sister. Just follow me."

He set off down the corridor opposite the one I had taken to reach the king's treasure room. As I scurried after him, he came to an abrupt halt and glanced back at me.

"Ella. Your shoes?"

"Oh!" I breathed, grateful for the reminder. "You keep going. I will catch up."

As I darted back toward the hall of armor, I reflected that this was the second time tonight I had nearly forgotten my dratted slippers. Fortunately, they were right where I had dropped them when I collided with Horatio.

As I bent to scoop them up, I thought I heard a door creak. I straightened abruptly, my heart quickening. The back of my neck prickled. I looked anxiously about me, but the hall seemed as silent and empty as it had ever been.

I hurried to put my slippers back on, wincing as I eased the left one over my sore heel. I hobbled along as best I could to catch up with Horatio. My sister was not exactly a lightweight. I marveled at how easily he could carry her and still maintain such a stride.

As I trailed after them, I reflected that, at least, Amy's drunken escapade had diverted the commander's attention from my own illicit activities. I was ashamed of the thought.

Horatio led the way up a narrow winding stair that brought us out into the bustling kitchen area of the palace. I was alarmed when everyone from the head cook to the pot boy stopped what they were doing to stare at us. Even though Horatio was only the commander of the Midtown garrison, he was clearly held in awe and respect by the palace denizens.

After he had a few quiet words with the head cook, the matronly woman offered up the use of her own private quarters. Horatio soon had us tucked away in a small sitting room, safe from prying eyes. As he deposited my sister on a cozy settee, he instructed a young page to go and fetch my stepmother.

I hovered just inside the door, feeling rather useless. Usually, I was the one having to rescue my family from the brink of disaster. It was an odd sensation to allow Horatio to take charge and assume that burden. I might have been able to enjoy it more except for my guilty conscience.

I thought Amy had fallen completely insensible. But as she nestled her head against the settee cushion, she murmured to Horatio, "You're a lovely man, Commander."

"Er... thank you."

"And my sishter likes you pro-prodig— quite a lot."

"Does she?"

"Yesh, but it won't do. Sorry, but you can't marry her 'cause you're a foundling, prob'ly part ogre. Not good enough for our Ella."

"I know that," Horatio replied sadly.

I flinched, wishing that my sister would just shut up and pass out. Horatio caught sight of my expression. Misinterpreting the cause of my dismay, he drew close to me and murmured, "You must not be anxious about your sister. I have sent for your step-mother and ordered your carriage to be brought round to the kitchen yard. Everything is going to be all right, Ella."

"Thanks to you, and I trust you will pay no heed to any of that nonsense Amy was spouting. She has no idea what she is saying when she is drunk.

"Not that my sister has ever been drunk before," I added hastily. "I fear that all the royal attention that she received tonight went to her head, along with the wine. Pray, do not think badly of

Amy. She can be impulsive at times, but she is not wicked. Ordinarily she is a very well-behaved girl."

Horatio smiled. "I am sure that she is. I only wish…" His smile faded as he continued, "Why did you not tell me at once the real reason you were down in the forbidden hall was to search for your sister?"

"Well, I…" I faltered, all too conscious of the stolen orb hidden in my pocket.

"Did you not think that I would help you, that I would not understand?"

"Well, um, it was very wrong for either Amy or I to be in that part of the palace and you are the king's sworn commander."

"You must believe the same as your sister does," he said in a voice thickened by hurt. "That I am part ogre, a most rigid, stiff-necked, unfeeling kind of brute."

"No, of course not! I would never believe that!"

"I hope not. Because I would do anything for you, Ella. Anything within my power."

He gathered my hand into the warmth of his own, but I could not even bring myself to look him in the eye. If I had felt guilty about deceiving him before, I was now utterly wretched.

"If you ever find yourself in such difficulty again, you must promise to come to me."

I hung my head and mumbled, "You are very kind, but I could not take advantage of—"

He pressed my hand. "Promise me!"

I forced myself to look up at him and the earnest intensity in his eyes was more than I could bear.

"Very well. I promise."

"Good." He rewarded me with a tender smile that I did not deserve.

The only way I could assuage my guilt was by vowing that from now on, I would do my utmost to be Arcady's most respectable law-abiding subject. No more teasing Mrs.

Biddlesworth that I might be an unlicensed witch. No more harassing royal heralds and above all else, no more involvement in Mal's dangerous schemes.

"Unfortunately, I must leave you now," Horatio said, although he made no move to release my hand. "I really do need to find Mercato and speak to him."

"Because you have other Midtown citizens to rescue from the consequences of their follies. You need not have any more worries about me. As soon as I have gathered up my stepmother and my other sister—"

I broke off in dismay. "Netta! I hardly caught sight of her all evening. I have no idea where she is. What a horrible sister I am! I should have been looking out for both girls instead of dancing with those silly princes and—"

"Calm yourself, Ella. Netta is fine." Horatio squeezed my hand reassuringly. "I chanced to see her myself earlier out walking the gardens. I believe she has been accompanying Sergeant Wharton while he makes his rounds."

Sergeant Wharton? The name sounded familiar. I recollected that he was the exceedingly tall young sentry that had comforted Netta when we had first arrived. My sister had seemed quite smitten with him, but I hardly thought my shy Netta would dare to seek him out. Exactly what had Mal put in that elixir he had given my sisters?

"You need have no fear for your sister in the company of Ned Wharton," Horatio said. "He was under my command before he transferred to the palace guard. I found him to be a most estimable and honorable man. But I will go find your sister and fetch her here at once."

"You have done more than enough for my family already. It is more important for you to seek out Mercato. I am sure I can manage to locate Netta without getting into any more trouble."

"I hope so." Horatio arched one brow dubiously. "It is nearly midnight. Finding your sister in the crowd after the fireworks start might prove more difficult."

"Nearly midnight?" I gasped. "No! It surely cannot be as late as that?"

"I fear that it is." Horatio gestured toward a clock ticking upon the mantelpiece.

Twenty minutes until twelve, the hour that I had agreed to meet Mal to hand over the stolen orb. Our last words as he had climbed out my bedchamber window echoed through my mind.

Midnight. Do not forget. If you are not there at the rendezvous, I will assume something has gone wrong and come looking for you.

And walk straight into the arms of the palace guard? Don't be ridiculous, Mal. Just be patient and wait for me. I will be there.

But patience had never been one of Malcolm Hawkridge's virtues.

"Ella?" Horatio's voice cut into my panicked thoughts. "Is something wrong?"

"Oh no. I had just forgotten about... the fireworks," I lied, wishing my face were not so transparent. "I will be sorry that I have to miss them."

To my relief, Horatio accepted that reason for my consternation. He emitted a rueful sigh. "I confess that when I came here this evening, I had hoped to watch the fireworks with you and perhaps take you to supper afterward. Presumptuous of me, I know. I have no reason to suppose you would—"

"I would have liked that very much," I said, adding with genuine regret, "We never even had our dance."

"Perhaps there will be another occasion. I hope you will permit me to call upon you again."

"Certainly, you may. I will be most anxious to hear about your meeting with Mercato."

"Then I promise I will come to see you first thing tomorrow morning." He paused, adding diffidently. "If you would like."

"I would like that very much." I smiled, trying not to sound anxious as the clock ticked off another minute. I tried to ease my hand from his, but his grip tightened.

Horatio glanced toward Amy who seemed oblivious to her surroundings. He drew me closer, and I could tell from the longing in his gaze how badly he wanted to kiss me again.

The man certainly deserved it after all he had done for me. I tilted up my head in silent invitation. As Horatio bent closer, my heart quickened with anticipation. I wondered if this kiss would be as heady as his last one had been.

Suddenly I forgot about the time, forgot about Mal, forgot everything as I lost myself in the smoky heat of Horatio's eyes. Our lips were but a breath away.

Unfortunately, at that moment, the page flung open the door, ushering my stepmother inside. Horatio and I sprang apart, but not quickly enough. Em drew up short, her mouth falling open.

I was further dismayed when I saw her old beau, Lord Redmond, trailing after her. When His Lordship also halted in surprise, I felt my cheeks burn bright red. Horatio colored a trifle, but he managed to snap off a military bow.

"Prunella Upton! What in the world is going on?" my step-mother cried, her indignation focused on me. "All that foolish page would tell me is that one of my daughters was in dire need of me." Her glare shifted to include Horatio. "I can see that the fellow did not exaggerate."

"I am fine, Em," I said. "But Amy is not."

Regrettably, for the second time that night, I found myself using my drunken sister as a distraction. I gestured toward the settee.

"Amy?" My stepmother frowned as she took in the sight of Amy's inert, disheveled form.

Amy roused at the sound of her mother's voice, enough to open one bleary eye. My sister had reached that stage when the ebullience produced by the wine had been replaced by the inevitable drinker's remorse.

She moaned. "Don't feel good, Mama."

"Oh, my dearest girl!" Em fluttered over to the settee. She bent down to caress Amy's brow only to reel back in shock at the strong whiff of spirits emanating from my sister's breath.

I exchanged a rueful look with Horatio before hastening toward Em to explain. I would have preferred to do so without Lord Redmond present. I knew nothing about Chuffy other than he was Em's former suitor and an accomplished flirt. He seemed fond of my stepmother, but I had no idea whether his discretion was to be trusted.

His Lordship appeared discomfited by our little family drama, enough that I hoped he would make his excuses and leave. When he did not do so, I was obliged to continue.

I told Em what had happened as succinctly as possible, all the while conscious of that clock ticking away. I braced myself for anything from a bout of tears to complete hysterics. I was surprised when Em only clucked her tongue at Amy.

"To be sure, Amy and Prince Dahl did behave imprudently—"

"Dashy," Amy mumbled.

"But if there is a possibility the young man has fallen in love with her and intends to make her his princess..."

"Won't live that long," Amy groaned. "Think I am dying, Mama."

From the gleam in my stepmother's eye, I surmised that she was already planning a royal wedding. Em could be rather foolish at times and indulge in the most preposterous fantasies, but this was a bit much, even for her.

"Em! Prince Dahl's intentions toward Amy were completely dishonorable," I said.

"Indeed!" Lord Redmond had listened to my account in grave silence. He startled me when he spoke up. "The young rascal ought to be thrashed."

"Chuffy!" Em protested. "You are speaking of a prince."

"Who did his best to ruin Amy's reputation and he would have succeeded if not for Commander Crushington. You must thank him…" I trailed off as I realized that at some point Horatio had stolen quietly out of the room.

"Of course, I shall express my gratitude to the commander," Em said. "I shall send him a note in the morning."

"A note? No, you must do it up proper and invite the young man to tea," Lord Redmond insisted.

"But, Chuffy!" Em lowered her voice and muttered something about not wanting to encourage the commander's attentions to me.

"Eh? Why not?"

"For one thing, the man is very likely a foundling," Em whispered.

"What of it? I never judge a man by his parentage or lack thereof. The commander appears to be a splendid, sensible fellow, honorable and all that." Chuffy winked at me. "And quite handsome."

My opinion of Em's old beau soared by a great many notches. I would be pleased to know him better, but now was not the time.

Quarter 'til midnight, the clock ticked. I backed away toward the door.

Em looked a little chastened and ashamed enough to concede, "I am sure Commander Crushington is a worthy young man, if you say so, Chuffy. I will invite him to call to express my gratitude." She added with a sigh. "If only he were a prince."

I made no retort, merely stated my intention to fetch Netta. But as I bolted out of the sitting room, I reflected that from what I had seen of the behavior of princes, I was very glad that Horatio was not one.

As I hurried down the palace steps toward the garden, I felt the blister on my heel break. I pulled up short, sucking in my breath at the pain, but I had to keep going. Above the ornate arch leading into the garden was a clock tower. The hands of the massive timepiece clicked up a notch.

Five minutes until midnight. I was never going to make the rendezvous in time. As I hobbled beneath the arch and down the flagstone walkway set between the colorful flower beds, I prayed, "I am coming, Mal. Please, please, please don't do anything stupid."

My sore heel prevented me from breaking into a run. My progress was also impeded by the number of other guests strolling the garden paths in anticipation of the fireworks. Ordinarily, I would have attracted too much attention, a wild-eyed limping woman, muttering to herself.

But everyone that I dodged past appeared to be young couples, entirely lost in each other. Some held hands, some walked arm in arm, heads bent close together while others playfully chased each other through the hedges, giggling and stealing kisses.

The palace gardens were a lovers' paradise, the moon shining softly overhead, the night sky spangled with stars, the air perfumed with the mingled scents of lilac, roses, and sweet honeysuckle. So many private nooks to choose from, wooden benches tucked in the shadows of tall yew hedges, hidden away from the glare of the lighted torches. The hushed burble of the fountains seemed to echo all the lovers' sighs.

I was surrounded by the sort of romance that Em had promised this ball would be. But not for me, I thought with a pang. I wondered how differently this evening might have gone, if I had not had to steal the orb for Mal, if I had never crossed paths with Harper again, rekindling poignant memories and tearing open that old wound. If I could have had my dance with Horatio and walked these garden paths with him... would my bruised heart have finally been open to the prospect of a new love?

I would never know. Nor did I have the time for such repining and speculation. I expected to hear the clock strike midnight at any moment, and I had only gotten as far as the green roundel of grass at the very center of the garden. As I paused to catch my breath, I spotted my missing sister.

The golden hews had been clipped to form a pediment and

just beyond that, Netta and Sergeant Wharton perched demurely side by side on a stone bench, an ugly aura cat curled up at the sergeant's feet. My sister leaned down and petted the fearsome beast.

Was this how Netta had spent the entire ball, in the company of this handsome young guard? Em would be horrified, but I had never seen our shy Netta look more animated or happier, not even when she was playing her harp. I recognized that starry-eyed expression. I had seen it reflected in the mirror the summer I had fallen in love with Harper.

Netta's tall, young swain appeared equally smitten. Neither of them noticed me observing them between the branches of the yew. Even the aura cat did no more than lift its head, peer lazily in my direction before settling back down onto its huge paws.

Em would have expected me to limp over there and order Netta back to the palace forthwith. My stepmother would never consent to Netta pursuing an acquaintance with a lowly Scutcheon even if he did work at the castle. His Majesty deemed it a privilege to serve in his palace guard, but everyone knew that was simply the king's excuse not to pay his sentries anything beyond bed and board. None of them could afford to take a wife.

There would be plenty of time to pry Netta away from her new admirer after I found Mal. Let my sister enjoy whatever moments remained of her romantic idyll, I thought sadly as I limped off in the opposite direction.

As Mal had instructed me, I headed deeper into the palace grounds where the garden had been fashioned to resemble a pretty wilderness, the shrubs and hedges less well trimmed. It was quiet and deserted here, not a good location for viewing the fireworks. No charming nooks with benches here, the towering oaks blocked any vista of the open sky.

The path was rougher as well, pebbles instead of flagstones. I swore when a particularly sharp stone poked the bottom of my dancing slipper. But there at long last, bathed in a ray of moonlight, was the old vine-covered gate that would lead me beyond the palace grounds to the woodland. I might just manage to make my rendezvous with Mal on time after all.

Heartened, I picked up my pace, despite my aching feet. I was feeling so jubilant; it took me a moment to realize I was being followed. I heard the crunch of pebbles dislodged. Before I could react, someone slung his arm over my shoulders. I let out a frightened squeak as I was yanked back against a hard wall of chest.

Horatio was my alarmed thought, but I knew the commander would never have grabbed me so roughly. If this was one of the palace guards, he was far exceeding his authority to be manhandling a guest in such fashion and so I would tell him.

"Bella." My skin prickled at the feel of hot breath on my neck as a familiar voice rasped in my ear.

I froze for a moment and then managed to squirm free. Spinning around, I came face-to-face with Prince Florian. His golden mane hung wildly about the chiseled planes of his face.

"Aha, there you are," he cried.

Yes, there I was. Unfortunately. Recovering from the fright he had given me; I bobbed a curtsy.

"I have been looking for you everywhere, beautiful Bella," he said.

"You have?"

Something about the way he smiled disquieted me. I took a wary step back only to have him follow.

"Yes. You stole something from me."

My heart stopped. He knew. Prince Florian knew I had taken the orb. How was that even possible?

The blood drained from my face. "No, Your Highness. I have taken nothing, I assure you."

"You have, you enchanting little thief." Florian almost tipped over backward as he struck one fist dramatically against his chest. "You stole my heart."

I went almost limp with relief. As soon as I could breathe

again, I gave a nervous titter and tried to jest. "Oh, that. Well, if you will just leave your heart lying about like that. I found it dropped along the herbaceous border. But I am happy to return it to you."

Florian flung back his head and emitted a... I could not really call it a laugh, more like a bizarre high-pitched giggle.

"You are amusing. I like that in a girl," he said as he teetered toward me.

Wonderful, I thought in disgust. The prince was as drunk as my sister.

But when a shaft of moonlight pierced the branches of the trees, I caught a glimmer of a silvery powder near his nostrils. As he moved closer, his pupils were so wide, they threatened to swallow up the rest of his eyes.

Not drunk. Even worse, the man had been snorting pixie dust.

"Keep my heart. Don't want it, don't need it," he declared in a singsong tone. "I have decided that you are the one, Bella. The one destined to be my bride."

"What!" I was so stunned; it took me a moment to gather my wits enough to protest.

"Oh, no, no, no. I am quite certain I am not."

"I have danced with many lovely ladies, but none can compare to you." He lunged, trying to take me into his arms. His movements were so clumsy, I evaded his grasp.

"There are a lot of women here tonight. You can't possibly have danced with all of them," I said. "You should go back to the ballroom and have another look around."

"Don't need to. I knew from the moment I saw you; you were the one."

Was that before or after he had started sniffing the pixie dust? I wondered. I retreated until my back struck up against the trunk of a massive oak, leaving me nowhere else to go. Florian leaned in, bracing one arm on either side of me.

"Will you be my princess, Bella? May I sweep you off to my castle to live happily ever after?"

"Frap, no! I… I mean, I am deeply honored and all that, but—"

His mouth crashed down hard against mine. I issued a muffled protest, but that was a huge mistake. When my lips parted, Florian thrust his tongue into my mouth.

It was like a warm wet eel darting about, trying to slither its way down my throat. I gagged, feeling like I was going to be sick or suffocate. I pounded on his back in a futile effort to make him stop. When that did not work, I seized two handfuls of his hair and pulled as hard as I could.

He ended the kiss with a gasp. "Ow! Ow! Ow!"

As he struggled to pry my hands out of his hair, he stumbled back and kept right on going until he fell, landing on his rump. I saw my chance and made a break for it. Florian rolled to his side and snagged hold of my skirt.

"Let go before you rip my gown," I cried, trying to disengage the fabric from his grasp.

Florian struggled to his knees and gazed up at me with a vacuous grin. "You're feisty. I like that in a girl." He lifted my skirt.

"Stop it, you great frapping oaf!" By this time, I was far beyond worrying about the respect due to royalty. I struck out wildly, kicking him in the chest. My blows might have been far more effective if I had been wearing the glass slippers instead of soft leather.

Florian only giggled. He released my skirt and grabbed hold of my foot. I jerked as hard as I could to pull free. My shoe came off in his hand and I went flying backward into a shrub. Florian flew in the opposite direction, smacking his head against a tree root.

The branches scraped my hands, and I heard my gown tear as I fought to regain my footing. From a great distance, I could hear the castle clock toll midnight, followed by a shrill whistle and the first burst of fireworks. I swore as I limped to my feet, bracing myself for another assault from Florian.

The prince had not moved from where he had fallen beneath

the tree. My first impulse was to flee toward the gate, but I was held back by a sense of uneasiness. The prince was still. Far too still.

"Your Highness?" I ventured.

No response. As another barrage of fireworks lit up the night sky, I called more loudly, "Prince Florian?"

I could discern no movement of the prince whatsoever, not even the rise and fall of his chest. I groaned. Could this night possibly get any worse? So much for all my vows to become Arcady's most respectable law-abiding subject. So much for my promise to Horatio to keep out of trouble.

I imagined myself going to him and saying, remember how you told me I should come to you if I found myself in difficulty? Well, I think I might have accidently killed the heir to the throne.

The thought almost caused me to break into hysterical laughter. I clapped my hand to my mouth to stifle the mad sound. Gathering up my nerve, I crept closer to the prince.

"Florian?" I tried again.

To my relief, he moaned, and his eyes fluttered open. Not dead, only dazed. He stared upward, a blank look on his face as another cascade of fireworks erupted above us, a shower of golden sparks visible through the foliage of the tree.

"What happened? Is the castle under attack?" he mumbled. "I should go get my sword."

"Yes, you do that and I... I will go rally the guards," I said, backing away. The idiot was still clutching my slipper, but I was not about to risk getting close enough to wrestle it away from him.

I turned and made for the gate as fast as I could hobble. The latch was rusted shut and I had to shove with all my strength. In my current state of mind, I think I could have kicked my way through a solid brick wall to get away.

The latch gave with a loud creak. I thrust the gate open and hopped through it into the parkland beyond. I could have moved faster if I had paused to shed my other shoe. I did not dare. I did not think that Prince Florian could rouse himself to pursue me, but I was not taking any chances.

During the days of Queen Anthea, the area beyond the castle had been designated common land, shared by cottagers for grazing their sheep. After King Cuthbert had claimed the throne, he had not wanted any peasants or their livestock that close to his palace. He had appropriated the commons to add to his hunting grounds and evicted the shepherds from their cottages.

Consequently, the meadow had become so overgrown, the tall grasses impeded my flight as though I waded through a stagnant pond. I shot a nervous look over my shoulder and was relieved that there was no Prince Florian lumbering after me. I appeared to be safe... for now.

I turned to discover a dark shadow looming over me. Before I could let out an alarmed shriek, another blaze of fireworks lit up the night sky and I realized it was Mal.

Clad all in black with a scarf knotted around his head and a cutlass strapped to his side, Mal looked more like a river pirate than ever. Recovering from my fright, I snapped at him, "Hawkridge! What the blazes do you think you are doing this close to the castle?"

"Coming for you. Where have you been?"

"I can't be more than ten minutes late. Why didn't you wait for me at the rendezvous?"

"I told you that if you weren't there by midnight, I would assume you were in trouble and come to help."

"Because getting yourself captured or killed would be so helpful. Idiot!" I socked him as hard as I could in the arm.

"Ow!" Mal rubbed his shoulder, eyeing me reproachfully.

I did not care. I had had all I could tolerate of masculine stupidity for one evening. I seized Mal's hand and dragged him along in my wake.

"Come on! Before you trigger some sort of magical alarm or one of those horrid aura cats get a sense of Hawkridge aura."

"All right. I'm coming. But why are you limping? And why do you look as though you are fleeing from a horde of goblins?"

"Worse than a goblin. Prince Florian."

"Florian? Why would the hair apparent be chasing after you?"

"Because he wants to marry me."

"What!"

I pulled up short and punched Mal again. He gasped. "What was that for?"

"That was for telling me that I had nothing to worry about, that there was no chance he would choose me for his bride."

"He shouldn't have, not if you gave him the sharp end of your tongue like you usually do me. Never tell me you were sweet to the man."

"No! When he proposed to me, I pulled his hair, and I kicked him and called him names."

"Not the usual response a fellow expects when he asks a girl to marry him. Perhaps it is a good thing I never tried to propose to you."

I was in no humor for any of Mal's jesting. I was too distressed by my recent encounter with Prince Florian. When I related the whole incident to Mal, I was infuriated to see his shoulders shake with suppressed mirth.

Doubling my hands into fists, I said, "I swear, Hawkridge, if you dare laugh, this time I will hit you so hard, your eyeballs will roll out of your head."

Mal seized my wrists to fend me off as a chuckle escaped him. "S-sorry, Ella, but when you look back on all this tomorrow, I am sure you will see how amusing it was."

"Oh yes, when I am arrested for assaulting the prince and dragged down to the Dismal Dungeons to be executed, I am sure I will die laughing."

"That will never happen. You don't understand what happens when you snort pixie dust, do you? Your brain goes completely fuzzy. When Florian wakes up tomorrow, he won't remember a thing that happened. He'll be so roaring hungry, his desire will be for a thick juicy beefsteak, not a bride."

"Just how do you know so much about the effects of pixie dust?"

"I may have tried it a time or two during my wilder days."

"When was that? Last week?" I groused.

Mal laughed. He loosened his grip on my wrists as he soothed me. "I promise you, Ella. Everything will be all right. Florian will forget all about you and go back to his one true love, his own reflection."

I felt partially reassured. It still worried me that Florian had my shoe, but if he woke up as confused as Mal said he would, the prince would likely take one bewildered look at my scuffed dancing slipper and toss it on the nearest rubbish heap.

I could tell Mal was bursting to ask me about the orb, but I was uneasy about Mal being this close to the palace gardens. He might blend into the night, but my silvery-gold gown would stand out like a white banner snapping in the breeze. I refused to discuss anything further until we had trudged across the open meadow and into trees to the place where Mal should have waited for me.

The cottage was little more than a ruin, deserted since the previous occupants had been driven out by the palace guard, evicted to dwell in Misty Bottoms or perhaps into the swampland beyond our border. The door hung off its hinges; the shutter-less windows were like gaping wounds. Thick vines grew in profusion, like greedy fingers, plucking away at the stone walls. I was not even tempted to enter the cottage, especially not after I caught the gleam of eyes and heard some nocturnal creature rustling in the darkened interior.

There was a rough wooden bench positioned outside and I sank gratefully down onto that, heedless of whatever further damage I might be doing to the delicate silk of my gown. I could hear the continued burst of fireworks, but it sounded faint and far away from this secluded spot.

Mal paced in front of me like a restless shadow. Moonlight pierced the trees, not enough for me to discern his expression, but I sensed his eagerness.

"Well?" he demanded.

"Well, what?" I responded grumpily. I was still feeling irritated with him for laughing about the episode with Florian.

"How was the ball? How did everything go?"

"I danced far too much."

"And?"

"My sister Amy got very drunk."

"And?" Mal's voice grew increasingly anxious.

"Myrtle Hanson fainted in front of the prince and a huge fight broke out."

"Ella!" Mal groaned. "You are killing me. The orb. What about the orb? Did you get it?"

I feigned a deep sigh. "Unfortunately, with one thing and another..."

When I saw Mal's shoulders slump with disappointment, I could not bear to tease him any longer.

"Yes, I got it." Delving into the pocket of my gown, I produced the orb. Considering everything I had been through tonight; I was relieved to see the tiny globe still intact.

"Happy birthday, Mal," I said.

Mal snatched the orb from me before I had a chance to hand it over. He reached upward and I realized there was a small lantern hanging from a hook by the cottage door. Mal had been keeping it cloaked, but he removed the cover, allowing the light to spill over the orb.

He cradled it reverently in the palm of his hand. "You did it, Ella, you darling girl. You really did it."

I could not resist getting in one last jab. "How do you know that I am not tricking you and just giving you the fake one back?"

"I can feel the difference. The real one is slightly heavier."

"What!" I sat upright in alarm. "You told me the fake one you had made was identical."

"I said the substitute was as alike as I could make it. No one could tell the difference between them, except perhaps another wizard."

"Another wizard like Mercato? Blast you, Hawkridge, why didn't you warn me that—"

"Relax, Ella. I do not think even Sidney Greenleaf is allowed to go poking about in the king's private treasure chamber. The orb has been gathering dust there for decades. No one is likely to have a sudden urge to inspect it now, so stop fretting."

I subsided, but the list of things that Mal kept telling me I did not have to worry about grew longer by the minute.

The lantern light played over Mal's face, illuminating his expression. I had expected him to be overjoyed to have this memento of his grandfather returned to him. But there was something that made me a little uneasy about the rapt light in Mal's eyes as he examined the orb, as though he was mesmerized.

"Exactly what did you say that thing does again?" I asked.

"It finds that which has been lost," Mal said, as though he was quoting from some ancient text.

"You mean like a missing glove or a shoe?"

"Something far more valuable."

"Like what? A buried treasure?"

"Yes, a lost treasure," Mal murmured. "I have to figure out how to use the orb first, but when I do— oh, Ella, just think how this could change all our lives."

"Um, hmm." I agreed halfheartedly. Ever the dreamer, Mal was probably imagining finding some lost cache of gold or jewels. I hated to disillusion him, but I was far too cynical to believe that little glass ball had that kind of magic or even if it did that Mal would be able to use it.

I struggled to my feet. "I really need to get back to the palace before my stepmother wonders what happened to me."

Mal snapped out of his trance and tucked the orb away in a small pouch affixed to his belt. "Thank you, Ella. I am so grateful; I could kiss you."

"No need for that. I have had quite enough kissing for one night."

"But you have no idea how much this means and— what!" Mal gaped as my words registered. "Who have you been kissing?"

I shrugged. "Commander Crushington and a couple of princes."

When Mal shot me an outraged look, I reminded him, "You did tell me to enjoy myself."

"Not that much!"

"Good night, Mal," I said, regretting my spurt of honesty. I could only blame it on my exhaustion, my mind too tired to control my mouth. I turned to make my escape, but there was no way Mal was going to be fobbed off that easily.

He caught hold of my arm and hauled me back to face him.

"Why were you kissing the Crusher?" he demanded.

"The commander caught me down in the forbidden part of the palace right after I had stolen the orb. He was asking me too many questions. I needed to do something to distract him."

And what a delicious, pulse pounding, blood warming distraction it had been. I barely managed to suppress a sigh at the memory.

"You couldn't have just hit him over the head or something?" Mal scowled. "And how could Crushington catch you when you were wearing the glass slippers? You would have been invisible."

"I wasn't wearing the glass shoes."

"What! Why not?"

"They hurt my feet."

"Ella—"

"Besides that, they didn't work."

"But I gave you explicit instructions."

"Which I followed exactly."

"You must have done something wrong because those shoes were well tested. They worked just fine in my shop."

"Well, they did not work for me."

Mal flung up his hands in a frustrated gesture, looking as though he wanted to shake me. "Blast it all, Ella. I would never have agreed to let you do this if I had not thought you would be protected. When you couldn't get the shoes to work, why didn't you just forget about stealing the orb?"

"Because I promised you and when the fight broke out, I saw my chance and oh, what does it matter? I managed well enough without the shoes, didn't I?"

"Except for being forced to get all cuddly with Crushington to keep from being arrested," Mal grumbled.

I could think of many words to describe Horatio's kiss. Breathtaking, passionate, tender, but definitely not cuddly. Since Mal was already looking jealous enough, I kept such reflections to myself.

"So, your kiss worked? Did your distraction allay the commander's suspicions?" Mal asked.

"Not entirely. It was really Amy who did that."

"Amy!" Mal looked confused as well he might. "What was she doing in the forbidden corridor? Did she kiss Crushington too?"

"No!" I explained briefly about Amy's drunken tryst with Prince Dahl in the king's wine cellar. I concluded by jabbing an accusing finger against Mal's chest. "I consider you partly to blame for my sister's behavior."

"Me? What did I do?"

"You gave my sisters a bottle of that infamous potion of yours. What were you thinking?"

"I told you; my Elixir of Love is completely harmless. If Amy ran wild, blame it on the king's cheap wine. It happens every year you know. Couples get tipsy at the ball and sneak off into the shrubbery. The royal ball is usually followed by any number of sword-point weddings and then months later an increase in the population."

"And you never thought to warn me about that either?"

"Amy insisted things never went that far with the prince, didn't she? I am sure you have nothing to worry about with her. The worst that will happen is she will wake up with a splitting headache tomorrow and be a sadder but wiser girl."

"You had better be right or after I choke the life out of that smirking prince, I will be coming after you. You swore to me how smoothly everything would go tonight—"

"Never mind about that," Mal cut me off. "Who else were you kissing? You said a couple of princes. Which ones?"

"Prince Florian, although it certainly wasn't my idea. When he proposed to me, he pounced and gave me the sloppiest, revolting kiss. Do you know he actually thrust his tongue in my mouth?"

"Ah!" Mal nodded. "Obviously our prince has been spending time on the Isle of Lothmara."

"What has that got to do with anything?"

"The island is mainly populated by these voluptuous beautiful women, sirens skilled in the arts of every imaginable seduction. The things these women can do with their tongues can reduce a full-grown man to a quivering mass of—" Mal broke off with a discreet cough. "Not that I would know much about such creatures."

"Oh no, of course not," I said drily. "I wish the prince did not either. Florian's kiss was utterly disgusting."

"Only because the prince did not learn how to do it right. If you like, I could demonstrate the proper way to do a siren's embrace."

"I thought you just said you didn't know much about such kisses."

Mal grinned. "I know enough. So, who was the other prince?"

"What?" My mind was still boggling over the information about those sirens and their magical tongues.

"You mentioned kissing a couple of princes. That implies two." Mal held up a pair of fingers. "Who was the second one?"

I gave a weary sigh. I really did not want to discuss my painful discovery that my long-lost lover had turned out to be Prince Ryland in disguise. But I had already hurt Mal enough by keeping Harper a secret from him in the first place. So, I told him about the scene on the balcony.

"That treacherous bastard!" Mal growled. "If I ever cross paths with him, he'll lose a lot more than his hand."

"Forget about him, Mal. I assure you that I have."

I tried to shrug, but some of the lingering ache I felt over Harper must have shown on my face. Either that or Mal simply knew me far too well. His grim expression softened, and he held out his arms.

"Come here."

When I regarded him warily, he gave a rueful laugh. "No kissing, I promise. But you've had a demon of a night, my dear friend. You look as though you need a hug."

I stumbled into his arms. I fit so comfortably against his shoulder and Mal stroked my hair, murmuring nonsense and consoling me as he had done so often over the course of our friendship. I felt so drained, I wished I could have closed my eyes and remained tucked in Mal's embrace for the rest of the night.

But I was too aware of the hard lean, musculature of his body, the tension in his arms. I could sense his desire for me, the effort that it cost him to restrain himself. I drew awkwardly away from him.

"I really do need to get back to my family," I insisted. But I recollected one more thing I had neglected to tell Mal about, and he was not going to like it.

As Mal moved to douse the lantern, I said, "Something else happened this evening that you should know about. Your witch friend attempted to attend the ball."

"Delphine? What was she doing there?"

"I think she had some notion of helping me get the orb for you."

"Silly witch. How did she think she was ever going to get past Mercato and those aura cats?"

"I don't know. She had barely set foot inside the palace gates when that magical alarm thing on Mercato's scepter went off and he sent the guards after her. She got away by conjuring up this mist and then she..." I winced, knowing how mad this was going to sound. "She transformed herself into a cat."

"She what?" Mal laughed. "My dear Ella, how much pixie dust have you been snorting this evening?"

"None! It's true, Mal. I watched her do it with my very own eyes." I went on to describe with greater detail Delphine's transformation into the black cat Ebony.

Mal folded his arms across his chest, looking skeptical. "You are trying to tell me that Ebony is really..."

"Delphine."

"The same cat that likes to follow me around and rub up against me?"

"Delphine."

A frown creased Mal's brow as he struggled to get his head around this disturbing revelation. "You mean the same cat that I sometimes allow to snuggle in bed with me?"

"Yes! That's Delphine."

"The cat that often tries to leap onto my lap and use her front paws to knead my... my..." Mal shuddered. "Oh, frapping fairies, Ebony really is Delphine."

He rubbed his arms as though his skin crawled with fleas. He groaned. "I need to go home and take a scalding hot bath."

Mal had teased me so many times during the years of our friendship. I fear that I enjoyed telling him about Delphine far more than I should have. Feeling slightly repentant for my glee, I gave him a quick peck on the cheek in parting. I left him still trying to come to grips with the realization he had been sharing his bed with a lascivious witch.

I approached the palace with trepidation, but the guardian

fairies, if there truly were such things, finally deigned to smile upon me. The fireworks were over, and all the guests had headed to the banqueting hall for the midnight supper. Prince Florian had either staggered off in search of his sword or been found by some of the palace guards and carted off to his bed. No doubt the poor fellows were accustomed to performing such duties for the royal family.

Either way, I was relieved to be spared another encounter with my pixified royal suitor. I wondered wistfully where Horatio was and hoped he was having some success in persuading Mercato to spare the Hanson family.

I found Netta bidding a sad farewell to her sergeant. I scooped her up and with Lord Redmond's help, managed to get my stepmother and sisters to our carriage. Our departure was somewhat enlivened by Amy puking all over His Lordship's shoes. I hoped the poor man was not repulsed by my sister's antics. I liked Chuffy and wanted him to call upon Em. Out of all of us, my stepmother was the only one who had enjoyed what might prove to be a promising romance.

Our hall clock chimed the hour of two before we were divested of our ballroom finery and in our nightgowns. After seeing Em and my sisters tucked in for the night, I retired to my own bedchamber. Even as exhausted as I was, I could not settle enough to sleep, my mind too full. I still could not believe out of all the women at that ball, Prince Florian had singled me out to be his bride. I prayed that Mal was right about the effect of that much pixie dust on the brain and by morning, that dolt Florian would forget he had ever met me. As for Ryland, the prince in disguise who had once won my heart, I hoped I could finally forget him.

Attending the royal ball had only left me with more questions about my parents' history, and then there was King August's strange reaction to me. Would I ever be able to learn the truth behind all of that? I fretted. I took down my hair and sought to calm myself by rhythmically brushing out the tangles, but I still felt like a pocket watch wound too tight.

Pacing over to my window, I opened it and perched upon the sill, allowing the cool night breeze to fan my cheeks. Coaches lumbered past in the street below as one by one, Midtown families straggled home from the ball. None of the carriages stopped at the Hansons' door. I worried about the fate of Ivy and Myrtle, their brothers, Fortescue Bafton and all of the other Midtown boys who had been arrested after the melee.

But I worried even more about Horatio. Our king had an unpredictable, vindictive nature. Even though Horatio was a Scutcheon commander, would his rank be enough to protect him if he angered His Majesty by trying to thwart August's cruel laws? Why had I not thought of this when I had begged Horatio to intervene on Myrtle's behalf? I regretted I had ever done so as the returning coaches became fewer and fewer until the street stood silent and empty.

The Hanson household remained shuttered and dark. There was no sign of Horatio either. He had to pass by this way to return to the garrison, but it was possible I had missed his return to town when I had been helping my sisters prepare for bed. I comforted myself with the thought of his promise to call upon me in the morning to let me know how everything had turned out. I had to believe that nothing would prevent him from doing that. Horatio Crushington was not the sort of man to make promises lightly.

A glance at my bedchamber clock warned me that the first light of dawn would be breaking soon. I needed to try to snatch a few hours' sleep. The grand ball that had so disrupted our lives was over and I would need to return to my workaday world and more practical considerations. Like what I could serve for dinner tomorrow besides another pot of stewed eel and how I was going to stretch what remained of our funds until next quarter day.

I shifted off the windowsill, rubbing my hip, sore and stiff from perching on the hard wood. I was just about to snuff out my candle when I heard the clatter of a horse's hooves upon the cobblestone street. Leaning out the window, I saw a lone rider approach from the direction of the Heights. My heart soared with relief as I recognized Horatio's stalwart frame, tall and upright in the saddle.

He slowed Loyal to a walk as he neared my house. Glancing toward my house, he reined the gelding to a halt. Horatio could likely see me better than I could him. Framed in my window, I was illuminated by the candle I was holding. Despite the flickering light from the streetlamps, Horatio's features were lost in shadow.

But I could discern when he nodded his head to reassure me all was well. Then he lifted his hand to his brow and snapped off a sharp salute, a rather playful gesture for the solemn commander. I grinned and waved back at him. Before he could ride off, I launched into a series of hand motions, pointing downward, moving two fingers to simulate walking, followed by a frantic beckoning.

He craned his neck to see me, and I was afraid he would not comprehend the meaning behind all my impulsive gestures. But understanding must have dawned upon him, and he dismounted, looping Loyal's reins about one of the fence's posts. I was not sure why he had bothered. I could not imagine anything short of a roaring fire would ever induce that horse to stray far from his master's side. Perhaps Horatio was more concerned that Loyal would attempt to follow him through the gate.

The hinges creaked loudly as Horatio entered my front garden. At the same moment, a low moan issued from Em's bedchamber next to mine, indicating that my stepmother was also passing a restless night. Being reunited with her old beau had left Em in a flustered, excited state. I cringed at the thought of waking her, imagining Em bursting into my room, demanding to know what I was doing. Trysting with Horatio Crushington at such an indecent hour, clad only in my nightgown! I could hardly explain the impulse that had come over me, even to myself.

All I knew was the way my heart quickened as Horatio picked his way through the wild tangle of my roses to stand beneath my window. Before he could call out to me, I placed a cautioning finger to my lips. Gesturing, I managed to convey to him that he should meet me in the back garden.

I closed my window and doused the candle. My childhood nocturnal adventures with Mal had gifted me with the ability to sneak through the dark house, stealthily and silently. I tiptoed through the upper hall and down the stairs, still remembering to avoid the boards that creaked. Ducking into the drawing room, I found my old shawl that I had left discarded on the settee. I draped it around my shoulders to maintain some semblance of modesty and then I slipped quietly out of the double doors.

Horatio was already there, his tall form a looming shadow beneath the pergola. I hastened toward him, my bare feet whispering through the damp grass. If my blistered heel still bothered me, I was hardly aware of it. My steps grew quicker, and I was nearly running as I closed the distance between us. I drew up short at the last moment, keenly aware of how disheveled I must look, dressed in my worn, much mended nightgown, my hair tumbling wildly about my shoulders.

The sky had lightened to a deep grey the same hue as Horatio's eyes. He looked exhausted, the bruise on his cheek that he had sustained during the fight more prominent. But his entire face lit up at the sight of me.

Seized by a rare attack of shyness, I felt my cheeks warm. Before I could speak, Horatio said, "I should not be disturbing you at such an unreasonable hour, Ella."

I smiled ruefully. "I am the one doing the disturbing. You look so tired, I should have allowed you to return to the garrison, but I was so anxious to hear the news."

"Of course." Horatio offered me a reassuring smile. "You need fret no longer. The Hansons and our other Midtown citizens will be obliged to spend another uncomfortable night in the King's Royal Prison until they have paid a hefty fine, but then they will be released. It took a great deal of arguing and persuading on my part, but Sidney Greenleaf has given his word that he will intercede with the king."

"And you trust Mercato? You are on such good terms with that wizard?" I asked in a troubled voice.

"I would not exactly call it good terms. But we seem to have developed a grudging respect for one another. This may be hard for you to believe, Ella, but Sidney— that is, Mercato can be reasonable if it does not jeopardize his own position. I convinced him that obtaining a pardon for the arrested Midtown citizens will enhance Sidney's reputation as a man of power and earn him the gratitude of all of Midtown."

"Humph!" I said indignantly. "You are the one they should all be grateful to. The Great Mercato would not have lifted a finger to help anyone if you had not intervened. The Hansons, especially, should get down upon their knees to thank you."

"The fairies forfend! I don't want their thanks or their gratitude." Horatio paused. His jaw worked, like a man wrestling with some momentous decision or trying to summon his courage. That was surely a ridiculous supposition on my part because Horatio had to be one of the bravest men I had ever known.

But when his eyes met mine, I had never seen him look so anxious or vulnerable as he said, "I have to admit I was thinking only of you when I leapt to the Hansons' defense."

"Me?" I asked, astonished.

"From the first of our acquaintance, you saw me a harsh, rigid kind of man. I fear perhaps you still might do so at times." Horatio flushed with embarrassment. "You will think me a great fool, but I wanted to play the role of hero before you."

I gave an incredulous laugh. "Oh, Horatio, you never have to play at that. You are already a hero in my eyes. You rescued me from that villain Iggy Burt, remember? You saved my sister from disgrace. But I am flattered you value my opinion of you so highly."

"Why would I not?" He stepped closer and gathered up my hand, drawing it close to the region of his heart. "I love you."

My jaw dropped. It was not as though I was unaware of Horatio's feelings for me. At one time, I had even dreaded him making such a declaration. But it was the way that he said it. I love you. So simply, so quietly, so sincerely. My heart raced wildly. I could scarce breathe, let alone speak.

I was silent so long that Horatio's face fell. "I am sorry. I spoke too soon. I knew I should have waited, given you time to know me better, but I am finding it more and more difficult to restrain myself when I am near you. But I should have. I am sorry if I have offended you."

He started to release my hand.

"No," I cried, finding my voice at last. I entwined my fingers through his to prevent him drawing away from me. "I am not offended." I released a shaky breath. "I am just a bit overwhelmed and— and cannot understand why."

Horatio's expression was lightened with hope, but confusion as well. "Why what?"

"Why would you ever fall in love with me, Horatio? I never cause you anything but trouble. You had to battle that huge brute on my behalf. I got you entangled in that situation with the Hansons, and you even got hurt in the fight." I touched the bruise on his cheek. "And then you caught me and my sister in the banned part of the palace, but you protected us and helped me get Amy to safety."

And I lied, deceiving you about the real reason I was in the forbidden area.

I still could not bring myself to confess that to Horatio. I concluded miserably, "I do not see in the least why you should love me at all."

Hope had returned to Horatio's eyes, but he blew out a deep breath as he sought an answer for my question. "Well, I—"

"And please do not say it is just because you think I am beautiful," I warned him.

"All right, although I do."

I pulled a face. "Even the way I usually look, tearing about in my faded gowns, my hair a flyaway mess?"

Horatio released my hand to caress his fingers through my hair, smoothing out a tangle as he did so. He smiled tenderly. "I prefer you with your hair down. It makes you look softer, approachable. I was rather in awe of you tonight at the ball. You were so dazzlingly beautiful in that silken gown, your hair pulled up in that crown of ringlets. You looked like a fairy princess far beyond the reach of a mere Scutcheon officer like me."

"Nonsense." I shook my head deprecatingly. "You should know by now that was not the real me. As for my appearance, there are many other women, even in Midtown, far more beautiful and elegant than me."

"Are there? I have never noticed." Horatio caressed my cheek, sending a shiver of warmth through me. "When I first was assigned to Midtown, it was your lovely face that attracted my notice. It gave me pleasure just to look at you as I rode by, making my rounds. As time went by, I observed you more closely and saw how kind you were, to your family, to others, even to me."

"Oh, come now, Horatio," I protested. "You cannot claim that you ever found me sweet. I recall more than one sarcastic remark that I made to you."

Horatio chuckled. "No, you are not sweet. But you do possess a sharp wit that I admire."

"But surely no man falls in love with a woman for a reason like that."

"No, not entirely. I was attracted by your beauty, your kindness and intelligence. But as to what caused my feelings for you to deepen?" He frowned. "I suppose it has more to do with the effect you have on me when I am with you. I cannot explain it."

"Please try." I rested my hands upon his shoulders and peered earnestly up at him, seeking to convey to him how important this was to me. Prince Ryland had once composed songs in praise of my beauty and charm. When his love for me had proved to be weak and fleeting, my world had been shattered. If I was ever to risk my heart again, I needed to know that Horatio's feelings were stronger than that.

Horatio sighed and lifted his gaze heavenward as though desperately seeking inspiration, struggling to find the words to answer my question. The glimpse of sky through the latticework of the pergola had lightened to a pearly grey. I could hear the distant call of a lark announcing that daybreak was almost upon us.

But time seemed to have stopped for me as I breathlessly awaited his answer. Finally, Horatio lowered his eyes to meet mine. He said haltingly, "I am a plain man, Ella. I tend to view things in black and white, occasionally shades of grey. But when I am with you, you make me see the world in vibrant color and— and it's glorious."

"Oh!"

If Horatio had overwhelmed me before, this time the sincerity in his eyes and his voice nearly moved me to tears. And humbled me as well as I fully realized the impact I had had upon the heart of this stern, proud and lonely man.

Once again mistaking my reaction, Horatio sought to apologize. "Forgive me, Ella. I am sure you wanted something far more eloquent than that. But I am not good at expressing my emotions or paying compliments to a lady or—"

I pressed my fingertips to his lips to silence him. Smiling up at him, I said in a voice thickened by emotion, "Yes, you are, Horatio Crushington. That is quite the most wonderful thing any man has ever said to me."

"Then there is a chance you might learn to return my regard?"

"Yes," I stammered. "I believe that I could."

I can hardly describe the expression that came over Horatio's face when I said this. A look of heartfelt wonder as though he could not believe his good fortune, as though I had indeed made his world erupt with a burst of color. Another man might have whooped with joy and snatched me up in his embrace.

But Horatio took my face between his hands, just drinking in the sight of me for a long moment before he touched his lips to mine. As though he feared if he was not careful, I could slip between his fingers and vanish.

But when I wrapped my arms around his neck and melted against him, that was all the encouragement he needed to kiss me in earnest. Passionately, tenderly, fiercely. If I had found magic the first time he had kissed me at the ball, this time it was pure enchantment. His lips moved over mine, causing my blood to sing through my veins, making me feel as though I was floating off the ground.

I did experience a twinge as I recalled I still had not told Horatio the truth about the stolen orb. And another pang as I thought of Mal, of how devastated he would be when he realized I was encouraging Horatio's pursuit of me. Would our friendship survive it?

But I determinedly thrust all thoughts of Mal and the orb out of my head. Because I refused to allow anything to spoil the magic of this moment, the wonder of what was happening to me. I had not just opened my arms to Horatio, I had opened my heart as well. That door I had slammed closed years ago to protect myself from ever being hurt again, slowly inched open, letting in the prospect of hope, joy, and love.

I reflected that in all the old romantic tales, this was where the story would end with "and they lived happily ever after." But I was still too practical to believe in that. I was sadly familiar with the kind of tragic things that can happen to shatter dreams, death and betrayal and the difficulty of merely trying to survive under the harsh rules of our kingdom.

The romance that had blossomed between Horatio and me was new and fragile. It had yet to be tested by time and hardship, perhaps even divided loyalties. We still had so much to learn about each other, so many discoveries to make and secrets to reveal, mostly mine.

For now, I was content just to lose myself in the magic of Horatio's kisses. We broke apart only long enough to catch our breath and to beam at each other before we fell to kissing again. I was still locked in his embrace when the sun rose over my garden, full of the promise of a bright new day.

Also by Susan Carroll

<u>The St. Legers Series:</u>

The Bride Finder

The Night Drifter

Midnight Bride

<u>The Daughters of the Earth Series</u>

The Dark Queen

The Courtesan

The Silver Rose

The Huntress

The Twilight of a Queen

The Lady of Secrets

<u>Regency Romances</u>

The Sugar Rose

Brighton Road

Hellfire Harry

The Wooing of Miss Masters

Mistress Mischief

Miss Prentiss and the Yankee

Christmas Belles

The Valentine's Day Ball

<u>Contemporary Paranormal</u>

The Gumshoe and the Ghost Whisperer

About the Author

Author Susan Carroll began her career in 1986, writing historical romance and regencies, two of which were honored by Romance Writers of America with the RITA award. She has written twenty six novels to date. Her St. Leger series received much acclaim. The Bride Finder was honored with a RITA for Best Paranormal Romance in 1999 and also received the Reviewers Choice Award from Romantic Times magazine for Historical Romance of the year. Two sequels followed, The Night Drifter and Midnight Bride.

Ms. Carroll launched a new series with the publication of The Dark Queen set during the turbulent days of the French Renaissance. A blend of history, romance and intrigue, these six books relate the saga of the Cheney sisters, three women of extraordinary abilities who live in constant peril of being accused of witchcraft.

Her most recent title, Disenchanted is a humorous retelling of the Cinderella story.

Want updates when Susan has new books out, fun goodies to share, and other news? Click here. As a FREE BONUS for signing up, you will receive an Historical Romance Crossword puzzle.

www.ingramcontent.com/pod-product-compliance
Lightning Source LLC
Chambersburg PA
CBHW050016120726
47903CB00006B/1789